THE COCKATOOS

~ঈঈ~

by the same author

Novels
RIDERS IN THE CHARIOT
VOSS
THE TREE OF MAN
THE AUNT'S STORY
THE LIVING AND THE DEAD
THE SOLID MANDALA
THE VIVISECTOR
THE EYE OF THE STORM

Short Stories
THE BURNT ONES

Plays
FOUR PLAYS

❧❦❧

THE
COCKATOOS

STORIES BY

PATRICK
WHITE

❧❦❧

THE
VIKING PRESS

NEW YORK

Copyright © 1966, 1968, 1974 by Patrick White

Published in 1975 by The Viking Press, Inc.
625 Madison Avenue, New York, N.Y. 10022

Published simultaneously in Canada by
The Macmillan Company of Canada Limited

Printed in U.S.A.

Second printing February 1975

Library of Congress Cataloging in Publication Data:

White, Patrick, 1912–
    The cockatoos.

    CONTENTS: A woman's hand.—The full belly.—The night the prowler. [etc.]
    I. Title.
PZ3.W58469Co3 [PR9619.3.W5] 823 74–3792
ISBN 0-670-22648-3

My thanks to the following publications, in which stories have appeared:
Australian Letters and Macmillan's *Winter's Tales* for 'A Woman's Hand';
Angus and Robertson's *Coast to Coast* for 'The Full Belly'; and *Southerly
Magazine* for 'Five-Twenty'.

To Ronald Waters
for having survived
forty-eight years
of friendship

Contents

THE COCKATOOS

A Woman's Hand

The wind was tearing into the rock-plants, slashing reflections
out of the leaves of the mirror-bush, torturing those professional
martyrs the native trees. What must originally have appeared
an austere landscape, one long rush of rock and scrub towards
the sea, was prevented from wearing its natural expression by
the parasite houses clinging to it as obstinately as wax on diseased orange branches. Not that the houses weren't, nearly all
of them, technically desirable, some of them even Lovely
Homes worth breaking into. Although the owners of the latter
were surely aware of this, they had almost completely exposed
their possessions behind unbroken plate-glass. To view the
view might have been their confessable intention, but they
had ended, seemingly, overwhelmed by it. Or bored. The
owners of the lovely seaside homes sat in their worldly cells
playing bridge, licking the chocolate off their fingers, in one
case copulating, on pink chenille, on the master bed.

Evelyn Fazackerley looked away. It was, in any case, what
she would have called a heavenly day. She was breathless
with it, from the pace at which Harold was walking, as much
as from the biting air.

'You should walk more slowly,' she suggested, because it
was time she asserted herself. 'That is what retirement is
for.'

It was the kind of remark Harold ignored. Their marriage
was strewn with such. It was not unagreeable that way.

Perhaps because he had been thrown into retirement so
unexpectedly, so abruptly, he had difficulty in believing in it,

and had taken refuge in perpetual motion, though they kept the flat as a pied-à-terre.

Evelyn was squinting back at the glass faces of the huddled houses. In the general dazzlement of the landscape and the physical exhaustion of an unnecessary but virtuous walk, she felt that warm surge of desire which only material things can provoke.

'How vulgar they all are!' she said.

And was automatically absolved.

'Nothing wrong in being well lined.'

If he sounded tired, it was not from their walk – he had remained a physically active man – but from remembering the ganglion of plumbing on the neo-Tudor wall across from their neo-Tudor flat.

'Oh, come!' Evelyn said. 'There are certain standards the ones who know can't afford to drop.'

Evelyn was one who knew. Harold knew too. Only he didn't care enough.

Harold was again involved with the mystical problem of his own retirement. Before it had happened he used to say: Retirement will be the time of life when I read the books I have bought and never read, when I shall re-read *War and Peace*, and perhaps understand Dostoevski. Probably write something myself, something solid and factual about cotton in Egypt, or a travel book. Perhaps one or two articles for *Blackwood's*. Whereas retirement had, in fact, meant nothing of this. If anything, it was more than ever a prolonged waiting for some moment of revelation or fulfilment, independent of books, of other minds, while depending only partly on himself.

He was lucky to have Evelyn.

'Do you think this road is going to lead anywhere?' she asked, and smiled at space.

Although she could have been mistaken for a delicate woman, and liked to think of herself as threatened, she was less fragile than wiry, or stringy. Certainly she experienced the odd head-ache on occasions when her sensibility was taxed, but she almost never suffered from physical fatigue. Her weakness, she claimed, was in never being able to find enough on which to exercise her over-active mind. Nor was she capable of simply sitting. She would really have to see about taking up a charity, like Meals on Wheels. She was good at talking to the aged, and it was so gratifying to see in their old faces the appreciation of advice.

'Why shouldn't it lead somewhere?' Harold asked.

'I beg your pardon?'

'The road. This is a day's outing, isn't it?'

'Yes,' she said. 'That was the intention.'

They had eaten a rather nasty lunch – charred chops and fried banana lumped together on a lettuce leaf – in a cemented rockery beside the highway. There was nothing after that but to follow one of the side roads.

Evelyn picked a bunch of shivery-grass, and breathed deep, too deep, on returning momentarily to the years before she knew the answers.

'Yes,' she said. 'We're lucky to have enough to eat. And the climate. The Australian climate. Fancy if we'd been the Burds. Running that awful service station. Quite apart from anything else, the Thames Valley is so damp.'

Harold continued crunching springily ahead. She could smell the acceptable smell of his pipe. Evelyn preferred the company of men for the simple reason that she enjoyed being liked back. Women did not like her honesty.

'In the long run,' she said, 'Australian nationality paid.'

But again Evelyn experienced a little twinge of guilt. She plunged her chin into the bunch of pale-silver shivery-grass.

'Do you think Win Burd really works in their service station?' she asked, but only casually. 'Sticking a petrol hose into strangers' cars?'

'If that's what she wrote you.'

'Some women are not strictly truthful,' Evelyn said. 'And you know Win,' she gave the laugh she kept for those whose faults she had to accept, 'she always loved to dramatize.'

It did not seem to bother Harold.

'Anyway, whether she works the hose or not, it's too dreadful to think about,' Evelyn continued, 'Win and Dudley reduced to a service station!'

Her mouth grew thin and appalled, as though the disaster had been her own.

'Most of them in the same boat – most of the English,' Harold said, 'after Suez.'

'But the Burds', Evelyn protested, 'could have bought and sold the lot. That staircase they brought from Italy must have cost more than most of the others *had*.'

She was careful not to include themselves.

'Wasn't it lovely!' She sighed. 'Rose marble.'

The guests resumed mounting the rosy stairs to be received, those the Burds had invited, with professional affection, the others, with irony disguised as tact. Evelyn – she was an intelligent woman – had seen through it all, and had always felt glad she was on the right side of Win and Dudley's irony. Harold's managing the business for them in a country of the wrong colour made her almost one of the family.

Win Burd had delighted in parties. She could not resist fancy dress. Her long lovely thighs and legs were made for display, and she always took advantage of them. That gold lamé Knave of Hearts the year the Fat Boy showed too warm an interest. Scandal notwithstanding, Win must have derived enormous satisfaction from snubbing a king. The summer the Fazackerleys spent an extended leave in Australia, Win had insisted on Evelyn's packing the Knave of Hearts: so useful on the ship, throw it overboard afterwards. Evelyn had only accepted because she couldn't very well refuse.

Though of course she hadn't worn anything so daring, not to say disgraceful, as Win's tinkling tunic. Both during the voyage, and after, Evelyn had brooded over their employer's generosity, while trying not to relate it to the image of her own, always rather skinny, thighs. She had sold the costume soon after landing.

'Perhaps Win can *put up with* the service station,' she said to Harold. 'She had a streak of something. Not exactly vulgarity. Toughness. It was probably true what people said.'

'What?'

'Oh, you know. About the chorus.'

'Can't remember,' said Harold, when she was sure he did.

'Poor Win, she had a heart of gold. But, my God, wasn't she plain!'

'The face of a goat and the body of a statue. Not all women are as lucky as that.'

'Oh, Harold, you shouldn't!'

'What's wrong? There are men who are partial to goats – even to statues, I'm told.'

'Oh, Harold! How dreadful! How *sick*!'

But she loved it. She loved an opportunity for using the *in* word.

The houses of success strung along the ridge seemed to leap in approval of her knowing mirth. But the houses were thinning out, she observed. The thinning process, together with the wind down her cleavage, turned her cold. Her laughter flickered and was extinguished.

Evelyn said, 'I do hope there won't be a war.'

'What put that into your head?'

'My few investments, naturally. Where should we be without them?'

'In the soup like anybody else.'

Evelyn wasn't prepared to argue. She wasn't just *anybody*, whatever Harold decided for himself.

The road had faded to a faint sandstone scar below the persisting razorback.

'There,' she said, 'I told you it would peter out. Nobody would be mad enough to build in such a barren spot as this, nobody but a suicide.'

Then the little, attenuated, clinging weatherboard offered itself at the last flick of the vanishing road.

Harold said, 'It suited somebody to build.'

'What? That! That *hutch*!'

Certainly the wooden house couldn't pretend to be much more. Clamped to what was practically a cliff, there was nothing to suggest ease or skill in its execution. It was the defenceless amateurishness of the house which roused Evelyn's dark-red scorn. It was a kind of honesty in its painfully achieved proportions, in its out-of-plumb match-stick stairway and exposed seaward balcony which moved Harold and filled him with a longing for something he could never accomplish. Perhaps it was just as well to see the house as a hutch, to imagine large soft animals turning on straw, or enormous satiny birds contemplating the ocean from behind wooden bars. Although he would never have confessed it to Evelyn, his imagination had often helped him out.

But just then Harold Fazackerley was confounded by reality.

The head, the face, the solid shoulders of a man appeared on the out-of-plumb outside stairway, rising above the level of the roof, the road, to look inside the letter-box for one of those letters, Harold could see, the man did not expect to find.

In the same manner, the expression on the anonymous face was directed towards the strangers on the road: doubting, but hopeful.

Then Evelyn Fazackerley heard her husband, not exactly call, bleat, rather, from unpreparedness. It was disconcerting, coming from such a man.

'Clem! Clem, isn't it? Dowson?'

From beneath his stubbly hair, the man's red, coarse-skinned face very diffidently admitted to the name. It infuriated Evelyn. She knew too much about him in advance. Slow people drew from her an irritation almost as visible as blood. Oh yes, she knew!

Excitement was making Harold's mouth lose control.

'You remember Clem, Evelyn!'

He turned.

Harold, she saw with a shock, had been rejuvenated. She would take her time.

'Clem Dowson?'

She might have been proud of her inability to remember.

'The *Simla*. The *Nepal*.' Harold helped.

Then she did begin, faintly, sighingly, allowing herself to recall a heavy engineer, in one liner, and in a second. Since then, she noticed, sun and wind had made him more transparent. In those days the steam and sweat of the engine-room had kept him the colour and texture of a suet crust. Opaque. Afterwards, on land, when she had been given the opportunity of getting to know him better, she hadn't succeeded.

'Ah yes why of course *yes*!'

Whatever your feelings, there were always the social obligations, so Evelyn was turning on what she knew to be her charm. But she had never cared for engineers. Pursers, now, were almost always jolly, first officers sometimes capable of fascinating, but engineers, even when shouting you a white lady, seemed to remain below with their engines, or whatever the things were called.

'And this is where you've hidden yourself away!' She would make it sound a charming joke.

'Yes,' said Dowson.

He did not attempt to excuse himself, though his solid body attached to the frail railings for support, trembled slightly. It might have been the wind buffeting him, if he had not been protected from it by his comic house. He had stood, she allowed herself to realize, on another still occasion, in an almost identical position, holding on to a mango tree.

So now, as she looked at him, she said, 'I wonder exactly how long it is since we took you with us to the Delta?'

'Long enough,' Dowson mumbled, getting a fresh grip of the rail with his thick, bristly fingers.

He had made himself look even cruder by wearing his hair shorn to a stubble, no doubt attempting to disguise his baldness. It made his eyes look bluer, his face more enormous and open to attack.

For that matter all three of them were temporarily somewhat exposed, unable to rely on the disguise of words, as they stood amongst the stones and silence, arrested in their moment of statuary.

Till Harold broke away with that candour which Evelyn had deplored before putting it down to innocence and his sex.

'Anyway, Clem,' he said, 'isn't it about time you showed us over your hide-out? I take it you built the house yourself.'

Dowson laughed. He turned. He was hanging his head and still heaving slightly as he went down the wooden stairs. If he did not reply to Harold, it was clearly because he was giving him the answers to his questions.

The Fazackerleys followed, as it was intended.

'But how *clever!*'

Even before crossing the threshold Evelyn knew which line to take. It was so easy. She was so expert. With shy, boring men.

'You don't mean to tell me you made *this*? This cunning little cupboard with revolving shelves!'

Dowson reached out with his hand and held her for a moment, firmly, even hurtfully, through her glove.

'Only with a finger,' he warned. 'The slightest touch is all it needs.'

Evelyn might have felt offended if the incident hadn't been so insignificant. In the circumstances, she simply passed on. 'And what is this?' she asked. 'This *surrealistic* contraption in wire?'

'That is one of my own inventions. That's to turn the egg out – automatically – as soon as it's boiled.'

'But how amusing!'

Or how pathetic.

'If Harold had half your talent. Now that we're retired, he only threatens to read books, and never gets around to that.'

She looked at her husband as though asking forgiveness for the slight wound she had been moved to inflict. But he did not seem aware of it. There was so much men failed to notice.

The kitchen was all very well. The living-room – she could not hope to see the bedroom – ought to be more rewarding, because more personal, revealing. But it was, in fact, a disappointment. Too bare, too glary. The two armchairs, their covers too tight. The desk: on it one or two instruments, in which she could not take an interest, bottles of coloured inks, what was probably a dictionary. Not even a photograph. Evelyn loved to be able to relate photographs to the owners of them, or better still, she loved the photographs which could not be explained.

But, on a little, ugly, yellow table, there was a basket of wools. And a sock stretched on a darning egg. It put the moisture back into Evelyn's drying lips.

In time they were sitting over Dowson's tea, the kind of dark-red brew you might have expected, in thick white common cups, which showed a rime of tannin as the tide receded. Harold was leaning forward very seriously above his tilted cup, his grey eyes – she had always been proud of their honesty – for the moment rather irritatingly abstracted, as his mouth struggled to convey an awkward preoccupation.

'And what do you *do* with yourself?' he asked when finally he dared.

It was almost as though he were embarrassed to discuss anything so personal in front of his wife.

Dowson sat pulling at the tufts of hair on the backs of his fingers. Then he drew in his mouth, and focused his shockingly blue eyes.

'I sit and watch the ocean,' he answered Harold straight.

Harold appeared to find it a perfectly normal reply, and a gust of breath rose in Evelyn's throat as though to protest against an immoral act.

'But it's so empty. Most of the time, anyway. Except for some uninteresting ship. Ships are only interesting when you're in them,' she managed to gasp.

Neither of the men noticed her.

'You're lucky to know how,' Harold continued.

Evelyn mightn't have been in the room.

Dowson laughed – for Harold. It sounded unexpectedly gentle.

'I won't say you don't need to practise. In the beginning.'

'Yes,' said Harold. 'But the beginning – that's the difficulty.'

Then Dowson leaned forward and asked, 'What about those poems you used to write?'

Evelyn raised her head.

'Poems?' Harold could have been afraid.

'At school.'

'Oh, yes. That was at school.'

Evelyn was swaying slightly.

'That was a beginning,' Dowson suggested.

Evelyn had a headache. Of course she knew, she had heard, but long ago, Clem Dowson and Harold had been together at that preparatory school. It was the wind giving her a head, or the atmosphere of boredom their host created just by his physical presence.

'Fancy your remembering about those poems,' Harold said, and laughed. 'I had forgotten.'
He hadn't.

Harold Fazackerley, the little leggy boy with protruding ears and blue, chilblained hands, used to write poems and things in his peculiar screwed-up writing on scraps of paper he was always terrified might blow about and have to be explained to someone. When he couldn't have explained half of what came out. But the poems were necessary to him at that stage. At a later date, when his reason had sorted things out, he related those creative skirmishes of his boyhood to a hot shower on a cold afternoon or a smooth stool on a warm morning. Often as a boy he had suffered from constipation for stretches of several days. The poems seemed to ease his fears.

All winter the school buildings had been victimized by the winds. But in summer, when the Virginia creeper was again in residence, and the dust thickened amongst tired laurels, and the smell of disinfectant rose piercingly from over-sodden urinals, small boys were fairly trampled by the possibilities of living.

There were the scandals. Harold Fazackerley had not understood them quite. And was frightened by all that. He would not have liked to hear it explained, so he avoided those who were on the point of telling.

Clem Dowson was that silent, slightly older, much sturdier boy: thick ankles in heather-mixture stockings, knees outgrown from knickerbockers. Clem would probably have started shaving early on. He did not go with anybody much, yet survived his isolation. He was not averse to anyone or anything, though it was hard to know whom or what he liked, beyond birds' eggs and grass-chewing and fried bread. He was probably, in fact he *was*, a funny sort of fish you would have been ashamed of meeting in the holidays.

Then Harold Fazackerley went up to Clem Dowson on an afternoon smelling of smoke and showed him two of those poems he had written. And Clem had read and handed them back. He smiled. He had broad teeth with grooves down them.

He said, 'They won't ever understand. Your writing's too hard to read.'

And at once Harold Fazackerley was reassured. They had a secret between them, besides, which was perhaps what he had wanted.

There was nothing between Clem and Harold, nothing you could be ashamed of. Harold had never done anything like that, or not that you could count. Nothing reprehensible, as he might have expressed it later, in his report-writing days. Not with Clem, anyway.

Sometimes they mucked around the paddocks looking for nests. How Clem shone, blowing a maggie's egg for Harold on a clear morning of spring, ankle-deep in dead grass, against the huge stringy bark. Held to his more-than-friend's lips the speckled eggshell increased in transparency, and reddish, palpitating light.

'My intellectual husband has kept the secrets you apparently share.'

Pleating her mouth, lowering her eyelids, Evelyn Fazackerley made an exquisite irony of it.

In abeyance for a short space out of respect for memory, the wind had begun again to torment the little room in which they were sitting. The tenure of the house perched above the sea was more than ever insecure.

Evelyn looked at Harold and forgave him any hurt he might have caused her. Forgiveness had always come easily to her.

She even turned to Dowson and asked, 'Shall we see you again?'

Though here she only half forgave. She was putting the man

in an awkward position. She knew. She wanted to. It was the best way of cutting a knot. And he shuffled slightly, his rubber soles, and gave a congested smile, not even to Harold, but the room.

Harold said, 'I don't expect we could ever tempt Clem inside our horrible flat.'

Although feeling it was unnecessarily sincere, Evelyn played up to it.

'With my cooking! No *suffragis* now, you know!'

She could enjoy the faint bitterness of it.

'I'll look in. Some time. Perhaps,' Dowson suggested, mastering each word except the last.

Nobody seemed to think of offering or receiving an address.

Harold Fazackerley could have been muddling again over some problem the elusiveness of which had become a worry. He was greyer than Evelyn knew him, as though bleached by the blazing ocean, shrunken and brittle in the presence of Dowson's resilient stillness. Could it be that Harold's manhood would desert him before the end?

Though the possibility did not bear investigating to any depth because of the terror in it, Evelyn often dared wish she might outlive her husband, whose virility still attracted other women. She could not complain really, herself contributing to this in choosing his more exciting clothes, and in many little, more intimate ways, such as taking her own nail-scissors to clip back an independent hair of his moustache, or those which were sprouting beyond his nostrils.

'I mean,' Harold was saying, or harping, 'Clem has come out of it with so much more than most of us. I mean, he has learnt to sit still. He has learnt to think.'

Not a thought in his head. You only had to look. Or did men, especially men together, experience something women couldn't?

She examined Dowson particularly closely, and disliked

more than ever what she saw. If she had prodded him hard she imagined he would have felt of hard rubber.

'Certainly Mr Dowson has made himself very comfortable. Charming. This cosy little house. All the inventions. That egg-boiling thing alone. But a bit lonely at times, I should have thought.'

There, she knew, she had put her finger on it.

Then Dowson looked at her; it was for the first time, she realized, for the first time, at least, since they had stood beneath the mango tree in the steaming Delta. 'A spell of loneliness never did anybody any harm.'

'If you are convinced,' she said.

Evelyn got up, sweeping out of her lap the non-existent crumbs, because there hadn't been even a bought biscuit.

Everybody had, in fact, got up.

'It's been fine seeing you, Clem,' Harold Fazackerley was saying. 'We must write. We must keep in touch.'

Although, to emphasize it, Harold had taken him by the elbow, Dowson hung his head, not believing it possible. Dowson, the elder, more stomachy, congested, preparing for a lonely stroke, had been transformed into the younger, Evelyn saw. She did not know whether she was pleased. The sight of Harold's youthful back often inclined her to invent youth for herself. Now his back was the wrong side.

As they clung to the rickety outside stairway, above the supine rockplants and the unfortunate, spinning fuchsias, she was battered into charity.

'How shall we find,' she began to ask through the veered wind, 'how can we get in touch with you?'

'Just put "Dowson",' Dowson answered incredibly. ' "Dowson",' he repeated, ' "Bandana Beach".'

Standing on the friable road, the wind spiralling round his legs inside the stuff of his trousers, Harold Fazackerley again visualized those large primeval animals and enormous satiny birds gravely observing the ocean from behind wooden bars. It was not possible to communicate with such removed creatures, except through silences, of which there were never enough.

Yet he had communicated a little, he thought, or hoped, with Dowson.

All the way, and especially in the bus, Evelyn kept repeating they had had a lovely day.

'Yes,' he agreed, at one stage, because it was expected of him, 'and what luck to come across old Clem.'

'I like him,' she said, firmly, holding up her chin.

He ignored it. Perhaps he thought nobody else capable of appreciating Dowson.

'I envy Clem,' Harold said.

'How?' she asked, drawing in her breath.

'He's happy.'

'Oh, come!' said Evelyn. 'You can't say *we* aren't happy.'

'No,' he agreed. 'Is the window too much for you?'

She shook her head, giving him her dreamy look, one of those relics of her girlhood.

'The air is so lovely,' she said; she would not let it be otherwise.

They were being jolted past the litter of matchbox houses waiting on that sweep of the coast for the tidal wave which hadn't yet materialized.

'I would have said,' she said, 'he wasn't all that happy. In his do-it-yourself house. With those unnecessary gadgets.'

'Why?'

Though he did not move, except as thrown by their onward motion, she could sense him rearing inside his constraining body beside her on the lumpy public-transport seat.

'Because,' she said, 'well – it lacks a woman's hand.'

She looked down at her own formally gloved ones. Whatever her other shortcomings she could afford to be proud of her hands. During the almost endless stretch between Colombo and Fremantle an artist had once asked to paint them, and she had been persuaded – with Harold's knowledge.

But now Harold was invisibly rearing, finally actually heaving and altering position, rather too uncomfortably, aggressively, on the bus seat.

'But you don't understand', he blurted, 'a man like Clem Dowson.'

'Then I don't,' she decided to agree.

Because to submit in a crisis was to subscribe to her own reasonableness.

Harold appeared convinced, and rightly. Nobody could have questioned her loyalty to him, in the larger sense, either in the squalid present, or the good old plushier days of power and respect. When Egypt had gone to so many women's heads.

Harold Fazackerley had returned to Egypt after the First World War. His friend Dudley Burd had kept his promise. First Dudley's father, then Dudley himself, became Harold Fazackerley's employer. Friends more than employers, though Evelyn always maintained friendship wasn't the elastic affair Harold liked to believe. Anyway, he was in the habit of calling his employer 'Dud' to his face, and of helping himself from the decanter before he had been invited; while to employ an 'Aussie', and to refer to his manager's wife as a 'Dink', seemed to entertain Dudley Burd.

All very well, and amusing, for an Englishman of Sir Dudley's wealth and rank to season his conversation with crude colonial salt; but Evelyn detested it. For a long time she couldn't avail herself of the familiarity the Burds appeared genuinely wanting to share. Her hand trembled holding gin. She was nervous, she supposed, in the beginning: it was agony to imagine the colours she had chosen clashed, or that she was making mistakes at dinner parties, or that her accent might be showing through. 'Oh no, Sir Dudley,' she might say. 'Thank you. Really. I'd rather not. Well, you see, not every Australian girl is at home on a horse. Just as', she added with a little giggle, 'not every Australian speaks with an accent.' She hated to hear her own giggle. But the scent of gin was anaesthetizing her gaucherie, giving her courage. She liked, she had to admit, the faint scent of leather and sweat, of horses, and the men who had been riding them.

Or Win: the trailing, the devastating, interchangeable scents of Win Burd.

'Ev, darling, what a bloody bore those Rockcliffes proposing to barge in for lunch! It would be much more fun to get ginned up a little together, and enjoy a siesta afterwards. But you're not *drink*-ing! Evelyn?'

'Oh yes, Lady Burd! Thank you. I'm doing nicely.'

Again that giggle. When she wasn't stupid. Probably less so than Lady Burd.

Early on, the Burds had suggested she drop the Sir and Lady. But she couldn't bring herself to. If she hadn't done it in her own time it might have seemed unnatural, and she would have felt embarrassed.

Also, perhaps, she did enjoy the sound of the title.

'That's so terribly kind of you, Lady Burd ... Yes, Lady Burd ... We'd be thrilled.'

Because Win used to telephone sometimes in that slurry, half-ginned voice, and suggest that Evelyn and Harold might like to spend the weekend in the Delta, which meant: use the house on what was referred to by the Burds' British dependants as the Estate. Evelyn was delighted for a time to receive its freedom, but she had to be so careful not to give anything like a display of girlish or vulgar enthusiasm, and she had to take particular care over her enunciation. She couldn't afford to throw accent and grammar over her shoulder like Win Burd. The upper-class English could get away with murder.

Sometimes when Harold had leave the Fazackerleys might spend a week or fortnight at the house on the Estate. The Burds found it a bit of a bore; they preferred the Aegean and the elaborately simple luxury of their converted caique. But in spite of the Egyptians and the flies Evelyn decided to love the Delta. She became the chatelaine. Of the Burds' certainly rather spartan, but cool, shuttered, whitewashed house. With lands stretching between canals. And mango trees heavy with nauseating fruit.

'You'd think they'd introduce some upholstery, at least, and a few modern conveniences,' Evelyn complained once. 'The mattresses are like lying on the ground.'

Harold had to make excuses for the Burds.

'They like to rough it now and again.'

'Oh, I suppose so,' Evelyn agreed, 'if you have something as smooth as rose marble to return to.'

But even without benefit of staircase, Evelyn Fazackerley came into her own as chatelaine, standing, for instance, in the doorway which separated dining-room from kitchen quarters, frowning, shouting, '*Gibbou wahed foutah, Mohammed!*' to the slave.

Harold might say, 'Darling – why do Anglo-Saxons have to shout at foreigners?'

'But I wasn't shouting,' Evelyn replied. 'I was making myself understood. And surely if you classify Arabs as "foreigners" it raises them to the level of Europeans? Not that I'm sticking up for Europeans! They're there – we know – but I don't know any, and don't particularly want to.'

'Aren't you being narrow minded?'

She looked at him. Because he was in love with her he was making it sound almost a virtue. So she was reassured.

'I am accused!' she said softly, looking down into the greasy bean soup.

Evelyn Fazackerley was slim. She wore a lot of white. In the reflective dark of the old Delta house, surrounded by a steamy, indolent landscape, she saw herself as the spirit of cool. If only her arms hadn't been quite so thin, or the pores hadn't stood so wide open in her otherwise immaculate skin.

But her power allowed her to forget such details. She was amazed, even shocked, by the passion she seemed to inspire in her husband during those steamy summer months.

'By the time October is here,' Win Burd used to say, 'I'm destroyed, I'm an Alexandrian whore.'

Win, of course, was extravagant in every way. She could afford to be.

One summer while they were all still comparatively young the Burds had lent the house in the Delta for the Fazackerleys to take a week's leave. The prospect no longer pleased Evelyn: the mango trees, the dark rooms, the smell, and worse, the taste of primus, Egyptian women afloat in black along the paths of the canals, laughing at what she was never going to discover – all would be the same as before, except that Mohammed had been replaced by Mustapha, and Mustapha by Osmin.

Moreover, Evelyn brooded, the Burds only lent the house in summer when the Delta was at its steamiest.

It was two nights to their departure. Harold had come in, she realized.

'You remember that cove, that Dowson, the engineer from the *Nepal?* The one I was at school with. Well, he's in Alex, Evelyn. Been sick. He's just discharged from hospital.'

It was far too sticky and undignified a night. Having to remember that engineer was to do so only irritably.

'I'd have taken him for a Scot,' she said. 'But he wasn't.'

Harold was in his kind mood. Its feelers were gently reaching out.

'I think he's hard up for something to do. A bit lonely, I'd say. He's got another ten days before joining his ship. I told him he'd better come out to Kafr el Zayat with us.'

'Oh, darling! That means I've got to set to and buy a whole

lot of extra *stuff*! You're most unreasonable at times.'

'You've only got to ring the Nile Cold in the morning,' Harold said.

She laughed rather high. She was wearing a lime sash.

'You do show me up, darling,' she said. 'And more often than not you're perfectly right.'

It was the sort of moment which made their relationship such a special one.

Harold kissed her. He had been drinking, but only the way everybody did. It added to his masculinity.

'Dowson has a friend,' he said.

'A friend? Then how can he be lonely?'

Harold was slowed down.

'Well, I mean. A manner of speaking. And anyway, the friend's a Greek. It isn't the same as your own kind.'

'A Greek? I've never met a Greek.'

'It may be an interesting experience. This one has just come from an archaeological dig somewhere in Upper Egypt.'

'*You don't mean to say you* ... ' Evelyn could only break off.

'Couldn't very well avoid it. He's a stranger, and Dowson's friend. I had to ask him.'

'I ask *you*! You sit drinking in some bar, and before you know, you've invited all the rag-tag in the bar! Darling, I do think you might have considered the position you're putting us in. Bad enough the stodgy engineer. I know he's honest, if uncouth in almost every way. But a Greek. In Win and Dudley's home.'

'Win and Dudley have been known to invite Armenians, and I never heard the silver was missing.'

'That is different. The Burds are responsible to themselves.'

Nothing was spoken at dinner, except when Evelyn said, '*Esh, Khalil. Gawam!*'

The drought from which she was suffering had grown so intense it was surprising such plentiful tears gushed over the coffee.

'Oh, darling, I am silly! I am silly!' she said, making it sillier. When he came and sat against her, the familiar outline of his body through the wringing shirt robbed her of her last control. She kissed his hands through the mess of tears. She and Harold were melting together in a scent of jasmine and moist flower-beds.

So next morning he promised to ring Dowson after Evelyn had rung the Nile Cold Storage. Reason had decided against the Greek. Evelyn said such a very simple man as Dowson would be easily persuaded. Harold said he hoped he would.

On the morning of the day, as Evelyn was discovering the Nile Cold had forgotten to include the *pâté* and the police were beating up a beggar in the street, the heavy man she remembered as Dowson the engineer appeared in the driveway. At his heels a second man. Evelyn froze inside her perspiration. Not, possibly, the Greek? Each of the men was carrying a small case.

Dowson shook hands much too firmly. The Greek, it was, pronounced his own name. Determined not to listen, Evelyn heard it going off like fireworks.

Then Evelyn, not with the assistance of her will, but in a gust of dizzying, and equally pyrotechnical, inspiration, began to say her piece, 'Oh, but what an embarrassing, such a terribly distressing mistake! Oh, but Harold surely, Mr Dowson? Or can it be another instance of the appalling Alexandrian telephone system? For Harold not to have made it clear that, much as we'd have liked it *ourselves*, we're hardly the masters in a *lent* house. It is kind of Sir Dudley and Lady Burd to allow us *our* friends – ' here she turned with evident graciousness to the engineer ' – but for us to go farther would, I feel, only be to impose on the Burds. Will Mr Dowson explain?' she appealed to Harold. 'More clearly? To his friend?'

In a morning which had already grown merciless enough to allow no shadows, she had stood the solid Dowson, like a wall, between herself and the situation.

Evelyn was smiling. Everyone was smiling. Harold was making noises as though somebody had punched him in the ribs. The Greek was smiling most of all. He was a small and, in every way, insignificant man. His necktie, which he had been in the habit of knotting always lower, and tried to restore for the occasion to even lengths, was looking chewed and stringy.

Evelyn turned away after that, but did just glance back once. Dowson had retreated along the drive with his friend, to where the hedge of blue plumbago was broken by the gateway. They were standing together in the white dust. Dowson's hand was on the Greek's shoulder.

'We've behaved rottenly,' Harold was saying. 'I expect we've hurt both of them.'

'Nonsense,' she said. 'People are thicker-skinned than you think.'

All the same, she was determined to be particularly nice to the Dowson man during his few days in the Delta.

She began already on the way. As Harold drove she would turn round towards the engineer, who was sitting on the edge of the rear seat, his hands firmly grasping the back of the one in front of him. It made them an intimate trio. Such a very simple man could only, she was certain, have forgiven her. Even so, she felt her face flicker with light and wind, also possibly with remembrance of a recent, if unimportant, 'scene'.

However she might be looking in the Egyptian glare, at least she would not see, nor, probably, would Dowson. Though she half-closed her eyes – a trick learnt from the mirror – whenever she turned to address their guest. Confidence seduced her mouth, the face she turned full on at him.

She was making that kind of conversation for visitors passing through: the water buffaloes and ibises, together with some of the cotton jargon and statistics picked up from listening interminably to experts.

When suddenly she was forced to remark, 'I do hope your friend wasn't hurt by the stupid mistake Harold – we, all of us, made.'

Dowson smiled his sandy smile.

'I don't think he's one who ever expects too much.'

Evelyn did not expect that.

'I've always been told the Greeks, the modern Greeks, that is, not the real ones,' she said, 'are practically orientals.'

'Protosingelopoulos is real enough,' Dowson answered. The windborne sun had set fire to his suety face.

'You should know,' said Evelyn. 'He's your friend. Have you known him long?'

'Three and – yes, half a day.'

'Oh, but really – are you always so sure?'

Dowson answered, 'Yes.'

She realized then that his sitting forward on the edge of the seat and clutching the back of theirs had not been to bring them all more closely together, but to help him coil more tightly inside his secretive mind. How repulsive the backs of his fingers were, with their tufts of reddish-blond hair. She had turned after that and watched the long, straight, boring road.

Dowson, surprisingly, seemed at home in the Burds' house. When he was not listening to, or out driving with Harold, the thick-walled rooms provided him with a silence the equivalent of his own; their rough proportions might have been designed to contain his crude form. As he strolled about the grounds, the landscape was perhaps more indifferent to his presence, though he appeared unaware of it, planting his heels firmly as he walked, in no particular direction but the one in which his thoughts were leading him.

She had to admit she was put out by what Dowson was becoming, so she looked for any weakness which might compensate for his rejecting the mould she had decided must be his. As in the case of so many visitors passing through from other climates, his clothes were quite unsuitable. When Dowson abandoned his blue serge coat, and went walking in his wrong shirt and serge trousers, she was more than amused: she was glad to see him look so out of place, hence vulnerable.

Sometimes as he wove thumping through the mango grove, or past the beds of reedy carnations, he would be carrying a book under his arm. There were occasions when she came across him, a core in the shadow of one of the closely shuttered rooms, at least sitting with, if not actually reading, the open book.

At last she reached the point where she couldn't resist taking it from him. To satisfy her curiosity.

'You'll ruin your eyes,' she said, not without gentleness, 'reading in such a dim light.'

It was a translation from the Greek, she discovered. Poems. By somebody called Cavafy.

'Surely you're not an intellectual!' She smiled a healing smile.

'Not exactly,' Dowson said.

'Harold has moments of fancying himself as an intellectual. Oh, I'm not trying to belittle him. He's much cleverer than I. I'm only a scatter-brained woman.'

She waited for him to handle that, but he didn't.

'What very difficult-looking, not to say peculiar, poems!' She handed back something she would have to make up her mind about. 'If you understand those, then it makes you most horribly intellectual, and I shall have to adopt a different attitude towards you.'

Dowson sat rubbing his hands together as if working tobacco for a pipe. The head on the bull-shoulders was averted, so that she found herself looking at his clumsy profile. Though she had been wrong in her assessment of his character, it was gratifying to know that his physical coarseness could not dissolve, and that his shirt, in keeping, smelt slightly of sweat.

'You don't have to understand,' she realized he was saying, 'not everything, not every word. I don't pretend to. It's something the professor gave me,' he added.

'Which professor?'

'Protosingelopoulos.'

'That little man a professor? You amaze me! Though I wonder why. When life is all surprises.'

Their talk was almost making her feel intellectual herself. But Dowson didn't seem aware of it, or was sensitive only to his own problems and reactions.

'Aren't I causing you trouble by being here?' he suddenly asked.

'Whatever put that into your head? I'm only afraid you may be bored. I think I know what forced unemployment must feel like to an active man. At least today Harold will be driving over to Mansoura, to look at a crop he's interested in. You'll be able to go with him. And talk about all the things you have in common.'

'What are those?' he asked unexpectedly, and tried to make it sound less strange by laughing.

She wondered whether he was cunning.

'If I knew,' she answered, 'then you might trust me more.'

Just then Harold flung open the door, and said, 'That idiot of an Arab tells me only now that the pump stopped working yesterday, and we're practically without water. Instead of going to Mansoura I'll have to drive over and fetch de Boisé. Do you want to come with me, Clem, on this errand, not that it's an interesting one?

'No, Harold,' said Dowson. 'I'll see what can be done about the pump. It's probably something just in my line. Then you can drive to Mansoura as arranged.'

A practical man, he was again happy, she saw, at the prospect of making himself useful. She was only scornful of the ease with which he and Harold called each other by their Christian names. What should have strengthened seemed to make them weak.

After Harold left, and Dowson had started tinkering with the pump, there was nothing to fill the morning but the steam which rose from the Delta. She sat down and again began looking through the book of poems, from which an occasional carved image formed glittering in her mind. First a word here and there, then whole phrases, breathed disconcertingly. Love was exchanged on terms she knew existed in theory, and which now in the half-light of poetry were too palpably fleshed, too suffocatingly scented. She remembered hearing of an English-woman raped by an Arab in Nouzha Gardens. Evelyn put the book down. There was no rape, she felt, which could not be avoided.

But the perfume persisted, of overblown words, sweat, and the dark red roses growing out of Delta silt the other side of the shutters.

In the course of the morning Dowson came and asked her for some rags. He looked so content and unselfconscious.

'What a mess you've made of your shirt,' she said, but completely detached.

'I'll give it a wash,' he said, 'afterwards.'

'Oh, no!' she said. '*They* will give it a wash.'

As she went to rummage for a suitable rag, her self-possession sat most agreeably on her. She came back with an old silk slip of Lady Burd's.

'Isn't it too good?' he asked.

'I shouldn't think so,' she replied, and laughed. 'Or if it is, it won't be missed.'

Not by Win. Who flew a hat from Paris for a wedding, and sent it back, and flew another.

'How is the *pump*?' she asked, deliberately impaling the word on her tongue.

'We'll fix it,' he said earnestly.

But she had not listened for his answer. She was fascinated by Win's silk slip hanging from his bare arm, and the skin of his arms dribbled with black machine-oil and daubed with greyer grease.

They met only briefly at lunch.

When she lay down for her siesta she could hear the intermittent sound of metal, tinny in competition with the dead weight of heat. He had been ill; he might get a sunstroke, she thought, but you could not persuade a man against what he wanted. How glad she was she had married Harold, whose wanting had less conviction in it. She wondered how she had found Harold, and where in sleep she would find him again.

For an instant she came across him or, no, Dowson, seated at a round, iron, slanted table. Dowson was stuffing his mouth with a mouse-trap variety of cheese. *Why must you eat like that?* she asked. *Because,* he mumbled through his bread, *you are starving, aren't you, Mrs Fazackerley?* She resented hearing her name, as much as she disapproved of the steadily falling crumbs.

On waking, she found that her right cheek had a crease in it. She was feeling irritable, but by the time she had bathed and powdered herself, she might have offered pity to anyone who asked for it. Old tangos persisted in her head, and the smell of a liner's deck at night. It was only natural. Half the life of so many Australians was spent at sea, getting somewhere, she reflected.

When she met Dowson she asked through her brightest lipstick, 'Hasn't my old Harold got back?'

'No,' said Dowson.

He was looking a caricature of himself, in a fresh shirt, and those blue serge trousers which, apparently, were the only ones he had with him.

'What a bore!' she said. 'The dinner will be awful. It would have been awful anyway.'

After pouring his whisky she asked, 'Are you glad to be an Australian?'

'I'd stopped thinking about it.'

'I'm glad I am,' she said, whether he believed it or not.

She was truly glad, though, for the reality of her healthy Australian girlhood. She was thankful for the apple she had bitten into, but thrown away extravagantly.

'Do you think Harold could have had an accident?' she asked.

'No. Why?' he said. 'There are too many reasons why he shouldn't have. People usually get back even when you're expecting them not to.'

It was the gin, she suspected, giving her morbid ideas. Although normally it was not the kind of thing she did, she had another one to quell them.

'You don't understand', she said, 'what Harold means to me. Although', she said, '*you* can talk to him, or not talk, and arrive at something I can never get at.'

Dowson looked puzzled and stupid.

He said, 'But, but?'

She suggested they stroll a bit. It was healthier than sitting drinking and having morbid ideas about car accidents and marriage.

'We didn't mention marriage,' said Dowson.

He was that kind of man.

Anyway, they began to tread the darkness down. Though the magic slide of the Delta had been withdrawn, the smell of it was there: exhausted clover and dung fires. When they told her it was dung, when she was newly arrived in Egypt, it had been one of the things to resent. Till by degrees it became a comfort of the nomadic existence, which was what the life of any foreigner in Egypt remained. Tonight there were also the stars, at which she used to look in the beginning, before she got into the habit of taking them for granted.

'Didn't we', she continued, tripping over something in the darkness, 'discuss marriage? I thought we were discussing it practically continuously.'

She could not help limping at first from the momentary pain in her ankle, but he did not attempt to support her.

'Not to my knowledge, Mrs Fazackerley,' he said, 'though I gather you're pretty obsessed by it.'

'Then *you* have never been married!' She shot it out.

'No,' he agreed.

She wondered whether the darkness would disguise the shape her mouth was taking.

'They say that if a man isn't married by the age of thirty, he's either very selfish, or very immoral. I wonder which you are!'

That at least convinced her she need not limp.

'Married or single,' Dowson said, 'most men seem to be moderately selfish and moderately immoral.'

'But you don't want to see!' she cried. 'It's the immoderate bachelors I'm talking about.'

'I don't see, Mrs Fazackerley,' he said, 'why it should interest you all that much. When you have what you want.'

'Oh I know! I know!'

Her face bumped against a mango in the dark. She was spattered with leaves and her own protests.

'But we are talking, aren't we,' she persisted, 'to keep our spirits up? And to get to know each other. Why don't I know you?'

'That I can't answer,' he said. 'If we are meant to know a person, then we do.'

In a glitter of starlight she saw a little of his face, and the expression had nothing for her. It was frightening.

'You are a man who strikes me as never being frightened,' she said. 'That in itself is frightening to anyone who is frightened.'

'What are you frightened of ?' he asked.

'Almost everything. Living in this country.' Her mind lurched. 'English accents. *Scorpions!*' She pounced on the scorpions. 'Even now, after years in Egypt, I'm terrified I shall forget to think, and step into a shoe which has a scorpion inside.'

And her hand, surprising to herself, seized his rough arm. It was as though she had never touched a man before, and the experience drew her towards him, closer still, to deeper experience of night and horror. Lurid and unconvincing in themselves, the scorpions had been necessary as a starting point. Just as Dowson's coarse and clumsy body might prove the kind of debasement she would return to in sober moments with all the drunkenness of remorse.

They had come out on the edge of the plantation, where a black water flowed through the greenish-silver light, and the raised Arab voices were splintering the cubes of village houses. Only Dowson remained solid.

'Did you ever find one?' he asked.

'What?' she spluttered.

'A scorpion.'

He laughed like a boy. With his free arm he was holding on to the trunk of a young mango tree.

'No,' she said. 'But it isn't any less frightening to expect.'

Although in the several light-years of their journey she had flattened, plastered herself against him according to the instructions she had somehow learnt, they both remained curiously objectiveless. Dowson might have withdrawn from his solid body, except, she realized, he was very slightly trembling.

'You expect *death*, don't you?' he was chattering, 'without even putting on your shoe. But you stop thinking about it. You'd never get on with living.'

'Oh yes, I'm silly, I know! It's my fate always to be re-minded of it!'

She was retreating by shivers of self-mortification.

'I know!' She gulped repeatedly.

She was standing crying beside him in the green Egyptian night. Now that her lust, it had not been lust, was no more than a tingling of coarse hair against her memory, she badly wanted him to believe in something more than her sterility.

'I'm sorry.' From a great distance she was listening to herself. 'I'm upset. Our little boy. You know we lost our child.'

'*No!*' said Dowson with the full weight of his astonishment. He was looking at her too heavily, too.

'Fell into one of the canals.' She was whimpering helplessly by now. 'You see, Mr Dowson? You *will* understand?'

Still the desire spurted in her to embrace her child's great stubbly head. Her lost child.

'What age was the little boy?'

It might have made her shriek with laughter if she herself hadn't created the solemnity. The green light was glittering in Dowson's earnest eyes.

'Five,' she calculated.

But he did not notice it was dragged out of her, and for a moment she got possession of his blunt, sweating fingers, which she no longer very much wanted, of which, in fact, she had a horror, as of herself.

'You must never – ' she was remembering how to give a command, 'never bring this up with Harold, who was more upset than I can tell,' she continued very rapidly. 'We don't talk about it ourselves.'

Dowson the fish was still goggling, and she still dissolved in the misery of deceit.

Shortly after, the headlights were approaching down the long straight road.

'Sorry, Evelyn darling,' Harold said, 'there's no excuse I can offer. I'm just late.'

She couldn't even feel badly used.

'We were beginning to worry about you,' said Dowson.

'Why?' asked Harold.

Neither could answer.

'No harm is done,' said Evelyn. 'Except in the kitchen. I can't be responsible for the dinner.'

Sweeping a spider out of her hair, she went into the house to restore her face.

In the morning Harold came to her and said, 'Dowson has decided to return to Alex. He wants to send for a car. But I told him I'd drive him over.'

'Oh?' she said. 'How peculiar he is! When he still has several days to put in.'

'Perhaps he wants to see something more of his friend before joining his ship at Port Said.'

When she went out to the front, Dowson was trying to refasten one of the locks of his suitcase.

'I'm so sorry you have to rush off,' she began. 'But I understand your wanting to see something of Professor Proto before you leave. I shall always feel he may have a grudge against me because it wasn't possible to invite him too.'

It was easier to sound sincere when obligations had been removed.

Dowson could have been mystified by the obviously broken lock of his cheap suitcase. He continued fiddling with the rusty clasp.

'Protosingelopoulos?' he said. 'I expect he'll have left for Greece by this.'

'But Harold said ... '

Harold was calling to the Arab to wipe the windscreen of the car. His back was turned. It was impossible to tell if he was aware of the snippet of conversation she was left holding with his friend. Harold was permanently preoccupied with the upkeep of cars. With cotton. Or, she admitted with a twinge, his wife.

And Dowson, she realized, was not at all mystified. He was looking away to hide what he knew, and would go off in possession of her secret. Fortunately the man was too stupid or too honest to make use of it.

'Goodbye, Mr Dowson,' she said. 'I hope you'll soon feel perfectly strong.'

He laughed oddly and, looking at his large feet, replied, 'I never felt sick. Nothing you could put your finger on. Only they told me I was.'

Then Harold was driving his friend or nuisance away. Dowson waved, or put up a blunt hand. Harold waved, and it was Harold on whom she focused, as he signalled that soon they would be uninterruptedly together. Sometimes she found herself wishing Harold might go down with a serious illness so that she could demonstrate a devotion which her surface concealed. She saw him lying in shaded light, in haggard, waxen profile, inside a mosquito net. While she drained the fever from him, into her own body.

But it was she who suffered illnesses, unimportant, fretful ones. It was humiliating.

At sixty Evelyn Fazackerley was tolerably preserved. Although she had looked skinny as a girl, by sixty her skinniness had become a figure, and she reinforced herself with hats. She was fortunate, the glass had told her, in having taste. Windows, the windows of buses, returned her conviction, as she allowed the motion of the bus to throw her lightly against her husband's shoulder because, in his retirement, Harold was almost always at her side.

Sometimes she wondered how much a man, a really mascu-

line man like Harold, was aware of the part a woman's
softness played in his life. She wondered on the afternoon they
were being carried back from that beach. She had on her coat
with the smoky-fox collar, less fashionable than timeless, like
something worn by the Queen Mother.

'There's the ironing,' Harold was saying. 'That'd be a bit of
a problem. But you could pay a woman to do it. I expect that's
how old Clem gets round it. There's still the shopping, though.
I can't stand the sight of a man with a string bag.'

'You surprise me,' Evelyn said, 'taking an interest in a person
so uninteresting as Mr Dowson.'

'Clem interests me tremendously.'

'There's no accounting for tastes, I suppose. Those books
you buy! I can't remember the *names* in a Russian novel from
one page to the next.'

She laughed tolerantly, however. She often did the most
boring things if Harold showed he wanted it.

'That Dowson,' she began afresh from behind half-closed
eyes, 'I remember seeing him with a book in his hands. But I
wonder whether he can really read.'

'Don't expect he needs to.'

'Oh, come, darling!'

The light in which Harold saw his friend made her close her
eyes completely.

'Clem strikes me as being as self-contained as – as some object – take,' he was straining at it awkwardly, 'a chunk of glass.'

Evelyn opened her eyes. Harold was positively sweating, as
though from embarrassment.

'But what was he?' she asked. 'A ship's engineer! Who
retired to an Australian beach. And what? And nothing!'

'He probably hasn't lived a life of any interest himself. But
absorbs – and reflects – experience.'

Harold was almost choking on his own words. In the end he
took out his pipe.

Evelyn felt most disturbed.

'What was that illness he had?' she asked. 'When his ship dropped him off in Egypt.'

'I believe it was a nervous breakdown.'

Evelyn moistened her lips.

'You didn't tell me,' she said.

'Didn't I? I don't suppose I tell everything. Do you?'

'I try to,' she said.

The bus was carrying them into the city. Now that they were looking at it again, each vaguely wondered whether they had chosen to live in it.

'What I admire most in Dowson,' Harold Fazackerly said abruptly, 'is his ability to choose.'

'You can't say we don't do practically everything we choose,' Evelyn murmured, drowsy from the bus.

But turned suddenly on her husband, and asked with the utmost earnestness, which was unusual for her, even when she felt earnest, 'Harold, do you think Dowson is queer?'

'What on earth makes you ask that?'

'I don't know,' she said, shrugging. 'The sea, they say, turns them queer.'

'It wasn't the Navy. On a liner the women don't give them much opportunity.'

'No!'

She giggled. She liked the way he put things. How glad she was to be married to Harold, who seldom ignored the openings she offered for a slightly oblique exchange. He respected in her the subtlety which lots of men might have pinched out on recognizing.

They were soon shut in the lift of the block in which they lived. Dust had settled on the branches of the iron roses, on the stems of originally gilded lilies, of the door which sometimes stuck. At different levels the same landing sank in striations of brown pine to meet the slowly rising lift. The Fazackerleys tried to count their lift among their blessings. But Evelyn always stood clear of its thicket of metal flowers, for fear of coming into contact with their slight fur, their greasy dew.

Tonight on blundering into their practically functionless hall, she sighed and said, 'There's nothing like your own home, is there?' without a qualm for the triteness of her own remark.

At least it would be a relief to relieve. Harold eased himself sideways into the lavatory's narrow stall, and stood like a horse gone at the knees. From down the well the sounds of night began exploding in Hungarian. For Harold Fazackerley, emptying a full bladder, the iron veins on the neo-Tudor wall opposite became the arteries of life.

'I expect even Mr Dowson feels attached', Evelyn said, resuming, as she often did, a dialogue with which he failed to re-connect, 'to that lonely little rickety house.'

Evelyn his wife was doing something to her hair. She had already, it appeared, attended to that first necessity, her mouth. Her lips dripped with light and crimson. He couldn't have done without Evelyn, of course. A vision of her death-mask on the last of the Egyptian pillow-slips made him switch on the radio.

Actors were acting out a play to which neither of them listened; because after Evelyn had brought the sherry, which neither of them really cared for, she turned towards him, flickering her eyelids, and began, 'I've had a brainwave – whatever you may think of it.'

'Let's have it, then,' he said, knocking back the Amontillado Dry.

Evelyn at first continued flickering her eyelids.

'Well,' she said, 'I don't want to meddle. But I suddenly thought of Nesta Pine – well, in connection with – now don't laugh – the Dowson man.'

Then Evelyn did exactly what she had told him not to: she tilted back her head and laughed, twiddling her surviving strand of pearls.

44

'Nesta Pine? Good God! Whatever made you? *Nesta Pine!*'
He could not join in Evelyn's laughter.

'There!' she said complacently. 'I knew you'd find it most
peculiar, but I'm prepared to persuade you it makes sense.'

She sat down, exposing those parts of her which had always
been much too thin, but he loved her. Only Harold knew how
Evelyn had envied Win Burd her legs.

'Surely Nesta', Evelyn was arguing, 'deserves in the end a
few of the good things of life?'

'But in your opinion Clem Dowson is far from being a good
thing.'

'Oh, my *opinion*!' She lowered her eyes. 'What do you care
about *my* opinion?'

He was by now too interested to contradict.

'Nesta's too quiet,' he said.

'Isn't *he*?'

'Yes.'

Although the situation was grave she did not seem to notice
it. Nor would he have expected her to. It was his concern. He
had observed Clem very closely, right down to that ingrown
hair which, Matron said, had caused the boil. Matron gave the
boil her Aberdonian squeeze, and Clem stood it. But could he
stand the kindliest, the cotton-wooliest intentions of Nesta
Pine?

'She's a jolly good cook,' Evelyn said.

If he allowed her to continue, it was because he had dropped
into the habit, from their being together so long. They still
slept together, perhaps once a fortnight. He did love her.

'I know,' Evelyn said, 'because I had lunch with them once
when she was with Mrs Boothroyd.'

'I wonder Nesta put up with that old bitch.'

'I don't know that the old thing was such a bitch,' said
Evelyn. 'Nesta can be trying too, in her own way. But it
would be different with a man. Anyhow, I was considering her

cooking. And that is most important to an elderly man. A nice cook. The digestion is so important.'

'Mm,' said Harold.

'Her mother trained her,' Evelyn said. 'I do feel sorry for Nesta. Once upon a time there was a place for a well-trained, practical, unmarried woman of good family and no income. Today there's simply no call for them – like parlour-maids.'

'She did pretty well with the Princess. No cooking in those days.'

Evelyn kicked up her feet and giggled.

'She had it good with the Princess!'

Evelyn loved it. They had been through it all before. After the second sherry Harold, too, quite enjoyed it.

'Lived on the fat of the land,' Evelyn said. 'Many lands!'

She nursed her refilled glass.

'And not a sign of it,' she sighed.

'You wouldn't expect it,' said Harold. 'Half those Australian women come back looking as though they hadn't been farther than Leura.'

Evelyn smiled and nodded her head.

'They were related, weren't they?' Harold asked. 'Nesta and the Princess?'

'What?' Evelyn exploded. 'But I told you, Harold, I *told* you!'

It was one of those games they played.

'Nesta Pine and Addie Woolcock were sort of cousins. On the maternal side. Melbourne. Old Mother Woolcock was most determined. Nobody was exactly surprised when Fernandini Lungo jumped at Addie their first season in Europe. A horrid little man, I believe, but he left her alone. Addie was happy with the title, and the Prince with her sausages.'

'I remember about the sausages.'

'Oh, yes. Very popular at one time. There was one variety had bits of tomato mixed with the beef. Horrid,' Evelyn said.

The Fazackerleys sipped their sherry and forgot the spirits it had replaced. They were themselves the spirits of a certain age.

'I should go and get dinner,' Evelyn sighed.

Harold didn't encourage her. Experience had taught him to lose interest in food. Besides, he was filled with his vision of Nesta Pine: a large, white, cloudy woman, usually carrying parcels. The parcels hung from her fingers like clusters of brown, bursting fruit. People allowed her to shop for them.

Evelyn was growing dreamier.

'I can see her knitting,' she would have rocked if the chair had allowed it, 'in that funny room above the sea. Such a comfort. Nesta was always a great knitter. She took to it as far back as school. None of the girls at Mount Palmerston liked her much. And I suppose the knitting was some kind of compensation. She used to offer to teach us stitches. It didn't appeal to us at all. Nasty little things we were!'

'I thought you liked Nesta.'

'Oh, but I do! You get to like people like Nesta. Life wouldn't be livable unless.'

'I shan't collaborate in any way.' Harold might have been rejecting a knife.

'I shan't ask you to,' said Evelyn. 'I don't propose to do an awful lot myself. You don't have to push men and women. Only assist nature a little. See they drift together. Mingle.'

She made it look like mist, and the remorselessly unconscious grey fingered coldly at Harold's joints.

While Evelyn sat forward, holding the points of her elbows. Smiling. A purposeful future made the lines in her face more distinct.

'Now I must really see about getting our dinner,' she said rather breathlessly.

And went out into the kitchen to open a tin of salmon.

It was the name, obviously, which helped Evelyn see Nesta sitting at the foot of one of the enormous pine trees which grew on the windy side of Mount Palmerston, or at least the trees had appeared enormous to the girls playing on the slippery needles underfoot. The scent, the sound of pine trees haunted Evelyn terribly as soon as she became involved again. She was haunted, too, by Nesta. Curiously, though, Nesta seated beneath the tree was not the older girl at school, but the large-breasted woman she had finally become, almost always in grey, straight, knitted dresses. Or twin-sets, with plaid skirts in other greys. Though time had had its way with her face, her hair had remained aggressively black without assistance from the bottle. Beneath the heavily-spiked branches her hair still glowed with startling lights, while the shade accoutred her thickening body with the greyish-brown armour of bark. She sat knitting, her smile filtering through her thoughts rather than directed outward at those who might be approaching.

But on one occasion Nesta was wearing, in Evelyn's mind, her older-girl's hair and body. The other children had drifted away. The long dark fall of hair was gathered at the back of Nesta's head by a thin brown-velvet ribbon. Or was it a snood? Evelyn couldn't quite see. It might have been that she was concentrating on the attitude: of Nesta holding the knitting-needles as though preparing for a rite.

'Why are you always knitting?' Evelyn asked.

Nesta did not seem to hear, though her broad face was beginning to offer itself from behind the web of her private smile. Evelyn noticed the fawn circles, of flannel, or chamois leather, in the whiter face. As Nesta suddenly leaned forward.

'I've only just started,' she said, fluffing out the knitted frill. 'I haven't decided. It could be for you, Evie.'

She applied the frill to Evelyn's bare, prickling neck.

'I'm not called "Evie",' Evelyn protested.

She was both fascinated and disgusted to see that Nesta's breasts were already almost fully formed. Like milk buns.

So she ran away. Through the scent of resin and the sound of pines. Her own footsteps chasing her over the slippery needles.

'Hold hard!' Harold was protesting from the other bed. 'You're shaking the whole room!'

'Ohhh,' she replied. 'I must have been dreaming.'

'Whatever about?' Harold asked from the dry ground of wakefulness.

'I don't know,' she said pitifully. 'Or was it about the Burds and their horrible service station?'

Her neck felt stiff. After a certain age there was really little more rest in sleep than in waking. The great difference, or doubtful advantage, was that in sleep you were planned for, in life you planned.

Whether she had dreamed about the Burds or not, and she was inclined to think she hadn't, Evelyn returned to a plan she was forming: for sending Win the blue dress she was about to discard. After all, it was a nice dress, certainly nothing in gold lamé, but so much wear left in it. Evelyn hadn't told Harold yet. She proposed to enjoy, to embroider her plan a little longer. Over and over again she visualized Win receiving the parcel, fiddling with the knots on a damp-cold morning in Surrey. She saw Win's face, as she remembered it: that of a shrewd goat nibbling at gossip, jabbing seldom, but with skill. Win would be old by now, though. A Nellie Wallace smelling of petrol.

Evelyn shivered on her corrugated bed.

'They're too short,' she grumbled, pulling the sheet up.

'Who?'

Harold could sound so dry at night, and distant, hinting at other allegiances joined in sleep. In the days when they had shared a bed his toe-nails used to make a dry, scraping, almost a tearing sound, as he turned.

'Cheap sheets,' she said bitterly. 'When all the good Egyptian ones wear out we'll have to decide which to sacrifice – our chests, or our feet.'

Harold was escaping her. She turned her head.

'Harold,' she said, 'I was dreaming about Nesta Pine. I suddenly remember.'

Her voice filled the room with the hopelessness, the helplessness of honesty in darkness.

'I thought I ought to tell you,' she said.

He was buzzing. His voice made an attempt, but remained disintegrated.

'Do you think Nesta is a lesbian?' she asked.

Harold was bundling, scraping the sheet.

'I don't believe there's any such thing. I don't believe it's possible,' he said.

He laughed. Evelyn did too.

'They say there are ways and means.' She yawned rather crooked. 'I was only wondering,' she managed between yawns. 'All those women she lived with. Most of them pretty harmless. But Addie Woolcock – the Princess – she was taken to Europe so early. And moved in more unconventional circles. She had the body of a boy. I can remember she had on a dress. Hand-painted by a famous artist, they said. A Futurist, I believe he was called. He was a kind of Movement. Well, he had done a hunting scene on Addie's dress. Some goddess or other. If you could fool yourself. They explained it to me. With Addie inside the dress. Like any common mannequin. She enjoyed that sort of thing. And took up with poor old boring Nesta. Who used to make the hotel reservations, and book the tours.'

Evelyn yawned.

'Of course it was only a matter of convenience. And even those who are successful cling to bits of the past.'

The room had filled with thickest darkness. Evelyn Fazackerley would have liked to wash her hot hands. And

anoint them with Dreaming Lotus. A nice drink of Alka-Seltzer.
'Are you awake, Harold?'
She slept.

On mornings when she left him to buy their chops and look round David Jones, Harold Fazackerley used to go to the parks, until suspecting that the elderly men seated on benches presented the more negative aspect of retirement. He must get a job, at least a part-time job. Until he made up his mind – strange, when so many had depended so long on his immediate decisions – he sometimes tried spending the morning in the flat. He took down a book. Or he simply sat in the creaking silence of shoddy woodwork, in the suffocating silence of Evelyn's blazing blue cushions.

Above the blaze of sea Harold would distinguish Clem Dowson clambering animal-wise amongst the flat rock-plants and combed-out scrub. Or Clem, similarly silent and intent, in the bare room built of silence. There were definitely those who could make use of silence, just as there were those who knew how to use tools. Harold had never made anything with his hands, and silence only used him up.

Half embarrassed he wondered whether Dowson believed in God. Probably didn't need to. He, Harold, had never needed or, when he had begun faintly to need, was diffident about embarking on a relationship of such large demands.

Instead he took down *War and Peace*, and although appalled by its length, was on several occasions about to return to its half-remembered riches. On the morning when he came closest, or at least had glanced through the list of characters involved, Evelyn burst in on him with that string bag which tried not to look like one.

'You'll never guess!' Haste and excitement had turned her pale under her complexion. 'I ran into Nesta – Pine – in the haberdashery at Jones's. She's living at – oh, some boarding house. She's promised to look in. So, *all that* looks more or less pre-ordained!'

Perhaps it was her happy choice of a word which gave her a look of triumph.

'You don't believe you're going to foist that woman on poor Dowson, do you?'

'Not really,' Evelyn said, and laughed. 'I'm not so presumptuous.'

Out of the string bag she emptied the reel of silk which had been her morning's mission, and went to put it away.

On the afternoon Nesta looked in on them it was fortunate they weren't away on one of their expeditions. Too vague, or too discreet, she had not been persuaded to choose a date. However, when she did appear, she came in almost with the air of being expected, and when she had arranged her parcels within sight, settled down as though the friendship had been a deeper and unbroken one.

Nesta, stirring her tea, said to Evelyn in that dead quiet voice which some remote part of her released, 'That day you lunched at Mrs Boothroyd's there was quite a little scene after you left.'

Nesta laughed to relive it in the depths of her inward-looking eyes.

'When you had gone, she said, "Do you think she liked me?" She attached great importance to being liked.'

'Isn't that natural?' Evelyn said. 'To me it's important. Though I don't imagine many people do like me,' she added expectantly.

Nesta continued since she had begun.

'I forget what I said to reassure her. In any case one never could. She started on the pork. You remember we had pork.'

Evelyn did not remember.

'Mrs Boothroyd said, "Anyway, your pork didn't turn out too well. Your crackling. A *cuirass*! When it's usually one of your star turns." '

Harold Fazackerley was about to yawn, but stopped himself, to be incensed.

'Wonder you didn't walk out on her.'

'After all,' said Evelyn, 'it was you who were doing the favour.'

The rather horrid little cakes in paper cups, all she had for Nesta Pine – it was Nesta's fault – looked, she hoped, better than they were.

'Oh, she *needed* me!' Nesta protested. 'And when you are needed.'

Evelyn looked up as though she had found the scent again.

Nesta was lighting a cigarette. They had forgotten about Nesta and the cigarettes. She had taken to a pair of tweezers in the days of their fashion, and had continued to smoke her cigarette with tweezers long after the fashion had passed. Evelyn remembered how strangers used to nudge one another as Nesta sat smoking in public places. Always oblivious of her silver tweezers. Now she was sitting, at a deliberate distance, the tweezers attached by their ring to an index finger, the cigarette slightly quivering, like a hawk on the falconer's wrist. As Nesta, the mistress of her cigarette, sat fastidiously smoking. Quietly absorbed. Smoke flowing, wreathing, through every crevice, it seemed, of her large face, white against white, except where the fawn circles round the eyes broke or emphasized the scheme.

Evelyn looked at Harold. She was so delighted with the apparition she had conjured up.

'How wonderful to be needed,' she said. 'Not only by Mrs Boothroyd. By all of them.'

Nesta looked as though Evelyn might have gone too far, but did not deny that ministering to the needs of others was her profession. She continued smoking. Only the cigarette in the grip of the little silver tweezers quivered more.

'Even the Princess,' Evelyn persisted.

Nesta's stomach rumbled from its distance.

'Addie didn't need anybody,' she said. 'But from time to time imagined she did.'

Harold should have felt sorrier for this large woman, all in black, whose hips were filling the narrow scuttle of a creaking rosewood chair. But Nesta's turnip flesh had not craved for sympathy.

'To imagine you need somebody is surely the same thing as to need.' The frills of the property cakes twitched as Evelyn manipulated them. 'And Addie was so fond of you besides.'

Then Nesta released her half-smoked cigarette from the silver tweezers. She got up. She was turning, searching for her only too obvious heap of parcels, presenting at moments the view of her broad black hips, at others her full white, goitrous throat. Evelyn could not remember ever having seen Nesta in black.

'She was not fond.' Nesta wrenched it out. 'I irritated Addie. I maddened her.'

Her throat was swallowing, her white cheeks were munching on the words, as she took up the parcels, and quickly bound them to her fingers with the string which cut.

Harold did not want to look.

Evelyn was made so nervous she laughed.

'That too', she giggled, 'can be a kind of necessity. Perhaps Addie needed someone to irritate her.'

Nesta was again composed. She stood smiling for the long comforter life had knitted, unevenly, but acceptably enough.

'Next time you come,' Evelyn said, 'you must warn us, and we shall be better prepared.'

She rubbed her cheek against Nesta's for an instant, as though ratifying something secret.

Evelyn was glowing, Harold saw, when they were alone.
'Next time I won't be caught,' he said.
Evelyn was laughing in little chugging bursts.
'Don't be silly, Harold dear. Dowson isn't a rabbit. And you see what a victim poor Nesta's always been.'
'You wouldn't do it!'
'No! No! No!' She threw back her head. 'Hasn't Dowson a will of his own? No man is *compelled*.'
She was looking at her husband whom she needed as much as any of those women had needed Nesta Pine. She could feel herself perspiring round the eyes.
'Not compelled,' Harold said. 'Compulsion is easier to resist.'
Unlike smoke. Smoke would drift in, suffocatingly at times, where the windows stood innocently open.
'You forget', he said, 'that Addie Woolcock, on at least two known occasions, slashed her own wrists.'
'Addie – what?' Evelyn was horrified; then she mumbled, 'I did – I suppose – know. I'd forgotten.'
To Evelyn Fazackerley, suicide, even of the half-hearted kind, was one of the great immoralities. Why, murder was more pardonable; murder showed guts.
'But all this', she said, 'is beside the point and my few harmless words.'
'All right, darling!' he said, laughingly kissing her.
She was reassured by his moustache.
That night while cleaning her teeth she called across the expanse of their intimate flat, 'I do remember about Addie – on one of the occasions. They said she did it with a little mother-o'-pearl penknife which had been a present from somebody. There was a picture of her in one of the papers, waving from the deck of a liner, leaving Southampton. There was a bandage round her wrist, under the bracelets. Nesta had come back. She was standing beside her.'

Evelyn had cut some remarkably thin, for once remarkably professional, cucumber sandwiches. When not too wet, they tasted so cool and refined. There was also one of those old-fashioned tea-cakes, extravagant with melted butter, made by Evelyn, as well as a really expensive Viennese *Torte*, which she had brought in, and admitted to it. She couldn't apologize enough for not having made the *Torte*.

Evelyn did the talking. Harold looked for the most part coerced, and began at once to get indigestion from the cucumber. Dowson and Nesta Pine addressed their hosts from time to time, and once Miss Pine, through these intermediaries, her fellow guest.

'Does Mr Dowson know,' she asked, averting her face, lowering her beige eyelids, 'does he know – living as he does in an exposed position – that geraniums stand up to wind better than pelargoniums?'

Dowson moved, and moaned, it sounded – low, however.

Nesta Pine blew the smoke through her nose.

'Pelargoniums', she said, 'are far too brittle.'

But Evelyn did not allow any more. Everyone should remain in character. She was doing her virtuoso stuff, and on such occasions Harold Fazackerley couldn't help admiring his wife.

'The little exquisite flowers of the Dolomites – ' they made her close her eyes as though in exquisite pain – 'the year we went there on leave from Egypt! One felt frustrated, not being able to transplant such masses of vivid, but *pure*, colour. Fatal in Egypt. Sydney would be almost as bad. Almost all alpine flowers are scorched by the heat of Sydney.' Acceptance of the fact made it appear more brutal. 'Mr Dowson,' she said, 'I shan't *force*, but *suggest*, another piece of this soggy tea-cake. Of course I'm not an expert cook.' Here she glanced at Nesta. 'But get away with it at times. And know what men like. Unless Harold is chivalrous. Or dishonest.'

Dowson had dressed himself up in clothes which did not

belong to his body, but which were obviously his best. He looked orange inside them, except for his eyes, which might have blazed if they hadn't been so innocent.

They were so intensely blue, it was this, probably, which prevented Nesta looking at them.

She had been persuaded to take off her hat, and a vagary of smoke from her fastidiously held cigarette made the coils and mats of dark fern-root hair and the brooding, chamois-leather eyelids appear separated from the rest of her. Today she was dressed in grey. To Evelyn's satisfaction. Grey was in keeping.

But Harold would have felt uneasy even without cucumber. He wished he was alone, like Clem Dowson knew how to be.

Dowson was sitting with his thick fingers stacked together, the orange tufts visible on the backs of them.

Then Evelyn Fazackerley, drawing down her mouth, asked, 'And what have you been doing with yourself lately, Mr Dowson?'

Because she had felt the thread of continuity sagging.

Dowson hoisted himself up and replied, 'As a matter of fact, I've been making cumquat jam.'

Suddenly Nesta Pine was writhing – yes, writhing – in Harold's mother's rosewood chair, which she had continued to favour although it was scarcely able to contain her.

'Not cumquat?' she rasped.

Evelyn had forgotten Nesta's eyes. They were topaz colour, glistening, even glittering.

'I have had failures with cumquat,' Nesta gasped.

The Fazackerleys realized Nesta Pine and Clem Dowson were addressing each other directly, as well as publicly.

'I almost always burn it,' Nesta was confessing.

'Not if you throw in three two-shilling pieces.'

'Ah!' She breathed out smoke. 'If you can remember to do it. My Aunt Mildred Todhunter taught me the trick with the two-shilling pieces.'

Then they sat looking at each other a while. When they realized they were being observed, they composed their clothes. Nesta's cigarette-tweezers ejected the extinct butt. Dowson's eyes dispensed with practically the entire room.

The chill had come too suddenly into a hitherto humid day.

Evelyn was saying, 'Of all the things these Egyptian devils think of, the submerging of temples is the most difficult to accept.'

Evelyn allowed several weeks to elapse before sitting down to a letter she had spent most of that time composing.

It began:

Dear Mr Dowson,

> To my mind, we who have reached a certain age are very dependent on our friends, and should foregather more frequently under the roof-tree ...

– she paused to admire it –

> ... of one or another of us. Actually, I am writing to suggest you come here to a little informal lunch ...

– those she feared and admired would have written 'luncheon', but on giving it thought she rejected the word on psychological grounds –

> ... if the prospect of deserting your beloved house and planned routine does not altogether bore you ...

'What are you doing, Evelyn?' Harold asked.

'Writing a letter.'

He did not inquire further because he knew.

Evelyn was disgusted on receiving no reply to her letter, while telling herself it was foolish to expect civilities from anyone so uncouth.

A Woman's Hand

When a note arrived:

Dear Madam,
 I am writing for Mr Dowson who is sick. I go
there Tuesdays for the ironing and he asked me to write
the letter. He is real sick. It is his heart sort of. They say
he will recover and he will, because he is not going not to.
I am only writing because he asked me and you are a
person he respect. But he does not want you or anyone
else to come. It is a long way.
                                   Yours sincerely,
                                   E. PERRY (Mrs)

Evelyn said, 'Dowson is seriously ill. His heart.'

'Poor old Clem,' said Harold, working his knuckles. 'We'd
better go down to him.'

'No,' she said. 'That kind of man, when sick, can't bear
people pouring in. But he's got to eat. To live. Perhaps I could
take him something.'

They both saw him trussed on his sickbed in that house of
the winds. So Harold agreed. Evelyn was, after all, the woman.

She bought a boiler, and took the soup in a billy-can which
slopped over on her blue skirt in the bus. It was in the best
cause, she had to remind herself all the way down that road as
her heels went over on the stones.

The gangway through the wind, down the side of the cliff,
over the passive succulents and nervous, wiry clumps of thyme,
led her at last to a still house. In the kitchen she heard the drip
of a tap, and regretted Harold's absence. The egg-boiling inven-
tion stood out far too sculpturally.

And Clem Dowson lying on his bed. He opened his eyes
very briefly but distinctly under the orange brows.

He said, 'I didn't expect anybody.'

The wind off the sea howled amongst the mauve-fleshed
rock-plants.

Her hair no doubt was looking terrible.

'But we can't *desert* you. Look, I've brought you some good nourishing soup.'

He did not look, however. He had resumed lying with his eyes closed, probably one of those men who sulk when they are ill, and must be wooed.

'Would you like me to warm some up?'

'No,' he said.

'Well, then,' her charity refusing to be extinguished, 'I'll put it in the refrigerator, and you can take some when you feel inclined.'

She went back into the kitchen, which she knew well enough by now. It was the bedroom she longed to examine. On the first occasion its owner had not taken them there.

The refrigerator was neither too well nor too poorly stocked. After pouring her soup into a bowl, Evelyn stood it amongst the usual necessities. There was a fish pudding, she noticed only then, of rather too professional a texture, delved into, as you might have expected, by a sick, clumsy man.

'That looks a jolly appetizing fish pudding,' she said on returning with her brightness to the bedroom. 'It looks so light. And such a creamy sauce. I expect your Mrs Perry, who wrote to us, made you that, didn't she?'

Dowson blew down his nose.

'Never cooked anything eatable in her life. Judging by what she brings me to try.'

He spoke with such vehemence Evelyn found it hard to believe he was seriously ill.

'No,' he said, and hesitated. 'Miss Pine brought the pudding,' he said.

'*Ohhh?*'

She was quite put out. But as she had started the thing, it was surely logical to accept it.

'I am so glad you have found something in common,' she

said, to follow through. 'Food, anyway. Most important. Nesta', she said, 'is such an excellent person. So reliable.'

As she sat on her upright, hospital-visitor's chair, intent on her wedding and engagement rings, she heard herself sound as though recommending a brand of goods from a store.

'Miss Pine's all right,' said Dowson, his eyes still closed, his nose swivelling to elude a non-existent fly.

Evelyn Fazackerley could imagine Nesta's visit. She could hear their joint silence. Yet, why should it not seem natural? Mushrooms congregate. And spawn together. Horrid expression.

In her unbalance and distaste she glanced round the room, which she had looked forward to exploring before this unpleasant discovery. Pathetic the inner rooms of solitary males. Chaster even than the cupboards of elderly virgin women. The darning egg, naked today. An almost used-up carpenter's pencil. Saved string, wound in impeccable hanks. A kerosene lamp, with opalescent shade, still in use. *The Conquest of Peru*. A pair of mittens which on winter mornings by the sea would half cover the raw, the knotty hands of Dowson.

The name, she saw, could have been carved into him by a knife.

Then he opened his eyes, and looked at her, and said, 'Miss Pine is a good sort.'

Evelyn Fazackerley sat moistening her lips. She had intended to offer to take on the mending. Instead she coughed and looked at her watch.

'I mustn't forget my bus.'

On the way back through the kitchen to collect her billy she reopened the refrigerator door, and gouged out with her index finger a little of Nesta's fish pudding. It tasted most delicate, flavoured with something she couldn't identify.

She went back into the bedroom and took him by that meaty hand.

'Oh, Clem dear,' she had never called him by his first name before, 'Harold and I would do anything for you – *anything* – for the sake of old times – if only you would tell us.'

Dowson half-smiled – he might have been falling asleep – turning his face to the wall, which had been washed a flat white.

She left him then, with the suspicion that she was the innocent one. As she stumbled back along the unmade road the forms of the yellow furniture remained solidly with her, together with the knowledge that on neither occasion had she managed to unlock anything in that ostensibly open house, and that she had never experienced the slightest response from his hand.

Evelyn put off telling Harold about Nesta Pine's visit to Dowson, and soon it was rather too late to tell. She waited instead for Nesta to give some shape to her intentions; the rules of friendship demanded it. But Nesta did not come. She has used us just enough, Evelyn began to see, and now that she has met this man she is off to the races on the sly. Well, if she wished to humiliate herself. The mystery of the woman's face, behind the smoke, the uneven powder, and web of sentimental loyalties, or of the precociously mature girl in the ugly Mount Palmerston tunic, knitting up wool at the foot of the armoured tree, was a mystery no longer: it was the expression of congenital cunning.

On an incongruous occasion – but the whole business was incongruous – Evelyn Fazackerley allowed herself a vision of the elderly Nesta in one of the more convulsive attitudes of love: a great jack-knife of sprung flesh, the saucered rump, breasts heaving and plopping like a pot of porridge come to the boil.

'How revolting!' Evelyn said out loud.

And her breath snapped back elastically.

Harold Fazackerley turned from the urgent operations of a

gang of men tunnelling into a mountain-side, towards the state of rapt unreality his wife had trailed with her into the open, out of their neo-Tudor cocoon. For the Fazackerleys were off on one of their 'jaunts', as Evelyn used to refer to them. They were doing the Snowy Scheme by coach.

'What is revolting?' Harold shouted.

Competing against a passage for men's raised voices and splitting rock, he sounded angrier than normally.

'I forgot to tell you,' Evelyn shouted back, at the same time looking over her shoulder to see whether she could trust the landscape, 'the day I went down to Dowson, I found that Nesta had taken him a fish – a fish *pudding!*'

She had eaten off her lipstick, and her lips looked pale. For an isolated moment Harold Fazackerley would have liked not to have been married to his wife.

'I often wonder, Evelyn,' he continued shouting, his voice as wobbly as an old man's, 'how you ever experience anything fresh for remembering what has happened already.'

But the drills, he realized, had fallen silent, and he regretted his voice, his crankiness.

That night at the hotel he ordered a bottle of claret to accompany their not-so-mixed-grill. To make a little occasion.

'Well, it isn't much chop, is it?' he apologized. 'None of it!'

'What did you expect?'

She smiled at him out of the worldliness which had returned to her with a change of dress. Glancing round the room at the other couples, thin and fat, moist and dry, their fellow-passengers from the coach, she tried to create the impression that she and Harold at their own little table – she always insisted on their own table – were brilliant lovers who had sailed the Nile.

When he shattered her attempt.

'That fish pudding of Nesta's,' he said, 'I wonder if it was any good.'

Her mouth, blossoming again with the glamour of their past, wilted abruptly on her face.

Then she said, 'Actually, I did taste it, and have to admit, it wasn't at all bad.'

At least it cracked the ice which had frozen her relationship with Nesta Pine and Clem Dowson. She began to refer to them again. Both during what she remembered as 'that *ghastly* trip', and after, Evelyn found she was able to make jokes at her own expense, especially with the assistance of the fish pudding, the soft white ludicrous substance of which clogged Nesta's cunning and diminished its power.

With melancholy reserve Harold talked about going down to see 'poor old Clem'. Evelyn said yes they must, both of them, it was their duty, however touchy and impatient his illness might have made him. But they were overcome by a paralysis. They would go when it was cooler, warmer, or when the patient would be sufficiently recovered to enjoy their visit. They did not go. That woman, that Mrs Perry, Evelyn said, no doubt came in to do for him, and sounded an excellent person.

Their debate might have continued if Harold hadn't received Clem's letter:

Dear Harold,
       This is to let you know Nesta Pine and I decided to make a go of it. We were married last month. We came straight home, because we both felt, at our age, it would have looked foolish to trip off somewhere on a honeymoon. Our habits have formed, I shan't go as far as to say 'set'! Neither of us expects too much.

You know I have never been a great hand at expressing myself, Harold, but can't let this opportunity pass without wondering how different it might have been if we had met more often – or if we hadn't met in the beginning. I suppose I have always been most influenced by what can never be contained. The sea, for instance. As for the human relationships of any importance, what is left of them after they have been sieved through words?

Funny sort of letter, I can hear you say! But you can forget it, and next time we meet, nothing will be changed.

Miss Pine – *he had crossed it out* – Nesta sends her regards to your wife, for whom she seems to have a deep affection.

If the Fazackerleys weren't stunned, at least their ears rang.

'How grotesque!' said Evelyn.

She kept returning to the letter, as though in search of a window through which she might catch sight of recognizable attitudes. It *was* grotesque. If she did not say 'obscene', that would have been going too far. When she herself was, however innocently, involved. For Evelyn Fazackerley affection meant something, not exactly material, but demonstrable. And Nesta Pine, of cloudy features and brooding breasts, had begun to demonstrate. She was reaching out a shade farther, from under the giant trees, offering the frill of grey knitting. Evelyn wondered, poundingly, how she felt about it. But she would not allow herself for long, or not after her skin began to prickle. As in childhood she was running away, over the slippery needles, back into the living room.

'I don't know *what* they "expect",' she said, hitting the letter and laughing hoarsely. 'Only they *may* find', she added hopefully, 'that it is more than they imagined. Most people do.'

But Harold Fazackerley had become a sieve through which the words ran like water, and experience, or more specifically, that which has not been experienced. The little boy crying in the fetor of disinfected latrines. *What's up, young Fazack?* The square, warty hand gently thumping his sorrows. *Nothing.* Then the exquisite bliss even of maggots seething through the dusk and urine-sodden sawdust. The wind at sea, scouring the skin, sweeping out all but the farthest corners of the mind. The burning-glass of a blue eye. The stationary question-mark of a white ibis amongst the papyrus. Dreams and prophecies beating on jerry-built pitch-pine doors.

But of course the implications of the letter with which he was vibrating as he sat in his appointed box were also the tremblings, the thunderings of age.

They were all, not what you would call old, but elderly, when, not so very long afterwards, the Fazackerleys were summoned to the house on the cliff. (*They couldn't very well avoid it,* as Evelyn put it.) They were all either scraggy or bulging. Clothes of a past elegance and cut hung too loosely on the scraggy ones. Whereas Clem, as well as Nesta Dowson (yes, Dowson) appeared stuffed into what should have been the appropriate loose, practical garments.

The Dowsons were terribly alike, and unlike, Evelyn saw.

What Harold saw he wasn't sure, beyond the sea still blazing through the windows. The wind blowing, of course. Through the windows of the Dowsons' house the wind was always visible.

The Fazackerleys had been invited to a cup of tea.

'I must say, Harold, it's pretty mean of Nesta, considering she's such a dab at cooking.'

'Perhaps it didn't suit Clem. Nesta's not the only one – not now – to be considered.'

'Oh, *Clem*!' Evelyn's head might have been mounted on ballbearings. 'She's a fool if she doesn't make a stand.'

The Fazackerleys had taken them a plated toast-rack, though Evelyn was afraid it might shame them to receive a present after their neglect and deceit.

Anyway, there they all were, cups precariously positioned, bread-and-butter plates uncomfortably balanced. Evelyn noticed the crockery was no longer Clem's common white, but a service Nesta had most probably inherited from one of the old ladies, or her mother.

The light touched the rather delicate cups and turned them into transparent eggshells from which the life was still only half-blown.

Harold's cup was rattling in its saucer. The wind was rattling the loose-fitting windows.

'Oh, what a lovely little brooch!' Evelyn's voice could not resist pouncing.

For Nesta had pinned a little bunch of mosaic flowers, most vivid on its black marble background, against the grey jumper of her twin-set, below the thick white goitre of her throat. Certainly not a wedding present. Evelyn could not visualize that man's meaty hands offering anything Italianate.

'Is it something the Princess – did she leave it to you?' she asked.

'Oh, no!' Nesta, lowering those beige eyelids, sounded shocked. 'Addie had nothing Italian to leave. She only *wore* the jewels. They belonged to the Fernandini Lungos. Besides,' she said, softening the rest of her reply, 'this little brooch is of no importance. Something I picked up. A souvenir shop. On the Ponte Vecchio.'

Her hands were suddenly too full of china.

'But it is pretty,' she apologized.

'Lovely,' Evelyn emphasized, though there was no cause for further interest.

There was no reason why she should feel screwed-up inside. The incident was far too trivial. Nesta herself had admitted to the ordinariness of her brooch while correcting a mistake anybody might have made. But Evelyn could have screamed, for her gaffe, for the Dowsons – no, the four of them.

Nesta broke one of the inherited cups. Distress froze her above it a fraction too long, in an attitude of knock-knees. She was wearing grey ribbed stockings, no doubt knitted by herself. Her legs, below the shaggy skirt, looked like those of a born misfit on the hockey field.

'That was very clumsy of you,' Dowson complained. (During the whole afternoon he did not once call her by name.)

'But you know I am clumsy,' she said – well, clumsily.

As he got down on his knees, on the boards, he was behaving as though the cup had been his, not his wife's. Watching the hands deal with the fragments, Harold was again reminded of the maggie's egg Clem had blown for him when they were boys.

'Don't forget – in the bin for the dump,' Dowson warned. 'We have three bins,' he was explaining to guests, 'one for the dump, one for the compost, and a third for the incinerator.'

Then they were silent for a little, except for the slither and chatter of the remains of Nesta's cup, as she swept them into, presumably, the right bin.

That afternoon Nesta made no attempt to smoke. She brought out her knitting instead, and as she coaxed the grey, or faintly sage, feelers of wool, it provided something of the same effect.

Dowson sat frowning, listening perhaps to the sound of the needles. They were both listening

Evelyn felt herself drowning in a situation, the shores of which were concealed from her.

Battered by her ear-rings, she turned towards the view, and began in her high, light, deliberately superficial voice, 'How perfectly *marvellous* the sunsets must look from up here. Out to sea.'

Dowson cleared his throat.

'The sun sets in the west, the other side of the ridge.'

Nesta was smiling rather painfully at her knitting.

'We watch the sun*rise*,' she said, 'most mornings. That is wonderful.'

'You must be early risers!' Evelyn gobbled her words, turning annoyance with herself into a comic disapproval of others.

'Oh, yes. We are up early,' said Nesta, with a proud inclination of the head. 'Both of us.'

Dowson got up. He moved away from his wife and stood by the window looking out. The sun had already abandoned the sea for a world the other side of the ridge, leaving a distillation of perfectly white light on the corrugated water.

The Fazackerleys were left to listen to Nesta's knitting-needles, the sound of which she accompanied with her head and a just visible motion of her pale lips. For Evelyn, who had always hated, not to say feared, the silences in empty rooms, the sound of the bone kneedles was another kind of silence, and she began to gather herself and Harold.

They looked back. It was extraordinary to see the Dowsons standing *together*, at the gate below road level, in the drained evening light.

Harold and Evelyn did not speak on the way home, blaming it on the sea air.

Evelyn should have written a letter of thanks on the thick white notepaper which was one of her extravagances. She was expert at such letters, dashing them off in a gallant hand. But this time she hesitated. It was the arthritis in her thumb.

Although she had never received more than one or two letters from Nesta, she recognized this one immediately it came, and saved it up till Harold should return. Then when he did, she thought better of it, and kept the letter until she was again alone.

Dear Evelyn [Evelyn herself would have written *Dearest*]
    I don't know why I am writing except to say,

how fond I am of you. Clem is fond of you, I believe, but would never admit it. Neither of us says much, which makes our relationship a strange one: I have lived with peacocks all my life!

Most people do not know the peacock also redeems. I began to realize when we visited that church above Salonika – or convent, was it? – so deserted we could not decide – when the evening was suddenly filled with silent peacocks – never before had I seen them in the air – then settling to roost, their tails turned to branches of cedar.

Clem, I think, does not believe in redemption because he has no need of it. His eyes are perfectly clear. You couldn't flaw them in competition with a crystal. Though he and I are in so many ways the same, there we differ.

Well, my poor Evelyn, you did not see the sunset! Let me tell you it mostly shrieks with the throats of peacocks – though sometimes it will open its veins, offering its blood from love rather than charity.

NESTA PINE

The signature alone was a hammer blow to Evelyn Fazackerley. She did not know what to do with Nesta's letter. If there had been an open fire she could have reduced the thing immediately. In the absence of one, she put the letter in a box, and there it burned, but continued burning.

Evelyn had never been so frightened. The dreadful part was: she would never be able to tell Harold; she had never told him anything, nothing of importance. If it had been possible to ring the police, or better still, the fire brigade, they might have carried her down out of her panic. But it was not possible, in spite of the telephone book, and the numbers she had drawn circles round. Instead of the clangour of approaching engines, what she had to listen to was the frightened clapper of her dry heart.

Harold came in only to say, 'See somebody about my back. At our age I suppose we must expect a certain number of aches.'

He sat pinching up the skin on the backs of his hands.

'Although I've rung the last three mornings,' Evelyn said, looking at the ridges of his blue skin, 'the Gas Company doesn't seem to realize it is under obligation.'

She continued watching the hands with which she had been familiar.

'Harold? It's the front left burner. If only you were handier.'

Harold said – at times he sounded like leather, 'Ought to send for old Clem Dowson. Clem could fix it.'

She shied away from what was less easy to avoid on a morning in one of the canyons progress had ground into their city. She would not be allowed, it seemed, to sidestep the Dowsons. Though it was only Clem present in the flesh. Under his coat he was wearing one of those tweed waistcoats she had not noticed for years. At least it gave her a certain advantage. And the face. Something had been subtracted from it.

'You're the last person, Clem, I'd imagine meeting in the city,' Evelyn said in the rakish voice she put on for masculine but harmless men.

He mumbled about his solicitor. Or was it Nesta's solicitor?

'I must tell you,' she said, 'I'm so happy to know Nesta is in your hands.' She looked away from them at once, however, the red fingers plaited helplessly against the tweed waistcoat. 'Poor Nesta has made so many homes for others, to say nothing of the suitcase life she led round Europe with Addie Woolcock, it's a joy to see her make a home of her own.'

It was a neat, even a pretty speech, and Evelyn felt she could be proud of it.

'She didn't make it. The home was there already,' said Dowson.

'But a woman adds those little touches.'

A wind, not the one which rocked the house on the cliff, had sprung up along the concrete canyon, and was creaking between them.

'She was not that kind of woman,' he said. 'No frills. Just as I'm not the kind of man who enjoys a fuss.'

'It has turned out perfectly! I'm so relieved.' Evelyn was glad to be sincere.

Till realizing Dowson had related Nesta to the past. She got the gooseflesh then.

Dowson's lips seemed to reach out; the tendons were stretched like wire in the contraption of his neck. He was like, she saw, one of his own inventions, or a piece of that disturbing modern sculpture. A piece which moved, without escaping by its own motion.

'Nesta is ill,' he was saying.

His lips still reaching for words under the bristly orange moustache gave the whole situation a permanent look.

She was the one who must make an attempt.

'There is so much sickness about,' she agreed. 'The virus 'flu. What did we suffer from, I sometimes wonder, before they discovered the viruses? The wind', she said, casting down her eyes, 'is so treacherous at this time of year to anybody in any way bronchial.'

She couldn't remember whether Nesta was. But she gave a cough for all those who were bronchially afflicted. While sympathizing, she was determined to keep her sympathy general. She wouldn't look at Dowson's fixed, watery eye.

'What I would like you to understand –' he was begging for something, 'Nesta herself asked to go in. For treatment. The treatment alone must be hellish. I would never have put her there – not otherwise – though we did have the argument on the way to the pit – she'd put the pieces in the wrong bin. That, I suppose, was the last touch. For both of us. Both too conscientious. And quiet. Two silences, you know, can cut each other in the end.'

Again she was staring at his hands. He was not peacock enough to have thought of slashing his wrists. He was suffering instead in some more corrosive, subterranean way.

'I am so – so – *sorry*,' Evelyn said. 'Which hospital – home, is it?'

He told her the name. Which she would forget. In fact, she had already forgotten.

If only Harold had been there. Harold was useless in a crisis, but somehow gave her the power to act more brilliantly.

As for Dowson, his grief, remorse, whatever it was, had grown embarrassing in its crude importunity. The rims of his eyes might have been touched up, to glitter as they did, with such an intensity of raw red.

As there was nothing she could do, Evelyn left him. She trod very softly along the street, as though it were carpeted, as though all the doors were locked, as though the unfortunate, yet fortunately helpless patients were sitting the other side, listening, in their trussed or shocked condition, for further reprisals.

When she got in she announced 'I met Dowson. Nesta is suffering from some kind of nervous collapse. She is in the – he told me the name, but I forget.'

She gabbled it, not to make it unintelligible, but to get it over.

Harold, who was usually astounded, didn't seem to be.

'Don't you think it odd?' she asked when she could bear it no longer.

'No,' he said slowly. 'I suppose not.'

'I hope you are right,' Evelyn said. 'So many people have breakdowns today. It's the strain we live under – always the threat of war – the pace,' she said, 'and no servants.'

Harold sat pinching up his skin.

73

'Dowson himself,' she said, 'had that breakdown, when they dropped him off in Egypt.'

It was about this time that Harold Fazackerley took to going farther afield, on his own, without telling Evelyn where. Perhaps if she hadn't had a fright she might have grown peevish, cross-questioned him, wondered whether he had started a mistress. Because she had had the fright and didn't want another, she kept quiet. So Harold was able for the time being, to make these solitary expeditions. He would turn up on deserted parts of the coast, amongst rocks and lantana. Once he came across a rubbish dump and got his breath back sitting in a burst armchair on the edge of a gully. He was greatly moved by the many liberated objects he discovered, in particular a broken music-box from an age of more elegant subterfuges. Sometimes sunsets overtook him, and their impersonal rage did him good.

None of it meant there was any question of his being disloyal to Evelyn. She was his wife. If long association had turned that into an abstract term, it had not prevented the abstract from eating in as unwaveringly as iron.

He was attracted also to those iron-coloured evenings which bring out the steel and oyster tones in the sea. He was drawn to the wind which swells a sea while coldly slicing the flesh off human bones. With motion not direction his motive, he liked to take a ferry in the late afternoon. The wind-infested waters of the harbour matched his grey, subaqueous thoughts. Nor would any other mind intrude. Of the race of ferry passengers, one half was too dedicated to its respectability and evening papers, the other sidled instinctively after those it recognized as fellow rakes.

Often as an older man Harold Fazackerley had been embarrassingly told he was 'distinguished-looking'. If he had been less conscious of his inadequacies, he might have basked in the flattery of it. As things were, he had to laugh it off. There was even a trace of disgust in the gesture of protest with which he drew the no longer fashionable overcoat of English tweed closer to his 'distinguished' figure. The mannerism became finally a tic, which would break out on his solitariness, as on the afternoon when, without any reason, he remembered the ridiculous tweezers Nesta Pine had used for holding her cigarette.

He was standing alone on the deck of the plunging ferry, above waves drained of their normally extrovert colours. It was too blustery, too rough, for the majority. They preferred to huddle, coddling their mushroom skins behind glass. Some of them had evidently looked to drink for additional protection. The only other venturesome or possessed human being besides Harold Fazackerley himself was hanging over the rail at the bows. This large, spread character, staring monotonously at the waves, was probably bilious, Harold decided, until, as he passed behind the leaning figure, he realized they were responding in much the same way to the motion of the ferry, that they were sharing the smell of ships at sea, and that the stranger was no stranger, but his friend Dowson.

Dowson looked round. He was dishevelled by the head-on wind, but not drunk. Like a schoolboy he had rolled up his hat and crammed it into the pocket of his coat, which was starting to break free of the single button holding it. His fiery stubble stared in the blast. His mouth looked loose, from the draughts of air he must have swallowed.

The meeting was too unexpected. Harold would not have chosen it. In spite of his long, and delicately intimate relationship with Dowson, he could not think how to open a convincing conversation.

'I've been over to see my wife,' Dowson plunged straight in, as though he had been waiting for the opportunity to tell.

'She must have been pleased,' Harold said, and at once heard how fatuous it sounded.

'I don't think she was,' said Dowson. 'She was in a pretty bad temper. And she never used to be bad-tempered. That was one of the things we were up against. But today she was, I won't say – spiteful. She kept complaining about the screech of peacocks. Of course the traffic does make a hell of a noise out there. And to anyone in her condition. She must have meant the traffic.'

Harold Fazackerley would have liked to inquire into the peacocks, if only of his own mind, but this wasn't the time. What he did understand was that Dowson had shrivelled inside his indestructible body. It was a shocking discovery, the more so because you felt yourself the stronger for it.

Such a state of affairs might have become repulsive if it hadn't been so temporary. Dowson, or the genius of his fleshy body, had decided to resume the wrestling match. He who had turned round to face an accusation, locking his arms through the rail, exposing his chest, his belly, to whatever thrust, his unguarded face to the fist, had heaved himself back in the direction they were headed. And at that moment the sun struck, slashing the smudgy drifts of cloud, opening the underbelly of the waves, so that the peacock-colours rose again in shrill display out of the depths.

'My God,' Dowson was gasping and mouthing, 'one day, Harold, when we meet – in different circumstances – I must try to tell you all I've experienced.' He was speaking from behind closed eyes. 'That was the trouble between us. Between myself and that woman. We had lived at the same level. It was too great a shock to discover there was someone who could read your thoughts.'

Harold Fazackerley did not look but knew the tears were running from under the red, scaly eyelids, the orange, salt-encrusted brows.

'That put an end to what should never have happened in the first place.'

Soon after, they were received into a calm, into a striped marquee of light. Passengers were walking up the gangways of gently swaying matchwood. Somewhere a brass band was rather tackily playing.

The two men shook hands out of habit. One of them went on, to catch the bus, to the house which was ostensibly his, the other returning in the same ferry, as he could not remember having any further plan.

Harold began by not mentioning he had met Dowson on the ferry, and once he had begun, it was easy enough not to mention; it was his own very private experience.

'Have a good walk?' Evelyn asked on his return, and bit through the silk with which she had just threaded the needle.

Needlework had been considered one of her accomplishments as a girl, but she had soon put away something which might have made others doubt her capacity for sophistication. Until latterly, in what she was amused to refer to as her 'old age', she would start, half ironic, half nostalgic, some piece of elaborate embroidery to occupy herself on occasions of neglect.

Seeing his wife at her work Harold felt appropriately guilty. All that evening his eye was on her needle rather than on what he was trying to read. He would have liked to be able to talk to her, but couldn't. At least winter was not far off, when they were due to leave for Cairns.

The following evening he bought her a bunch of roses.

'Oh, dearest, how *sweet!*' Evelyn said with a spontaneity which overlooked the bruised condition of the buds inside the tissue cornet.

Harold grew guiltier than ever on seeing he had chosen such a bad bunch, and to realize he had been swindled again.

He had also brought her the evening paper.

'I don't know why we waste our money,' Evelyn Fazackerley always said.

But she read the evening papers. She liked to look at the
horoscope, 'just for fun', and she enjoyed – you couldn't say
'enjoyed' because it would have sounded too sick – it was
because she took an interest in the 'quirks of human nature'
that she read, or at least glanced at, the murders.

'Any good murders tonight?' Harold asked as a matter of
course.

'No,' she said. 'Murderers,' she said, in that voice she used
to put on to amuse them on board ship, 'murderers are running
out of ideas.'

When Evelyn's paper began to rustle.

'Harold,' she said, 'Clem – Clem Dowson is dead.'

It ripped into Harold Fazackerley.

'What?' he said stupidly. 'How – *Clem?*'

'An accident – it appears.' She was holding the paper as far
away from her as possible. 'How shocking!'

She was determined to make it anybody's death, and
Harold should have felt grateful.

' " ... walking yesterday evening from the direction of the
ferry, Clement Perrotet Dowson" ', she read aloud, ' "was
knocked down by a passing bus. He is thought to have died
instantly ... " '

But the muted voice did not spare Harold any of it.

'Instantly! What a mercy!' Evelyn said.

It was incredible to him the strength some women had, or
the convention they obeyed, which could transform an apoc-
alypse into a platitude.

'Apparently,' said Evelyn, still dealing with it, 'the driver
put on his brakes, and at least two pedestrians tried to prevent
poor – Clem, who didn't seem to realize. Apparently,' she
clung to the word she had recently discovered, 'he walked on,
stumbled, they say, and fell under the bus.'

The paper escaped from her hands in so many disordered sheets.

'Crushed!'

'Did they write "crushed"?' Harold asked.

Because he wanted to visualize Clem's great fiery head still glaring, blaring a revelation, not rubbed into pulp like a melon dropped on the tarred road.

'No,' said Evelyn. 'Not precisely.'

The walls of the flat were threatening them.

'Oh dear, the poor man! What can we do?' Evelyn protested.

She was wiping her hands on the little guest towel she had been embroidering so exquisitely.

'Is there any family?' she asked.

'I don't know.'

Evelyn was desolate, because who would break it to Nesta in the cell to which her absence of vocation had withdrawn her.

'Did you know Clem was a Perrotet?' Evelyn asked.

It was the hour when night began to take over in foreign tongues.

'Harold?'

Harold had not known, nor did they hear how Clem Dowson's remains were tidied up.

Or not until Evelyn received a note from the Perry woman

Dear Mrs Ferzackly,

   I have been in and done all I can do, all clothes to Salvation Army and such like, because the poor thing is too sick and will stay there they say. The young solicitor has been lovely. He and Mr Tompson have arranged, so now the house is shut up till Mr Tompson finds a buyer, it may take long, it isn't everybody's cup of tea. (Mr Tompson is Estate Agent Bandana.) So that is how it is, and if you would like to have a look, I thought I had better inform you where to find the key.

Knowing of the long friendship with the late Mr D. I am enclosing a snap I took after they was married. I would be happy for you to keep the snap. Sorry if the snap is blurred, I think the camera isn't up to much, but it is always a bit of a gamble.

Yours as ever,

E. PERRY (Mrs)

Evelyn would have preferred to ignore the snapshot, but took a quick disapproving look. The badly developed photograph was already discoloured. The figures of two large and shapeless people were arrested in the middle of nowhere. Although they might have been connected they were standing rather apart, undecided whether they should face each other or the camera. At least the photographer acted as some kind of focus point for smiles which might otherwise have remained directionless. Blur and all, she had caught her subjects wearing that expression of timeless innocence approaching imbecility, of those on whom the axe has still to fall. Like the photographs of murdered people in the papers.

Evelyn could not have kept Mrs Perry's snap. She would have torn it up immediately if Harold hadn't been there, not exactly watching, but knowing.

'A letter from that woman,' she said, because there was no way out, 'from Mrs Perry. She doesn't add anything – or nothing of importance – to what we know.'

How could she? There was nothing left.

Harold, Evelyn suspected as she made for the bathroom cupboard, was going to settle down to a prolonged sentimental-morbid session with Mrs Perry's snapshot. Well, men were less sensitive.

Harold did, in fact, allow himself to be drawn into the photographic haze. And read the letter several times. If he had had the courage – he realized late in life he was no more than physically brave – he might have gone down to Bandana, collected the key from the estate agent, and had a last look over the house. But – Evelyn might have got to know. He couldn't have borne that. Any more than his entry into the still warm, the gently creaking house – or hutch, they had perhaps rightly called it, in which some soft but wise primeval animal used to turn gravely on his straw, absorbing from between the wooden bars a limitless abstraction of blue, and a giant satiny bird had settled and resettled her wings, her uncommunicative eye concentrated on some prehistory of her own.

Fur and feather never lie together.

Harold Fazackerley made the noise with the mucus in his nose which his wife Evelyn deplored. He put the letter, together with the snap, inside his wallet, where the heat of his body had united many other documents by the time they were forgotten.

When Harold announced he had booked a room for a week at the Currawong Palace, Evelyn felt it her duty to disapprove and produce reasons why he shouldn't have, while secretly aware how relieved she would be to escape from the little box which contained too many confused emotions.

'But isn't that extravagant,' she protested, 'to say the least? When we are leaving for Cairns in July. And autumn,' she said, 'in the Mountains, can be depressing. Besides, nobody I can think of ever stayed at the Currawong Palace. Well, perhaps one person – a typist – though quite a decent girl.'

Harold said, 'Anyhow, I've done it, so we'll leave on Thursday.'

The weeks left to their departure for Cairns would be easily countable after their return from Currawong.

The Currawong Palace was one of those follies built in the shape of a castle by somebody who went broke from it.

Business enterprise had extended the castle by trailing more practical wings through a conflicting landscape, and by dotting pavilions amongst the evergreens intended to daunt the native scrub. There were guests who patronized Currawong in spring, briefly to admire rhododendrons, or in autumn to be dazzled by a splendour of lit maples. But such individuals were too few and discreet to count as clientele: the honeymoon couples who stared speechless over food, gathering strength for the next clinch; the young lady typists (typistes was perhaps nearer the mark) who perched on gilt in the ballroom while the business executives stalked up and down, rigid in their dark-suits-for-evening; and the foreigners – the foreigners were everywhere, lamenting Vienna and Budapest, filling all the most comfortable chairs.

After one glance the first evening Evelyn could see what a mistake Harold had made.

'We shall just have to put up with it,' she sighed, 'and close our eyes – and ears – and enjoy each other's company.'

She gave him one of those consuming looks she sometimes managed to construct when she was feeling consumed.

'Do you suppose there will be *anyone*?' she asked as they were changing into fresh things for dinner. 'There must be *someone*.'

'I expect so,' Harold said.

His thinning shanks ached as he pulled on the too-expensive socks he continued to buy out of habit.

As they prepared to go down she patted his back. Harold's back, she was pleased to think, would be the most presentable in a roomful of riffraff. Modesty prevented her dwelling on her own donkey brown under the musquash stole – once a coat – jolly smart; she only glanced obliquely at the wardrobe door in passing.

Downstairs, antlers presided; the velvet had worn off by now. The melon was terrible. There were some splinters of fish done in sawdust. She refused to wrestle with her cartilage of mutton. Over their helpings of marshmallow and tinned pineapple-ring the honeymoon couples were beginning to uncoil.

But afterwards, in the lounge, during the rite of coffee essence – ugh! – Evelyn discovered old Mrs Haggart, the widow of a grazier.

'Delicious coffee,' said Mrs Haggart, fitting her mouth to the space above the cup.

'*Yes!*' Evelyn gnashed a smile.

But found the old lady innocent.

She was one of those elderly Australian ladies innocent of a great deal, in particular the manifestations of their wealth. (Evelyn became at once passionately devoted to what she recognized as the kolinsky cape.) Yellowed by the sun, Mrs Haggart's skin had the texture of a lizard's. Her voice, as though thinned by drought, persisted not much above a whisper in the same dusty monotone. But she was kind. She would smile at the rudest waiter, asking, it seemed, for his forgiveness. The old thing was so kind it was a wonder she had managed to hang on to the kolinsky cape and the Cadillac.

'We used to drive out of the city', she confessed to Evelyn after clearing her throat of dust, 'always – while my husband was alive – and even now I drive out with Bill – ' Evelyn did not think she would have liked to refer to her chauffeur as 'Bill,' but Mrs Haggart was so democratic, 'we drive around the outskirts, looking for a fresh cabbage, or any other vegetable. I do enjoy a fresh-picked vegetable.'

Evelyn was entranced by the strangeness of it. She held her head brightly on one side, and gurgled for her new friend.

'Don't you?' asked Mrs Haggart, turning quite vehement.

'Oh, indeed, vegetables are very important!'

Evelyn was fascinated by the string of naked diamonds hanging innocently round Mrs Haggart's slack neck.

The old lady looked down, and was reassured by the sight of her own interlock cutting across the velvet V.

Then she raised her head and said, 'My husband was not so fond of vegetables.'

Suddenly for no reason Evelyn felt angry.

'Harold – my husband and I,' she said, 'have more or less similar tastes. Where – ' she asked, 'where is Harold?'

Mrs Haggart glanced over the arm of the sofa at the floor. She almost toppled. But recovered herself. At once it became obvious that she had contributed enough to the search.

'Perhaps he isn't feeling well,' she said.

'It would be most unusual,' Evelyn replied. 'Harold is never ill. I am the one.'

Mrs Haggart couldn't stop looking at Evelyn's arms. Then she suggested something quite horrid, but senile of course.

'Perhaps he's looking over the partners for the dance.'

'Oh, but there's only dancing on Saturday. I understood.'

'I thought there was dancing *every* night at Currawong,' said Mrs Haggart, introducing slight colour into her monotone. '*Every* night,' she repeated. 'But I can't say for *certain*, as I don't know where I put the brochure.'

She resigned herself to the kolinsky cape.

'Now, my husband,' she sat twangling faintly.

'Ah, there he is!' Evelyn said.

Some kind of expectation was making her tremble.

'Who?'

'Harold. My husband.'

Mrs Haggart's washed-out curiosity flickered behind her thickish glasses, investigating the cause of her new acquaintance's agitation. Mrs Fazackerley was sitting on the edge of the sofa trembling like a young girl.

Then Mrs Haggart made out the husband – there was no other possible candidate in sight – a cut above most in more distinguished company, still plenty of wear in him too, advancing on them in no hurry. While Mrs Fazackerley waved those gold bracelets. Egyptian, hadn't she said?

'There, you see, you didn't lose him,' Mrs Haggart consoled. 'And probably won't. Unless in an accident. If an accident has been arranged there's nothing you can do about it.'

But Mrs Fazackerley didn't hear, or else she had heard too much. Her neck had grown stringier. Now that she had attracted his attention, and he was picking his way through the Jewesses, she sat forward further still, gathering her knees into her arms, her throat straining red.

Mrs Haggart was not a woman who cultivated undue luxury but did enjoy a good stare.

'I'd begun to worry. Where on earth have you been?' Mrs Fazackerley almost called.

'Nowhere,' he said.

Staring luxuriously out of her moon-shaped glasses Mrs Haggart saw that he was smiling at his wife as though he only half-remembered her.

'Just wandering,' Mr Fazackerley said.

He had not, in fact, wandered any distance. Why he had not gone farther, he would have been too embarrassed to admit. Nor could he bring himself to accept Evelyn's girlish intensity as she craned up at him from the sofa trying to penetrate his thoughts. A nonchalance protected him, which he found rather agreeable.

The hotel, which should have desolated, mildly pleased. As he strolled, it had muted his footsteps with enormous flesh-coloured roses. He had easily navigated the gilt islands on which stranded typists sat, plumping out their mouths in anticipation, combing their hair with opalescent fingernails. There had been no sign that a chunk of the ornamental mouldings, which had obviously crumbled over the years, would be aimed at him deliberately if it should happen again.

Only when he stepped outside into the still more impersonal

dark, with its solider, blacker rhododendrons, and the disembodied voices, did Harold Fazackerley begin to have doubts for his safety. Or not exactly that. To feel he might be in danger, without having earned the right to regret it. Evelyn had been sensible enough to advise against autumn in the Mountains. The mist, for one thing, had begun to finger between him and his clothes.

Not all the ritual passion of lovers could warm the beds of rotten leaves or humanize the undergrowth as he advanced towards the line of native scrub. Where, on the edge, he knew he still wasn't ready for disclosures which might be made. To his shame, he felt he had been gone too long, and that his wife would be waiting for him. So he went back to the lounge, stepping over any bodies which lay in the way.

Evelyn had turned to the old lady beside her on the sofa.

'It has been so charming,' his wife was saying. 'But the journey has given me a headache. I think it is time we went to bed.'

With as much interest as she seemed capable of, Mrs Haggart examined the man who had been included in her friend's decision. Well, it had never been altogether unusual to include. Which perhaps decided Mrs Haggart to smile one of those filtered smiles, less for the present than for the past.

'I shall stay a little longer, and watch the people enjoying themselves,' she announced. 'I shall listen to the community singing.'

Then the Fazackerleys became aware that *Click Go the Shears* had started up at the end of one of the spokes which radiated from the hub of the lounge. A plaster shell encrusted with coloured electric bulbs increased the volume and fanned it outwards.

Enclosed in their varnished bedroom Evelyn could let herself go.

'As I expected,' she said, 'It's all perfectly ghastly.'

She took off her imitation pearl ear-rings, the increased weight of which was threatening to pull her under. Her string of *real* pearls she wore day and night for safety.

'Even the old lady.' She sighed. 'Although to some extent refined. Wasn't it a gorgeous kolinsky cape?'

She let her own tired musquash draggle across the ottoman.

'Can't you see Nesta – Nesta Pine,' said Evelyn Fazackerley, creaming herself at the dressing-table, 'sitting with an old creature like that in a whole series of ghastly hotels.' In its gulf the mirror was breeding other mirrors. 'Mrs Haggart is straight out of Nesta's stable. Nesta would have been just the thing for Mrs Haggart.' Evelyn could have been working it up, a fresh phase, in Elizabeth Arden, on her own face. 'If Nesta were ever to recover. Lots of people do, you know, from nervous disorders. Nesta – now she's a widow ... Oh, no, Harold, don't please! Not when I'm all covered with cream.'

In any case passion with the lights on, she had always found it embarrassing. But Harold's hands, she realized, were heavy cold outside the film of warm grease with which she had begun to revive her throat.

'Why must you start on Nesta?'

As she sat at the flimsy dressing-table he was addressing her reflection in the glass.

'She was our friend, wasn't she?' Evelyn replied, also in reflection. 'It's natural that she should crop up. Never more natural than in a place like this.'

'But Nesta is suffering,' Harold said, 'we can't begin to guess, in what kind of hell.'

Because his hands were so gentle in the angles of her neck it made Evelyn angry.

'It isn't my fault, is it, that Nesta Pine went round the bend? It was you – your – that man – that dead weight – that *Dowson*. I caught him reading a book once when he was staying with us at Kafr el Zayet. A book – oh, I can't explain it. Did it ever occur to you that red-haired men have a most distinctive smell? Oh, there's nothing I can accuse him of. Nothing of which you can say, that was the root of the trouble. He sort of seeped. We had several talks – you couldn't call them conversations because he was incapable of expressing himself. On one occasion we were strolling, I remember – one evening – through that mango grove – I can never see, let alone smell the beastly fruit, without getting the horrors – Dowson was not exactly telling but hinting. Poor old Nesta! I can just imagine! With that orange orangutang! And after all she'd gone through with someone as cold and egotistical as Addie Woolcock Fernandini Thingummy.'

'Don't shriek,' he advised. 'They'll think a peacock ... Yes, Addie and Nesta', he said, 'must have burnt each other up. But what does it matter, provided you blaze together – but *blaze*,' he was searching, ' – in peacock colours.'

He ended up sounding ashamed.

It made Evelyn turn round. 'Harold how loathsome! And why peacocks? It means,' she said, 'you must have been reading my private papers!'

It was no longer a matter of reflections. They were facing each other in the flesh.

'Ever since the day we read how Clem Dowson died I think I've been trying to forgive you, Evelyn.'

'Oh,' she shouted, 'indeed! I suppose *I* pushed Dowson under the bus! As well as putting Nesta where she is. Blame me, my dear. After all, I'm your wife.'

'No,' he said. 'I'm to blame. We never got a child. But *I* got *you*. I made you – more than likely! My only creative achievement!'

She looked at him.

'Oh, my darling,' she said, coughing up a noise which normally would have worried her in case anybody heard, 'my darling,' she spluttered, coughing, 'if you wanted to kill me, you couldn't have done it more effectively.'

But in front of this scraggy woman his wife, death, he felt, was no longer such a threat.

He hated what he was looking at, what he had caused. He took hold of the string of pearls, which, in the beginning, when it had been one of several strands wound into a rope, had given joy out of proportion. To both of them. He took the pearls, and twisted and jerked. And jerked. The string broke easily enough. He listened to the pearls scamper skittishly away against and behind lacquered veneer.

Evelyn didn't resist. She was too terrified. Not to recognize her husband. She had never known Harold. Was there also, possibly, ultimately, something hitherto unsuspected to recognize in herself? That was far more terrifying.

So she could not stop her dry cough, or retching. If she had been more supple she would have flung herself on the floor, but as she wasn't, she got down groggily, on all fours. She found herself, like some animal, on the hotel carpet.

It could have been that death no longer appeared so very important to Evelyn either.

'The pearls,' she whimpered, and it was a relief to admit her practical nature.

He looked down at her. Inside the slip her breasts continued shrivelling. The hotel lamp, rose-shaded to assist the diffident, couldn't help Evelyn's breasts: they remained a shabby yellow.

Nor himself: an old brittler man.

Or animal down beside the other rootling and grovelling after pearls.

'Poor Evelyn!' he found himself beginning again, to encourage them both in a predicament. 'We'll come across them. It was my fault. Better when it's daylight. Move the furniture. So that the maid won't sweep them up. Mistake them for beads. Throw them out. Or tread on them.'

They were at times kneeling, at times trampling on the pearls themselves, in the indiscriminate business of picking their way through what remained of their life together.

When she finally got to bed, the grit was still in Evelyn's knees, but she could not bother about it.

She said, 'I could do with a good stiff brandy. If I could face the staff. If they would come at this hour of night. Anyway it would cost the earth.'

He fondled her breasts a little, but suspected she didn't realize it was happening, just as it wasn't happening to him.

So he went out, unable, besides, to embrace the ritual of undressing. Evelyn did not protest. She was lying on the bed, half revealed by the hotel linen. She had started to give a performance of sleep, looking, he noticed, like a badly carved serving of steamed fowl.

Harold heard the beige roses responding to his footsteps in the passages. Although life was being lived spasmodically, at times even violently, behind closed doors, the passages were deserted and only economically lit.

In an open doorway Mrs Haggart in a black kimono was putting out her shoes as though she believed something would be done about them.

'In Harrogate,' she said to the one guest who offered himself, 'we used to see bottles of spa-water standing outside the doors with the boots. We had gone there, my husband and I, for the cure.'

Something shook her.

'Melon', she said, 'is the worst gas-maker of all.'

Her neck still flickering with blue fire, Mrs Haggart covered up her combinations with the rather elusive black kimono before withdrawing.

The whole hotel was beginning to subside into a detritus of pleasure: the stuffed egg someone had trodden into the carpet, shreds of lettuce and mauve Kleenex, the click of slow ping-pong balls, last phrases of *The Little Brown Jug.* None of it held Harold up. Reaching for the glass doors. Bursting out. Finally running. He couldn't help hearing himself: youth would have given it a sound of cattle, whereas age transposed it into the dry scuttle of a cockroach.

His movements emphasized the intense stillness of the shrubberies. Moisture was dripping from the rhododendrons. The animal intruder scattering gravel and tearing beaded spider-web did not interrupt the dripping bushes. He was the least of that cavern of dark which night was filling with the stalactites of silence. Realization spurred him to blunder deeper in, to try to shake off something which, by light, could only have appeared an exhibition of panic.

Harold Fazackerley's teeth confessed, *I am an old man with the wind up looking for what.*

And then he began to come across it. Where the congested shrubberies gave out, he plunged across the boundary into the scrub. In which the whips lashed. In which the rocks sprang up under his papery soles. A rapier was raised to slash his cheek. He could feel the flesh receding. Or he was freed of some inessential part of him as he blundered on, no longer troubling to tear off the cold webs of mist. The mist clothed his fingers, and clung to his bared cheekbone.

As he stumbled through the mists, they were beginning, he saw, as though for his special benefit, to give up the moon. He was standing on the edge of a great gorge, into which there was no need to throw himself because he had experienced every stone of it already. He was the black water trickling, trickling, at the bottom of it. He was the cliffside pocked with hidden caves. He was the deformed elbows of stalwart trees.

And all the time in the gorge, the mists were lying together, dreaming together, fur and feather gently touching, on which the healing moon rode. It was not that any of them had abandoned their material forms, but that night and mist had melted those broad faces, making more accessible the soothingly similar features, to which he had never dared demonstrate his love.

He went back presently. There was a single voice singing in the kitchens, and a clash of late crockery. In the fuzzy halflight of the hotel there was nobody to notice that Harold Fazackerley's kneecap was showing through his dark suit. Evelyn was sleeping, really sleeping, under a glitter of cold cream and tears. Her mouth was sucking at life with the desperation of rubber.

When Harold had undressed his somewhat unfamiliar body, and scrubbed his teeth, and put them back, he got into the other bed.

The rest of their stay at the Currawong Palace was agreeable enough, thanks chiefly to Mrs Haggart, who had taken a fancy to Evelyn. And you couldn't deny the old thing her little pleasures.

Evelyn and Mrs Haggart would be driven most afternoons, in the Cadillac, by Mrs Haggart's Bill, to look-outs, waterfalls, ghost towns, and the entrances to caves. (If they didn't venture inside the latter, it was because all caves are much alike.) The two women most enjoyed pulling up in front of a view, where Evelyn would tell about the Nile, and Mrs Haggart remember the vegetables she had bought. They would sit there until a swirl of mist gave them warning.

Sometimes Mr Fazackerley was persuaded to accompany the ladies, in his tweed cap set straight, and the English overcoat which wouldn't wear out. Mrs Haggart made him sit beside Bill, and her world was once again orderly and masculine.

'When he was younger,' she remarked, 'my husband had a leather motoring coat. It smelt most delicious.'

Evelyn continued to worship the kolinsky cape, which its

owner wore only at night, and the string of naked diamonds, which sometimes overlapped with day, because Mrs Haggart forgot to take it off.

Once Evelyn Fazackerley began, 'Nesta Pine...' and stopped.

'Who?' Mrs Haggart asked, although she wasn't interested.

'A friend,' said Mrs Fazackerley, noticing how the changed light was carving the sandstone into other shapes.

And soon the week was up. The two women exchanged addresses, which even Mrs Haggart suspected they would never use.

It could not have been more agreeable, however.

'I have so much enjoyed,' Mrs Haggart said.

Looking to the husband, she wove one of those smiles over her almost colourless lips.

'I envy you,' she added as colourlessly. 'Anyone can see you are such mates.'

Harold had learnt, no doubt in the Army, to hold himself erect. It made Evelyn proud.

The Fazackerleys continued making their trips. That winter they went to Cairns. You couldn't expect them to sit at home listening to their creaking cupboard and the leaking tap. They went twice to the Barrier Reef. They were lucky that, as age increased, their mechanism seemed to have been built for life. They flew to the Adelaide Festival, once only, because Evelyn cracked her ribs in the shower at that motel. She suffered perfect agonies, but the toughest moment was always when, hats held down, they walked into the wind across the tarmac. One year they did that cruise round the Pacific, beyond their means, and a mistake in other ways besides: for the scent of mangoes, and the drowned thoughts the sea kept washing up at them. They flew to New Zealand, but really it was antiquated. (On the way back, one of the engines conked out.) The winter Evelyn's arthritis played up – her hands were pretty twisted by now – and Harold's turn gave her a scare, they started off earlier than usual; they visited the Dead Heart.

Harold always arranged her rug.

He would ask, 'You're sure you're feeling comfortable, dear?'

Couples from Coffs Harbour and Hay, Wollongong and Peak Hill, never stopped asking one another who those people could possibly be, as the Fazackerleys continued to enjoy their retirement, preferably in seats up forward, so that nothing might obstruct.

Only on one occasion, above an aerial landscape of lashing trees, Harold Fazackerley, his limbs again fleshed, straddling the globe, returned for an instant to the solitary condition he remembered as normal, and the faces of those who were missing, the faces he had never touched.

But he was quick to inquire, 'You're sure you're comfortable, darling?'

As they sat out their travelogue, they became so inured to technicolour, it was hoped they would not be startled if it ended in a flack flacker of transparent film.

The Full Belly

Not many months after the Germans walked in, the elder Miss Makridis began to fail. She spoke rarely, which was distressing enough for those around her, but worse still, what she said was to the point. She said to her younger sister, 'If only we could go off quickly, Pronoë, there would be two mouths less, but age has toughened us, if anything, and we'll probably spend a long time dying.'

Pronoë, pinker, softer, less ascetic than her sister, naturally protested. Raising her furry upper lip, she whimpered back, 'Ach, Maro, you speak as though we were no longer human beings, but cattle!'

Miss Makridis didn't contradict. Ladies of perfect hearing liked to discuss Maro's increasing deafness, whereas the family recognized her silences as a kind of curtain behind which she chose to withdraw.

'And I don't want to die!' Pronoë insisted, who all her life had resented the hard corners designed for her hurt and humiliation.

As the two elderly ladies continued standing at the window, in the clear light which often seemed all that was left to them of the city they had known, Costa was sitting, warming his hands between his thighs, the other side of the folding doors. It was one of those afternoons which congealed the blood in his raw fingers, one of the days, frequent now, when he failed to turn the piano from furniture into instrument. The conversation in the next room might have sounded more ominous if it hadn't been for his faith in the aunts' permanence. It was as unthinkable that the Parthenon, say, should disappear. The real world must obviously survive even these explosive times, because his will would not allow it not to.

The light was already playing its game of coloured slides with the old ladies at the window. From girlhood it had been accepted that Maro was the intellectual one. Pronoë grew up artistic: there were the high-lit bowls of fruit, in oils, her *Cypresses against a Wall* (a whole series); there were the yards of crochet lace she hadn't succeeded in giving away. While Maro dealt, rather, in ideas. She used to exchange ideas, passionately, with men. She accepted men as intellects, she admired them as scholars, as poets, as priests. Otherwise, the whole thing was inconceivable. Between the wars Goethe had been her great love. She spoke English, Italian, French, reckless Russian, and with the greatest pedantic accuracy, though her conscience now hushed it up – *German*.

After Eleni's marriage, the two remaining sisters had wandered about Europe with Mother, in search of the kind of employment nice people expected. They visited watering places, for Mother's liver, her asthma, and her gout. There were museums for Maro. She had taken courses at some of the universities. While Pronoë had her little social flutter, in Greek circles, in Paris, and Vienna. She tried on hats, and sketched the easier monuments. Mother had died at Rome, after which they brought her back to Greece, for Christian burial, and because they suddenly realized, their money was running out.

Through the folded doors Costa watched the fading light strew his aunts' crumbling cheeks with ashes of violets. Light, it seemed, turned marble to pumice, flesh into grey pottery. There was a certain light by which his own genius became suspect: he couldn't believe in the music congealed in his mottled sausages of fingers.

So he was glad enough when Anna gave him a rough kiss in passing through the dining-room. (Acquaintances considered Anna cold, simply because she was too busy, too much depended on her.) This evening she was wearing her brownest, her most livery look, which meant she had spent most of the day hunting for food. On the whole Costa enjoyed being the practical Anna's younger brother. He got up now and followed her sturdy calves, which had something in common with his own hands. He was anxious to see what she had got in the bundle.

Anna kept for her aunts a gentleness she seldom showed to others, probably not even to Stavro.

'Did you take your tablets?' Her face changed shape, she lowered her voice, to indulge Aunt Pronoë's imagined heart. 'Are you cold, Maroula?' She touched the other old woman's hand as though it were of the flimsiest material.

Aunt Maro answered, 'No. But if I were, nothing could be done about it.'

It was the kind of realism which had begun to upset ladies of their acquaintance.

Aunt Pronoë let a sharp little whine escape; she couldn't wait to see what Anna had found.

'What is it?' she breathed, gasped, her watering eyes focused on the bundle.

'What have you brought?' Paraskevi came shuffling, slit-slat, over the honey-coloured parquet.

Springing from such different sources the maid and her mistresses had united far back. They had aged together querulously.

'It's the same.' Handing over the ragful of uprooted dandelion, Anna sounded apologetic.

'Weeds again? It's always weeds. I'm all wind from eating weeds,' the maid grumbled from out of her seamed leather, and went back, slip-slop, across the no longer polished parquet.

Aunt Pronoë advised her, through an overflow of tears, to give thanks to God.

'Poh! If He's feeding the other side?' Paraskevi was cranky this evening.

Aunt Maro recollected, 'He sent us the lamb from Vitina. It wasn't His fault if some pig of a man stole it out of the sack.'

It was true. And left a dog's carcass in its place.

Aunt Maro laughed. It still amused her, because it was the kind of incident which illustrates what one can expect. But almost at once her face grew stern, her eyes glittered: she remembered that she was in love with God.

A smell of cold moist earth lingered in the room, from the weeds Paraskevi had carried off to wash and boil. Costa used the prospect of a meal as an excuse to postpone working on the Haydn sonata. He promised himself that the wad of boiled dandelion he was going to eat, without oil, without salt, without anything, would endow him with a strength to overcome physical obstacles and lift him to pinnacles of understanding.

While knowing that Paraskevi was right: the weeds would turn to wind in their stomachs; just as the same thin notes would continue twittering out of his fingers.

'But we shall eat, at least!' Aunt Pronoë was filled in advance with a kind of hectic gaiety.

'Not I.' Aunt Maro's decision landed amongst them like a stone. 'Not when every mouthful counts. Remember the children. Who am I to deny them food?'

Possibly everyone had become a bit feverish. Costa's hair was permanently damp. Old Paraskevi muttered, and repeated; her eyes burned holes in anyone she looked at. And it was on this same evening that Aunt Maro took to her bed.

From there during the days which followed, she continued to conjure up those unconvincing, over-idealized children. The flame she had kept burning under the icons, in spite of shortages, at great expense, was more substantial than Aunt Maro's children.

At first his ailing aunt was the perfect excuse for Costa not to practise. In that small flat.

But she began insisting from her bed, 'Play to me, Costaki. Music is more nourishing than food.'

So he played for her, and at times the music ascended some of the way towards the heights he was determined to reach.

After they had learnt to admit to the Occupation, and the first knife-thrusts of hunger had developed into a permanent ache of emptiness, he had decided to utilize, to *spiritualize*, his physical distress. (He even made a memo of it, in French, in his neatest hand, at the back of his *Wohltemperiertes Klavier*.) To a certain extent he had succeeded, he liked to think. For instance, a detached, hungry melancholy, arising out of his physical condition, helped his Chopin. Out of the ebb and flow of his altered blood, his own *submergence*, his *Cathédrale engloutie* rose with a glowing conviction he hadn't achieved before. The architecture, some of the austerities of Bach, he had begun to grasp, if not yet the epiphanies. Pronoë suggested these depended on 'maturity of soul'. He no longer had the strength to feel irritated by his aunt. Instead he was amused to visualize his 'soul' rounding out, like a football bladder suspended in air, in a space beside the Parthenon.

Costa Iordanou was a serious stubble-headed boy with broad muscular hands. His hands were surprising to those who could recite his pedigree.

Consider his mother alone: Eleni – so dazzling from many worldly angles, her *toilettes* from Worth, her long sheaths of hands, her judgments, her generosity, her malice, her abandoned hair, her throat, her eyes. Her eyes. It was not so extraordinary that Iordanou, a cold, upright man, should have accepted her without a dowry. No doubt it was Eleni who had helped him to the Presidency. Tragic how leukaemia shortened his term of office, far more tragic that Eleni, driving her own car, should crash at that bend in the Kakia Skala.

For Costa his parents had never been more than photographs and myths. His aunts were what his touch confirmed. Only natural that those good souls should have taken Eleni's Anna and Costaki. (It's always sad for the children.) Anna was a brown sulky girl, Costa an amusing child making up his little tunes at Pronoë's piano not long after he began to toddle.

Until now, from her bed, under the icon of the Panayia, Maro was reminding him of her favourite.

'Play for me, Costaki, *La Cathédrale*.'

His aunt's voice rising slowly in sonorities of green masonry out of his tremulous belly out of the iridescent waters glowed with the light of rose-windows resurrected.

From the beginning the aunts had decided the children should inherit the brilliance of their parents. Anna would marry an ambassador, on a dowry provided – it was hoped – by Cousin Stepho Mavromati. But Anna the brown girl had thrown herself away on that young doctor, Stavro Vlachos, from Vitina. Months later ladies of the aunts' acquaintance were still putting on their kindest voices, as though to help the poor things over another bereavement, or an operation.

Fortunate for them, in the circumstances, that Costaki was born a prodigy. Nina Zakinthinou, one heard, had grown jealous of her own pupil. At the Odeion, Antoniadis finally informed Miss Makridis that Costa must study with someone able to take him farther. Maro returned looking even more haggard than her usual self. Until it was arranged, with the help of Cousin Stepho, that Costa should go to Cortambert in Paris.

When the house of Europe incredibly collapsed.

Costa taught himself not to remember the details of his pretended future. Though he kept the steamer ticket at the bottom of his handkerchief drawer. And his music remained, which nothing could devalue or destroy. Its flow continued, perhaps more uneven than formerly, reduced at times to a frustrated stammer, at others forcing itself with the glug-glug of water escaping through a hole.

If ever in the over-intimate flat the atmosphere of cloying love, of suffocating thoughtfulness, dried the music up, he used to refresh himself by invoking a fantasy of property: a studio just large enough to hold his piano, a divan besides, on the cushions of which he might occasionally undress some girl, not yet completely visualized, let alone possessed, her buttresses of thighs, her gargoyle breasts, rising slowly out of the oil-smeared waters and sumptuous lights of his imagination. Or discuss with his friend Loukas some of the theories of love over the frayed halves of a come-by cigarette. Fingers smelling of nicotine. Loukas said there was a sexual position in which the two bodies made a kind of boat together. So.

Loukas, who had in his left groin a birthmark like the map of Crete, disappeared on a November night the way people did nowadays. The map of Crete was no advantage; nobody had identified him. Costa found himself forgetting Loukas, not even caring. That, too, was the way it happened now. Mourning belonged to the age of visiting-cards and maiden ladies of sufficient means.

Or was he self-centred, as Aunt Pronoë, in moments of extreme hunger, accused? At least he didn't flinch on recognizing his own flaws, moral as well as physical, when he caught sight of them in the glass: that spot on the chin of an over-indulged puppy face; eyes which tormented nights had stamped with circles of sticky brown flannel. To this extent he was realistic; or was he self-congratulatory? He longed to be as old, as wily, as inviolable as Goethe, say, at the end of his sensuality, when his vices passed for experience, and his platitudes were accepted as gold.

'It is so *satisfying*', Aunt Maro called, as she got control of her machinery, 'to realize that music can be French as well. Thank you, dear Costaki. For your *Cathédrale*.'

And Aunt Pronoë, that elderly baby, gurgled, '*Ravissant, ravissant!*' on her way to disturb Maroula's pillows.

Very briefly as a young girl Pronoë was engaged to an officer. Nobody knew why the engagement had been broken off. Something mysterious, never discussed, had happened to Maro in Munich. After which, the two ladies gave themselves to Athene and the Panayia. Perhaps their names had designed them for it. Neither of them was in any way resentful of their fate. Each, in fact, would have protested her fulfilment. And her devotion to the other.

'Leave me, Pronoë!' Maro's voice began to grate as she sawed with her neck against the pillow. 'You are such a *fiddler!*'

'When all I think about is your comfort!'

Comfort was an immorality Maro proposed to resist.

'Oh, no, no, Pronoë! *Go*, Pronoë!' Her voice moaned and reverberated round the marble peaks; while her sister remained standing on the plain.

'As you hate me, I shall leave you,' Pronoë promised. 'All our life you have tried to hurt me.'

Then Maro laughed, and called down, 'My memory isn't as good as yours.'

On overhearing Aunt Pronoë as she passed, 'What are we going to do if we lose her? What then?' Costa understood he wasn't being addressed.

Immediately she saw him she said, 'When I was a girl I played the piano hoping to give pleasure to others. But *professional* musicians become so egocentric they forget they have an audience. Excepting, of course, when they hear the applause.'

Everybody drew a circle Pronoë was unable to enter. Even Paraskevi her maid.

'What are you standing there for?' Pronoë called. 'Standing and standing!' Perhaps it was hunger that made her voice so thin and shrill. 'What do you think about,' on one occasion she inquired, 'while you are standing?'

'I am thinking,' said Paraskevi, her slow thoughts voluptuous for one so old and dry, 'I am thinking how it felt in the days when our bellies were full.'

'Oh, our bell- - our stomachs - that is all we can think about? When they are so low down? And unimportant?'

'Important enough,' said Paraskevi.

Answering back made her mistress rush at the *bibelots*, dust the *potiches* her maid neglected, the books in which forgotten authors had written compliments for ladies of distinction, the icons which deteriorated whatever care was taken of them.

Pronoë always wore gloves for dusting. Once in her rage for cleanliness and order she put out the flame beneath the icons, flickering in the drop of oil Maro had got from the Armenian for four silver spoons. Pronoë could not blame herself enough; it was as though she had committed sacrilege.

But Maro opened her eyes and said, 'Why, Pronoë, all lights are extinguishable. Except, apparently, my own.'

She only opened her eyes now when there was reason for doing so. The lids seemed to creak back, uncovering a vision of old, brown, uncommon amber. Time might have passed unbroken, a long, slow, empty, soporific cold, if it hadn't been for the machinery of Maro's eyelids, and the shots they sometimes heard after curfew.

That winter, the house in which they had always lived impressed itself on Costa Iordanou with a vividness which only sickness or hunger kindles. To turn the corner of the street was to re-enact a first glimpse: of this ochreous face which poverty had blotched and history pitted, under its tiara of terracotta tiles. Dun shutters on rusty hinges could be forced open to admit the sun, or dragged shut to bar the enemy. Any pretensions to grandeur the house ever had were somewhat reduced by the fact that it was now shared, admittedly by members of the same family, but in altered circumstances. Since Dr Stavro Vlachos and his wife Anna had taken over the ground floor, there was a hugger-mugger public air, of patients hanging around outside. Scabby old men could be seen sitting on the steps, awaiting their turn, under the doctor's plate. But there was no longer any question of billeting, and whenever it was thought necessary to slam and bolt the shutters, there were no suspects amongst those who listened for approaching footsteps.

Otherwise, living together didn't make all that difference. Though Anna could be pretty bossy. They heard her moving about below, and she came upstairs and organized them. Their flat might have been a dolls' house when Anna began pushing them around. Stavro was a busy man, who would more than likely die of his patients, Pronoë said. (Though they had never known how to exchange more than a few words, Costa loved his brother-in-law.)

Upstairs the sloping rooms had been darkened by string-coloured net curtains and too much inherited furniture. Some of the furniture was so frail the sisters wordlessly dared callers to use it. There were the inscribed photographs of gentlemen in starched collars, ladies in *demi-décolletage*, everybody's nose impeccably aristocratic without being ostentatious. President Iordanou's photograph was set apart in a silver frame, which added to the cold distinction of his figure. Costa avoided looking at it, as though his father were present in the flesh. It shocked him to think he had once been a drop of sperm in the presidential pants. He preferred the crackled portraits of more distantly related admirals and noble brigands who had fought the Turk. His aunts' conversation had always glittered with words such as 'independence' and 'liberation'. They made them sound peculiarly theirs, till now, after bartering their other jewels, they brought these out more guardedly.

Over Maro's bed hung the tremendous small icon of the Panayia. As a little boy he used to climb on the bed, to rub his nose against the Virgin's brown Byzantine beak. Once when nobody was looking he scratched a flake of gold off the nimbus;

it tasted disappointing, and made him cough. By the time his pimples came, She had grown sullen towards him, he too conscious of the acne of wormholes in the wooden cheeks of the Mother of God. Their relationship finally settled down, half formal, half ironical. (From visits to the museum he suspected his aunt's icon was not a very good one.)

Till on a night of their present winter spattered with bullets smelling of damp cold of boiled weeds of blood his own love or hunger overflowed the eyes of his Panayia and he was drawn towards her like a drop of water to another into one crystal radiance.

Aunt Maro opened her eyes and asked, 'What are you looking at, Costaki?'

He stood trembling in a shamefully uncontrollable glandular stench of dripping armpits.

'You!' He lied smiling, ashamed equally of his cowardice and his unconfessable experience.

Maro made an almost flirtatious grimace, which did not fit her hewn-out features or her old hair. He ran at her, and began to work her hands: they might have been tokens in plaster or wood articulated by leather thongs. At the same time he looked into her eyes, the opacity of brown amber he had always known. It was possible that he had never communicated with his aunt, but he worshipped her imperishability, if not that same radiance of his Panayia.

In the morning the doctor came.

Most mornings Dr Vlachos, a stocky man from a village of pine-trees and rock, visited Miss Makridis. His heavy footsteps on the stairs were something Costa took for granted.

Maro would never have admitted to her niece's husband that he was the person she most respected, just as she wouldn't admit she could never forgive him for marrying Anna, thus thwarting a grand design.

As he went through his early-morning scales, Costa could

hear his brother-in-law. If he turned on the stool, he could see
the back of Stavro's large head, his thick, unyielding neck.

'It is a matter of willpower,' Stavro was explaining. 'There
is nothing wrong with you, Maroula. Except – where is your
will?'

Costa knew that Maro's head would be beating time on the
pillow as she spoke. 'I know all about will. My own in particular. When to use it. And to what extent. If I decide not to,
that is my own business.' She began to mumble. 'My contribution. To the children.'

Anna was always tempting their aunt, for some of the
doctor's patients were in a position to pay him: a couple of
eggs, a medicine-bottle filled with oil, once a goat cutlet which
drove the household wild.

That morning Anna had brought a soup-plate with watery
rice. It was mostly dust from the bottom of the sack, more than
usually glutinous. Mrs Vassilopoulo had got it – no one would
have asked how – and it pleased her sense of vengeful charity
to offer the little Vlachos a handful for that old creaking snob,
her aunt.

Anna said, blowing on the rice, 'Just a little mouthful,
Maroula.' Then she added, with a touch of the brilliance she
hadn't otherwise inherited, 'It is so insipid, no one should
suffer any moral qualms.'

At least they were able to laugh together.

But Costa could tell his sister had failed. He heard the dring
of spoon on porcelain, followed by Anna's demonstrative sigh.

Presently the Vlachos went downstairs to begin plodding
through the stages of their morning. Patients' voices floated
up from the surgery. Costa could recognize the extra-cheerful,
while tremulous, tone of those who were unable to pay.

He willed himself to believe in music. The blood of music
flowed through their veins as his hands splattered through pre-
liminary scales. If he could only live for music, music would

give him life in return – spirit, as old man Bach had demonstrated so sensibly. It was consoling to realize sense and not
daemon led to God.

When suddenly he had to run, the ways so tortuous, so dark,
in their cramped flat. He had to reach the bathroom. Scarcely
had time to arrange himself. It was the weeds they mostly had
to eat. The spirit was finally reduced to a stream of green
slime.

Or not finally.

Finally he sat pulling at himself, without an image, scarcely
erect. So much for sense, for Bach, for Maro and Pronoë – for
the worm-holed Panayia. He bowed his head at last above his
impoverished stickiness.

And remembered the afternoon not long after the enemy
had taken possession, when Pronoë began springing from room
to room, an obscene, elderly ballerina inspired by expectation
or fear. His own heart exploding. Glad he was only the young
nephew.

Paraskevi returned upstairs. It surprised him that anyone so
tough and fibrous as their maid could tremble quite so violently.
'A German officer,' she announced.

'Of what rank?' babbled Pronoë.

Though her fingers were performing all the arpeggios of
fear, there were certain formalities to be observed.

But Paraskevi had never been able to learn about rank, and
in any case, a German was a German.

Suddenly too old to react any more, Pronoë let fall, 'They
have come for us, then.'

All three continued *in extremis* awaiting guidance if the saints
hadn't turned to wooden boards since God withdrew His
favour.

Maro got up from her chair. Everybody realized this was
what they had been hoping for. Maro was the one saviour
who might possibly deliver them.

They all went down. As a mere hoplite, Costa breathed more easily.

There was a wind blowing. That winter the wind never stopped blowing on Lykavittos. Stavro had been called to a patient, Anna was out digging dandelion. So the phalanx faced the whole cold afternoon opening blue and rainy at them through the doorway.

The mortal gravity of the situation drove all four of them out of the house into the street. Pronoë held her hair to her head, but Maro's hair blew. She might have appeared cloudy if it hadn't been for her features: their cutting-edge was of weathered stone.

The young lieutenant – everyone but Maro afterwards admitted there was nothing objectionable about the lieutenant – standing unnaturally upright outside their house in Patriarch Isaïou, was offering a neat, oblong parcel.

'Miss Makridis,' he began composing in timid Greek, 'please accept with the greetings of Professor Schloszhauer, of whom I have been a student – in Munich – this small parcel of genuine coffee.'

The silence swelled in Patriarch Isaïou.

Then Miss Makridis, in a German stiff from disuse, though still thrillingly accurate, said, 'Professor Schloszhauer could not have realized he would force me to commit treason by accepting his parcel of coffee. I am sure the professor would not wish me to.'

Above her marble face, her hair was blowing about in tormented streamers of white cloud.

Paraskevi did not stop grunting and muttering.

Maro was actually moistening human lips. 'Tell him,' she began. '*Tell*,' she practically sang. But the rising voice had a flaw in it. It cracked on its highest, purest note. And shattered.

The German lieutenant clicked. Saluted. Turned. Still carrying the parcel of coffee. Routed by the phalanx.

The victorious Greeks went upstairs. It was not an evening for celebration. Pronoë snivelled on and off; she had a permanent cold since they were without heating. Old Paraskevi kept calculating aloud how many little cupfuls she might have squeezed out of the parcel. Where a scent of coffee should have floated, there hung a stench of boiling nettles.

As Costa Iordanou sat in the bathroom mopping at his thighs with a handkerchief on the morning of his shame, there wasn't even the stench of weeds. There was a smell of cold. And excrement. The flat was empty by now. Paraskevi, Pronoë, each had gone in her chosen direction – to hunt. One day somebody might kill. In the meantime, it was hoped, they would all survive on weeds.

Costa went into Maro's room. After hoisting her higher on the pillows, he embraced his cold aunt. The plateful of tepid rice on the bedside table gave him a whiff or two of aged, human flesh. His aunt's eyelids reminded him of hens he had seen peasants tying by the legs, but her lips had the bluish, gelatinous look of old, resigned, human lips. He couldn't look any longer. He went out, he didn't know, nor care, where. Slamming their front door. He was the disgusting genius whose shortcomings embittered his throat, and stuck to his thighs.

Even so, the little pure notes of truth trickled at intervals through his eyes into his mind: a sky still tolerated the scurfy roofs of the houses below, a geranium still burned in a pot, a donkey dropped a poor, but still sweet-smelling, turd.

He went down Callerghi Street buttoning his jacket. He went down Thessalogenous. His ankle twisted on a stone, and nearly threw him. He glanced back to curse the stone. In Meleagrou, Mrs Vassilopoulo looked out from the ground floor of the block she owned. She had been putting on her hat, but took it off, and called Costaki in.

Mrs Vassilopoulo explained, 'Somebody is giving me a

lift. To my sister at Porto Rafti. Where I go if possible once a week. It is from my sister's – at Porto Rafti – that the eggs come.'

Mrs Vassilopoulo made a phlegmy noise in her throat, a gesture with her head to indicate the bowl of eggs. Eggs today had acquired the status of flowers. Their smooth, passive forms disturbed. The sister's hens gave brown eggs. There was a bloom on their porous shells. They were the perfection of eggs: not for eating.

Perhaps for that reason you started to hate Mrs Vassilopoulo's eggs. She had a greasy skin, particularly about the eyelids. She had a just noticeable goitre. She smelt of body, and looked like bruised, browning pears.

While she spoke she kept on lowering her black eyelids.

'My sister at Porto Rafti.'

Flickering and smiling behind the powder.

'Where the eggs come from.'

Then Mrs Vassilopoulo stopped smiling. She drew down the corners of her mouth, her eyeballs straining out of her head, her face darkening as she screwed it up into a tight ball of wrinkles. You would have said Mrs Vassilopoulo was suffering from a belly-ache.

'Costaki,' she began panting in short sharp peppermint gusts, 'every day you pass I ask myself what have I done that he never looks. Of course,' she said, 'I know,' she said, 'young boys go through a brutal phase. And realize too late –' the tear-drops were bounding out of Mrs Vassilopoulo's eyes, ' – what they have missed.'

All at once she took his hand and stuck it right inside her nest of rotting pears. The sweat began prickling on him, and he had never felt so cold, so limp, between his legs.

Mrs Vassilopoulo was smiling again. It was more alarming than her belly-ache. The smell of body lying in ambush under powder shot up his nostrils as she moved in.

'I don't believe', she breathed, 'you are all that brutal. Not such an angel. Not underneath.'

Just then he succeeded in tearing his paralysed hand out from between her hot pears.

'You and your old eggs!'

Under the influence of the emotions which were swirling round them, the eggs in the bowl seemed to have swelled, to have increased in number, just as he and Mrs Vassilopoulo had begun to overcrowd the small palpitating room.

'My eggs?' she shrieked. 'You know there were never larger! Or fresher!'

Her breasts were bounding between her shrieks.

'But what are eggs?' As though to illustrate, she began picking them up. 'That', she bellowed, 'is all I care for eggs!' She threw. 'And you!' She threw and threw. 'And your stuck-up, crazy aunts!' Always throwing. 'Nasty *pousti* boy! Every sign. From away back.'

He went out. It was fortunate Mrs Vassilopoulo had worked herself into such a state she could only hit the walls of her own *saloni*.

He walked down the hill, down the narrowing, the practically deserted streets, which bobbed about under him like gangways over a rough sea. The clearest mornings were perhaps the bitterest in their city now, their fragility a constant warning.

In a gutter in Bouboulinas Street an old lady was lying. The hat she should have been wearing had disappeared from the neat swathes of her hair. The shoes were gone from her stockinged feet. Her legs, sticking out too straight, too wide apart, marked her as a carcass rather than a corpse, yet her decent black-silk, white-spotted dress, everything about her except the face, was that of his own, living aunts.

Death had not parted her from her handbag. Costa had a look inside the bag, because nowadays nobody, excepting no doubt his aunts, let an opportunity slip. Naturally the bag was empty.

He walked on through the labyrinth, between the blanks made by iron shutters. In the entrance to an empty arcade stood a German corporal offering a tin of something on the palm of his red hand.

'*Guck mal!*' he coaxed. '*Fleisch kaloh.*'

The unopened tin was so dazzlingly immaculate it could have contained the true answers to all the riddles.

Costa was fascinated by the tin.

Then the corporal compressed his voice in a lower, straining, hopefully seductive key.

'*Seh gamo kaloh, paithee. Ehla! Nimm's doch!*'

The corporal's hand, perhaps once-bitten, was trembling like his voice.

Never given the time, never, to think of historic replies, Costa Iordanou simply said, 'Go and stuff it up your own arse.'

It should have sounded thunderous as it rebounded off the peeling walls, but came out thin, wavering, schoolboyish, finally a warning of danger.

So he was running. Running from his own pseudo-thunder. Through the empty market. Running on his too short, once muscular, now watery, staggery legs.

The wind and the silence were against him.

He ploughed on till streets petering out in those choppy waves around the Agora tore into the last of his strength. He fell panting, grunting, amongst the earthworks, on the withered caper vines. There in past summers he had meandered with Loukas his friend, laughing at the lovers as they undulated amongst the twining capers, in a smell of dust still warm with sun, under a yellow moon. Now the capers only rustled as a gritty wind tweaked at their husks; the lovers had vanished with the velvet nights. Of melon ices melting trickling. Of swelling, bursting, golden moons. This year, all those who pushed with their bellies against the wind were thin girls tragically loaded.

From being thumped by his breathlessness against the winter grass, he was suddenly lying still, he realized. Not from exhaustion, or not altogether. It was the dish of roasted kid he had eaten somewhere out Halandri way. Memory made a museum piece of it: bronze skin incised with no particular myth beyond that of succulence, then the streaks of ivory in rosy, grained flesh, the bones not yet cast in their final sculpture. As crux, an exquisite small kidney.

Tears ran out from under his eyelids into the whispering capers. The most agonizingly live juices had begun to flow again through his veins his muscles wiry as green vines his cock fighting against his flies.

He sat up. Of course he had earned eggs in the past, and a tin or two of German meat. Bach only titupped along beside the need to stuff your mouth with food. Always eventually transformed into that same slobbering beast, the spirit stood grinning at him in the Agora.

He got on his feet after clawing at sand and a shard or two. The German corporal would be less messy, if more painful. In any case Mrs Vassilopoulo, of bruised pears and perfect eggs, would have already left for her sister's after mopping out the *saloni*. It was the German corporal of huge meaty hands.

Costa (they called him Costaki, but he saw himself as IORDANOU in print) was apparently walking away, in the direction of his dubious intention, though uneven ground and a cloudy mind helped him remain unconvinced. A little longer. In normal times he would have crossed the Agora with care, listening for the crunch of treasure. Now he ought to hurry, though. He started hobbling. He might have been lame. A noose set by a weed trapped him by the ankle. He jerked. Stumbled. Ran clacking at last along the street which led to Monastiraki.

He ran.

Swallowing the air.

He was running past the iron shutters. Flat faces of whores and spivs flickered in the entrances to alleys. They didn't seem in any way surprised. Wasn't he of their world? His own smell was married to that of crumbling plaster, damp cardboard, rags not fit to steal, shit. As he searched for the corporal who should have awaited his intentions. He couldn't believe the statue might have melted away. Or the tin of German meat.

That alone had been far too solid. His mouth was becoming furred, but gummy buds were swelling on his tongue. Hands throbbing already with cuts from tearing the tin apart. To get at the marbled meat beyond the jags.

All the while he was running houses shops he had been passing all his life that one dusty divided cypress the monument to Diogenes were rooted in reason a practical life could still be led and was. He, for instance, was only being practical. He could never have swallowed a raw egg. He would have had to carry eggs home, to share, boiled, with aunts whose devotion had made him so vulnerable, and a maid whose man's appetite hadn't been dulled by age. So. Eggs. Meat he could scoff down, face to a wall, on the way up, from behind fulfilled lips ignore the pain of getting it.

Meat.

It was distressing ludicrous as he ran to realize what he was doing peering down arcades up culs-de-sac for the figure of an illusory corporal. If ever they met he would greedily kiss the meaty mouth. Force the issue too hard perhaps. But *all* Germans love to talk Wagner, and no Greek could accuse music of treason.

There, you see, the spirit does survive the shit-pit, and the orthodox faith need not be so orthodox.

While he ran she had begun loping beside him. She had discarded her blue for the short white pleated kilt. Each one of her movements was performed with the utmost grace and ease. Health. She would have lobbed an accurate ball into her opponent's court. His Panayia. He searched her eyes, with a love he had never experienced and perhaps never would, her hair streaming in strands of palest sunlight.

Weakness on his part finally caused the milky dimples in the knees of his Valkyrie-Virgin to thin out and blur.

He was passing the little Church of the Annunciation at the bottom of the hill, a brown, lesser, chunk of a church favoured by Pronoë: 'the poorer saints are always saintlier.' He had come there with his aunt during their last Easter of peace. Now he pushed the tottering door, and was at once received into an enclosed emptiness.

He leaned, or flopped, against the stassidion, to get his breath, and the ancient wood did give him support of a kind as he lay spread-eagle, his Byzantine ribs cruelly creaking, while the professionally hungry stared at him out of the iconostasis: dog-headed saviour, lion-happy troglodytes, evangelists in cloaks of cruciform check – the whole luxury of consecrated poverty.

He might have prayed if he hadn't forgotten the language, all but a few burnt-in phrases. In moments of indolence or joy he liked to believe that being was prayer, but this did not help on occasions of guilt or desperation. So now he locked his hands together. He snuffed up the smell of dead incense, he rocked his head, and shuffled with his slanted feet. One anaemic candle was burning amongst the grubby pellets, the sickly stalactites, of last year's wax. The gold liturgies of then still hung carved in the grey, fluctuating atmosphere of now. From which his lips were hopefully sucking for sustenance.

And there in the centre stood his own wooden Panayia, sternly encased, however the wind tormented her orthodox hair, her supernal eagle's beak. Until it seemed his familiar Virgin was flowing through the whorls of his ears into the sanctuary of his brain.

Take, eat, She said, *this is my body, my mess of watery black-market rice, which is given for you.*

And at once he saw clearly through the cloud of his exhaustion the cloud not of incense but of steam rising out of a plateful of boiled rice.

The heavy lids of his Panayia confirmed her decision.

Costa Iordanou elbowed himself away from the stassidion. He stood himself on his props of legs. If not exactly restored to strength, he was again distinct, his own will, as he faced the last lap up the mountain, zigzag here, between the staggered cypresses, up up the streets of ochreous houses, through what had once been a good address.

Towards the dish of sacramental rice already gumming up his lips with opalescent goo.

On and off he tried to give thanks to his stern Virgin, but rising slowly higher on this half-deliberate, half-mystical ascent, he invoked, rather, Debussy. Another cobby little swollen-headed fellow, Debussy was eaten in the end, he had read, by a cancer. There was a wall to the right on which Costa, long enough ago, had written amongst the other scribble – *Iordanou.* The writing existed still. Death was something which happened to others Debussy or others. For Iordanou rising in swimming chords on weighted feet a submerged future must surely emerge out of the slurp of soupy rice.

He broke roughly into the house. It did not sound as though Stavro or Anna was at home. It made him joyous, if not cocky. Racketing up the dark stairs.

What would he say if she opened her eyes? But She had already opened Hers. And revealed.

He hadn't realized there were so many doors to overcome before you reached the innermost.

The knob on Aunt Maro's door gave. He seemed to have expended unnecessary breath as he threw open the easiest of doors. The long thin old woman was lying as usual nowadays:

stretched straight, eyes closed, the sheet under her cold chin. What was unorthodox shocking shattering was the chip chip of spoon against porcelain.

It was Aunt Pronoë guzzling at a wobbly plate of rice.

Pronoë rolled her eyes in her old chalky downy face as she rammed the spoon into a mouth he had never seen before. She rammed again. He could hear the metal striking her still pretty little teeth. But *rammed*. Desecrating her sister's room with a clatter. Obviously Pronoë had never understood the respect due to sanctity.

'*You!*' Though he heard his voice a thin hiss, his tongue felt shaped like a radish.

As he pounced on the plate.

Then they were wrestling together.

'You don't understand!' She was deafening. 'I feel so terribly hungry!'

In any glimpses he got, his aunt's face was that of an aged greedy girl. The strength in her deceiving hands enraged him. She was cold as lizards, but her stiff satiny agility suggested a large bird refusing to give up its prey. Her breath came at him in waves, sweetly scented with masticated rice. Her ugly tongue stuck out of her mouth.

'Costaki! No! No!' shrieked his gentle aunt. 'Haven't you any pity – respect?'

As they scrambled and fought, the veins in her eyeballs were terrible. At least her rings didn't scratch; they had gone to the Armenian. The spoon fell bouncing on worn carpet finally tinkling into silence over boards.

'No, no, Costa! Cost-*ah*-ki!'

The name lashed.

'You're a criminal then!' Her vehemence made it sound like laughter.

It strengthened him, if anything; it almost persuaded him he had a mission.

The plate fell: Anna's plate. In the absence of a dowry, they had given her a good dinner service, with a few things besides. Anna had been very proud of her household belongings.

The plate falling amongst their feet trampling scuffing the last of the pile from the carpet smashed.

'Costa you will suffer!' Pronoë the gentle aunt couldn't shriek enough to accuse someone other than herself.

Like some kind of black-and-white insect, she had begun hopping beyond his reach. Out of the room. Suppressing any afterthought of a shriek because of the maid, who was shifting the pots around in their empty kitchen.

When his aunt had gone, Costa Iordanou plumped on the carpet, intent on stuffing his mouth with rice. If only the few surviving grains. Sometimes fluff got in. Or a coarse thread. His lips were as swollen as cooked rice. The grains stuck to the tips of his fingers, the palms of his hands. He licked the grains. He sucked them up. The splinters of porcelain cutting his lips. The good goo. The blood running. Even blood was nourishment.

At one point, he could never remember which, his aunt Maro must have opened her eyes.

'Eat, poor souls,' she said. 'Fill your stomachs, children.'

He had been too engrossed to look. But continued hearing. 'I only pray you'll know how to forgive each other.'

Towards evening Paraskevi came calling through the house, 'Miss Pronoë? Costaki! Can you smell it? Anna was given the head of a lamb, two feet, and the lights! My God! My little Panayia! We're going to have a feast.'

During the night Costa Iordanou, in his emptiness, went back into that same shameful room hoping the oracle might reassure him that none of what had happend had happened. He touched the bones of her fingers. But her eyelids didn't stir. He stood for a little, gratefully listening to her slight breathing. Otherwise, there was the sound of silence and furniture.

Fortunately there were distant corners in their strait flat, in which those who needed to, could hide. The funeral, however, forced them out. It stood them face to face. After which, they were alone together – the heart, it seemed, of their mortified city.

The Night the Prowler

Mrs Bannister reached the bathroom in time to vomit into the wash-basin. She had meant to use the lavatory, but the night had been so ghastly it wasn't surprising her plan misfired. She stood running the taps while her reflection fluctuated at her in the glass. In *their own* bathroom. *Her* reflection. She shuddered, and turned the taps off. She almost dabbed herself with Humphrey's mouthwash before the shape of the bottle suggested it wasn't her eau de Cologne.

Though it was already nine-thirty Felicity was still in her room. Sleeping? Lying awake on her bed? Only God knew. Mrs Bannister preferred not to dwell on her daughter's probable state of mind for fear of churning up her own barely controlled distress. At least Felicity had consented to take Dr Herborn's sedative. They had all, even Humphrey, accepted pills.

Mrs Bannister couldn't hold back what sounded like a mew. She had never been one of those women who expect the superhuman in a husband, but what made the whole affair far more ghastly was to discover the limits of her own powers: when she had always secretly believed that, with the exception of cancer, air disasters, and war, she had circumstances under control.

Her self-confidence had suffered so badly she would have rung hours ago to confide in Madge Hopkirk, if Humphrey's ideas about what you can tell even your most trusted friend hadn't been so rigid. Humphrey himself had warned the office that he would be late, and was now she couldn't imagine where.

The incinerator, possibly. Some men wasted endless time burning things. Did they perhaps find solace in it? The thought would have been less irritating if she had dared ring Madge to tell about their experience.

Frustration had dried Mrs Bannister's cheeks to chalk when she twitched aside a curtain in the still darkened living-room, and there was her husband, stooping, snipping the deadheads off the geraniums in the tubs beyond the sill. His rather thick fingers, his methodically shaven cheeks, all the visible signs of male insensitiveness, sent her in a rush to the telephone. She dialled with such force she half wondered whether an unfamiliar voice would answer. But it didn't; and mentally, she flung herself into her friend's arms, without her normal reservations when Madge was audibly munching toast.

'Darling ... Yes, I know it's later than usual, but you can't imagine what we've been through ... what a night ... hardly a wink, though Dr Herborn gave a pill ... Well, I'll tell you, Madge, in *strictest* confidence, as you'll soon understand ... because Humphrey ... You must be patient with me, Madge dear.'

Mrs Bannister took fright at the sound of herself, but through a revival of will, got the better of her voice.

'It was like this, as far as I can remember, because you will realize what a shock. It was about two-thirty. I woke from one of my light sleeps. I heard Felicity crying, but *sobbing*, in the dining-room. I went in. She seemed quite hysterical. She was wearing only her torn night-dress. She told me she had woken to find someone beside her in her bed. One of these prowlers, intruders, we read about, who break into girls' bedrooms, and ... A psychologically deranged person ... A *man*, Madge – Felicity found a MAN in her bed ... Yes ... Well, I can hardly bring myself to say it. He – raped – my little – Felicity!'

For some moments Mrs Bannister sobbed into the telephone. It occurred to her it might sound frightening to Madge, but those who are closest to anyone are always the most frightening in the end.

'I can imagine the agonies my poor darling must have suffered. When it was all over,' Mrs Bannister couldn't help hearing her own voice make a disagreeable sucking noise, 'he dragged her into the dining-room. He had a knife, Madge ... No ... I know they do, but he didn't. He menaced her ... He smoked one of Humphrey's best cigars. He drank a tumblerful of brandy. He forced her to drink with him – while insulting her in the vilest language – all at the point of the knife ... Yes ... Yes ... Oh, well, yes, yes!'

While Madge ran on Mrs Bannister remained aware of the dreadful weight of events bumping around in her own mind. Of course Madge was incapable of realizing. One had to admit it: she was superficial.

'You needn't ask ... But give me a chance, darling. Everything possible has been, and will be, done. Humphrey would sleep through the Last Trump, but when I succeeded in rousing him, he knew exactly what steps ought to be taken. He dialled an emergency number, and the police threw a cordon round the neighbourhood. Two detectives came to the house. We were allowed to send for our own doctor. That was a great comfort. Felicity has known Dr Herborn since she was a tot.'

Madge had to have another go.

As soon as she was given an opportunity, Mrs Bannister managed, 'One of the detectives was such a charming little fellow. Clever too, I'd say. He grows staghorn ferns as a hobby.' She glanced at the chair in which the sympathetic detective had sat: there was still a depression in it, which made her throat knot again.

'But of course they didn't catch that *brute* ... Probably escaped through the park – through the gaps in the railings ... They won't catch him. And if any of this leaks out, we'll have the scandal on our hands without the cause ... The second detective I didn't take to at all – not exactly insolent, but as close to it as cynicism can get. You know how the Law takes pleasure in *insinuating*, regardless of the fact that *you're* the innocent party. It was like that. The second detective, for some reason – probably political – didn't want to be on our side ... Madge? You'll be discreet, dear. Humphrey would never forgive me.'

Such a spate of protest poured out of the receiver Mrs Bannister was forced to remove it from her ear; then when the crackle showed signs of letting up, she nerved herself to introduce a less dramatic, though major issue.

'John hasn't been told yet.'

Perhaps one had launched it too casually: Madge sounded distressingly remote.

'And who should tell him ?' Mrs Bannister was considering aloud rather than asking for the advice nobody would be able to give. 'Who will make it sound – not *acceptable* – less *ugly*? The right person would soften the blow. Because it will be an immense shock to – to the *psyche* – of even a sophisticated young man, to hear a month from the wedding that his bride has been raped ... Madge? ... Oh dear, I'm sorry! It's horrid when you upset it on the sheets.' Mrs Bannister could afford to show sympathy: her vision of Madge Hopkirk sitting in a squalor of spilt coffee made her feel superior. 'But returning to this question of who shall tell – Humphrey shouldn't attempt it – or so I consider. I mean – two men blundering round such a delicate situation would probably end up making it appear vulgar.' Mrs Bannister moistened her lips. 'I began to think, in the course of this sleepless night, that I might tell John myself. Such a splendid relationship has developed between us during their long engagement. Oh, these long engagements! But he was so firm about sparing Felicity the climate when he was appointed to Djakarta. As soon as he heard he was to be posted somewhere else ... we don't know where – not officially, though I have it from somebody at Canberra – somebody *high up* – they're making him First Secretary at Rome ... Yes, dear, I know I didn't tell you: Humphrey wouldn't have approved of it. And now this dreadful thing! ... Who is going to tell *John* ... at *this* point ... in his *career?*'

Mrs Bannister hugged the telephone and moaned.

'Yes, Madge? ... Yes ... Ye-ehs – I know what girls are like nowadays. I know there's all this sleeping around. But I'm *certain* – from her upbringing, and the little one's own child confides – I'm pretty sure Felicity was chaste. And John I suspect of having the highest principles.' Here Mrs Bannister used her 'ethical' tone. 'Of course a decent man might *persuade* himself on the wedding night that everything was as it ought to be. But wouldn't the most decent of them feel reproachful, anyway, by twinges? And Felicity is *my* child!'

So utterly hers, for one bleeding moment Mrs Bannister almost underwent the shocking act of violation to which her daughter had been subjected. Though a fairly solid woman she tottered at the telephone, but recovered enough of her balance and voice to cough and grunt farther through the moral labyrinth in which she found herself astray.

'Do you know, Madge, what I've decided?'

Because she had. Now. It was as though the moment of empathy with her ravished child had recharged her with the powers of decision.

Moist-eyed with inspiration, Mrs Bannister continued, 'Felicity herself must tell. What could be more touching than for a young girl to confess the most shameful experience of all to her future husband? No honest man could fail to respond, and cherish her for life. What might rankle and turn to disgust if the parents told – you know, "soiled goods" and all that – can only convince as frank courage if the girl herself takes the plunge.'

Mrs Bannister was so carried away she knocked off a silver

salver left over from the days of visiting-cards and parlour-maids.

'Of *course* ... everything depends on Felicity. But I know my child, Madge!'

The crash of metal had made her reckless; till Humphrey coming in so quietly – it was those wretched rubber soles – quenched the Roman matron in her.

'Bye now, dear,' she chirped, if it wasn't croaked. 'I must organize my morning.'

'Who was that?' Humphrey could only have known.

'Madge Hopkirk.'

She clothed her reply in lead; she aimed it at the back of her husband's skull, which on this of all mornings he might have been at pains to burnish: its nakedness shone so aggressively. Mrs Bannister felt contempt for what had often been an object of compassion, and sometimes, she shuddered to think, desire.

Humphrey said, 'I hope you've left nothing to that woman's discretion – nothing she could make the worst of.'

Because Humphrey had always been jealous of loyal old Madge she ignored his remark, and asked in an imitation of kindness, 'Aren't you going to the office, dear? You know how it upsets you when others don't rise to their responsibilities.'

Humphrey answered, 'Yes.' Its submissive tone made her flinch by playing on her own helplessness.

As if this weren't enough, he followed it up by doing something appalling: he sat down so heavily in one of the royal-blue armchairs he might have been relinquishing the Stock Exchange for ever, and worse, he covered his eyes with a hand – bald Humphrey was a hairy man – and began making sounds such as his wife had never heard, so dry, dusty, torn, she couldn't associate them with his familiar fleshy body.

'Oh, darling!' she whimpered in conventional terms; herself an old blowing rag, she moved to touch him, then didn't, for fear of letting loose some more terrifying cataclysm. 'This won't help Felicity!' she blubbed.

But who was Felicity today? Or, for that matter, who was Felicity ever?

To correct her feelings the mother began running at the curtains: she let light into the house; and at once regretted doing so. Almost worse than what had happened that night, her religion of orderliness and taste was disputed: by the broached bottle of Courvoisier, cigar-ash like noblets of neat excreta (the detectives had carried off the butt), smeared glasses from which two crude knockabouts had guzzled their beer. (By this present brooding light, all thought of the nice little staghorn man became a blasphemy.)

When the sound of somebody moving through remoter rooms froze the foreground in its every anarchic detail.

'That's Felicity,' the father said, as though hoping somebody might contradict.

In her desire to return to the rhythmic past, the mother reminded, 'It's garbage day, Humphrey. Did you remember to put the bin out?'

He was doing what, normally, she disliked to hear: clearing his throat of morning catarrh. Now it was almost a comfort.

'I rang Mrs Pomfrett,' he said, 'and told them not to expect her at work. I told them she'd sprained an ankle.'

His wife pleated her forehead and drew in her lips. If it had been herself, she would have made an excuse that was more vague, less a lie: she abhorred lies, while respecting the ways of getting round them.

As the sounds of movement increased, if not approaching appreciably, the lights in the parents' faces grew more hectic.

'I wish John wasn't such a decent bloke. It would mean less to someone with a touch of the shyster in him.'

'Oh, dear Humphrey – virginity isn't a sheet of iron!'

'In my day it was.'

'But isn't any more. Virginity isn't fashionable.' She was quoting Madge Hopkirk, but decided it might be imprudent to mention the source.

'A man isn't all that impressed by his wife's following the fashion. Not when it makes him look a fool.'

'Nobody, surely, will laugh at an outrage?' But she knew it wasn't true, however shocked she tried to sound: given a different target, she and Madge might have enjoyed a laugh on the phone; so she took a chance, 'I expect it will bring John and Felicity closer together. They'll try harder to please each other.' She wasn't sure, but thought she had received another inspiration.

Humphrey only sucked his teeth, before snapping them shut.

What they had both been dreading had begun to happen: Felicity was coming into the room. For the first time since the night of their common disaster they were face to face with their changed child. Each hoped she might say something to relieve them of the responsibility of speaking first.

But Felicity abruptly lowered her eyelids, more from distaste, it appeared, than out of modesty or distress. She didn't hesitate in her progress, except to diverge slightly where the living- became the dining-room, to pick up the salver which was still lying where it had fallen. She replaced it on the mahogany console, and continued with a firm heaviness – she was barefooted – towards the kitchen.

'Where are your slippers, darling? You might catch cold, mightn't you?' Mrs Bannister almost seemed to wish it might happen.

'I don't think so.' It wasn't unusual for Felicity to act a bit lumpish before she had drunk her coffee.

Humphrey Bannister looked at his watch: for an instant he could have persuaded himself that this was one of their normal mornings.

Certainly the mother was trying hard. 'Would you like me to boil you an egg? Or two? Or grill you a kidney? There's such a nice-looking kidney.'

'You know I don't eat breakfast.'

'I only thought', Mrs Bannister babbled, 'you might be – hungry.' At once she wished herself dead of her own foolishness.

Her daughter either didn't, or wouldn't let herself, see the point. She was in any case engrossed by her immediate activities: warming up the coffee, choosing an apple, deciding whether the milk had turned; while the parents, who had followed her in on mechanical legs, stood around, large and noticeably useless.

Healthy rather than pretty, Felicity herself was fairly large. Her complexion, considered her greatest asset, was somewhat muddy by the present light, her pale-pink dressing-gown crushed, not to say grubby. She almost always dressed in pink – or blue – to show off the fair complexion, and because they were the colours she had been taught by Mummy to wear.

This morning, the mother noticed, her child wasn't wearing anything underneath her gown. Thought of the ripped nightie reduced her own throat to a hank of grey tatters.

The coffee plopped over on the stove, and at once there was something for somebody to do: Felicity got there first, and unfairly did it.

She sat peeling, then eating her apple: it sounded and looked cool. The very pale-pink dressing-gown only half hid the shapes of her breasts, their nipples not at all: these might have appeared less chaste if it hadn't been for a certain candour of the whole body; the mother was not exactly hanging on the nipples, but nearly.

Humphrey Bannister on the other hand began his move towards the office. The sight of his girl's breasts made him feel shy, almost virginal. What he murmured was full of half-

formed endearment, of 'ptt-ptt', or 'pet-pet', as he planted the
ritual kiss.

She must have felt his lips trembling on her forehead. An
already acute situation was intensified by the scent of crunched
apple. He was positively glad to steal away from it on rubber
toes; while his wife stood dabbing at what might develop into
a cold. There was so much they had failed to make together:
not even a child; this one was less than ever theirs.

Because he was always expecting something of them, his
withdrawal inspired the women to behave more naturally at
least: Mrs Bannister even began scratching one of her buttocks,
a luxury she would never have allowed herself in any presence
but her daughter's.

'What I'd do if I were you, I'd take myself to the hair-
dresser's,' the mother suggested practically; 'I'd treat myself to
everything – facial, manicure – *everything*. It would do you a
world of good, dear.'

'But I don't need good done to me' – in spite of the fact that
her hair, a light mouse, was looking a mess.

As she shrugged off her mother's advice, the pale pink fell
farther open.

'I'm only thinking of your happiness, darling,' the mother
mumbled to disguise the fascination her daughter's breasts were
exercising.

She had hardly caught sight of them since they were formed,
and now these were not only Felicity's breasts, they were also
what 'that man' must have done to them; even more fascinating
than the flesh of her flesh were the shadows on it, or could they
be horrid bruises?

'Cover yourself up, Felicity.' It was as much an order to her
own imagination. 'It isn't nice.'

It probably suited Felicity to do so, but Mrs Bannister
liked to think she had been obeyed. She had always congrat-
ulated herself on having a reasonably tractable daughter, till

remembered details of the ghastly Business they had just been through made her wonder whether her luck had left her.

'There's something I've thought and thought about, and still fail to understand.' She was returning in bitter triumph to a subject she might not be able to bear.

'Don't harp on it, Mummy. There'll always be the things which you – or anybody else – won't understand.'

'But why, why, wouldn't you let kind old Dr Herborn examine you when it came to the point?'

'I know! I know!'

She threw the apple core into a corner. More from habit than disapproval, her mother went and picked it up.

'Apart from anything else,' Mrs Bannister was clutching the retrieved core, 'it makes us all look ridiculous. I could see that nasty big detective immediately begin laughing up his sleeve. If they catch the beastly pervert, we shan't have a case, don't you see?'

'I know! I know! But they won't catch him.'

Over her shoulder Felicity threw the apple skin she had peeled in one long skilful streamer. She glanced round to see what it spelt, but the ribbon hadn't survived: it lay in pieces. She laughed slightly, down her nose.

This time Mrs Bannister let the rubbish lie. 'They have every chance of tracing the man. So I feel. You described him so vividly – horribly. Then to refuse our own doctor!'

'Can't you understand that what happened was humiliating enough? without a doctor messing about.'

'Oh, but darling – what if there are consequences?'

'I don't think I'm so helpless I can't deal with consequences.'

So the mother no longer knew what she might say, or do, but cry. She even wished her husband back: she would make use of him at least.

'Daddy was so upset by your strange behaviour. You know what you mean to him.'

'Oh, Daddy! My virginity means more to him than anything else about me. All those lectures! Thank God I'm rid of the rotten thing.'

Outrage made Mrs Bannister's sobs knock against her teeth, almost battering them down.

'I can't believe, Felicity, you're the girl Daddy and I brought up.'

'No. It's unbelievable.'

'Who agreed to marry an honourable man like John.'

'John's so honourable – so kind – so *perfect* – I couldn't live up to him. I've been writing to him this morning.'

She brought the envelope, less cool than it should have been, out of her dressing-gown pocket, and stood it against the empty cup.

Mrs Bannister could hardly prevent herself pouncing. 'What have you written? Felicity? While your mind's disturbed!' Fortunately she didn't say 'unsound'.

'I've written breaking off the engagement. For a number of reasons. The least of them being the loss of Daddy's old virginity.'

They looked at each other: each seemed to dread the sound of something still more delicate tearing; they would have liked to hold the moment off. Then they were tottering, most ungainly, towards the inevitable thwack of flesh. They were melting together, clawing after something they might still grab hold of and share, while the aseptic kitchen reverberated with their cries of helplessness, the skin from the peeled apple browning in coils around their ankles.

Early in their married life Humphrey and Doris Bannister had established themselves on the edge of the park. It was a comfortable rather than a fashionable quarter: its large, undesirable houses, in Sydney Tudor, late Victorian Byzantine, Bette Davis Colonial, suggested wealth without flaunting it, just as the inhabitants seemed agreed by the smiles in their eyes never to mention money, and the odd Jaguar or Daimler silently apologized. It suited Humphrey Bannister down to the ground: solid, and only ten minutes' drive from the GPO; Doris, who might have liked to cut a dash, hedged her enthusiasm with reservations. She had married late; she had time to make up for; but settled down to solidity and quiet, and park air. On the occasions when she arranged a bridge luncheon for some of her more fashionable friends, she allowed them to turn her neighbourhood into no more than a mild, party joke; no one could accuse her of disloyalty.

And when their only child Felicity was born, the near-by park was such a blessing: to push the pram through the ragged grass around the silted lake (you couldn't expect upkeep of parks with a war on and the men away); to sit on the balding slopes under the araucarias, and look deep into her little girl's eyes; to surprise each other's cheeks with the delicious flicker of eyelashes. Exchanging the breath of laughter and contentment it was as though they were still one; in the drowsy park, there seemed no reason why they should ever be anything else.

Every other week Doris Bannister took a snap of their child to send Humphrey in New Guinea, and Humphrey described in return a formal nostalgia for home which failed to persuade her he wasn't a fairly fulfilled adjutant.

Humphrey was a man's man: though he mightn't have known what to do about a son, he would have preferred one. A girl was breakable, you felt, while he held theirs in his large hands. 'Do you think', he might ask, 'she's making the right kind of noise?' or 'I don't feel she's happy about the way I hold her. I haven't the right touch. Oughtn't you to take her back?' as he held her out and away from himself.

In the beginning Humphrey usually referred to Felicity as She. It was absurd, touching, his attitude to the child, but also gratifying: it convinced Doris that Felicity would always be hers. So she could afford to be generous; she would make it up to poor old Humphrey.

When he came back for good, and the little girl was staggering about she used to say, 'Run to Daddy, darling. You've forgotten the kisses you've been saving for him. He's waiting, Tchitchy. He does think the world of you.'

Once or twice she persuaded him to give Felicity her bath. It was never a success, if amusing to watch: Humphrey worked almost despairingly, dribbling the water from the sponge over the little flowers of flesh, powdering the self-absorbed wrinkle.

The mother would receive her child back, give her a playful slap or two, and quickly slip the nightie on, to demonstrate how skilful she was.

Of course it was never her intention to claim all Felicity's affection. The child obviously loved her father. She would lie in ambush for him, and spring out of the salvia after he had locked the garage. She would fasten her arms round his legs, and even try to climb higher up: as though she were a cat and he a tree. Once as he was lying in his big squelchy leather chair relaxing after a busy day, she flung herself on his chest, and lay curled, eyes closed waiting for somebody to make a move.

'Oh dear,' the mother protested, 'I'm sure Daddy's too tired and hot to enjoy a heavy girl on his chest.'

But at least, if he didn't act, Daddy didn't resist.

Then Felicity sprang, and by some chance, bit the lobe of one of his ears. She actually drew blood. And grew sulky. The blood had frightened her.

Mummy was annoyed; but Daddy laughed. 'What have we got here? A little tiger?' They had to fetch his styptic pencil to stop the bleeding.

That night when he kissed her in bed, she mumbled back, 'It's "tigress".'

'It's what?' he laughed.

He had forgotten, or didn't see the point; so she didn't

explain: she lowered her eyes from what Mummy described as 'Daddy's splendid teeth'.

When Humphrey Bannister began asking his wife, 'Do you think Felicity's happy?' she answered spontaneously, 'Why ever not? She's got everything a girl could wish for.'

Humphrey had grown somewhat heavy. 'She doesn't seem to speak any more.'

'Girls don't at her age. They like to have secrets together. Though certainly Felicity hasn't many friends. That's because we've always been so close as a family.' It explained the situation perfectly.

No one could deny Felicity was quiet. She had those spots, too. Her former lollipop of a face had turned, if you wanted to be unkind, or truthful, into an unsuccessful pudding.

She would lock herself in the lavatory.

'What are you doing, darling?' Mummy asked.

'Having a read.'

'Oh, but dearest, it's so unhealthy – I mean, stuffy in there – when you've got your nice airy room.'

There was tension each side of the door.

When Felicity was sixteen Mrs Bannister organized a small dance, with hired music, a catered supper, and Japanese lanterns on the lawn. Forsaking pink and blue, Felicity might have looked pretty in her pale primrose and a string of Mummy's pearls if she hadn't been so awkward; but all the young people were awkward, it seemed, excepting two or three youths who set out to impress by a loud, vulgar braying, in spite of the good addresses they came from. Finally Mrs Bannister was too busy to bother, unless when her guests were wasting the music. But you couldn't say they weren't enjoying themselves: all the awkward taffetas and damp shirts exploding under the big bull-magnolia at the bottom of the garden.

From time to time Humphrey went down, and at once the young people grew silent. He tried to revive the party spirit with bits of slang remembered from his schooldays. A couple of the boys sniggered, but ambiguously, at his attempts; on the whole he didn't succeed in jollying the young back to where he had found them.

Not long after the dance Daddy delivered the first lecture on 'keeping clean and pure for the man who will eventually put all his faith in a girl'.

'Do you understand me, Felicity?'

She only grunted and scowled. She had never been so acutely conscious of her spots: she could feel unborn clusters forcing their way needle-headed towards the surface of her prickling skin; while Daddy sat crouching in the leather chair concentrating on his mission.

'Because to the right man, Felicity, a girl probably means even more than she does to her parents.'

The sweat was trickling down Humphrey Bannister's ribs. If only he could have left Doris to deal with the matter like any other; but you couldn't afford to take any risks: however high her moral standards, a mother's hand might be too gentle to turn the key on virginity.

So Humphrey sweated it out, and Felicity prickled.

When it was over they might have been made of rubber the way they sprang out of the room by separate doors. Felicity rushed straight to the bathroom to look at her face, and discovered several hitherto invisible spots. She tried to pop one or two of them.

'Oh darling, you may do your skin some *irreparable* injury!' Mummy was close behind her in the glass.

The following morning Mrs Bannister went on a special expedition to buy her daughter a lotion and a cream which she sensibly accepted.

Felicity, all three of them realized, had finally sloughed her old skin. What had been agonizing seemed so simple now. It was Doris Bannister's proudest moment when her friend Madge Hopkirk pronounced her daughter a 'radiant young woman'. Certainly Felicity looked very cool and pleasant, with her transparent, *English* complexion, the mother liked to think. Even more important, she had learnt to speak a language everybody understood: it gratified Mrs Bannister to find that Felicity could distinguish instinctively between what was 'marvellous' and what was 'ghastly'. The neighbourhood took a pride in the girl. She adored children. And old people. Elderly men didn't cock their legs – she was too refined – but their heads beat like metronomes in time with her weather predictions, which were almost always what they themselves predicted.

The old people of the neighbourhood continued calling her 'Tchitchy' to show they had known and cherished her from the beginning.

Mrs Burstall, who was what Mrs Bannister would have called 'ordinary' if she had allowed herself such an undemocratic thought, was also perhaps their most interested neighbour, 'Now we must find Mr Right, Tchitchy; then we'll really be off to the races.'

It was the more embarrassing in that John Galbraith had already arrived on the scene, had progressed in fact, from tentative overtures, to something more sustained and noticeable.

Mrs Bannister barely breathed at the telephone, '... Department of External Affairs ... Yes, Madge. Between posts ... John never mentions it but I know from a reliable source that the Prime Minister has taken him up ... Oh, I shan't presume to hope, but time will show ... No. She hasn't given me a single clue, but I wouldn't ask. Felicity is a girl of delicate sensibility.'

Doris Bannister's own sensibility was charmed by the erect young man in charcoal flannel; his wristwatch made her feel quite drunk; his receding hair saddened her as she realized how history repeats itself.

'Canberra,' her lips dared to mould the plastic word, 'so cold – *empty* I've always found. Of course there are the lovely trees – but one can't live with trees alone – not indefinitely, anyway.'

He enjoyed her little epigram enough to laugh at it. Had she gone a shade too far, though? She would venture anything for her child. Or for this intolerably desirable young man.

It was high time Felicity took matters into her own hands.

Though it had been Felicity who accepted John Galbraith's proposal, the engagement became a communal triumph. Mrs Bannister didn't know her neighbours socially, but almost every one of them had stopped different members of the family in the street to offer congratulations, and in Felicity's case, admire the ring.

Everybody was impressed, except perhaps Mrs Burstall, who would have preferred a larger stone in a more important setting. Anyone else could see the ring was in the best of taste, as you would have expected from a young man who was a B.A. and diplomat, and Tchitchy Bannister, who had started work with Moira Pomfrett in the interior decorating business – all the most exclusive homes. The lovely sapphire, moreover, was the exact shade of Tchitchy's eyes. Even when, owing to the fiancé's posting to Djakarta, the engagement became so drawn-out you sometimes wondered whether it was on, the ring was still there to remind: it would suddenly flare up in the neigh-bourhood's imagination to illuminate otherwise lustreless lives.

To those who had shared in this romantic efflorescence it was all the greater shock the night that fiend the prowler climbed into Tchitchy Bannister's room some said got into bed though it wasn't in the papers they all bought the *Sun* that evening the *Herald* next morning it was not in any of the papers to confirm the prowler had slashed at Tchitchy with a knife but decent people were so upset they couldn't eat a mouthful for several days for participating in the night the prowler tore apart the long white perfect thighs as though they had been a boiler's flesh only luck it wasn't your own Trish or Wendy or yes it might have been yourself in Tchitchy Bannister's bed while as for the elderly prostate-stricken gentlemen they drove it home as never before and certainly never after.

So it was very terrible for everyone.

In its actual relationship with the Bannisters, the neighbourhood strictly ignored facts: you could only treat the matter as though the whole family had gone through a serious illness; you asked about their health and what they were eating to keep their strength up, and recommended a nice invalid's programme on the box. That was for the parents only: with the girl it was more difficult because you yourself had seen her wrestling in bed with a randy stranger, the tattooes on his arms, her vaccination marks, as she tried to hold off the knife.

So, on the whole, the neighbourhood tended to avoid Tchitchy Bannister. In any case, Tchitchy herself had changed. For one thing, she began to dress different, though you couldn't say it wasn't in the fashion: it was in the style of no style. But apart from all that black, which after all was what a great many of the young girls were wearing, her face was different, as you might have expected, if you could get a look at it, because she had taken to doing her hair different. Come to think of it this Felicity had always been a girl you couldn't say you exactly knew, although you knew her. Talking to her was like as if the real Felicity was something, some sort of metal, say, shimmering and changing under the water as you looked down from the solid jetty. Now even this tantalizing and distant object had been eclipsed by the event which had passed over it, and the hair which she had begun wearing in the carefully messed-up style of today.

Most important, the ring had gone, claimed Mrs Burstall, who was the bravest, or the least ashamed. She had got a good look at Felicity's hand, only incidentally, on stopping her to ask, 'How's the job going, Felicity?'

'Oh, I gave it away – that one.' She twitched at the tangle of hair, which could be used as a curtain if necessary.

But for the moment she was exposed to anybody interested, and Mrs Burstall thought she had never seen such a naked face: she had never come across such loaded eyes.

'Well, if that's what you feel,' said Mrs Burstall. 'A person's independence is what matters, isn't it?'

'If there's any such thing, I guess it does.' She laughed too, through her colourless lips, and it sounded cool, not to say cold.

If Mrs Burstall hadn't been ever so slightly frightened she might have taken offence: Tchitchy Bannister, always straight-forward and pleasant in her conversation, had started talking clever. Even taking into account that the girl must have been changed by what had happened to her, Mrs Burstall was glad to be alone again with the dahlias after the young person had marched off in her high boots and black suit. Mrs Burstall gathered her house-gown tight around her. Anyway, she had found that Felicity was no longer wearing the diplomatist's ring.

The young man had not been seen in those parts since the unpleasantness. Except once, by Mr Jerrold. Mr Jerrold, now retired, had been taking his little dog for its lunchtime outing when he noticed some English make of car drawn up farther down, on the park side of the street. The car's uncommonness made him want to inspect it, when he realized the individual in the driving seat was Felicity Bannister's young man, and that the girl herself was there beside him. It might have been very embarrassing for Mr Jerrold if all three of them hadn't been facing in the same direction. At least he could walk on,

only half looking while listening, and frustrating his dog's
desire to pee on one of the flashing hub-caps.

Actually Mr Jerrold saw and heard very little because the
young couple's heads were inclined: they seemed to be silently
examining the dashboard, as though some delicate instrument
incorporated in it had been giving trouble; or they could
simply have come to the end of what they had to say.

Immediately on receiving her letter John Galbraith had tele-
phoned Felicity Bannister and announced she could expect
him on a day and at a time named. His voice in Canberra,
though faint, sounded more than ever warm and kind. Neither
of the reasons for her letter was mentioned during the telephone call.

Mrs Bannister said, 'I know John will be understanding.'

Seeing her mother's face, hearing her voice, Felicity was
determined to avoid the pitfalls 'understanding' might lead
her into, just as she would resist any attempt on her mother's
part to woo her lover. Mrs Bannister had done up her mouth,
and was rather scented for eleven o'clock in the morning.

So, while the car could still only just be heard, Felicity
began not exactly running, but almost, down the sloping path
in the front garden, managing the two short flights of steps
with what her speed made look like finical skill, and arrived
by contrast with a thumping burst of gracelessness amongst
the hibiscus at the bottom. Her dress was the simplest: an old
white cotton tennis frock her mother disapproved of.

She felt a heart-rending thrill of pleasure as the grey Aston
Martin drew up.

John embraced Felicity with a warmth which must have
enslaved Mrs Bannister afresh if she had been watching, which
no doubt she was.

'Now, darling,' he said, 'we can talk the sense we don't write
in the heat of the moment.'

It sounded so blandly reasonable.

'Yes, at least we can talk.' If she agreed on that point, Felicity was also aware that reason might not protect her from the shape of his back and the texture of its cloth, not to mention the leather of the Aston Martin's upholstery. 'That is why I've come down here,' she added too breathlessly, 'so that we can discuss – sensibly – without interruptions.'

They drove a little way along the parkside. Beyond the railing, mounted police were carrying out a morning exercise in support of reason. In more normal circumstances the landscape would have been too familiar to notice. Now it amazed: burnt and ragged, with sheets of escaped newspaper trapped again in the pine-scrub.

As the police wove their orderly patterns, wheeling and re-forming in accordance with commands from the voice of a superior, a second voice was superimposed: that of a dog-trainer bullying a pale young Labrador into obedience amongst the hummocks of dirty sand. Suddenly the man cursed, the dog squealed once or twice before bolting on a wide and hysterical trajectory, the trainer following, pitting a foolish wheedle against the torn screams of his dog, while the rocking-horse policemen continued to revolve, uneasy in their manliness.

It might have been more disturbing if the usual morning silence hadn't taken over soon after; till the silence itself disturbed, when you thought how it would make personal decisions clang.

John Galbraith said, when they had more or less settled down, 'I've found a buyer for the car – the chef at the Brazilian Embassy.'

'Is he paying you a good price?'

'Not good enough. But I'm lucky to be let off so lightly. And I've lived it up in the Aston Martin.'

'Yes. You've lived it up.'

As he took her hand in his assured, larger one, she thought how comfortably happy they might have been together, like those minor couples at dinner parties whose affection for each other seems to have protected them not only against the attacks of lust, but also the exigencies of love.

'The Aston Martin was an extravagance, of course.' She said it so equably. 'But it was what you wanted. I wonder what you'll get in Rome to replace it.'

'That's for you to – *half* decide.' He turned on one of the smiles she felt he must have been practising on the drive from Canberra. (Did a corner of his mouth twitch?) 'Because you can't believe, can you? that anything – that whatever happened – can make any difference to us – Felicity – darling.'

It had made enough difference for him to be looking at her with a curiosity he had prevented himself showing till now. He was trying to visualize the minutest detail of what the man had done to her. His hand bound to hers had grown sweaty. His rather colourless, fleshy, but pleasing, and to no extent sensual lips looked clumsy for once. John Galbraith's mouth had been formed by tactful conversation, foreign languages, and the strategic smile, though he enjoyed doing his duty by a kiss.

'I mean – you don't imagine I can love you less?' He was now doing his duty by words.

'Yes,' she said. 'I know.' She didn't believe him passionate enough ever to be unfaithful to her.

'Then I take it you think the letter you wrote as unreasonable as I do. But you felt you had to write it.'

'Oh, I had to write it.'

'In case I was the kind of bastard who might go back on an agreement.'

'Oh, I knew you'd keep your word, John. But I suddenly felt I mightn't be able to keep mine. That's why I wrote the letters: because I found I didn't love you in the way you imagine and expect me to.'

'But if you love me?'

'Yes. I love you. Only it isn't what *I* expect of love.'

He took away his hand. It might have looked less hurried if he hadn't been holding hers.

'Did this man's lust make it so clear?'

'No. It certainly wasn't his lust. I don't think it was anything that happened between us – only the fact that it happened. And I had had no part in it.'

'Surely the thing about marriage is that two people do take part in it?'

'They can – and sometimes they don't. As in a rape.'

'I can't see the analogy.'

She must persist. 'So I had to break the engagement. Incidentally, how can love be "engaged"?' She laughed because she had just that moment thought of it. 'And how can an engagement be "broken"? Anything big enough ought to be *"shattered"*!'

She must have leant towards him, because he was retreating: barely perceptibly. His face was so still and wooden he must have been holding his breath.

While she continued laughing. ' "Break" is a miserable little verb!'

His Adam's apple went up and down, twice, like a fast lift; then he asked, 'Is there anything we ought to do? Anything formal, I mean. To show that it's off?'

It must have been the first time in her life anybody had asked her what to do.

'I shouldn't think so,' she said. 'I'll tell my mother. Otherwise, I guess you just let it fade out.'

He was looking at her with the moist eyes of a grateful dog. 'Well, if that's what you feel, Felicity. I'll be only too glad to do anything you want.'

All that needed to be done now was to slip the ring off and put it in the glove compartment of his car, which she did with the minimum of demonstration, and he was tactful enough not to notice.

They sat for a while. Their talk was of Rome, which she could discuss intelligently because she had been reading it up.

'The parasol pines,' she was saying, when she remembered, 'I ought to go, or my mother will draw the wrong conclusions.'

'We're the ones who could be wrong, couldn't we?'

'Oh, no! Not if that's how you feel!'

He did make a further effort to tempt her, with his eyes, which had grown clearer since release, and a kiss which even entered her mouth. She could feel a whimper forming in her throat, and had to force herself to strangle it, together with the longing for that eiderdowniness he had to offer.

'Thank you – darling.' She returned his kiss with such force their teeth collided uglily.

She saw she had left a bad taste, and that they were both saved.

When she got in, her mother came out to meet her in the hall, in the pair of rubber gloves she wore as protection against the nastier details of domestic martyrdom.

'Oh dear, what have you done to me!' Mrs Bannister immediately wailed.

'But I'm the one who was engaged.'

'I can only say, Felicity, you've done something wicked and perverse. Why, I wonder, do you want to destroy us?'

Looking her mother in the face it was impossible to prevent herself shouting back, 'Why – WHY? If I knew the answers! But I don't! I'm not the record you'd like to play!'

As soon as her daughter had slammed her door, Mrs Bannister tore off the flesh-coloured gloves. She must talk, she must tell Madge. But her finger slipped halfway through the number. She might have sounded too old, too ugly. The transparent, torn-off gloves were as distasteful to her as her own skin.

In the past when she had run to the phone, it might have been to a lover's arms. Now she began to dread the call. Those hours of blandishment, of flirtation with the reported woes of others, no longer titillated: what had begun as a delicious sensual luxury was turning into an inquisition. She had even begun to admit that Humphrey was right: that Madge Hopkirk made the worst of things. Certainly Madge put some hard questions.

And the telephone continued to ring. And you had to answer, because it would have been immoral to pretend you were not there when you were: nobody would ever accuse you of disobeying the basic rules of the social code.

'No, Madge ... No. You are interrupting nothing – one or two little routine chores ... Of course, dear, I shall be glad to hear it if you really feel you have to tell ... With another young man? ... Well, Madge, if it's only another. If Felicity was with the *same* awful young man instead of the *several* you've seen her with, we might have something to worry about. As it is, I shan't let worry enter my head ... I know some of her friends are of doubtful character. It's since she left her good job with Moira Pomfrett, and went to work at this place, this *boutique*, or old clothes shop. Whatever it is, it's hardly my business ... I *told* you – they call it *Pot Luck* ... I'm sure there's no significance in the name. It's only a silly, tasteless joke. Everyone is tasteless nowadays ... But Felicity's a clean, healthy girl. If her appearance has changed – her clothes a bit "different" – it's because of this set she runs around with. And because ... yes ... she's changed – since ... You don't have to tell me, Madge. Humphrey's suggested we get Dr Herborn to put her in touch with a reputable psychoanalyst. But she says she can psychoanalyse herself as well as anyone else could do it for her.

Why not? An educated girl. And I always say, nobody knows a person better than she knows herself. It stands to reason ... I agree there *are* people who don't understand themselves. There will always be the simple ones. That is another matter ... Whether she's happy? Oh, really, Madge! I'm too discreet to ask her. I've learnt my lesson ... I must go now, dear. Something's boiling over. I can smell it ...'

When she had brushed off her accuser, Doris Bannister went straight into the dining-room and poured herself a tot of Humphrey's brandy. It was in the wrong glass, but she didn't care, or whether her breath would give her away if anybody came to the door ...

It was a wet night, no longer raining, though the rain was hanging about above the black, patent-leather leaves. If you opened a window, a cold, almost liquid air rushed in, and forced you to gulp it quickly down. It had the effect of making you feel you were standing inside a flannel tunnel with Daddy's snores at the other end; Mummy, convinced she was awake, would be lying asleep in the twin mahogany bed. Between them in the dark hung the ticking of a clock which would restore them to life in the morning.

Once or twice Mummy called, but it sounded of grey flannel. Once the word emerged, 'Feugh – *lisss?*' before being muffled by the overhang of sleep.

Mummy couldn't have twigged that the others called you 'Liss' unless she had picked it up somewhere in the bumpy tunnel along which she was being dragged. If so, sleep had lessened, or at least drugged, her disapproval.

A tendency to disapprove was probably the most you had inherited from the parents. Nothing could be done about it, except to pacify the conscience by disapproving of yourself.

She threw down the brush with which she had been sleeking her dank hair: it was the night, the damp. The brush contributed the one positive sound in all the sleeping, flannel house. The brush was in solid ivory, part of the set Daddy had given as a twenty-first, the FB in gold to remind you who you were – when names are the least part of it.

Now that she had done her hair she went downstairs. Here and there, on the landing, and below, she barged against the shapes of furniture in spite of knowing the geography by heart; she might have wounded herself if the corners hadn't been felted, or her flesh contemptuous of pain.

In the street she became more purposeful, her mind less blurred by memory and the instincts. Her body grew muscular inside the protective skin of slithery leather, her face contracting with the spasms of wet leaves, in the currents of air, as she bowed her head to cleave the otherwise empty streets. All the normal, timid virtues had homed, though the ice-blue lights continued blooming, under civic instruction to protect stragglers from the kinds of violence they most expected.

As she walked through the streets her ice-cold skin increased her sense of inviolacy.

Those intruding on her separate existence, some old feeble derelict, or band of stumbling Masons, or even an occasional brute male, lowered their eyes. She had made a joke or game of it in the beginning; a pocket-mirror might have explained, but vanity hadn't sold her one; she had ended by accepting the lowered eyes as part of the inevitable situation.

One of her young men – Gary, was it? or Barry? had come out with the accusation, 'You've got some idea, Liss, that you can make everyone dip their lights. Well, we're bloody well not going to dip.'

At first she hadn't been conscious of the effect she had on others, except on the anonymous night faces. So she had laughed at the accusation, and the young man, the Barry or Gary her friend, hadn't been able to avoid lowering his eyes, if only for an instant.

All the young men and girls of her new acquaintance, whom she attempted so earnestly, at least in the beginning, to imitate, had similar names and interchangeable bodies. They were happiest in clusters on floors in a state of euphoria she found touching and enviable. She longed to conform, at the same time to illuminate their rather sleazy faces with some revelation of the love they believed in but couldn't discover. Once or twice she had gone so far as to turn on with them, and take part in their childlike, almost sexless rituals. She must have been the only one who remained distinct: a menace in fact; some of them, on recognizing an outline which refused to melt into their common blur, started abusing her. There was nothing she could do about it. She was incapable of laying down her will in their field of flowers, or of calming their fear that she might engulf them in a flow of lava which would petrify their bliss.

She herself couldn't at first accept that frightening, still partly dormant, cone of her own will.

It was on this night of suspended rain that it began erupting, not for the first, but for the second time. It was on this night too, that she faced, or began to accept, the other occasion. As she walked along the hillside, any of the pompous houses dumped there over the years would have opened to her if she had willed it; but she postponed the enjoyment of her strength till unable to resist a house not unlike their own in its ugly splendour and convinced inviolacy.

A porch lamp had been left burning to show the occupants were away from home.

One small stone, a splatter of glass, and her hand easily turned the catch. She hitched herself over the sill, and at once identified the familiar flannel smell of such houses at night. At first she went, not so much cautiously as experimentally, through the living-rooms: casually knocking on a goblet to hear it ring; gently enough, kicking a silly little footstool.

There was the portrait of a woman in a fashionable dress no longer fashionable, smiling the smile of success and riches. Furniture overwhelmed an originally enormous room; for the moment you no more than combed the flesh-coloured upholstery with your nails, as an initiation.

A second rich room smelt of male and leather. She lit a cheroot for company. She straddled a leather arm to inspect the prints of horses, calendars, paper knives, books of reference, bottles, and other aids to masculine authority. Then she spat out on the carpet a shred of the tobacco which was making her feel sick. Supposing she was? She would have liked to be.

The rooms upstairs, because more private, seemed even more relinquished. They were also uglier, in that fantasies of youth and sex dangled in the wardrobes and clung to the muslin skirts of a dressing-table. In the hollow of a double bed a boy and a girl doll were entwined in a sawdust impersonation of lovers.

Throughout the house there were the sounds of furniture, and clocks, and silence.

So she began to revel in it. She lay down and rolled on a frizzed-out sheepskin rug till clouds of powder started her coughing. She bent a feathered mule double, and shot it at an alabaster shade which reacted like a donged gong. After disposing of the limp dolls she trampled on the great bed, up to the ankles in its blonde buttocks and breasts; the satin skin was easily ripped off. She turned her back on a photograph she would investigate, but later, and more seriously. Drawers and cupboards collaborated with the sheepskin rug to give her the secrets of the big powdery woman in the portrait below: because they were of little interest, in their trite luxury, and occasional grubbiness, and anxious hankering after sex, she let them fall with indifference. They flopped and lay, or skidded with metallic explosions into corners. A book of art photographs must have broken its spine: it looked so collapsed, exposed and passive; she ground a heel into the Twenty-Seventh Position of Love.

She made a quick tour of several smaller rooms filled with the toys, the trophies and aspirations of youths, or boy-men: pennants; silver-plated cups; rows of footballers promoting their own muscles; sheets of technicolour girls, heavily mammiferous.

Bursting into the bathroom she flung a cast-iron athlete at the mirror with shattering results: it was her own head transfixed at the centre of the crystal web. She might have stripped herself, and stretched out in the receptive bath, and experienced all kinds of guiltily voluptuous embrasses, if there had been time; but there wasn't.

She remembered the photograph in Florentine-style art-leather on the dressing-table of the master bedroom: the face of the man, the master, the owner of the woman, for whom his features would have grown too familiar to be any longer meaningful.

She went running back her leather suit slightly gasping along the landing. She was longing to eat to devour something meat after a surfeit of Turkish delight.

Snatching up the photograph from its place on the frilly dressing-table, she held it unnaturally close, as though her distended nostrils craved the rich, masculine scents of all such faces: of shaving lotion, brilliantine, alcohol, tobacco, which intermittently disguise the ranker smell of natural hide.

God I look a starving imbecile! She saw herself glance up from her meal; for that was what it had become: a feast of prime beef.

But the unconscious man continued smiling back at her out of the photograph, the smile in which he had been set for ever, from above the inscription, in the language of executive chivalry,

The Night the Prowler

To Darl
with love and nibbles
from
Harvey

'You look a real Harvey,' she muttered; while he continued smiling at each and every Darl.

In the end she was forced to break the glass protecting the expertly shaven smile of all soft, fleshy, successful men. The smile she tore like pasteboard. All men were soft.

And Darl: her most personal attributes, like brushes, scent-sprays, a half-open powder box, were easily scattered; the frilly skirt yanked off the dressing-table, gave away the bandy, reproduction legs.

To hear the sound of your own breathing can breed a kind of lust.

So she began to run hurtle down the thundering stairs might have crashed if she hadn't been holding so tightly to the knife at her waist (*What's it for? That's my shark-knife; I carry it for emergencies*) the bone handle tightly clutched helped her recover her balance her scattered thoughts.

On arrival at the bottom she walked firmly, soberly, in what must be the direction of the kitchen, to satisfy her next need. She came back. She began smearing *Portrait of Darl*: first the floury face with its twin patches of triumphant rouge, then the floral chiffon torso, then the face again, for luck – with rasp-berry jam. Darl was outrouged.

Some of the flesh-coloured chairs she smeared. And Harvey's tooled-leather desk-top; though here, crimson was lost on crimson. She would have liked – frankly – to smear Harvey's desk with shit; only there wasn't any.

Instead she took her knife. The desk-top turned the blow: might have broken her raspberry-spattered bloody wrist. The chairs gave more easily: like the flesh of big soft smiling and finally frightened men. Darl's skin in peach-toned satin was hardly worth the trouble; but the leather pretensions of men were a different matter.

Riding their thick thighs, still slashing, jerking with her free hand at the reins, sawing at the mouth which held the bit, she was to some extent vindicated, if guiltily racked by the terrible spasms which finally took possession of her.

She fell back in the leather arms, half expecting Mummy to walk through the door with that look on her face: Mummy wanting her own little girl whom not even Daddy must sponge.

She lay there only half credulous of what was after its fashion a consummation.

She had not been frightened the night the prowler, not really, not from the very beginning. Certainly the unexpectedness of it made her lie rigid; but she wasn't afraid; she wouldn't have been afraid if he had stuck the knife, as you read they do; but he didn't.

He climbed in clumsily, not to say noisily, almost tripped by his own shoe on the sill: like some amateur. There were bits of the performance where he showed himself to be more experienced: he was adept, for instance, at twitching back the sheet. Then he was getting down beside her. It was so natural. As it was what she had always been expecting, she now realized, she turned her face towards that side of the dark from which his eyes must be looking at her. She was ready to grapple with him in the glorious but exacting game in which she had never taken part, only rehearsed move by move in the most secret reaches of her mind, knuckles cracking, their legs plaited together into a single, strong rope. Then, according to the rules, she would dare him with her wordless mouth to plunge deeper. She would feel his strength depending on her, and whenever it hesitated, she would urge him on with her most pervasive kiss to scale other peaks of her choosing. It was she who would ordain the death thrust.

So she kept her face turned towards her desired intruder; and waited for the first move; while his sandshoes, through which she could feel the shape of his toes, stubbed her naked feet, and the rather greasy surface of his jeans caught at Mummy's present of a 'lovely nightie'.

It would only be a matter of instants before he opened the attack; but as she waited, a sick, sour, miserable smell, or suspicion, began to drift against her expectations: what if, after all, it wasn't a trial of strength, but an outrage by impotence?

She put out her hands. She took his arms: they had the feel of damp plumage over bones. Only then he began slobbering her mouth with taut lips which smelt of dripping. He bit into her cheek with what she visualized as little jagged decalcified teeth.

She was so shocked she punched the mouth and his head dropped hissing on *her* pillow.

It was such an intolerable situation she nearly upset the lamp reaching out to switch it on. It righted itself. It clicked.

The head on the pillow was moaning. She saw a blue stubble, open on what she had rightly guessed were small, pointed, decalcified teeth. A smell of decay shot out of the open mouth.

Her sense of dedication was affronted by such an unsavoury votary. 'What do you expect to get?' she hectored, 'crawling in like some kind of insect – and so bloody clumsily!'

He turned his face away from her, as though to suggest the glare from the lamp was too much for his eyes. Though she was addressing him in a louder than normal voice, he might have been pretending she didn't exist.

'*What!*' It wasn't a question. 'Oh, I know you do get it. You savage some feeble hysterical creature, or frightened schoolgirl, or half-paralysed old woman. I shouldn't be asking you: I read the papers.'

Still he didn't answer. In the silence they were making together she thought she heard the movements of his eyelids.

'If one didn't know, it would be difficult to believe.' The recoiled intruder suddenly filled her with a great rage. 'Even if I'd wanted you, you wouldn't have been capable. You're too – mingy!'

And she began hitting this *man* with the back of her hand, with swinging blows, on his stubbly cheeks, so that his head flung to and fro on the pillow.

'*You!*'

She knelt up and punched with her fists against his ribs; while the man whinged and writhed and groaned.

'Have a heart! What's yer game?'

'None!' She couldn't have explained her behaviour, but muttered back, 'No *game!*'

Then for an instant the flame rose in her: she fell on him, caressing his cheeks with hers, veiling his already anonymous face with her hair, and plunged her tongue into his mouth. His terror snored deafening around her before she left off: a nausea, brought on by rancid dripping and her loathing of limp potato chips, forced her back on her knees.

If he had been moved to kill her she couldn't have cared at this point.

'Is this the knife you slash them with?'

She pulled it from the sheath hanging from his belt, and presented the handle on the flat palms of her hands, the blade appropriately aimed.

'Go on!' he said. 'You win!'

She didn't want to confirm that the eyes flickering at her in the shaded light showed themselves to be small oily black piteous.

'Nobody *wins!*' She had to use all her strength not to answer piteousness out of her own frustration. 'That's the depressing part of it.'

Then when she had tossed back her hair, and drawn up the mucus sharply through her nostrils – a habit Mummy deplored in Daddy – she said, 'Come on, you! We're going to celebrate a failure!'

A short man was pattering childlike behind her as she dragged him by the wrist, the knife still held in her other hand; only sleep could have made their transit credible.

Together and apart they burst into the dining-room.

'Never touch a drop meself,' he insisted when she had poured out the half tumbler of 'Daddy's good brandy'.

'But just a mouthful.' She tried forcing the glass against his clenched teeth. 'Normally it isn't necessary, I know. This is an unusual situation.'

But the man was growing firmer, and she recovered her contempt: this time, unreasonably, for his reasonableness.

'You don't smoke either, I expect.' She was choking on a throatful of brandy.

The man agreed that he didn't smoke.

She lit one of the cigars, according to the way she had seen. The fumes of her rage had begun floating directionlessly inside her.

'Then I can't invite you to celebrate in any way?'

'Eh?'

It didn't matter.

As she drifted up and down, half fuming, half tearful, the man leant across the table, and asked, 'What are you gunner do with me? If you're gunner call them in, let's get it over. I'd only like to say I've got a wife, and a coupler kids: we adopted 'em – two little girls.'

'Not *girls*!' she protested.

For a moment she was afraid he might begin to tell her the story of his ordinariness: she couldn't have borne that while her half-strangled desire was still squirming around inside her.

'I don't expect you to tell me,' she said. 'I don't expect anything of you – or anybody.'

She continued nurturing her half-lie after she had let him

out. He had gone past her like the electrician or the plumber.

Only on returning to the dining-room, the slopped brandy and smouldering cigar emphasized her failed intention: to destroy perhaps in one violent burst the nothing she was, to live, to be, to know. Now she might have mortified her already over-mortified will by wounding herself physically, if she hadn't heard another self bellowing like a deprived cow. Walking up and down she was tearing a nightdress she couldn't very well 'rend' in circumstances so far removed from the tragi-classic.

Till Mummy came in with that look on her face.

'Oh, Felicity! Oh, my darling! My baby! Do tell me!'

She let them tell her what to do, and obeyed them to the extent of giving the answers they expected: not all of those.

'The knife? Why, he took it – didn't he? Yes, he took the knife he threatened me with.'

It was important for her to keep this one memento, which she had slipped behind the sideboard for safety; just as she must conceal the heart of a moral predicament they couldn't possibly understand.

She could have continued lying in the shambles of Harvey's leather chair, luxuriating in a chaos reflected around her, if the pulse of the violated house hadn't very slightly quickened: the slack silence was tautening; time had audibly recovered its steel. As she dragged her hands out of the hot bowels of the chair, she heard a key gnawing at a lock, and voices obsessed by trivialities: Daddy was trumping Mummy all over again, while Mummy resented being trumped.

It would have been almost too comforting to let them catch you.

Then the lights in other rooms were blaring out; the owners had begun stampeding amongst their possessions, the unsuspected ugliness of which made them adopt voices they probably hadn't used for years. As they ran, so you ran. There wasn't even time to exchange with Harvey that long love-look, half horror, half fulfilment.

She ducked beneath the clothes-lines and slid down, leather-slick, over the back wall. Speed and danger, and the wet night, lent her professional ease – or indifference. Running along the lane, she picked the thorns out of her hands, and rejoiced in the scent which had rubbed off on her from bruised lemons.

Perhaps remembering advice to others on sound minds, her father Humphrey Bannister mowed the lawn more regularly; he weeded the garden more assiduously than ever; he pricked out seedlings with an embroiderer's precision, and when snails slavered them away, or cutworm got them, or cats pawed them up in covering excreta, he planted afresh, with a patience which would have been admirable if it hadn't also been self-defence. She used to watch, while taking care not to approach, because to have done so might have involved them in an exchange of those least convincing subterfuges, words. Outwardly occupied as he knelt, his mind, she suspected, was making tentative advances, just as her mother, in the suede gloves she wore for dusting, would be standing at an upper window contemplating a void in which the three of them existed.

Once she went so far as to inquire of her father, with a coldness she had intended as warmth, 'What are you putting this time?'

'Portulaca.'

All her life she had watched him planting portulaca; she should have recognized these scraps of plant flesh.

'Of course. Don't you get tired of them?'

'They're reliable, Tchitchy.'

She bit her mouth for the chance implication.

As he continued transplanting the seedlings, her father

157

remarked, 'A cove I know – Harvey Makin – had his house burgled the other night. Though 'burgle' is hardly the right word. They don't seem to have taken a thing. Anyway, whatever the motive, a gang of thugs broke in, and just about wrecked the place.' His laugh sounded strangely thick, almost approving. 'Well, good luck to 'em. I hope they got their thrill. Harvey was always a smooth, self-satisfied beggar, and his house the kind of mausoleum asking for rape.'

She could see him shrink on realizing his blunder, sweat gathering on the back of his neck, fingers blenching as they firmed the soil round a seedling.

'As a matter of fact, that's how the *Sun* referred to it.' He badly needed somebody to share his callousness.

Lacking the courage to look up, he couldn't have known that she was shocked. She was, though: not for his use of a word with unfortunate personal overtones, nor his casual mention of an incident for which she was responsible, but for his pleasure in what was a brutal act by his own standards.

'I'm surprised you didn't recognize the old portulaca,' he said when he had recovered himself.

She kicked at a rejected seedling. 'I wasn't thinking. And they're insignificant little things.'

'They have their unexpected moments.'

At that moment what she most resented was the unexpected, at any rate in a father who had shown her a flaw in his hitherto predictable character. Looking at the backs of withering hands, and creases in the nape of a neck, she could accept physical decay, but not the rot attacking what should have remained indestructible. Her father's confession started in her a fresh train of unhappiness, as though she herself were responsible for infecting the innocent with a moral disease.

However much she might regret an imperfection in her desirably straight father, she continued in her efforts to expend, by acts of violence, the passive self others had created for her;

though this behaviour too, she suspected, was ending in conformity. Nor did she ever find fulfilment, or establish her supremacy, in the defenceless houses she entered and wrecked. There remained the possibility, finally the hope, that she might be caught. She never was. Over and over, she demonstrated the stupidity of those who were out to catch her: men, of course.

There was a night when her instinct for unattended houses failed her. As her torchlight picked out a sleeping figure, her breath rasped, not because she had slipped up, but because she might at last have found. Or was she about to debunk another of her illusions in the naked body of this young man, lightly sleeping in coils of sheet up to the shins? Her superior in physical strength, he could not disguise the defenceless pathos of a human being asleep: slightly open, suppliant lips; tender eyelids; innocent muscles; the male breast no longer an aggressive fraud under its hackles; the secret fruits exposed to theft by marauding hands. Was this perhaps too little of a man, too much the wax effigy of a god? Her hovering torchlight expressed doubts as well as longing wherever it touched the golden surface; till the sleeper awoke.

Recovering its strength too quickly, the body appeared agonisingly muscle-bound; lips gulped at elusive air; petrified eyes blindly glittered.

'What are you after?' asked the god in rather a high, directionless voice; and spread trembling leaves of hands to conceal a shrivelling.

'What do you want?' he repeated on an even higher note; then getting down to business, 'If it's money, there's a couple of notes and some silver on the dressing-table.'

'No.' She lowered her chin. 'It isn't money.'

She switched off her light, floundered through the open window, and escaped from the ruins of a vision as quickly as she could.

From now on she would glut herself on whatever reality had to offer, however abysmal and degrading. She took to roaming the park by night (' ... never at night, Felicity ... only drunkards, cut-throats, and perverts ... nobody in their right mind, not even a trained athlete, would cross the park after sundown ... ') preferably the blackest nights, branches of trees slashing at her cheeks, a network of grass alternating with sandy pitfalls, the lake reduced to a presence and the reedy cries of waterfowl.

She would edge herself between the railings in one of the many places where the iron had been torn from its stone sockets, and stride off beneath the holm-oaks and pines, often twisting an ankle on the empty bottles left behind by drunks. The park offered a variety of solutions: perhaps this explained why it was so well patronized at night. She could hear her heart bumping towards a fulfilment she had not yet experienced. As she plodded through the sand, her stature was increasing, it seemed; her boots had been reinforced with the soles of buskins; at any moment, she felt, she might call out in a heroic voice and be answered by her opposite from what was normally a red-brick suburb on the other side. She imagined how the voices would advance, calling to each other from time to time, for guidance, and to give each other the strength to face ugliness in any form.

So she went plodding and stumbling, collecting herself for the moment when she would need her courage; and sometimes the moon would freeze her by rising and catching her out in her thoughts, her intention: she could not immediately reconcile a world of beauty with the images of reality she wished to invoke.

By such a light she came across a man's body floating gravely face down amongst the reeds: his back shone with waterproofing; the hair at the neck had been gathered into rats' tails; if the hulk rolled just perceptibly inside the widening circles, it was only because it had been animated by some form of underwater life. She decided to respect the man's secret death as if it had been a secret of her own.

On the other hand she would listen quietly and patiently to those who positively wished to tell: drunks, for instance, waving their bottles at her like flags, from under the paperbarks and figs. She would lie beside them, uncritical of the stench from rotten teeth, alcohol, and feet; she would put up with anything, provided it did not offend against her sense of scale, and promised some kind of revelation.

One old girl confided in her, 'You've no idea how the nuns made me suffer – at our Lady of Mercy. Dear me, no mercy *there*! I would never of believed there's bitches of nuns as well as women. It all began with a safety-pin I use to keep the cold out from the rear of my underwears. No, dear, it wasn't – I think – it was because of the spotted dog – because spotted dog is my favourite pud. It was because of Sister Mary Perpetua. Sister Perpetual I called 'er. Didn't I tell yer? Perhaps I didn't. P'raps it wouldn't be of interest – not to anyone oo 'asn't experienced a bloody amateur from Cunnamulla Queensland.'

'You didn't tell me. Tell me, though – if it will be a comfort.'

But the old woman had already lost the key to her suffering in the mouth of her bottle: her story was never heard, except as a cryptic glug glug between blasts of metho.

Some of the drunks offered love, as if it were some old junk they could pull out of their pockets at will, from amongst the lengths of grey string, snotty handkerchiefs, and scraps of crumpled tote ticket. 'Keep it till morning,' she advised, 'and look it over to see whether you were right.' None of them ever cursed her, or tried to bash her up: they understood that someone of the same derelict condition could only respect their serious aspirations.

It was she who cursed when necessary. When she stumbled over some mesmerized girl stretched on top of her languid lover, she would put the boot into them, and shout, 'You wouldn't know if you were half dead – if you were already standing in the knacker's yard! Well, take that – and drop to yourselves!'

As she shouted and booted, they would scramble up, worming their way into panties, jerking at zippers, to protect their offended parts from possible indignities, faces which had no more than guessed at love expressing a virtuosity of hate and fear.

One pursy bookmaker, or alderman of Irish extraction, spattered her with threats as the thin girl he was dandling bounced out from between his thighs, 'I'll give you in charge... the police ... the ranger ... Anyone of your sort is a menace to the community!'

'Like hell I am! All of us in here at night are the wrong side of the railings. The difference is only in the purpose.'

But he didn't appear to understand; none of them really understood, whichever language you chose to speak.

If she ran after a mob of leatherjackets, trumpeting, 'Hold on, youse! P'raps we got somethun to say to each other,' the whole push made a smart getaway; while she continued in pursuit, whirling in the air above her head a bicycle chain she had won during another such encounter.

As the chain savaged the air, she called, 'We don't know till we find out whether we don't see eye to eye.'

More truthfully, she could see without looking into the straining eyeballs of any of these hoods, she could tell without pressing with her fingers to locate the pulses in a throbbing throat, that it was her own soul struggling to escape from their frantically catapulted bodies.

It was different with the singers: she was all gentleness as she approached the distance and their brooding voices. The young singers were sitting in the damp tussocks amongst the formations of stunted pine. At that hour, before morning, the trees on the farther outskirts of the park were at their blackest. Time did not seem to have exhausted the singers; though they must have sung all night, and were picking the music languidly enough out of their guitars, the voices were still strung with passion, and the foreign words expressed their themes most lucidly.

'Tell me what you are singing about?' she asked with appropriately soft respect; in fact she knew by instinct, but hoped to encourage their confidence.

By that first watery light there was a shocked stillness in the young men's washed-out faces. She might have cut into the first guitarist's hairy wrist: as a result of her brutal interruption, his whole physical attitude seemed to express the despair which, till then, his song had been conveying.

A voice answered, 'This is a song about one love.'

It was a valid enough answer, she realized.

'About loneliness,' another of the singers contributed.

That too.

When one who had been turning the words over in his mouth rid himself of them at last. 'It is about a man who open up her corm – her body – and plant stones where her heart no be.'

She fell on her knees in the sand beside the group of singers. 'That isn't true! Nobody is born without. Those are just the silly words of a song. You'd recognise that if you were more than a bunch of milk-bar kids getting a kick out of false pathos. You'd know the heart was in anybody – only waiting to be torn into – by somebody big enough to perform the bloody act. See?'

She had never made such a reasoned appeal. She should have felt ashamed.

But it was the young milk-bar Greeks who were; they got to their feet, and trooped off, their leader trailing his guitar: it bumped against the dew-sodden tussocks, emphasizing its hollowness.

The white light increased. Because there was nobody left to accuse, she could only rage against that radiance which had begun to rise and overflow with the magnificence of perfect equanimity. Standing beneath the remnants of a moon she was thrashing with helpless, wooden arms, throwing back her pumpkin of a head, ejaculating, 'I fuck you, God, for holding out on me!'

Spurred out of the convulsive stupor in which she found herself lying, she might have blamed her own will for her survival if she could have respected it enough. She was threatened besides, by a fit of nervous hiccups. So she dragged herself up from the wiry grass, and continued to function through some force of necessity. Strands of Japanese mist were still loosely strung above the lake, against a light which had resolved itself into a tingling of transparent, almost audible, gold leaf. Through this euphoric world she went stumbling, weighted with her load of stones.

Other people's houses, looming beyond the park railings, reminded her that her father, the least of clowns, would be wearing the clown's mouth which the toothpaste gave him, and that the cheek on which her mother had been lying last would still be crumpled. The row of unfamiliar houses looked so blameless it increased the sense of guilt in anyone susceptible. She slunk along the pavement aware of strangers already aiming accusations at her from inside curtained rooms. Some of these once pretentious houses had been converted from residences into residentials, with bits added on in weatherboard, and balconies enclosed in warped asbestos. Others in the row of mansions could only be classed as derelict. In one instance, she noticed, the shutters were sagging on their hinges; scrolls of ornamental woodwork had either rotted, or been torn off for fuel; glass was glittering on tiles and flagging like splinters of permanently frozen ice.

Her vanity was moved to remember her own superior techniques in destruction as she dawdled up the path of the abandoned house, snapping obstructive branches of woodbine and laurustinus, skirting a starling's corpse on the once tesselated veranda.

A smell of cold mould from out of the window she looked inside took away her breath at first. Other smells began to reach her, from rags, sacking, finally, she realized, as her eyes grappled with the tortoiseshell gloom, aged human flesh.

It might have been wiser to have resisted looking deeper; but she had to look.

'What are you doing there?' she asked as soon as she could stop herself feeling disgusted.

'Living. Or at any rate, this is where I what they call live.'

She was so horrified she went inside the house, and after blundering through its emptiness, found her way to the mingled smells of the room where the old man lay stretched out on a stained mattress.

'You're not very well covered,' she said, looking for something with which to hide his nakedness.

'I left off clothes some time back. It's less trouble without. If you want to scratch yourself, for instance. Or pee. Or if somebody comes to the door, they go away; they leave you alone.'

She might have taken the hint if it hadn't been for his age. He would probably have looked unbearable at an earlier stage in life, but by living long enough, had been admitted to time's museum: an objective intelligence could accept the scrotum equably enough, along with sharks' eggs and Egyptiana.

'That may be so. But surely you must have somebody – somebody who comes – somebody you want to see you at your best?'

Half-remembered precepts from a code of popular morality made her feel she ought to bully him back into a proper frame of mind.

'This is my best,' he said. 'And there isn't anybody now – not since they got what they wanted. I gave that away about the same time as the clothes and the prostate.'

She looked around desperately. If only she could lay hands on – alcohol, say, she might find bedsores to rub. Unlike the old man, she badly needed to justify her existence. But the bottles in one corner of the room all looked empty.

'Not even grog,' he confirmed. 'Never would have thought. The grog was my most faithful enemy in a lifetime.'

'Oh, come! A lifetime!' The bright nurse she had discovered in herself was making her bare her teeth in a professionally encouraging smile. 'You, with so much life in you still! Wouldn't you like me to give you a wash?'

She would too, without a tremor, but as she knelt on the boards beside him, anxious for his approval, the old man closed his eyes and drew down his mouth, and answered with a waking snore; so the most she could do was attempt to comfort the fetid skin, with its crust and semi-cancerous moles.

The old man lay smiling, but not in the present, she suspected.

'At least you have your memories,' she dared hope.

He opened his eyes. 'I was thinking of the days when I could still enjoy an easy piss. And stools came easy. That's the two most important things, you find out.'

Oh no, she mustn't allow him to drag her down to his own level of negation and squalor; she needed him more than any of the others who had eluded her.

'Trouble is,' he continued, 'you find out too late to appreciate the advantages.'

She would wrestle with him. 'But you must have *something*. Everybody – or almost everybody – eventually finds somebody or something, whether it's another human being – or cat – or *plant*. Don't they? Or some great idea. To believe in.'

She was as desperate as that.

'I can honestly say I never believed in or expected anything of anyone. I never loved, not even myself – which is more than can be said of most people.' When he laughed he showed his gums; they were a milky mauve. 'I always saw myself as a shit. I am nothing. I believe in nothing. And nothing's a noble faith. Nobody can hurt nothing. So you've no reason for being afraid.'

'I am afraid,' she admitted.

But she was as much distressed for this old man she had on her hands. She would have liked to remind him of something miraculous. From out of her limited experience she tried to remember. As her mind blundered and lumbered around, all she could think of was a double-yolked egg they had shown her in her infancy: the egg had been broken into a basin, the twin perfections in gold gold. How to convey it, though? She was so incapable.

In her helplessness she began blurting words in the shape of colourless bubbles, till at last she was able to give them substance. 'I could stay here with you and help you, if you'd let me. I could show you then, perhaps.'

'What?'

Not love: that had already been proved far too arrogant a word.

'Oh, I don't know,' she cried; she was literally weeping: her tears fell amongst the scabs and cancerous moles, and on the perished nipples of this old man who was slipping from her, she could sense. 'This light, for instance.' She was almost physically clutching at it. 'Look! Do you see how it's changing?'

In fact the masses of hitherto colourless, or at most dust-coloured wall, were illuminated: the tributaries of decay had begun to flow with rose; the barren continents were heaped with gold.

But as the old man kept his eyes shut, she couldn't show him.

'Light don't do away with the rats,' he suddenly said. 'Or only for the time being.'

'The rats?'

'At night the rats come. They sit here looking at you in the dark. They put the wind up you at times.'

'Not if I stay.' She took his hand and held it as though she had got possession of all knowledge. 'At least I can keep the rats at bay, and you needn't expect more of me than of anyone else.'

'Yes,' he said.

In his relief he slightly jogged a tea chest on which his teeth were standing.

'No rats,' he sighed. 'And an easy pee.'

For he had begun to urinate; and as she watched it trickle over the withered thighs, her own being was flooded with pity.

'That's *something*, isn't it?' She was so grateful for their common release from the myths to which they had been enslaved, she only slowly realized the hand she was holding in hers had died.

When she had put it down, and her face had tightened sufficiently, she went out through the garden to the street. None of those engaged in their business of opening up houses, delivering bread, running scooters at the pavement, appeared to find her presence in any way questionable. Between two of the concrete paving-slabs, a colony of ants wove without end, through a navel of sand, into the body of the earth. So she continued up the hill to report the death of an old man she had discovered a few moments before, but knew as intimately as she knew herself, in solitariness, in desolation, as well as in what would seem to be the dizzy course of perpetual becoming.

Five-Twenty

Most evenings, weather permitting, the Natwicks sat on the front veranda to watch the traffic. During the day the stream flowed, but towards five it began to thicken, it sometimes jammed solid like: the semi-trailers and refrigeration units, the decent old-style sedans, the mini-cars, the bombs, the Holdens and the Holdens. She didn't know most of the names. Royal did, he was a man, though never ever mechanical himself. She liked him to tell her about the vehicles, or listen to him take part in conversation with anyone who stopped at the fence. He could hold his own, on account of he was more educated, and an invalid has time to think.

They used to sit side by side on the tiled veranda, him in his wheelchair she had got him after the artheritis took over, her in the old cane. The old cane chair wasn't hardly presentable any more; she had torn her winter cardy on a nail and laddered several pair of stockings. You hadn't the heart to get rid of it, though. They brought it with them from Sarsaparilla after they sold the business. And now they could sit in comfort to watch the traffic, the big steel insects of nowadays, which put the wind up her at times.

Royal said, 'I reckon we're a shingle short to'uv ended up on the Parramatta Road.'

'You said we'd still see life,' she reminded, 'even if we lost the use of our legs.'

'But look at the traffic! Worse every year. And air. Rot a man's lungs quicker than the cigarettes. You should'uv headed me off. You who's supposed to be practical!'

'I thought it was what you wanted,' she said, keeping it soft; she had never been one to crow.

'Anyway, I already lost the use of me legs.'

As if she was to blame for that too. She was so shocked the chair sort of jumped. It made her blood run cold to hear the metal feet screak against the little draught-board tiles.

'Well, I 'aven't!' she protested. 'I got me legs, and will be able to get from 'ere to anywhere and bring 'ome the shopping. While I got me strength.'

She tried never to upset him by any show of emotion, but now she was so upset herself.

They watched the traffic in the evenings, as the orange light was stacked up in thick slabs, and the neon signs were coming on.

'See that bloke down there in the parti-coloured Holden?'

'Which?' she asked.

'The one level with our own gate.'

'The pink and brown?' She couldn't take all that interest tonight, only you must never stop humouring a sick man.

'Yairs. Pink. Fancy a man in a pink car!'

'Dusty pink is fashionable.' She knew that for sure.

'But a man!'

'Perhaps his wife chose it. Perhaps he's got a domineering wife.'

Royal laughed low. 'Looks the sort of coot who might like to be domineered, and if that's what he wants, it's none of our business, is it?'

She laughed to keep him company. They were such mates, everybody said. And it was true. She didn't know what she would do if Royal passed on first.

That evening the traffic had jammed. Some of the drivers began tooting. Some of them stuck their heads out, and yarned to one another. But the man in the pink-and-brown Holden just sat. He didn't look to either side.

Come to think of it, she had noticed him pass before. Yes. Though he wasn't in no way a noticeable man. Yes. She looked at her watch.

'Five-twenty,' she said. 'I seen that man in the pink-and-brown before. He's pretty regular. Looks like a business executive.'

Royal cleared his throat and spat. It didn't make the edge of the veranda. Better not to notice it, because he'd only create if she did. She'd get out the watering-can after she had pushed him inside.

'Business executives!' she heard. 'They're afraid people are gunner think they're poor class without they *execute*. In our day nobody was ashamed to *do*. Isn't that about right, eh?'

She didn't answer because she knew she wasn't meant to.

'Funny sort of head that cove's got. Like it was half squashed. Silly-lookun bloody head!'

'Could have been born with it,' she suggested. 'Can't help what you're born with. Like your religion.'

There was the evening the Chev got crushed, only a young fellow too. Ahhh, it had stuck in her throat, thinking of the wife and kiddies. She ran in, and out again as quick as she could, with a couple of blankets, and the rug that was a present from Hazel. She had grabbed a pillow off their own bed.

She only faintly heard Royal shouting from the wheel-chair.

She arranged the blankets and the pillow on the pavement, under the orange sky. The young fellow was looking pretty sick, kept on turning his head as though he recognized and wanted to tell her something. Then the photographer from the *Mirror* took his picture, said she ought to be in it to add a touch of human interest, but she wouldn't. A priest came, the *Mirror* took his picture, administering what Mrs Dolan said they call Extreme Unkshun. Well, you couldn't poke fun at a person's religion any more than the shape of their head, and Mrs Dolan was a decent neighbour, the whole family, and clean.

When she got back to the veranda, Royal, a big man, had slipped down in his wheel-chair.

He said, or gasped, 'Wotcher wanter do that for, Ella? How are we gunner get the blood off?'

She hadn't thought about the blood, when of course she was all smeared with it, and the blankets, and Hazel's good Onkaparinka. Anyway, it was her who would get the blood off.

'You soak it in milk or something,' she said. 'I'll ask. Don't you worry.'

Then she did something. She bent down and kissed Royal on the forehead in front of the whole Parramatta Road. She regretted it at once, because he looked that powerless in his invalid chair, and his forehead felt cold and sweaty.

But you can't undo things that are done.

It was a blessing they could sit on the front veranda. Royal suffered a lot by now. He had his long-standing hernia, which they couldn't have operated on, on account of he was afraid of his heart. And then the artheritis.

'Arthritis.'

'All right,' she accepted the correction. 'Arth-er-itis.'

It was all very well for men, they could manage more of the hard words.

'What have we got for tea?' he asked.

'Well,' she said, fanning out her hands on the points of her elbows, and smiling, 'it's a surprise.'

She looked at her watch. It was five-twenty.

'It's a coupler nice little bits of fillet Mr Ballard let me have.'

'Wotcher mean let you have? Didn't you pay for them?'

She had to laugh. 'Anything I have I pay for!'

'Well? Think we're in the fillet-eating class?'

'It's only a treat, Royal,' she said. 'I got a chump chop for myself. I like a nice chop.'

He stopped complaining, and she was relieved.

'There's that gentleman,' she said, 'in the Holden.'
They watched him pass, as sober as their own habits.

Royal – he had been his mother's little king. Most of his mates
called him 'Roy'. Perhaps only her and Mrs Natwick had stuck
to the christened name, they felt it suited.

She often wondered how Royal had ever fancied her: such
a big man, with glossy hair, black, and a nose like on someone
historical. She would never have said it, but she was proud of
Royal's nose. She was proud of the photo he had of the old
family home in Kent, the thatch so lovely, and Grannie Natwick
sitting in her apron on a rush-bottom chair in front, looking
certainly not all that different from Mum, with the aunts
gathered round in leggermutton sleeves, all big nosey women
like Royal.

She had heard Mum telling Royal's mother, 'Ella's a plain
little thing, but what's better than cheerful and willing?' She
had always been on the mousey side, she supposed, which
didn't mean she couldn't chatter with the right person. She
heard Mum telling Mrs Natwick, 'My Ella can wash and bake
against any comers. Clever with her needle too.' She had never
entered any of the competitions, like they told her she ought
to, it would have made her nervous.

It was all the stranger that Royal had ever fancied her.

Once as they sat on the veranda watching the evening
traffic, she said, 'Remember how you used to ride out in the
old days from "Bugilbar" to Cootramundra?'

'Cootamundra.'

'Yes,' she said. 'Cootramundra.' (That's why they'd called
the house 'Coota' when they moved to the Parramatta Road.)

She had been so dazzled on one occasion by his parti-coloured
forehead and his black hair, after he had got down from the
saddle, after he had taken off his hat, she had run and fetched
a duster, and dusted Royal Natwick's boots. The pair of new

elastic-sides was white with dust from the long ride. It only occurred to her as she polished she might be doing something shameful, but when she looked up, it seemed as though Royal Natwick saw nothing peculiar in Ella McWhirter dusting his boots. He might even have expected it. She was so glad she could have cried.

Old Mr Natwick had come out from Kent when a youth, and after working at several uncongenial jobs, and studying at night, had been taken on as book-keeper at 'Bugilbar'. He was much valued in the end by the owners, and always made use of. The father would have liked his son to follow in his footsteps, and taught him how to keep the books, but Royal wasn't going to hang around any family of purse-proud squatters, telling them the things they wanted to hear. He had ideas of his own for becoming rich and important.

So when he married Ella McWhirter, which nobody could ever understand, not even Ella herself, perhaps only Royal, who never bothered to explain (why should he?) they moved to Juggerawa, and took over the general store. It was in a bad way, and soon was in a worse, because Royal's ideas were above those of his customers.

Fulbrook was the next stage. He found employment as book-keeper on a grazing property outside. She felt so humiliated on account of his humiliation. It didn't matter about herself because she always expected less. She took a job in Fulbrook from the start, at the 'Dixie Cafe' in High Street. She worked there several years as waitress, helping out with the scrubbing for the sake of the extra money. She had never hated anything, but got to hate the flies trampling in the sugar and on the necks of the tomato sauce bottles.

At weekends her husband usually came in, and when she wasn't needed in the shop, they lay on the bed in her upstairs room, listening to the corrugated iron and the warping whitewashed weatherboard. She would have loved to do something

for him, but in his distress he complained about 'wet kisses'.
It surprised her. She had always been afraid he might find her
a bit too dry in her show of affection.

Those years at the 'Dixie Cafe' certainly dried her up. She
got those freckly patches and seams in her skin in spite of the
lotions used as directed. Not that it matters so much in anyone
born plain. Perhaps her plainness helped her save. There was
never a day when she didn't study her savings-book, it became
her favourite recreation.

Royal, on the other hand, wasn't the type that dries up,
being fleshier, and dark. He even put on weight out at the
grazing property, where they soon thought the world of him.
When the young ladies were short of a man for tennis the
book-keeper was often invited, and to a ball once at the home-
stead. He was earning good money, and he too saved a bit,
though his instincts weren't as mean as hers. For instance, he
fancied a choice cigar. In his youth Royal was a natty dresser.

Sometimes the young ladies, if they decided to inspect the
latest at Ryan's Emporium, or Mr Philup, if he felt like
grogging up with the locals, would drive him in, and as he got
out they would look funny at the book-keeper's wife they
had heard about, they must have, serving out the plates of
frizzled steak and limp chips. Royal always waited to see his
employers drive off before coming in.

In spite of the savings, this might have gone on much
longer than it did if old Mr Natwick hadn't died. It appeared
he had been a very prudent man. He left them a nice little
legacy. The evening of the news, Royal was driven in by Mr
Philup and they had a few at the Imperial. Afterwards the
book-keeper was dropped off, because he proposed to spend
the night with his wife and catch the early train to attend his
father's funeral.

They lay in the hot little room and discussed the future. She
had never felt so hectic. Royal got the idea he would like to

develop a grocery business in one of the posh outer suburbs of Sydney. 'Interest the monied residents in some of the luxury lines. Appeal to the imagination as well as the stomach.'

She was impressed, of course, but not as much as she should have been. She wasn't sure, but perhaps she was short on imagination. Certainly their prospects had made her downright feverish, but for no distinct, sufficient reason.

'And have a baby.' She heard her own unnatural voice.

'Eh?'

'We could start a baby.' Her voice grew word by word drier.

'There's no reason why we couldn't have a baby. Or two.'

He laughed. 'But starting a new life isn't the time to start a baby.' He dug her in the ribs. 'And you the practical one!'

She agreed it would be foolish, and presently Royal fell asleep.

What could she do for him? As he lay there breathing she would have loved to stroke his nose she could see faintly in the light from the window. Again unpractical, she would have liked to kiss it. Or bite it suddenly off.

She was so disgusted with herself she got creaking off the bed and walked flat across the boards to the washstand and swallowed a couple of Aspros to put her solidly to sleep.

All their life together she had to try in some way to make amends to Royal, not only for her foolishness, but for some of the thoughts that got into her head. Because she hadn't the imagination, the thoughts couldn't have been her own. They must have been put into her.

It was easier of course in later life, after he had cracked up, what with his hernia, and heart, and the artheritis taking over. Fortunately she was given the strength to help him into the wheel-chair, and later still, to lift, or drag him up on the pillows and over, to rub the bed-sores, and stick the pan under him. But even during the years at Sarsaparilla she could make amends in many little ways, though with him still in his prime, naturally he mustn't know of them. So all her acts were mostly for her own self-gratification.

The store at Sarsaparilla, if it didn't exactly flourish, gave them a decent living. She had her problems, though. Some of the locals just couldn't accept that Royal was a superior man. Perhaps she had been partly to blame, she hardly dared admit it, for showing one or two 'friends' the photo of the family home in Kent. She couldn't resist telling the story of one of the aunts, Miss Ethel Natwick, who followed her brother to New South Wales. Ethel was persuaded to accept a situation at Government House, but didn't like it and went back, in spite of the Governor's lady insisting she valued Ethel as a close personal friend. When people began to laugh at Royal on account of his auntie and the family home, as you couldn't help finding out in a place like Sarsaparilla, it was her, she knew, it was her to blame. It hurt her deeply.

Of course Royal could be difficult. Said stockbrokers had no palate and less imagination. Royal said no Australian grocer could make a go of it if it wasn't for flour, granulated sugar, and tomato sauce. Some of the customers turned nasty in retaliation. This was where she could help, and did, because Royal was out on delivery more often than not. It embarrassed her only when some of them took it for granted she was on their side. As if he wasn't her husband. Once or twice she had gone out crying afterwards, amongst the wormy wattles and hens' droppings. Anyone across the gully could have heard her blowing her nose behind the store, but she didn't care. Poor Royal.

There was that Mr Ogburn said, 'A selfish, swollen-headed slob who'll chew you up and swallow you down.' She wouldn't let herself hear any more of what he had to say. Mr Ogburn had a hare-lip, badly sewn, opening and closing. There was nothing frightened her so much as even a well-disguised hare-lip. She got the palpitations after the scene with Mr Ogburn.

Not that there was anything wrong with her.

She only hadn't had the baby. It was her secret grief on black evenings as she walked slowly looking for the eggs a flighty hen might have hid in the bracken.

Dr Bamforth said, looking at the nib of his fountain pen, 'You know, don't you, it's sometimes the man?'

She didn't even want to hear, let alone think about it. In any case she wouldn't tell Royal, because a man's pride could be so easily hurt.

After they had sold out at Sarsaparilla and come to live at what they called 'Coota' on the Parramatta Road, it was both easier and more difficult, because if they were not exactly elderly they were getting on. Royal used to potter about in the beginning, while taking care, on account of the hernia and his heart. There was the business of the lawn-mowing, not that you could call it lawn, but it was what she had. She loved her garden. In front certainly there was only the two square of rather sooty grass which she would keep in order with the push-mower. The lawn seemed to get on Royal's nerves until the artheritis took hold of him. He had never liked mowing. He would lean against the veranda post, and shout, 'Don't know why we don't do what they've done down the street. Root the stuff out. Put down a green concrete lawn.'

'That would be copying,' she answered back.

She hoped it didn't sound stubborn. As she pushed the mower she bent her head, and smiled, waiting for him to cool off. The scent of grass and a few clippings flew up through the traffic fumes reminding you of summer.

While Royal shuffled along the veranda and leaned against another post. 'Or pebbles. You can buy clean, river pebbles. A few plastic shrubs, and there's the answer.'

He only gave up when his trouble forced him into the chair. You couldn't drive yourself up and down a veranda shouting at someone from a wheel-chair without the passers-by thinking you was a nut. So he quietened.

He watched her, though. From under the peak of his cap. Because she felt he might still resent her mowing the lawn, she would try to reassure him as she pushed. 'What's wrong, *eh*? While I still have me health, me *strength* – I was always what they call *wiry* – why shouldn't I cut the *grass*?'

She would come and sit beside him, to keep him company in watching the traffic, and invent games to amuse her invalid husband.

'Isn't that the feller we expect?' she might ask. 'The one that passes at five-twenty,' looking at her watch, 'in the old pink-and-brown Holden?'

They enjoyed their snort of amusement all the better because no one else knew the reason for it.

Once when the traffic was particularly dense, and that sort of chemical smell from one of the factories was thickening in the evening air, Royal drew her attention. 'Looks like he's got something on his mind.'

Could have too. Or it might have been the traffic block. The way he held his hands curved listlessly around the inactive wheel reminded her of possums and monkeys she had seen in cages. She shifted a bit. Her squeaky old chair. She felt uneasy for ever having found the man, not a joke, but half of one.

Royal's chair moved so smoothly on its rubber-tyred wheels it was easy to push him, specially after her practice with the mower. There were ramps where necessary now, to cover steps, and she would sometimes wheel him out to the back, where she grew hollyhock and sunflower against the palings, and a vegetable or two on raised beds.

Royal would sit not looking at the garden from under the peak of his cap.

She never attempted to take him down the shady side, between them and Dolans, because the path was narrow from plants spilling over, and the shade might have lowered his spirits.

She loved her garden.

The shady side was where she kept her staghorn ferns, and fishbones, and the pots of maidenhair. The water lay sparkling on the maidenhair even in the middle of the day. In the blaze of summer the light at either end of the tunnel was like you were looking through a sheet of yellow cellophane, but as the days shortened, the light deepened to a cold, tingling green, which might have made a person nervous who didn't know the tunnel by heart.

Take Mrs Dolan the evening she came in to ask for the loan of a cupful of sugar. 'You gave me a shock, Mrs Natwick. What ever are you up to?'

'Looking at the plants,' Mrs Natwick answered, whether Mrs Dolan would think it peculiar or not.

It was the season of cinerarias, which she always planted on that side, it was sheltered and cold-green. The wind couldn't bash the big spires and umbrellas of blue and purple. Visiting cats were the only danger, messing and pouncing. She disliked cats for the smell they left, but didn't have the heart to disturb their elastic forms curled at the cineraria roots, exposing their colourless pads, and sometimes pink, swollen teats. Blushing only slightly for it, she would stand and examine the details of the sleeping cats.

If Royal called she could hear his voice through the window. 'Where'uv you got to, Ella?'

After he was forced to take to his bed, his voice began to sort of dry up like his body. There were times when it sounded less like a voice than a breath of drowsiness or pain.

'Ella?' he was calling. 'I dropped the paper. Where are yer all this time? You know I can't pick up the paper.'

She knew. Guilt sent her scuttling to him, deliberately composing her eyes and mouth so as to arrive looking cheerful.

'I was in the garden,' she confessed, 'looking at the cinerarias.'

'The what?' It was a name Royal could never learn.

The room was smelling of sickness and the bottles standing on odd plates.

'It fell,' he complained.

She picked up the paper as quick as she could.

'Want to go la-la first?' she asked, because by now he depended on her to raise him and stick the pan under.

But she couldn't distract him from her shortcomings; he was shaking the paper at her. 'Haven't you lived with me long enough to know how to treat a newspaper?'

He hit it with his set hand, and certainly the paper looked a mess, like an old white battered brolly.

'Mucked up! You gotter keep the pages *aligned*. A paper's not readable otherwise. Of course you wouldn't understand because you don't read it, without it's to see who's died.' He began to cough.

'Like me to bring you some Bovril?' she asked him as tenderly as she knew.

'Bovril's the morning,' he coughed.

She knew that, but wanted to do something for him.

After she had rearranged the paper she walked out so carefully it made her go lopsided, out to the front veranda. Nothing would halt the traffic, not sickness, not death even.

She sat with her arms folded, realizing at last how they were aching.

'He hasn't been,' she had to call after looking at her watch.

'Who?' she heard the voice rustling back.

'The gentleman in the pink Holden.'

She listened to the silence, wondering whether she had done right.

When Royal called back, 'Could'uv had a blow-out.' Then

he laughed. 'Could'uv stopped to get grogged up.' She heard the frail rustling of the paper. 'Or taken an axe to somebody like they do nowadays.'

She closed her eyes, whether for Royal, or what she remembered of the man sitting in the Holden.

Although it was cold she continued watching after dark. Might have caught a chill, when she couldn't afford to. She only went inside to make the bread-and-milk Royal fancied of an evening.

She watched most attentively, always at the time, but he didn't pass, and didn't pass.

'Who?'

'The gentleman in the Holden.'

'Gone on holiday.' Royal sighed, and she knew it was the point where a normal person would have turned over, so she went to turn him.

One morning she said on going in, 'Fancy, I had a dream, it was about that man! He was standing on the side path alongside the cinerarias. I know it was him because of his funny-shaped head.'

'What happened in the dream?' Royal hadn't opened his eyes yet; she hadn't helped him in with his teeth.

'I dunno,' she said, 'it was just a dream.'

That wasn't strictly truthful, because the Holden gentleman had looked at her, she had seen his eyes. Nothing was spoken, though.

'It was a sort of red and purple dream. That was the cinerarias,' she said.

'I don't dream. You don't when you don't sleep. Pills aren't sleep.'

She was horrified at her reverberating dream. 'Would you like a nice soft-boiled egg?'

'Eggs all have a taste.'

'But you gotter eat *something*!'

On another morning she told him – she could have bitten off her tongue – she *was* stupid, *stupid*, 'I had a dream.'

'What sort of dream?'

'Oh,' she said, 'a silly one. Not worth telling. I dreamed I dropped an egg on the side path, and it turned into two. Not two. A double-yolker.'

She never realized Royal was so much like Mrs Natwick. It was as she raised him on his pillows. Or he had got like that in his sickness. Old men and old women were not unlike.

'Wasn't that a silly one?' she coaxed.

Every evening she sat on the front veranda and watched the traffic as though Royal had been beside her. Looked at her watch. And turned her face away from the steady-flowing stream. The way she bunched her small chest she could have had a sour breath mounting in her throat. Sometimes she had, it was nervousness.

When she went inside she announced, 'He didn't pass.'

Royal said – he had taken to speaking from behind his eyelids, 'Something muster happened to 'im. He didn't go on holiday. He went and died.'

'Oh, no! He wasn't of an age!'

At once she saw how stupid she was, and went out to get the bread-and-milk.

She would sit at the bedside, almost crouching against the edge of the mattress, because she wanted Royal to feel she was close, and he seemed to realize, though he mostly kept his eyelids down.

Then one evening she came running, she felt silly, her calves felt silly, her voice, 'He's come! At five-twenty! In a new cream Holden!'

Royal said without opening his eyes, 'See? I said 'e'd gone on holiday.'

More than ever she saw the look of Mrs Natwick.

Now every evening Royal asked, 'Has he been, Ella?'

Trying not to make it sound irritable or superior, she would answer, 'Not yet. It's only five.'

Every evening she sat watching, and sometimes would turn proud, arching her back, as she looked down from the veranda. The man was so small and ordinary.

She went in on one occasion, into the more than electric light, lowering her eyelids against the dazzle. 'You know, Royal, you could feel prouder of men when they rode horses. As they looked down at yer from under the brim of their hats. Remember that hat you used to wear? Riding in to Coot-ramundra?'

Royal died quietly that same year before the cinerarias had folded, while the cold westerlies were still blowing; the back page of the *Herald* was full of those who had been carried off. She was left with his hand, already set, in her own. They hadn't spoken, except about whether she had put out the garbage.

Everybody was very kind. She wouldn't have liked to admit it was enjoyable being a widow. She sat around for longer than she had ever sat, and let the dust gather. In the beginning acquaintances and neighbours brought her little presents of food: a billy-can of giblet soup, moulded veal with hard-boiled egg making a pattern in the jelly, cakes so dainty you couldn't taste them. But when she was no longer a novelty they left off coming. She didn't care any more than she cared about the dust. Sometimes she would catch sight of her face in the glass, and was surprised to see herself looking so calm and white.

Of course she was calm. The feeling part of her had been removed. What remained was a slack, discardable eiderdown. Must have been the pills Doctor gave.

Well-meaning people would call to her over the front fence, 'Don't you feel lonely, Mrs Natwick?' They spoke with a restrained horror, as though she had been suffering from an incurable disease.

But she called back proud and slow, 'I'm under sedation.' 'Arrr!' They nodded thoughtfully. 'What's 'e given yer?' She shook her head. 'Pills,' she called back. 'They say they're the ones the actress died of.'

The people walked on, impressed.

As the evenings grew longer and heavier she sat later on the front veranda watching the traffic of the Parramatta Road, its flow becoming syrupy and almost benign: big bulbous sedate buses, chrysalis cars still without a life of their own, clinging in line to the back of their host-articulator, trucks loaded for distances, empty loose-sounding jolly lorries. Sometimes women, looking out from the cabins of trucks from beside their men, shared her lack of curiosity. The light was so fluid nobody lasted long enough. You would never have thought boys could kick a person to death, seeing their long soft hair floating behind their sports models.

Every evening she watched the cream Holden pass. And looked at her watch. It was like Royal was sitting beside her. Once she heard herself, 'Thought he was gunner look round tonight, in our direction.' How could a person feel lonely?

She was, though. She came face to face with it walking through the wreckage of her garden in the long slow steamy late summer. The Holden didn't pass of course of a Saturday or Sunday. Something, something had tricked her, not the pills, before the pills. She couldn't blame anybody, probably only herself. Everything depended on yourself. Take the garden. It was a shambles. She would have liked to protest, but began to cough from running her head against some powdery mildew. She could only blunder at first, like a cow, or runty starved heifer, on breaking into a garden. She had lost her old wiriness. She shambled, snapping dead stems, uprooting. Along the bleached palings there was a fretwork of hollyhock, the brown fur of rotting sunflower. She rushed at a praying mantis, a big pale one, and deliberately broke its back, and was sorry afterwards for what was done so easy and thoughtless.

As she stood panting in her black, finally yawning, she saw all she had to repair. The thought of the seasons piling up ahead made her feel tired but necessary, and she went in to bathe her face. Royal's denture in a tumbler on top of the medicine cabinet, she ought to move, or give to the Sallies. In the meantime she changed the water. She never forgot it. The teeth looked amazingly alive.

All that autumn, winter, she was continually amazed, at the dust she had let gather in the house, at old photographs, books, clothes. There was a feather she couldn't remember wearing, a scarlet feather, she *can't* have worn, and gloves with little fussy ruffles at the wrists, silver piping, like a snail had laid its trail round the edges. There was, she knew, funny things she had bought at times, and never worn, but she couldn't remember the gloves or the feather. And books. She had collected a few, though never a reader herself. Old people liked to give old books, and you took them so as not to hurt anybody's feelings. *Hubert's Crusade*, for instance. Lovely golden curls. Could have been Royal's father's book. Everybody was a child once. And almost everybody had one. At least if she had had a child she would have known it wasn't a white turnip, more of a praying mantis, which snaps too easy.

In the same box she had put away a coloured picture, *Cities of the Plain*, she couldn't remember seeing it before. The people escaping from the burning cities had committed some sin or other nobody ever thought, let alone talked, about. As they hurried between rocks, through what must have been the 'desert places', their faces looked long and wooden. All they had recently experienced could have shocked the expression out of them. She was fascinated by what made her shiver. And the couples with their arms still around one another. Well, if you were damned, better hang on to your sin. She didn't blame them.

She put the box away. Its inlay as well as its contents made it something secret and precious.

The autumn was still and golden, the winter vicious only in fits. It was what you could call a good winter. The cold floods of air and more concentrated streams of dark-green light poured along the shady side of the house where her cinerarias had massed. She had never seen such cinerarias: some of the spired ones reached almost as high as her chin, the solid heads of others waited in the tunnel of dark light to club you with their colours, of purple and drenching blue, and what they called 'wine'. She couldn't believe wine would have made her drunker.

Just as she would sit every evening watching the traffic, evening was the time she liked best to visit the cinerarias, when the icy cold seemed to make the flowers burn their deepest, purest. So it was again evening when her two objects converged: for some blissfully confident reason she hadn't bothered to ask herself whether she had seen the car pass, till here was this figure coming towards her along the tunnel. She knew at once who it was, although she had never seen him on his feet; she had never seen him full-face, but knew from the funny shape of his head as Royal had been the first to notice. He was not at all an impressive man, not much taller than herself, but broad. His footsteps on the brickwork sounded purposeful.

'Will you let me use your phone, please, madam?' he asked in a prepared voice. 'I'm having trouble with the Holden.'

This was the situation she had always been expecting: somebody asking to use the phone as a way to afterwards murdering you. Now that it might be about to happen she couldn't care.

She said yes. She thought her voice sounded muzzy. Perhaps he would think she was drunk.

She went on looking at him, at his eyes. His nose, like the shape of his head, wasn't up to much, but his eyes, his eyes, she dared to think, were filled with kindness.

'Cold, eh? but clean cold!' He laughed friendly, shuffling on the brick paving because she was keeping him waiting.

Only then she noticed his mouth. He had a hare-lip, there was no mistaking, although it was well sewn. She felt so calm in the circumstances. She would have even liked to touch it.

But said, 'Why, yes – the telephone,' she said, 'it's this way,' she said, 'it's just off the kitchen – because that's where you spend most of your life. Or in bed,' she ended.

She wished she hadn't added that. For the first time since they had been together she felt upset, thinking he might suspect her of wrong intentions.

But he laughed and said, 'That's correct! You got something there!' It sounded manly rather than educated.

She realized he was still waiting, and took him to the telephone.

While he was phoning she didn't listen. She never listened when other people were talking on the phone. The sight of her own kitchen surprised her. While his familiar voice went on. It was the voice she had held conversations with.

But he was ugly, real ugly, *deformed*. If it wasn't for the voice, the eyes. She couldn't remember the eyes, but seemed to know about them.

Then she heard him laying the coins beside the phone, extra loud, to show.

He came back into the kitchen smiling and looking. She could smell him now, and he had the smell of a clean man.

She became embarrassed at herself, and took him quickly out.

'Fair bit of garden you got.' He stood with his calves curved through his trousers. A cocky little chap, but nice.

'Oh,' she said, 'this', she said, angrily almost, 'is nothing. You oughter see it. There's sunflower and hollyhock all along the palings. I'm famous for me hollyhocks!' She had never boasted in her life. 'But not now – it isn't the season. And I let it go. Mr Natwick passed on. You should'uv seen the cassia this autumn. Now it's only sticks, of course. And hibiscus. There's cream, gold, cerise, scarlet – double and single.'

She was dressing in them for him, revolving on high heels and changing frilly skirts.

He said, 'Gardening's not in my line,' turning his head to hide something, perhaps he was ashamed of his hare-lip.

'No,' she agreed. 'Not everybody's a gardener.'

'But like a garden.'

'My husband didn't even like it. He didn't have to tell me,' she added.

As they moved across the wintry grass, past the empty clothes-line, the man looked at his watch, and said, 'I was reckoning on visiting somebody in hospital tonight. Looks like I shan't make it if the N.R.M.A. takes as long as usual.'

'Do they?' she said, clearing her throat. 'It isn't somebody close, I hope? The sick person?'

Yes he said they was close.

'Nothing serious?' she almost bellowed.

He said it was serious.

Oh she nearly burst out laughing at the bandaged figure they were sitting beside particularly at the bandaged face. She would have laughed at a brain tumour.

'I'm sorry,' she said. 'I understand. Mr Natwick was for many years an invalid.'

Those teeth in the tumbler on top of the medicine cabinet. Looking at her. Teeth can look, worse than eyes. But she couldn't help it, she meant everything she said, and thought.

At this moment they were pressing inside the dark-green tunnel, her sleeve rubbing his, as the crimson-to-purple light was dying.

'These are the cinerarias,' she said.

'The what?' He didn't know, any more than Royal.

As she was about to explain she got switched to another language. Her throat became a long palpitating funnel through which the words she expected to use were poured out in a stream of almost formless agonized sound.

'What is it?' he asked, touching her.

If it had happened to herself she would have felt frightened, it occurred to her, but he didn't seem to be.

'What is it?' he kept repeating in his familiar voice, touching, even holding her.

And for answer, in the new language, she was holding him. They were holding each other, his hard body against her eiderdowny one. As the silence closed round them again, inside the tunnel of light, his face, to which she was very close, seemed to be unlocking, the wound of his mouth, which should have been more horrible, struggling to open. She could see he had recognized her.

She kissed above his mouth. She kissed as though she might never succeed in healing all the wounds they had ever suffered.

How long they stood together she wasn't interested in knowing. Outside them the river of traffic continued to flow between its brick and concrete banks. Even if it overflowed it couldn't have drowned them.

When the man said in his gentlest voice, 'Better go out in front. The N.R.M.A. might have come.'

'Yes,' she agreed. 'The N.R.M.A.'

So they shuffled, still holding each other, along the narrow path. She imagined how long and wooden their faces must look. She wouldn't look at him now, though, just as she wouldn't look back at the still faintly smouldering joys they had experienced together in the past.

When they came out, apart, and into the night, there was the N.R.M.A., his pointed ruby of a light burning on top of the cabin.

'When will you come?' she asked.

'Tomorrow.'

'Tomorrow. You'll stay to tea.'

He couldn't stay.

'I'll make you a *pot* of tea?'

But he didn't drink it.

'Coffee, then?'

He said, 'I like a nice cup of coffee.'

Going down the path he didn't look back, or opening the gate. She would not let herself think of reasons or possibilities, she would not think, but stood planted in the path, swayed slightly by the motion of the night.

Mrs Dolan said, 'You bring the saucepan to the boil. You got that?'

'Yeeehs.' Mrs Natwick had never been a dab at coffee.

'Then you throw in some cold water. That's what sends the gravel to the bottom.' This morning Mrs Dolan had to laugh at he own jokes.

'That's the part that frightens me,' Mrs Natwick admitted.

'Well, you just do it, and see,' said Mrs Dolan; she was too busy.

After she had bought the coffee Mrs Natwick stayed in the city to muck around. If she had stayed at home her nerves might have wound themselves tighter, waiting for evening to come. Though mucking around only irritated in the end. She had never been an idle woman. So she stopped at the cosmetics as though she didn't have to decide, this was her purpose, and said to the young lady lounging behind one of the counters, 'I'm thinking of investing in a lipstick, dear. Can you please advise me?'

As a concession to the girl she tried to make it a laughing matter, but the young person was bored, she didn't bat a silver eyelid. 'Elderly ladies', she said, 'go for the brighter stuff.'

Mrs Natwick ('my little Ella') had never felt so meek. Mum must be turning in her grave.

'This is a favourite.' With a flick of her long fingers the girl exposed the weapon. It looked too slippery-pointed, crimson-purple, out of its golden sheath.

Mrs Natwick's knees were shaking. 'Isn't it a bit noticeable?' she asked, again trying to make it a joke.

But the white-haired girl gave a serious laugh. 'What's wrong with noticeable?'

As Mrs Natwick tried it out on the back of her hand the way she had seen others do, the girl was jogging from foot to foot behind the counter. She was humming between her teeth, behind her white-smeared lips, probably thinking about a lover. Mrs Natwick blushed. What if she couldn't learn to get the tip of her lipstick back inside its sheath?

She might have gone quickly away without another word if the young lady hadn't been so professional and bored. Still humming, she brought out a little pack of rouge.

'Never saw myself with mauve cheeks!' It was at least dry, and easy to handle.

'It's what they wear.'

Mrs Natwick didn't dare refuse. She watched the long fingers with their silver nails doing up the parcel. The fingers looked as though they might resent touching anything but cosmetics; a lover was probably beneath contempt.

The girl gave her the change, and she went away without counting it.

She wasn't quiet, though, not a bit, booming and clanging in front of the toilet mirror. She tried to make a thin line, but her mouth exploded into a purple flower. She dabbed the dry-feeling pad on either cheek, and thick, mauve-scented shadows fell. She could hear and feel her heart behaving like a squeezed, rubber ball as she stood looking. Then she got at the lipstick again, still unsheathed. Her mouth was becoming enormous, so thick with grease she could hardly close her own lips underneath. A visible dew was gathering round the purple shadows on her cheeks.

She began to retch like, but dry, and rub, over the basin, scrubbing with the nailbrush. More than likely some would stay behind in the pores and be seen. Though you didn't have to see, to see.

There were Royal's teeth in the tumbler on top of the medicine cabinet. Ought to hide the teeth. What if somebody wanted to use the toilet? She must move the teeth. But didn't. In the present circumstances she couldn't have raised her arms that high.

Around five she made the coffee, throwing in the cold water at the end with a gesture copied from Mrs Dolan. If the gravel hadn't sunk to the bottom he wouldn't notice the first time. provided the coffee was hot. She could warm up the made coffee in a jiffy.

As she sat on the veranda waiting, the cane chair shifted and squealed under her. If it hadn't been for her weight it might have run away across the tiles, like one of those old planchette boards, writing the answers to questions.

There was an accident this evening down at the intersection. A head-on collision. Bodies were carried out of the crumpled cars, and she remembered a past occasion when she had run with blankets, and Hazel's Onkaparinka, and a pillow from their own bed. She had been so grateful to the victim. She could not give him enough, or receive enough of the warm blood. She had come back, she remembered, sprinkled.

This evening she had to save herself up. Kept on looking at her watch. The old cane chair squealing, ready to write the answers if she let it. Was he hurt? Was he killed, then? Was he – what?

Mrs Dolan it was, sticking her head over the palings. 'Don't

like the accidents, Mrs Natwick. It's the blood. The blood
turns me up.'

Mrs Natwick averted her face. Though unmoved by present
blood. If only the squealing chair would stop trying to buck her
off.

'Did your friend enjoy the coffee?' Mrs Dolan shouted;
nothing nasty in her: Mrs Dolan was sincere.

'Hasn't been yet,' Mrs Natwick mumbled from glancing at
her watch. 'Got held up.'

'It's the traffic. The traffic at this time of evenun.'

'Always on the dot before.'

'Working back. Or made a mistake over the day.'

Could you make a mistake? Mrs Natwick contemplated.
Tomorrow had always meant tomorrow.

'Or he could'uv,' Mrs Dolan shouted, but didn't say it. 'I better
go inside,' she said instead. 'They'll be wonderun where I am.'

Down at the intersection the bodies were lying wrapped in
someone else's blankets, looking like the grey parcels of mice
cats sometimes vomit up.

It was long past five-twenty, not all that long really, but drawing in. The sky was heaped with cold fire. Her city was burning.

She got up finally, and the chair escaped with a last squeal,
writing its answer on the tiles.

No, it wasn't lust, not if the Royal God Almighty with
bared teeth should strike her down. Or yes, though, it was.
She was lusting after the expression of eyes she could hardly
remember for seeing so briefly.

In the effort to see, she drove her memory wildly, while her
body stumbled around and around the paths of the burning city
there was now no point in escaping. You would shrivel up in
time along with the polyanthers and out-of-season hibiscus. All
the randy mouths would be stopped sooner or later with black.

The cinerarias seemed to have grown so luxuriant she had
to force her way past them, down the narrow brick path. When

she heard the latch click, and saw him coming towards her.

'Why,' she screamed laughing though it sounded angry, she *was*, 'I'd given you up, you know! It's long after five-twenty!'

As she pushed fiercely towards him, past the cinerarias, snapping one or two of those which were most heavily loaded, she realized he couldn't have known that she set her watch, her life, by his constant behaviour. He wouldn't have dawdled so.

'What is it?' she called at last, in exasperation at the distance which continued separating them.

He was far too slow, treading the slippery moss of her too shaded path. While she floundered on. She couldn't reach the expression of his eyes.

He said, and she could hardly recognize the faded voice, 'There's something – I been feeling off colour most of the day.' His mis-shapen head was certainly lolling as he advanced.

'Tell me!' She heard her voice commanding, like that of a man, or a mother, when she had practised to be a lover; she could still smell the smell of rouge. 'Won't you tell me – *dearest*?' It was thin and unconvincing now. (As a girl she had once got a letter from her cousin Kath Salter, who she hardly knew: *Dearest Ella* ...)

Oh dear. She had reached him. And was given all strength – that of the lover she had aimed at being.

Straddling the path, unequally matched – he couldn't compete against her strength – she spoke with an acquired, a deafening softness, as the inclining cinerarias snapped.

'You will tell me what is wrong – dear, dear.' She breathed with trumpets.

He hung his head. 'It's all right. It's the pain – here – in my arm – no, the shoulder.'

'Ohhhhh!' She ground her face into his shoulder forgetting it wasn't *her* pain.

Then she remembered, and looked into his eyes and said, 'We'll save you. You'll see.'

It was she who needed saving. She knew she was trying to enter by his eyes. To drown in them rather than be left.

Because, in spite of her will to hold him, he was slipping from her, down amongst the cinerarias, which were snapping off one by one around them.

A cat shot out. At one time she had been so poor in spirit she had wished she was a cat.

'It's all right,' either voice was saying.

Lying amongst the smashed plants, he was smiling at her dreadfully, not his mouth, she no longer bothered about that lip, but with his eyes.

'More air!' she cried. 'What you need is air!' hacking at one or two cinerarias which remained erect.

Their sap was stifling, their bristling columns callous.

'Oh! Oh!' she panted. 'Oh God! Dear love!' comforting with hands and hair and words.

Words.

While all he could say was, 'It's all right.'

Or not that at last. He folded his lips into a white seam. His eyes were swimming out of reach.

'Eh? Dear – dearest – darl – darlig – darling love – *love* – LOVE?' All the new words still stiff in her mouth, that she had heard so far only from the mouths of actors.

The words were too strong she could see. She was losing him. The traffic was hanging together only by charred silences.

She flung herself and covered his body, trying to force kisses – no, breath, into his mouth, she had heard about it.

She had seen turkeys, feathers sawing against each other's feathers, rising afterwards like new noisy silk.

She knelt up, and the wing-tips of her hair still dabbled limply in his cheeks. 'Eh? Ohh luff!' She could hardly breathe it.

She hadn't had time to ask his name, before she must have killed him by loving too deep, and too adulterously.

Sicilian Vespers

Too constricted from the beginning, their room could have been further reduced by the throbbing in his jaw. If he had stretched out an arm, he might have touched any of the four walls, the lurching wardrobe, or the air conditioner which did not cool. But he could not bring himself to carry out the experiment. He lay and sweated, or turned in the loosely jointed bed, and the tooth which possessed his body and mind seemed to probe deeper than ever with its fluorescent roots.

'Oh, God!' Some comfort to hear it sound no more than a formality. And Ivy down in the lounge. He had advised her to stay there after finishing her coffee. In the lounge the air conditioning worked, provided the management had turned it on and there wasn't an influx of hot bodies.

'God, God!' he repeated with a vehemence he would not have liked his wife to interpret.

He so shocked himself he switched the light on. The bed groaned once or twice before the springs surrendered him and he began the long-short trek to the bathroom. He was wearing his underpants. Though he had reached the scraggy stage in life, and the corrugations in his scalp exposed by a disarrangement of hair suggested he was playing the part of a withered loon in some cruel farce, his right cheek bloomed with a feverish jollity of risen flesh as he stood between the strip-lighting and swallowed an unwilling Veganin.

He coughed dry, and swallowed a mouthful of probably infected tap-water instead of the *acqua minerale* recommended by Ivy.

Prudence was a virtue normally present in both of them. What had made their marriage such an exceptionally happy one was its balance. Each respected the other's right to an opinion (actually, there were few they didn't share). Though she hadn't taken up golf, Ivy could follow a game with interest; she enjoyed a mild flutter at the races; while he had made a point of not allowing a busy practice to prevent his putting in an appearance on nights when her discussion group met. His retirement had made it easier for them to indulge a passion for history and to air their knowledge of the French language: they travelled 'extensively', as the papers say, 'extravagantly and too frequently', according to some of their friends, who waited for news of a coronary or stroke. If Ivy had started Italian on her own, it was perhaps because he could not hear himself, a mature Australian male, producing some of those Italian sounds.

So Italian became Ivy's individual accomplishment. He was proud of it. Standing at the wash-basin, he visualized the somewhat tremulous motion of her upper lip as she sat by herself downstairs in the lounge: *vorrei un caffè – solo – per favore.* She had always managed it very nicely.

He was sixty-six, he was reminded by his tooth, and by the hairs hatching the division of his chest. Ivy was fifty-eight, though some, he knew, or perhaps he didn't – he *sensed* when somebody suspected Ivy of cheating on her age. He personally didn't like to think they looked anything but equal.

Laughter sounded farther down the corridor. He trudged back to the glaring room the management must have reserved for them out of spite (foreigners do, you know, discriminate against Australians). He stood at the glass door he had forced open earlier that evening against the waves of dust-clogged carpet. Lights along the waterfront flickered blue in time with his fluorescent tooth. A Sicilian stench of rotting mussels, excrement, and sweat (his own, alas) made him clamp his nostrils down, to unclamp almost immediately, to breathe in, to swell with putrid air; he did not mind if he died of it.

A face in the street took fright at something happening on a balcony, and *Dr Charles Simpson, 27 Wongaburra Road, Bellevue Hill, Sydney* (there it was on the labels at least, in Ivy's large, innocent hand) withdrew out of sight. He began not lying down again but doing a belly-flop on this yellow modernistic bed. No trampoline, it tossed him only feebly as he groaned for the pain in his possessive tooth and for what he alone knew of himself. What if all the patients who had brought him their forebodings as well as their actual cancers – what if *Ivy* were to realize that inside the responsible man there had always lurked this diffident, whimpering boy?

He must concentrate on Ivy the immaculate. A plain woman, she had given him the courage to propose. Infinite trustworthiness as a wife had even inspired in him what passed for faith in himself. It was a fake, however. While he was parading this impersonation of what she and others expected of him, Ivy had never cheated. Or would he recognize it if she were to cheat, when she had never been aware of his true self inside the man she took for granted?

It was all very morbid and part of this Sicilian nightmare. The tooth flamed up in him, and died, and flamed. Incidentally, he must not hate Sicilians when Ivy and he had loved each other not passionately irreproachably always and for ever ah dear amen.

She must have come in while he was dozing. Proof against the traffic, its teeth gnashing and snarling past his ear, a still centre had formed in the surrounding dark.

'Who is it?' Certainty made him sound irritated.

He switched on. Standing beneath an inverted acrylic turban from which the light swayed and splintered, she was too noticeably upright, too deliberately controlled. Sympathy gave her powdered skin a more than usually crumpled look.

'Oh, darling,' her upper lip was venturing out, 'is it still hurting?'

'You would have done better to stay down there as I suggested.' Self-sacrifice softened his voice.

'How could I – in the circumstances – and amongst all those tourists!'

For a moment they were so perfectly agreed they might have been dove-tailed; his tooth was still; his swelling smiled. To celebrate their empathy, she sat beside him on the edge of the bed, and took his hand, and gently laid it against her cheek of crumpled kid.

'Those Dutch!' She didn't snicker, because Ivy wasn't malicious.

'The French are better.'

'Some of the French. An American couple', Ivy did giggle a little, 'insisted, *à l'Américaine*, in coming to my table and having coffee with me.'

'What sort of Americans?'

'Big and juicy. Not bad. Getting on. No, about our age, I should think. We'd probably find the man noisy in the long run. She's his female counterpart, but quiet. She has a smile.'

'What sort of smile?'

'I don't know. I think she's probably sat around all their life together smiling to disguise her feelings. Or perhaps she hasn't anything to say.'

Though normally he trusted his wife's judgment, Charles Simpson's tooth would not allow him to accept Ivy's Americans. The roots of the monstrous tooth had started flaming again. Any time now, the bulb swathed by the acryllic turban was going to give up, or so its flickering warned.

When she had got into her nightie – whether she was ready for bed or not, this was the coolest proposition – Ivy Simpson stood at the door which the rucked-up carpet was holding open. She might have sat awhile on the small triangular balcony, but looked down her front and decided against it. Ribbons of oily light, or just perceptible motion, suggested sea where darkness lay. Palms were shivering. Now and then a plastic bag amongst the litter strewing the dead grass between sea and roadway half inflated, but flopped back into inertia. Ivy might almost have taken pleasure in the languid squalor of night if the furious activities of man roaring down the Foro Italico had allowed her. And Charles's tooth: she caught herself whimpering, raising a drooped shoulder to ward off renewed pain.

The toothache seemed, like nothing ever had, an affront to their relationship; which was ridiculous in two mature individuals who had survived the tests of time, who had agreed from the beginning to depend on their faith in each other rather than the man-concocted fallacies believers bunch together and label Faith.

There had been moments in their married life when she might have proposed a trial of this personal faith, if she had been less rational, and ashamed of the shocked expression she would have brought to his physician's eyes. Just as now she would not have confessed to her own spasmodic attempts to will into her body the physical pain he was suffering. Other people, including Charles, she suspected, believe only theoretically in the efficacy of love. And she did not want to damage his affection for her: it was too precious.

Standing on the verge of the horrid little modernistic balcony and the baroque nightscape beyond, Ivy Simpson nursed the perfect lifetime relationship. None of the minor stresses had hitherto threatened it. What should have been the major tragedy of childlessness had only increased the kindness with which they treated each other. As far back as their youth they had been considerate rather than sensual lovers. As Father's daughter she was grateful for it.

Ivy could never dismiss completely the humiliations of her childhood. There were wounds so deep, even Charles had not succeeded in healing them. She was glad the old corsair her father had died before she met her husband; Aubrey wouldn't have approved of Charles.

'What are you doing, Ivy?'

'Nothing.' Her throat had dried; her voice sounded unlike itself. 'Is there anything you want, darling?'

There wasn't, it seemed, unless to keep in touch. He didn't answer.

She stood a while longer, frowning now, not at the past, but at the red sports car, at the young Sicilians luxuriating in their brilliantine and open shirts. Normally broadminded, scarcely prudish, she realized how she loathed body hair.

'I was only looking,' she said. 'And thinking.'

He was lying, eyes closed, immersed in pain, or the first waves of sleep. She risked kissing him on the forehead. He didn't respond. There was no need.

She continued moving about their room, in search of an occupation, when Charles asked, 'Those Americans of yours – what does he do?'

'I don't know. I think he's rich.'

'They can't have told you much – not for Americans.'

'Oh, they did! They told me lots. He did, that is. He's the one who does the talking.'

Behind closed eyelids, Charles was looking peevish for Charles. It was his tooth, of course.

'Their name is Shacklock – Clark and Imelda.' She laughed. 'Did you tell them ours?'

'No.'

'You should have played their American game.'

'It wouldn't have come naturally,' she said.

In spite of his closed eyelids she could tell Charles approved of that.

Even so, his drowsy lips took the trouble to remind her, 'There's nothing wrong with our name – though after Shacklock – you can't say it – swashbuckles.'

'There *is* something piratical about him. That, I think, is why I couldn't altogether take to Mr Shacklock. You'll understand what I mean when you meet him.'

Charles remembered his tooth. He turned away, on to his side. One shoulder was protecting him. She would have liked to demonstrate her love if she could have thought of some modest way of doing so.

She was tired by now. She could think of nothing. Not the merest duty. She had made out the laundry list before lunch and given their bundle to the *cameriera*.

'*Due camicii*,' she murmured as the second yellow bed started creaking around her, 'or is it *-ie?*' She couldn't remember: she was too tired; and Charles didn't answer, who hadn't taken lessons in Italian.

But Charles often didn't bother to answer. Nor did she resent what she interpreted as trust rather than apathy; and wasn't it a privilege of their kind of marriage to be able to ask the questions for which you neither expect nor require an answer? The better you knew each other the thicker these questions piled up, agreeably, acceptably, passionlessly. And would, she imagined, thicker and thicker, till the end.

About to switch off the light, she realized Charles had turned again, and was not exactly looking at her, but his eyes so intent she could not ignore them. He jumped her into telling what she had planned to keep at least till morning.

'Those Shacklocks', she said, 'have a car. They suggested they take us tomorrow on an expedition to Agrigento. I told them we'd see. I didn't expect your tooth.'

He closed his eyes. 'There's no reason why you shouldn't go.' He sounded so relaxed she wondered whether the pain had left him.

'Oh no, darling, you know I wouldn't!' It was she who experienced a twinge: that he should have suspected her of it.

She couldn't. She couldn't sleep. Sand on the sheets. Her breasts itching. Nobody could find fault with her figure. 'Svelte' is the secret word she has never dared use. Kind people apply all the milder words to your face; only Father ever called it ugly. *Ugly Ivy mingy as her name.* Father himself was handsome and drunken. Mother had wanted 'Ivy' *simple and yet pretty* and for once stuck to her guns. You wished she hadn't. Because you hated your father, you wished you could have loved Mother: her squashed smile. Mother was made unhappy by penury, and adulteries, and the time he exposed himself at Manly. Oh yes, Mother deserved her full share of sympathy. You hadn't been able to make it up to her before she died. After that, Father too, a shabby-skinned, once gorgeous male, or god. If you withheld love, it was because a parent's behaviour encourages miserliness in children. Even Mother was greedy. Everything was left unsaid and undone, there was all the more reason for pouring it into Charles. To love my husband: his honest, un-Sicilian eyes. Might never have known reason for nursing disgust, shame, despair. All all dissolved in love. Or the sober affection which is better than.

What is too precious is more breakable she sighed when you dropped the Lalique bowl a wedding present. For Father *that middle-class monstrosity.* Aubrey was the artist. He had *panache* said one of the ladies who bought him hoping to experience in the flesh a vitalist bravura absent from his turgid nudes. *His daughter is it one would never.*

To be something special *superba donna* work of art better a whippet than nothing. He caressed his whippet. Then Charles waiting for the ferry made none of it any longer necessary.

No abrasions beyond the sand of non-sleep.

The plastic lilies raise their heads from out of it flop back loll

and recover slightly. Contrary to opinion sand isn't sterile.
Fertilized by putrid shells rotting mussels black mesh of
mattresses the mounds of sea lettuce and excrement of various
kinds the human splurges best between *ugh* the naked toes my
poor *lavata camicia da* nightie still doing its duty in spite of
will the red car plough the plastic lilies the biggest the
acryllic already crushed you next unless you can uproot the
whippet legs are pale mauve onyx nails enmeshed in a Sicilian
plot the red glove will burst its buttons if Dr Wongaburra
Simpson can't prevent its evil spilling
　　true as blue he solves *the plot is not to fear darling*
what plot Americans don't they are on our side
do we know?
Ivy should
　　the Simpson lips eject is it a kiss at any rate an offering
glistening white never remember which is honesty which thrift
it hovers between us
　　take this Ivy I am only its temporary host this for you is more
than a rotten tooth a token of my trust
　　what is too precious breaks or spills it is I who spit at Charles
Swimson my hus my lover it swings for ever between us a
chain hanging from his chin
　　it is out Ivy at last
　　from its chaste scabbard the Arabs brought from Africa the
sword is only to expect he has sharpened
　　oh why God you will save me Mr Cutlack there's no other reason
for your being between us oh oh Clark save me from Aubrey my
frightening husband

'Clark? Clark!' Ivy Simpson had almost rocked the bed apart.
　　'What's the trouble, Ivy?' The eyes looked afraid in his
lopsided face, the light making an ungainly, circular motion
from his having hit the reading lamp.
　　'My leg!' Ivy was gasping, biting mouthfuls of the warm

flannel the air had become as she fought the pain she was obviously suffering from.

Then as her mind resumed control, she thought to explain, 'I've got the most excruciating cramp!' And jumped up, hobbling, stretching, contorting, again stretching, tiptoe if possible.

'Better if you lie still now.' Dr Simpson was only incidentally the husband she had left with toothache.

She obeyed, and he began massaging her calf; her legs, like her breasts, were still youthful. In that appalling dream she had become for an instant Father's whippet – *Emma*; he had loved her for her elegance.

A whippet is at least clean and neat. She was glad she could not remember any of the formlessness, the gibberish – and relieved to have thought of the cramp.

Charles accepted it. Why shouldn't he? She could tell she had been convincing. She lay, eyelids fluttering; once or twice she whinged, back still arched, as he stroked her calf with kind, regular hand. It was a comfort. Though she had no vestige of a cramp, she was still suffering from a dream.

Aubrey Tyndall. He liked to see his name engraved on expensive, superfluous objects, like the cigarette case Mother said was vulgar because the donor had never been more than half explained. He would sit polishing his own engraved name with the ball of a thumb, its whorls black with nicotine. Invited you to call him 'Aubrey', but you never had – not to his face. *Why not, Ivy?* Couldn't answer. *'Dad' is a cosy all-time bore they'll think you're my girl if you call me 'Aubrey'.* His voice had never struck deeper. He laughed to hurt as he lowered lids over eyes the expression of which seldom went with what he had been saying. His beard, a tarnished gold, would tingle with sand from the beaches where he spent whole afternoons lying breast down.

'Has it passed?' It was Dr Simpson.

'I think it has. Yes. You've saved me.' Still weak-eyed, she smiled at him, flickering; because it was Charles he wouldn't see that her eyelids, her cheeks were withered, papery, probably greasy where the skin had devoured the powder.

Kindness isn't breakable. She closed her eyes, reassured, and now it was she rubbing rubbing Aubrey's shoulder because of the rheumatic pain he had from running round without his clothes he said after the southerly came she was his ugly daughter but good for something at last she had he said the soothing touch her hand sliding over the shoulder down the ribs almost to the thigh the skin not quite gold sea-light gave it a tinge of green of verdigris she rubbed in the embrocation relieved when it vanished the skin less easy to the hand rubbing this disgusting man *your father* his breasts fattening in a fuzz of dirty gold.

'I think you could leave off, darling,' Ivy remembered to tell Charles. 'It's so – kind,' she sighed, and scuffed her cheek against the pillow.

She should have asked after his tooth, but felt too exhausted, or fulfilled, falling asleep.

They started off with what was scarcely a row, an argument, between the Shacklocks over which road they should take for Agrigento: Clark so obviously knew, and she was complacent in her ignorance. Ivy, who had studied the map before leaving, would not have liked to admit that Mr Shacklock was right: she kept quiet.

'Do you mean to say you've spent three whole days here and not been outside that *albergo*?' The rented Fiat could hardly contain Clark Shacklock's incredulity.

On the back seat, Charles Simpson raised a buttock preparatory to answering. 'The other evening we went for a bit of a stroll as far as the Villa Giulia.'

'We didn't go inside, though,' Ivy added.

Mr Shacklock admitted that a toothache can be pretty

traumatic. 'But how I envy you your self-sufficiency! Like a couple of plants – needless to say, nice, sensitive ones – all these days in a room at the Hotel Gattopardo!'

Mrs Shacklock turned her head. 'My husband doesn't mean to be offensive. He has always loved and envied plants.' Then she subsided to observe the landscape, herself not unlike a plant, more of a vegetable, a large creamy gourd with overtones of gold.

Mr Shacklock, on the other hand, was of the animal kingdom: too compulsive by far.

Seated behind their hosts, the Simpsons' contained irony communicated itself through loosely linked hands. Once or twice Ivy glanced at Charles without, she thought, giving them away, though you can never be sure of those driver's mirrors. She was only surprised Charles had accepted the invitation to drive with unknown Americans to Agrigento after their frankly hideous night. She gave him an extra look to see whether it was truly he who had plunged the sword into her – tummy. Memories of her dream were so gross and frightening she put them out of her head again.

'Are you comfortable, Charles and Ivy?' Clark Shacklock called. 'Fiat cars are designed – back seat, anyway – for the dangling legs of dwarfs.'

The Simpsons could not have felt more relaxed, though they did not come at Christian names, or not until Lercara Friddi.

Along the road Clark Shacklock drew their attention to points of interest. Ivy Simpson, who had read the guidebook in advance, could have confirmed that most of what he told was truthful.

Sometimes his natural exuberance drove him to add extravagant touches. 'See that church on the escarpment? They say Our Lady put in an appearance there before the last elections. It helped the Christian Democrats a lot.'

The Simpsons looked at each other. They enjoyed that. They

were prepared to admit Clark Shacklock, if shyly, to their own Enlightenment, not that he wouldn't have barged in sooner or later regardless of whether they allowed him. It was less certain what beliefs Mrs Shacklock held. She was probably moody – or dumb, Ivy Simpson decided.

As they drove, Imelda Shacklock continued looking from side to side at the landscape. From the back seat you caught sight of her rather full, creamy cheeks; otherwise, when she stared ahead you had only the view of a strong neck and tawny hair in the tousled style. Clark, by contrast, attempted repeatedly to face his back-seat passengers while driving. If it had been her own husband, Ivy Simpson might have felt shocked and frightened, but as it was someone of whom she knew nothing, his driver's daring became an acceptable technique, and she could listen calmly to his tales of Shacklock travels. He told these in such detail you wondered what he could be gleaning at present. Perhaps he would be briefed by his wife: she was absorbing the landscape with such obvious concentration.

It was certainly a very fine one, immense and dusty in the heat of morning. Human or even animal activity hardly belonged, though there were clues to both: in the stubble recurring patterns, geometrical to the point where they suggested rites; the neat architecture of a haystack, a slice carved out of its pediment; cow-pats in an olive grove; a hovel teetering against the sky. In spite of the fact that she was holding hands – loosely and discreetly – with Charles, who had begun asking Mr Shacklock the kind of statistical questions men are moved to ask each other, and for which Clark seemed to have all the answers, the landscape through which they were hurtling might have been for Ivy Simpson alone. She would not have cared to admit to Charles that this was the kind of experience he could never share. Fortunately it was a possibility which would never arise in conversation, but if it did, she would almost certainly deny that she had ever aspired to, let alone experienced, any form of levitation. Immersed in his pragmatic exchange with Mr Shacklock, Charles did not notice her hair was streaming, or realize that her skirt was catching in the branches she skimmed, and that the door of a barn, huddled in the bushes of an airless hollow beside the road, scarcely made her nails blench as she tore at the rusty hasp to explore the darkness inside.

It was Mrs Shacklock who disturbed one's sense of sole possession. The strong neck with the creases in it, the large but by no means flabby torso, performed heavy obeisances to left and right as the car sprang with them through a pass. Ivy Simpson wondered whether Imelda Shacklock was a person she would ever get to know. She did not think she could actively dislike the woman, because it wasn't in her nature to dislike others (hate for her father had exhausted her capacity for dislikes) till for a moment, and alarmingly, she visualized Imelda's white body spread-eagle in a patch of grass, her fleshy necklaces quite distinct, and still more startling, the black tuft where her thighs forked.

Ivy Simpson felt so guilty she sat forward on the edge of her seat. 'I shall never be grateful enough, Mrs Shacklock, for your persuading us to come on this fantastic drive.'

Now it was Mrs Shacklock's turn to look alarmed as she hesitated to expose her own state of mind. 'Yes,' she mumbled over practically incapable lips, 'it is a – a *generous* landscape, isn't it?' ashamed of her opaqueness and inadequacy.

While Clark Shacklock chose that moment to turn round and, between statistics, wink. 'Don't tell me, Ivy, you're a member of the Romantics' Club!' His face was too burnt and jolly for his remark to have been in any way an accusation or sneer – though it might have been.

His glance lingered long enough to remind her of her reputation as a plain woman. What apparently he failed to notice were the flashes of gold which came and went in her streaming hair, and the shape she could feel her lips taking inside the confines of an actually small mouth.

She resettled herself in her seat, and only now remembered she was still holding Charles's hand.

Whatever her attitude to the Shacklocks, it was soon after, at Lercara Friddi, that Ivy decided to plump for Christian names.

Mrs Shacklock, who seemed to make all the minor decisions, murmured that this was probably as good as anywhere for a stop. A juke box was hammering home its message in the unfinished concrete roadhouse where her husband drew up amongst the rubble. As they entered through a plastic curtain, its fly-spotted strips slithered on their faces, and Ivy asked, 'Do you think we dare risk the *gabinetti*, Imelda?'

'I guess we'll have to – or last out till Agrigento.'

'Better a bush, perhaps!'

Ivy Simpson would have liked to use her daring, together with the threatening horrors of the *gabinetti*, as the cement for an alliance with Imelda Shacklock. But as Imelda either wouldn't, or didn't know how to play, Ivy was saddled with her own rakishness at the moment when the mirror showed her the cracks in her lips and the knots in her swag of dust-laden hair.

Clark Shacklock only half looked at the two women on their return; he was telling Charles about discovering certain Caravaggios. 'What makes them a bonus is finding them unexpectedly in these obscure and, on the whole, mediocre churches. Like suddenly coming across the Goya in San Anton, Madrid.'

The Simpsons looked appropriately grave, and Charles coughed, and remarked, 'Yes.' Art made him nervous; he was always reading books about it, trying to learn, but hadn't succeeded in bringing it alive. 'We haven't been to Madrid,' he admitted.

Ivy blushed.

'But you must!' Clark Shacklock's thighs heaved; the Shack-locks had been everywhere it seemed, and sometimes more than once. 'If only for the Goyas. That *Communion of San José* is *the* greatest *spiritual* experience.' He glanced from one Simpson to the other, to see if they would dare disbelieve.

If Charles was uneasy, his swollen face increased his expression of earnestness.

'I still prefer the Burtonville Goya.' Imelda Shacklock was smiling into the large old handbag she had opened.

It must have been a great comfort to own such a capacious, though shabby, bag. On her otherwise naked, plump hands, she was wearing an enormous slumberous stone Ivy could not identify.

Imelda appeared elated to hold an opinion of her own, but Clark wanted to demolish her. 'The Burtonville Goya? The hell it is! Our intentions were of the best. We just hadn't been around. And didn't know Goya. We didn't know ourselves.'

But Imelda Shacklock smiled as she stirred up the contents of her handbag. 'I have always known what I am. And what I want.'

'You're so goddam stubborn. It's three to one that the Burtonville Goya's a fake. We have that in writing if you'd care to open your eyes to it.'

Rudeness in a marriage always pained Ivy Simpson. She looked unhappily at Charles. She would have to persuade herself that Americans obey a different set of rules.

'What is Burtonville?' she asked rather carefully.

Clark Shacklock continued frowning: it was too soon for him to avoid including Mrs Simpson in the anger his wife had roused in him. 'Burtonville? There's a small collection – a museum, I suppose you'd call it – we founded back home – I and Imelda – when we first laid hands on money, in our ideal-istic youth. Some of our intentions misfired, as you must have gathered, though Imelda is still determined to Christian Science the truth.'

Imelda laughed and snapped her handbag shut; there were moments when she seemed hardly to belong to Clark.

'Oh, I *would* like to see the Burtonville Museum!' Ivy wanted genuinely to console, so she avoided mentioning the dubious Goya (a painter she thought she might find morbid, whether fake or real) and made her desire an innocuously collective one.

'So you shall – when you visit the States.' That he put some slight value on their friendship did not help her to believe that she – or Charles – would ever see the Burtonville collection.

Nor perhaps did Clark Shacklock himself believe. He put an end to anything equivocal or unresolved by slapping down payment, together with an extravagant tip, for the *acqua minerale* they had just finished. He appeared to be paying, more than anything, for the physical pleasure of a return to natural amiability. This may have been what he was inviting Ivy Simpson to share. The cushion of his lower lip, with its slight dent swelled and glowed. Over the V of his shirt a glistening wave of black hair curved quivering without breaking. Ivy wondered how far she could believe in Clark Shacklock's 'great *spiritual* experience'.

But it was time to push on to Agrigento.

A curtain of brown heat had been lowered between them and the mountains. They looked down at a dry stream, a pale wrinkle at the bottom of a valley. Neither houses, nor even a power station, any longer convinced. The passengers in the car with an egg-shell chassis had reached a stage where their own suffering flesh was the real proof of human continuance. Though probably none of them would have admitted to such a negative conclusion. Because all four were educated. Hadn't they exchanged the names of universities, or colleges, they had attended in Australia, or the States?

As the large Americans were bounced onward, and the skinnier Australians slithered stickily against each other on the back seat, Charles Shacklock began telling over his shoulder how he had read in some magazine that Sicilian boys of the deprived class sat masturbating in the schoolroom under their teacher's nose.

Charles Simpson deplored, sociologically and medically, what he was able to laugh at as a man, while Ivy was proud to appear broadminded, though the scene she visualized brought the gooseflesh out on her, and she wondered how she might have reacted if her own husband had told the story. Imelda Shacklock seemed unmoved, or else she was inured.

Very practically, Mrs Shacklock had brought a picnic basket along ('you can never be sure in Sicily'). After the rigours of the Archaeological Museum and the scramble up to the Sanctuary of Demeter, when Ivy might have more than grazed her knee if Clark hadn't steadied her, it was decided to open their basket in the shadow of the Temple of Concord.

Charles whispered, 'Isn't this great, Ivy?' but she suspected it was less for the temple than the sight of food which the poor darling's tooth might allow him to enjoy only in the abstract.

She whispered back, 'Is it hurting, dearest?' but Charles avoided answering.

Imelda Shacklock conjured her picnic lunch: there were foie gras sandwiches, and a cold chicken, and some enormous peaches only slightly bruised, and a thermos of chilled wine.

Clark almost at once began complaining in the half-angry, half-jocular voice he used on his wife – that is, when he wasn't wholly angry, 'Sicily rides again, Imelda! Something in this basket downright stinks.'

'The chicken, I guess,' Imelda said. 'But it's only a chicken's normal smell. No worse than some underwear.'

Ivy flinched.

'That's your goddam Christian Science again!' Clark

grumbled on. 'I wonder how many are born Christian Scientists without ever realizing.'

Embarrassment made Ivy's voice sound more than usually girlish. 'As far as I'm concerned, I can't smell a thing. Excepting peaches!' She inhaled ecstatically.

Each Simpson found the food 'delicious', though if they had been as callously truthful as Clark Shacklock they might have admitted the chicken was tainted.

For the sake of his tooth, Charles concentrated on the foie gras sandwiches, which at other times, Ivy knew, he would have considered far too rich. She herself drank a second glass, more than her share, of the chilled wine, hoping it might protect her from the chicken.

Whether this were high or not, Clark Shacklock devoured a drumstick, then another, spitting out the gristle on the dead grass, and afterwards unashamedly licking his glossier, seemingly fuller lips, while he told them the history of the temple – which the Simpsons already knew.

'During the Sixth Century,' he finished, 'they turned this perfectly respectable temple into a Christian church.'

'As so often happened!' To express her disapproval Ivy made it extra dry.

Tact prevented the Simpsons from developing the theme. Apart from his references to Christian Science and a crack at Our Lady, their host had given them no clue to Shacklock beliefs or lack of them. The Simpsons were inclined to hope for the best, not that they hadn't met with some nasty surprises: American 'enthusiasm' will out fairly soon, but the popish spectre sometimes lurks indefinitely behind the most deceptive façade.

After Imelda Shacklock had gathered up the scraps from their feast with rather ostentatious gestures – 'so as not to contribute to this earth's pollution' – they began to ascend the steps of the temple. Imelda led the way, very light for one so large. Her white, stockingless calves bulged and shone in motion. Climbing several steps behind, Ivy was reminded, not without guilt, of the chicken they had eaten at lunch: she saw again the fragments of unctuous flesh lying on the rosy cushion of Clark Shacklock's lower lip.

So she increased her efforts to concentrate on the Temple of Concord rising around them out of the dust and heat, its golden-pink columns supporting the beaten gold of the sky. The glare made her half close her eyes, and for a moment the columns shuddered – like flesh: dry and pocked, of course, which did take some of the fleshiness out of them. But not enough. And of all flesh, she had to remember that of her father on the occasions when she had massaged his shoulder. There is nothing wrong with rubbing embrocation into your father's rheumatic shoulder. Then why had she hated him most of all while kneading him? It must have been the rank smell of overheated male, and of the white goo welling up from between her fingers.

She realized, with not as much surprise as she would have expected, that Clark Shacklock had taken her by the hand, and was leading her out upon the southern podium. Was Charles throbbing somewhere behind them? In any case, short of pulling out the tooth, nothing can be done for a man with toothache.

Clark was pointing into the vast golden haze beyond which the sea lay, according to the maps. She was almost cracking with a situation she must prepare herself for managing shortly. Because in spite of being youthful and supple, she was also old and brittle. Her smile, she could tell, was becoming a visible tic in her face.

Till her guide decided it was time for her to share his secret 'Down there,' he was still pointing, 'is the house where Pirandello was born.'

'Ohhh!' she moaned spontaneously. 'He does terrify me!

Somebody lent him to me,' she confided, 'while I was at university.' She paused for him to appreciate the significance, then realized this was a secret they had shared already on the drive. 'At first I could only read him in English.' She was babbling now, her tic leaping. 'Till recently – during a course I took – I started on him in Italian. I read – well, after a fashion– *The Rules of the Game*.'

'So you're studying Italian.' Clark smiled.

'Oh, I'm only a lame linguist,' Ivy Simpson protested.

He had a brown, quizzical, or was it a Roman Catholic, eye?

Turning away at that moment Ivy Simpson might have asked, 'Where is Charles?' if the shadow of a pocked column hadn't become Imelda Shacklock.

'I'd like to remind everybody,' Imelda said in her differently inflected American voice, 'we've got three more temples and a long drive back.' She was so composed, or apathetic.

Perhaps only Mrs Shacklock appreciated the three remaining temples. The sun was battering everybody else, though only Mr Shacklock admitted.

Clark groaned. 'Find me a big, moist-leaved plane-tree and a kilo of figs, and let me drink a couple of gallons – of ice-cold water straight from the spring.' In spite of his size, he suggested a dehydrated schoolboy; the heavy gold bracelet dangling from his wrist could do nothing for him.

Ivy Simpson had noticed the bracelet in the beginning; she had seen the medallion, with the name CLARK deeply engraved; she supposed this was a habit peculiar to Americans, and decided she must get used to it.

The room was unchanged, except that the bulb in the acryllic turban no longer functioned. They had to rely on the bed lamps. At once fluff seemed to flower in the feeble gasps fluttering out of the air conditioner.

'Oh, dearest, that drive must have been ghastly for you!'

She was making little whimpering sounds into the fiery gristle of his neck.

Charles reacted not unlike a shaken deck-chair. 'I'd have called it a memorable day, Ivy.' As he righted himself he could have been rejecting a sympathetic wife.

'I'm not saying it wasn't *interesting* – the landscape – the archaeological *sites*. But could you, darling, suffer the Shacklocks?'

'They're not bad. In fact, I liked them.' His Adam's apple supported him.

'Did you? I shouldn't have thought you'd care for them at all. How wrong one can be! She's definitely dull. He's – well, cultivated in a sense. Yes. They both are to some degree. No, I suppose they're not *bad*.'

Remembering the chicken, Ivy Simpson went into the bathroom and cleaned her teeth; she took an Entero-Vioform. Charles grimaced at his reflection in the dressing-table glass. To hide what he saw, he took off his shirt and tested the armpits, to decide whether it would last another day.

'That *cameriera*,' Ivy called, savouring the rich word on her tongue, 'I wonder whether she's going to produce our washing – *domani*? I think she looked too much a Sicilian.'

Charles did not answer, and presently his wife returned, and they lay on their separate beds, their familiar limbs in their familiar underclothes, as though at last in possession of something which had been eluding them.

They dozed.

The following morning Charles Simpson had a relapse, if you could say that of a toothache which, in Ivy's opinion, had never really let up, only it was in Charles's nature to play it down. Now as he lay in the citron light, in the moist Sicilian heat, on the brutal tide of traffic noise, he had a greyer, patient look.

'What is it, Ivy?'

'But what? You're the one who should be able to tell!'
Considering the circumstances, she answered sharply.

On occasions when there hadn't been the remotest possibility
she had imagined herself a widow. She mustn't think about it
now. But grey, but patient: he hadn't shaved yet, of course; it
was only the stubble showing.

Ivy Simpson sat down too emphatically on the edge of the
yellow modernistic bed and the springs whinged. 'Darling,
I'm going down to Alitalia – to book. Better a Roman than a
Sicilian dentist. Wouldn't you agree?'

But Charles visibly recoiled, as though pain had sapped the
natural desire for deliverance. 'Give it another day, Ivy. There's
still so much to see. San Fabrizio alone.'

'How can we see San Fabrizio or anywhere else while you're
lying in this ghastly room?' Her hand made the fluff fly upward.

'You've got the Shacklocks, haven't you?'

'The *Shacklocks*!' She couldn't bear the thought of them this
morning: those white, straining calves; the engraved medallion
on a heavily dangling, gold bracelet.

Ivy Simpson picked up her bag. In spite of the heat, she felt
energetic: her mission demanded it. She took a taxi. The driver
robbed her, as she should have expected of any Sicilian bandit.
She did not care, though pride in her Italian vocabulary was
momentarily hurt.

They were charming at Alitalia. She booked the two seats
for the following day. Hadn't he said *give it another day Ivy*?
Her own instincts might have persuaded her to hasten their
departure, make it that evening at least, if Charles hadn't
wanted to defer, and the man at Alitalia hadn't been so charming. At any rate, she had reserved the seats: her conscience
could feel at rest.

She walked through the streets. The bag she was carrying
under her arm had become a cherished object. (*That old thing
of Imelda Shacklock's: almost a Gladstone.*) She took a bus for

219

some distance. (*My darling Charles to nourish him with love when pasta fails if you could masticate it first without causing revulsion in the patient.*) She walked some more.

In these back streets of crumbling palazzi and cloacal smells, the cold blast from a church doorway might be the greatest danger of all. She must hurry past the churches, the trails of stale incense, the saints seduced by their own torments. Toenails can be torture enough. Would Imelda neglect her toenails while coping with his toothache? Marriages, like teeth, are deceptive.

From luxuriating in her own thoughts, Ivy Simpson's attention was diverted by something attached to this rusty nail, dripping brown, like honeycomb. She was so intent on investigating, she went up, and almost had her nose on the wall, on the bunch of tripe, the knots of intestines, no bees, but flies, sipping at the brown juices as they dripped.

She was not running, tottering. Perhaps she would vomit in the gutter. She didn't; and as she retreated, her mind returned and hovered over the bouquet of brown tripe suspended from its brittle, rusty nail: she was so disgusted.

Naturally she said nothing about the suppurating tripe to her invalid husband. What is more, she decided not to mention the tickets she had in her bag; at this stage the step she had taken might worry or over-excite Charles.

He was looking at her, smiling the smile she knew.

She smiled back. 'Shall we ask them, darling, to send you up some *pasta in brodo*? That will be soft at least.'

'Not yet. It's too hot. Tonight perhaps.' He made the sheet rustle. 'I'll give it a go tonight.'

They exchanged one of the light, token kisses of a relationship founded on mutual understanding.

Then the husband remembered a duty. 'Go down, Ivy,' he advised; 'you don't want to miss your lunch.'

And she did as she was told.

She sat in the dining-room amongst the Dutch, the French, even a few Italians. She stirred a fork furred with cheese in the *lasagne* she couldn't persuade herself to swallow. (Perhaps she should have ordered *agnolotti*.)

From staring at the door through which she must escape, she finally did. Her relief was probably groundless, because anyone as inveterate as the Shacklocks would have set forth on an expedition today too – a conjecture refuted as she crossed the lounge and saw them squeezed out of the lift: their size and the narrow door made simple emergence an elaborate operation. Apart from a nervous and irrational wish not to become involved with them, the thought of missing the ascending lift assumed for Ivy tragic proportions.

Perhaps sensing distress, the Shacklocks looked embarrassed; though large and confidently American, they might have wanted to tiptoe past; their opening words nudged each other.

'Not seeing you anywhere around,' Mrs Shacklock felt her way, 'we guessed you were taking a group tour.'

'It's Selinunte today.' Balanced on the balls of his feet, a subdued Clark ever so slightly toppled as he spoke, with the result that Ivy was admitted to the invisible envelope of warmth with which he was surrounded.

Each Shacklock was smiling a condolent smile, though neither seemed inclined to mention Charles's indisposition, which Ivy supposed natural in anyone as independent, rich, and apparently healthy as Clark and Imelda.

'Hardly up to an excursion today.' Ivy laughed and left it at that.

'We spent the morning doing San Fabrizio.' Mrs Shacklock appeared even less moved than usual.

'That', her husband admitted, 'is something!'

As when he had stood pointing from the Temple of Concord in the direction of Porto Empedocle, he might have been preparing to share a secret with Ivy Simpson, this time a deeper one.

'Though everything is against it, I'm determined to see San Fabrizio!' Mrs Simpson petered out in hoarseness, from meaning what she said, and the flight tickets in the bag beneath her arm.

For an instant, an almost tangible longing flickered out of her towards the wall these non-friends presented, and her knees trembled as they had on her discovering it was flies, not bees, swarming on the combs of oozing tripe.

Then she was gathered together again, and did not really care whether she saw San Fabrizio or not. Hadn't she and Charles read about it, and looked at the photographs, and discussed it rationally in their own home in Wongaburra Road? That was what mattered.

'I hope you enjoy your lunch,' she said, more specifically to Mrs Shacklock, who lowered her thick, creamy eyelids.

'At least we know what we can expect,' Mr Shacklock confided.

As they trod away from a delicate situation – it was obvious they were only too aware of Charles's suffering, but were determined, out of respect for their own well-being, not to inquire – Clark Shacklock looked back smiling at Ivy Simpson. Noticing the tartar staining his otherwise excellent teeth, she knew exactly how they would smell.

Curiously enough the lift was still waiting, when it had seemed inevitable that she would be left behind.

Charles Simpson was immobilized in his siesta dream if it was that and not an extension of his waking fever. Whichever it might be, and however threatening, he tried to prolong his vision, piece it together at the widening cracks. Of course he must lose in the end. The cracks continued widening, whitening like bone. His jaw-bone. His suppurating tooth, in the shape of a bulbous, bursting fig, was the root of the matter. When it was all over, Ivy gave up sitting astride him. There was no longer any necessity. Their only need was to sort out the wreckage littering this long beach: the driftwood, ribs of whales, brine-pickled apples; to select, and construct. Well, no, the structure is of its own choosing, of never-ending white arches.

Actually it is Ivy sitting on this yellow stool looking ahead of her into the mirror, which is also the room they share, permanently. She has put on her dress. She has finished combing her hair. Her cervical vertebrae are unusually salient above the collar of the white dress. She strips the comb of hair, and throws the combings where normally the wastepaper basket would have been standing.

At a time of day into which neither of them fitted perfectly, long past its zenith and far too close to night for a broken dream to amount to more than an immoral luxury, their relationship had never seemed reduced to such heart-freezing fragility.

Ivy said, looking away from him into the dressing-table glass, which meant that she was also looking at him, as he lay in the distance in their small room, 'You must have had a jolly good sleep, darling. Nothing would wake you. Not even my hairbrush when I dropped it.'

'I suppose I must have slept. It's later than usual.' He heard his stubble grate against the pillow; perfection, aesthetic or moral, made him shy, because it was such a chancy affair, whereas he had only ever arrived at the perfect medical solution by comparatively straight, established paths.

Though she had worn it often enough, perhaps it was the white dress making her look so elusive and timeless. She hadn't looked more a girl the day of their meeting on the jetty at Cremorne, her thin mouth traced in what was intended as a firm line. Now, as then, the coral wavered. Only the hair had altered, not so much in style as in tone: the mouse had gone dusty, though that could have been Sicily.

He hoped his love for her never embarrassed Ivy. Possibly it did. She had turned round, still seated on the dressing-table stool, holding the ivory comb in her hand. She was looking noticeably grave, her stare liquid, but that was usual after sleep.

'I'm going out for a little,' she said. 'A breeze has come.'

Yes, the light had changed; its yellow might have seemed congealed, like throat lozenges, if it hadn't moved constantly: he was reminded of the flapping of Moreton Bay fig leaves.

'If it's all the same to you, I'll let you go on your own,' he told her. 'I'll probably get up later, and dress. I think I could face some food tonight.'

'Yes, we'll slip in before the mob.'

Ivy made a habit of sifting words from out of the expressions men use, perhaps thinking it would put her on an equal footing with him. He had often considered how to tell her it introduced what almost amounted to a false note in their relationship, but he had never brought himself to the point; he was afraid of hurting her feelings.

'Something soft, but nourishing.' She was all thoughtfulness. 'And I've heard the Sicilians make exceptionally good ices;' as though there were anything she had heard or read which they hadn't heard or read together. (But marriage is forgetful, from whichever side you look at it.)

Charles is asking, 'Where do you think of going?'

'To the Villa Giulia.' Gravely and without the least hesitation.

'The where?'

'The Villa Giulia,' she repeated more carefully than before, with an accent she hoped would not sound pretentious.

'Isn't that Rome?'

She knew they had both been thinking of the *Etruscan Spouses*, so called, when they were more truthfully Charles and Ivy.

'No, darling.' Her voice had grown fretful now. 'You

remember the gardens along the street? We looked through the railings the first night. I'm sure they're horribly Sicilian, but they're the only breathing space I can think of.'

It was as reasonable as he would have expected. Then she came, she stooped over him, she kissed him, but on the mouth, and that too, he would have expected, though she had never done it before, anyway not at six o'clock.

Ivy Simpson, in her white dress, might have hurried to reach the Villa Giulia if she had not remembered that the farther south the later the gates are closed, and that her legs, for all their apparent youthfulness, might have gone prop prop past the iron railings. So she strolled through the adamantine dust, and this more indigenous manner got her there just as inevitably.

Inside the gardens she glanced round once or twice in spite of a determination not to do so. She would have liked to catch sight of something which convinces. A child, for instance. There were, in fact, bands of children click clacking in different directions. But she had never been much good at children, if she were to be honest: she closed them up. Nor were the trees in this tattered garden more revealing: they had become too dry, too brittle, inside bark which resembled diseased cork or very old basketwork. Only in one corner, where the dust had been replaced by a saucer of mud, apparently the result of flooding from a small ornamental duck pond, a lushness had been achieved, of dark, fleshy leaves, and voices escaping from their normal constriction to curdle and cling on marble benches.

Her gooseflesh broke out. She was too afraid to enter this thicket with its stench of duck-infested mud.

She was even more alarmed to hear what sounded like the roaring of a lion, at close quarters, behind some bushes. What chance would she stand, her breakable legs, her conspicuously white dress, in this small park? And what then would become of Charles?

She noticed that the hitherto random children had begun to stream in the one direction, that of the lion, whose roars were increasing. The other side of a screen of laurels, in one of a row of empty cages, she came across him: bald buttocks, matted mane, one eye extinguished, the survivor still prepared to blaze. As the children tried to climb the loose and irregular net woven out of barbed wire in front of the cage, the tired lion lashed and roared. In spite of his general dilapidation, his jaws might have been dripping blood, his throat choking with raw flesh. Overjoyed by the smell of danger at a safe distance, or out of contempt for shabbiness, the children climbing the barbed wire were baiting their prey, one with a bulrush, others with branches torn from the near-by laurels. A group of parents, skin and teeth made yellower by the black they were wearing, stood smiling their apathy, or else approval.

Ivy Simpson knew she ought to do something – but what?

'Non avete pietà per questo animale disgraziato che soffre?' Her Italian came out stilted, when it should have soared passionately.

One or two of the black adults smiled and frowned at the same time, no more than half comprehending the crazy *Inglesa*, who was waving arms thin as wishbones, while her laughably insignificant breasts palpitated inside a dress more suited to a girl at her first communion.

To make things worse, Ivy herself knew that her compassion had been learnt, like her Italian, and that she was distressed, or excited, by some more personal contingency.

So she moved on, along the row of empty cages, towards where he was standing, mopping the hair at the nape of his neck, while staring with exaggerated interest at the bars in front of him. This last amongst the unoccupied cages was occupied, she now saw, by a sick, skulking wolf.

Ivy Simpson immediately said, 'Isn't it disgraceful! What

can be done?' She spoke too loudly so as to be heard above the roars, as she gesticulated in the direction of the lion-baiting.

'Nothing can be done,' he assured her. 'If we were natives, I guess it would be different. We'd do even less.'

They laughed together in enjoyment of their superior foreign status, then fell to observing in silence the cage in front of which they were standing.

The starved and worm-infested wolf, Ivy Simpson suddenly realized, was as irrelevant as the lion farther down. The only point in the sick wolf's existence was that she and Clark Shacklock should be standing together in front of his cage. He would cease to exist as soon as they turned their backs.

She wondered briefly whether she should comment on their meeting to her companion, but decided not to. Harping on coincidence, if it wasn't, might have turned the situation into a joke, when life as well as damnation hinges on seriousness.

Clark Shacklock seemed to understand. He wasn't wearing his jokey look. He was sweating so seriously, the water bounded off him in blobs, and great waves of heat, rising from his fleshy depths, broke on Ivy almost as though she had been a rock.

When he offered with some relevance, 'We might, I thought, drive up to San Fabrizio before dinner. It's a sight nobody ought to miss.'

'There's no reason why I should miss it. But weren't you there already this morning?'

'On a first visit Imelda checks the inventory.'

'In that case,' Ivy agreed.

If no reference was made to the absence of Charles and Imelda, she could at least reassure herself that she and Clark each knew that Charles was sick.

As the moist grey heat streamed past the open windows of the car, she was moved to remark, 'I've read that the panorama is superb.'

'If you can see it for the haze.'

It seemed doubtful that they would: the fumes of the city were rising below them as solid as fungus.

'Oh, I do *hope*,' was jolted out of Ivy Simpson as the car, reaching a curve, must have flung her hand between Clark Shacklock's thighs.

He could not have put it there himself, for he was glancing at what lay for the moment in his lap, his detachment too pronounced, his surprise too obvious: at this faintly freckled, woman's skin; at the ring time had thinned and refined, while shrivelling the finger which was wearing it.

If it had been her own impulse, it would have appeared a vulgar one, Ivy realized, though she was no great expert on vulgarity: she ignored farts, and refused to react to men's jokes when they verged on coarseness; nor had she ever been drunk, while sometimes wondering what it would feel like. It was not her own mechanism, but the jolting Fiat, which knocked the non-giggles out of her. (How much more reliable their own solid Rover!) In fact the only out-and-out laughter pursuing them round the curves was, not surprisingly, Aubrey Tyndall's: Father would have wanted this.

'Did you say "before dinner"?' she gasped when again in possession of her hand.

This time it was Clark Shacklock, a large man, who had the giggles (or was it farts?) shaken out of him. 'The *agnolotti*,' he bellowed, 'at the *Gattopardo!*'

The recurring curve in the road laid her head on his shoulder, but a bump helped her recover it at once.

Oh my grey my suffering husband! For several kilometres Ivy Simpson sat recalling her actual life. But what is actual?

She held herself erect in spite of the jolting and her embrocated thoughts, and soon they were drawing up in one of the spaces authorized for cars in front of the *duomo*.

'The cloister first!' Clark would have flung himself out more youthfully if part of him hadn't caught on something.

Ivy emerged with greater strategic caution, lowering her head, stretching the legs which could still surprise her pleasurably. (She had never understood his love for his Emma his whippet little more than an emblem of chilly grace and controlled movement *perfection* he called her.)

When she had patted her hair she said, 'I wonder whether I shall be disappointed.'

It must have made Clark Shacklock anxious. 'The cloister's more austere,' he warned. 'But wait till you see the *duomo*. It's my guess you'll be bowled over – not by the façade – by the apparition you'll find inside.'

She shook herself after that, for having behaved like a capricious whippet, and shivered in advance for the apparition promised her.

Aubrey Tyndall was allowing them to move decently, primly in her own case, towards the cloister. She might even catalogue the details by heart for poor Charles who was having the toothache.

Ivy Simpson noticed her hands, and knew she had always despised them, whether skinny-old in a wedding ring, or slithering on Aubrey's shoulder, or picking her nose as a nail-bitten schoolgirl. *Not my Lalique Ivy!* The same hands dropped Mother's precious bowl which *call me Aubrey* had scorned.

'I expect it will all be fascinating,' she assured him, and linked an arm with his thicker, fleshier one.

They advanced by synchronized strides on the cloister she might find austere.

Clark looked over his shoulder once, and she forgave him; it might have presaged worse if he had marched too straight and too jauntily. As for herself, she didn't look back. She unlinked her arm, bowed her head, and dabbed at her sticky eyes, not with a handkerchief, but a tissue she found in her bag, and which she let fall after use in spite of her own disapproval.

The cloister of San Fabrizio was, if anything, more austere than he had told her to expect. The rays from a copper disc were striking through tumid cloud and gathering dusk to pierce its heart – without drawing blood, it would seem: the baked earth of a wilting garden was scored with fissures, and only plants able to endure permanent drought and complete neglect had survived the Sicilian summer. Coupled columns elegantly twisted should have writhed with sensuous life instead of standing passively. Here and there the late sunlight did kindle a glitter, of glass rather than fire, in the eyes with which a creator had endowed their stone forms, but more often than not, empty sockets returned a grey, stony stare. Hoarse Arab affirmations of faith would have echoed through this cloister more convincingly, one felt, than the rippled ecstasies of Christian mystics.

'I am not disappointed. It is different, though,' she protested, with the smile, and in the voice, of the tasteful amateur of culture.

Clark's laughter was appropriately lacking in mirth. 'Wait! This isn't what we came here for!'

Again confidence faltered in her: would she be equal to the *duomo*? could she destroy enough of what she loved to come to grips with what she feared? the *Godhead*: as a mere word leaping at her from off the printed page, it made her turn over quickly, to escape something far beyond what Charles and she had agreed to find acceptable.

So she was rattled by Clark's reminder. 'No,' she answered, giggling; 'not what we came for!' To snigger gave her the courage to become still further unlike herself; this way she might overcome the remorse of an Arab asceticism which lingered in the draughty cloister alongside her own rational principles.

'I can't guarantee you'll like it,' he was practically shouting, 'if the Romanesque doesn't turn you on.'

She thought she could detect a trembling in him, and put out a dry hand to confirm. When she had hoped to make use of a resilient, rubbery voluptuary to collaborate with her in a moral suicide more brilliant than any her mind had hitherto conceived, was he planning to lead her to safety over some frail suspension bridge of his own?

'That remains to be seen,' she decided.

Renewed spasms of sniggers on her part bumped her against him. That they should stay pressed together longer than was physically congruous, her burning drought against his streaming shirt, and yes – *rubbery* breasts, was less shocking than reassuring.

'Hold hard, girlie!' Whether or not she had actually heard it as he withdrew, her assurance was increased.

She could now face the *duomo*, and whatever might be in store for her in the way of illumination or damnation.

'But *Clark*,' she heard that her r had perceptibly altered as she became more adaptable, 'this isn't the *way*, is it? Where are we going, Cla*rr*k?'

'The terrace first. The lights should be coming out.'

She complained, but followed, mumbling grumbles. He might have been dragging her away from the dance at which she was fated to disgrace herself, his heavy, moist hand wrapping her dry, brittle one, her white skirt brushing against the dusk, the cymbidium leaves, the knowing laughter from jam-packed benches. She stumbled so clumsily. (What if she developed polio? In Sicily!)

'There's magnificence for you!' He was offering her a different genre, or the opportunity to make the end a truly physical one, splattered on rock.

'It's cold, Clark.' Arranging a fretful, invisible gauze. 'We ought to go inside the *duomo*. We'll find it *chiuso* if we put it off much longer.'

A breeze had come, dispersing some of the steam from the

cauldron of the city. Lights simmered. Immediately around them a smell of growth, as well as rotting, assaulted the nostrils. It could have been black hair hanging from pockets in a giant ficus which began rustily swinging in the night. Her breasts might have been swelling behind the pleats of the white dress.

'You're right. We ought to go in. We don't want to miss vespers.' Was Clark's voice crossing itself in the dark?

Men should be braver. They were on the whole. It was she who was jittering with terror, as though her father had proposed an indecency of which she might be capable. She would have to be, on the heights, or in the chasms, towards which she was being propelled by her own choice.

They scuttled through the thickening dark as fast as her club foot or incipient polio allowed, and reached the door which was standing open for them.

As they entered she sidestepped. A loathing returned out of childhood, when one of them had flown out of the fly-proof meat-safe and hit her in the face. She dreaded what the carapace contained. And here it was – her *scarafaggio*! a black one. She could not avoid she was grinding it into smearing it over the jewels of marble.

After Charles had shaved (it was tricky on the swollen side) he pasted his armpits with the deodorant stick, and put on the dark suit they had sent for pressing, more out of habit than for any celebration. He was wearing a dark tie too, with narrow white stripe, which might have been a club or school tie, but wasn't. (Ivy had bought it for him, thinking it was something he would like.) While sprinkling eau-de-Cologne on a handkerchief to carry in his breast pocket, it occurred to him, looking in the glass, that strangers, particularly foreign ones, might suspect him of being in disguise. It was partly his lopsided face. He had been having a toothache, he remembered.

He went in to wash his hands a second time. Whatever he did, it seemed, became a ritual of sorts: he might have been preparing to examine a patient.

Ivy was good with patients; they sent flowers to her telephone voice. Going down in the narrow lift he was almost suffocated by a perfume. But burst out in time. To find the urnful of tuberoses, and a live bee working their plastic flesh.

The lounge was practically deserted. Unavoidably, one or two Dutch. In a far corner, the woman, their American, sat reading a book (two books in fact), her capacious leather bag lying on the carpet beside her. If he did not approach her it was to some extent out of respect for her un-American activity, but more because friendship was something Ivy conducted for them both.

Seated in a corner opposite this Mrs – Scudamore? Charles Simpson ordered a Scotch and soda, and expected the worst. (If Ivy had been with him they might have enjoyed a *Campari – so much cheaper darling*. Hardly, but he wouldn't have contradicted her for the world.)

He began waiting, well, it was for Ivy, then they would go in to dinner. An eclipse of the moon had been predicted: he had witnessed several, and one of the sun at the age of twelve through a piece of glass smoked over a candle flame. Several times the end of the world had passed him by, till now it was prophesied again by an organization which busied itself with esoteric matters. Why was he born an unbeliever? He wished he could have at any rate half believed – not in God; that would be unnecessarily pretentious – but in the end of the world, for instance.

He cleared his throat and wondered whether he should go across and speak to the American woman, but didn't.

Would Ivy, in those ragged gardens, remember to look for the moon? He was sorry he hadn't reminded her. If they hadn't discussed the world's end, it was because each would have taken it for granted that the other had dismissed such an irrational event. Nature and their education had miraculously absolved them from looking for apocalyptic solutions.

Only in dreams, or half sleep, or spasms of pain, did Charles Simpson experience doubts. But the toothache had left him temporarily.

Now he was sitting on the edge of his chair, not so much contemplating, as examining his hands. He liked to think of them as practical rather than sensitive, for that again would have been pretentious; if they were not creative, they had in numerous instances helped prolong life, whether that was desirable or not, in the present light.

In the present light he was shivering, so he locked his hands, and glanced across at the American woman to see whether she had noticed. It was unlikely that she would have. Ivy never had. Not the least trace of blood on his thoughts. His murders were all too methodically conceived. His only real fear was that the official voice might lay at his door some compulsive mayhem he had committed unconsciously: little girls; old unsuspecting women with pulses in their goitrous throats; Ivy whose love was too precious – her trachea glugging and spluttering in the dust.

He glanced again at Mrs – Shacklock? but she continued turning the pages of her books, as though the answers might be contained in the smaller of the two. He was surprised that she, that almost anyone but Charles Simpson, should find themselves in need of confirmation.

Presently he went over and asked, 'Did you know that an eclipse is predicted for tonight?'

'I believe Clark said something about it.'

She smiled, but Charles Simpson could not feel it was intended for him in particular. At the same time she laid down the book she was holding, and stretched her arms above her head, and pressed her white, muscular calves in a curve against

the chair, as though she found his presence in her orbit fortuit-
ous rather than deliberately suppliant.

Charles consulted his wrist. 'If we went outside we might
get a look at it.'

'I'll leave that to Clark. Astronomy isn't one of my subjects.'

'Which are your subjects?' He found himself sitting down,
speaking like a turgid pedant, grimacing with what must
appear amateurish gallantry.

Imelda Shacklock said, 'I guess I'm ignorant on the whole.'

He was sitting almost knee to knee with this creamy goddess,
whose composure inspired her yawns, the flexing of her calves,
even her professed ignorance, with a vegetable dignity.

'And that's how Clark wants it,' she brooded. 'I can learn
up anything he – or anybody else – expects of me, because I'm
not all that dumb. But I'm content, I've found, just with being.
Why not? Isn't that a worthy occupation?'

Whether she was inspired, or simply vegetable, he felt
himself to be the ignorant one. Though Imelda Shacklock
seemed unconscious of it. Perhaps she was too intent on what
she liked to refer to as 'being'.

'I was happiest,' she said, 'just after we married and went to
live in Vermont. We had a frame house, and not much money
– or not much compared with later. I used to bake our bread.
The smell of bread and the smell of snow – those are the two
purest smells. We were snowed in most of the winter, and I'd
put food for the animals that came. I got to know the animals.
And I was familiar with every inch of the road to town,
from the miles I walked humping the supplies home on my
back.'

'What about your husband – didn't he help?'

'Yes. But Clark tires of things. And he was trying to be a
writer then.'

'Didn't he become one?'

'Oh, no. He was fortunate to realize early on. And came into the money, and bought the Burtonville Goya. You already know about that.' Her big creamy face seemed to take it for granted that he was a member of the cult.

'It's always a matter of how you see it,' she went on, 'of what you make it. Goya anyway – even the real – isn't everybody's dish. That doesn't cancel him out, does it? If it did, it would mean the world is a sense missing – of poetry – or madness – or whatever. So my Burtonville Goya must be allowed to exist for me, and perhaps one or two others – because it's one of our windows. You see, don't you? Clark won't let himself.'

Charles Simpson did not see, but because he could not understand art and his deficiency made him nervous, he answered 'Yes' indistinctly enough for it to be interpreted as 'No'; in this way his conscience was eased.

'Clark would like to worship,' Imelda Shacklock continued, 'but he can't accept the flaws. Whether in a work of art. Or men. Particularly in women.' (In different circumstances Charles Simpson might have felt lulled by the goddess's marble attitudes, most of all by the palimpsest of her confidences.) 'It makes him restless: he's always off on another voyage of discovery.' She looked at Charles with a gravity the more intense for being detached. 'Whether it's actual travel, and God knows, we never stop. But I also mean in his personal relationships. And the paintings he collects. After he gave up all idea of ever becoming a writer, he thought there might be a painter in him. But he always ends up where he started: obsessed and inhibited by flaws, and the greatest flaw of all – himself.'

Just then Charles Simpson conceived such a personal vision of Clark Shacklock he might have painted him if he had known how to begin: the eye feverish from perpetual search, lips polished by too many relationships, and a pair of transparent testicles, one of them slung considerably lower than the other.

Charles coughed for his own thoughts.

'I love him,' Imelda said with that contralto seriousness in which American women specialize.

Charles and Ivy would never have spoken openly of 'love', not together, let alone to a stranger.

So he asked, 'Do you find the Fiat a satisfactory car? In performance,' he added unnecessarily.

Mrs Shacklock dealt with the question as though it were the natural outcome of their conversation. 'Fair enough. Considering it's a rented machine. If it was your own, that would be another situation.' She spoke with the same seriousness she had used while dwelling on the subject of her husband.

Then she turned her wrist to look at her watch, an ordinary one she was wearing on a man's old sloppy strap. 'I guess Clark will have run up to take another look at San Fabrizio. There are those who consider him superficial. But I know, Dr Simpson – I ought to know by now – just what makes Clark Shacklock tick. Clark is a law unto himself and his own sensitivity. Whether it's a church or – or a *person* – he's got to explore them in his own fashion.'

Charles Simpson sat farther forward on the edge of his chair. 'Does he share his reactions with you?'

'I don't encourage it,' Imelda Shacklock said, 'never ever. A sensitive soul's reactions are too sensitive, don't you think? Besides, if you take a stick and start stirring around, you can fetch out something which doesn't appeal. As we know from experience, don't we, Doctor? from experience of our own selves.'

Mrs Shacklock shook back her loosely strapped watch to where she wore it, on her wrist's under side. On the same hand she was wearing that slumberous stone which must have cost a discreet fortune. Charles Simpson felt tempted to ask whether the ring was a love token, or simply an object with which her husband had formed a sensitive, but temporary, attachment. It was a thought which might have amused Ivy, in different circumstances.

Ivy Simpson and Clark Shacklock were received inside this jewel of light and refracted sound. The words of psalms were falling slumberously as wax (... *il suo cuore è saldo perché confida nel Signore, il suo animo è tranquillo; non temerà ed infine vedrà la rovina dei nemici...*) when they were not ascending in smoke (... *ma il desiderio dell'empio è destinato a perire ...*) Here and there an individual word scintillated perceptibly before it splintered into fragments of glass. The saints primly contained by their golden mirrors might not have believed all they had heard and witnessed over the centuries, least of all in the present. She averted her face from them. If she succeeded in fainting, she would be carried out, and avoid the shame reserved for her; though of course what she feared worst of all was the alternative: a shaky apotheosis under the eye of the Pantocrator. (How would she ever confess her apostasy to Charles?) Lie down then along this row of chairs. Too tidy for a faint, it might be accepted as the prelude to a coronary. But her other plan weighed so heavily on her, it was this which must prevail. Aubrey would make sure that Clark didn't miss his cue, one gross male prompting another to fall into the trap she had helped devise. In advance she could hear chairs creaking, rush bottoms disintegrating, legs tottering giving way under the double weight. Faces turn, breath hisses as the silken ladder of liturgy is snapped. Eyes hunger to assist at a common adultery, the officiating priest most involved of all on finding himself under instruction.

Actually the priest, another fat, hairy man, continued concentrating on his office, his flock of the kind one would have expected: elderly or crippled women, two or three thin, fluting men, a girl suffering from acne, another from chlorosis, a pair of nuns, the contours of their backs straining against their blue habits, only the forehead and the eyes of a brachycephalous dwarf.

(*Am I one of them? If I am only faintly prospective I must make every effort not to be.*)

Clark Shacklock had lowered his voice out of respect for the devotions of the faithful. 'From one standpoint, Ivy, we couldn't have come at a worse time. We can't very well barge through to the apse, and I'd like to show you, amongst other things, the sarcophagi. Still, it's the overall impression, I think you'll agree, that counts at San Fabrizio. Daylight and a guidebook don't do justice to it.'

If he were preparing to convert her through the reverential humdrum she would resist him on his own ground.

Screwing up her mouth and eyes as she stared heavenward, Ivy Simpson ricked her neck. 'Architecturally,' she mumbled, 'it's very fine. I'll grant you that.'

Charles Shacklock boggled so hugely she might have been his wife. 'You're surely the first person who had reservations about San Fabrizio.'

'Not reservations. I have my limitations, Clark, even if you despise me for them.'

'But the mosaics alone!' To persuade her he fumbled for her hand. 'See here in the nave – The Story of Genesis ...'

Restricted by the observances of others (... *come era in principio, ora e sempre e nei secoli dei secoli ...*) their progress was crabwise.

'And there's The Evangelizing of St Peter and St Paul. In the sanctuary – if we could take a proper look – which we can't, all considered – we'd find a very beautiful Passion.'

(*Oh the Passion frightening word the tears of blood you have never shed stillborn is not a real one not a dead husband either in that incredible event you might bow your head along with the dust-coloured gentlewomen the cripples the male lost souls and learn from nuns how to climb a ladder of prayer.*)

'... but the most magnificent of all, Ivy, is the Pantocrator.'

239

This was not why she had come to San Fabrizio with Clark Shacklock, the commonplace, perspiring American. She would not look at the Pantocrator. She would rather shut her eyes tight, close her mind to intellectual duplicity. Or discover her own, vulgar, fleshly self.

She dropped her bag. Unlike Mother's Lalique bowl, it didn't break, but she knew it was a measure Aubrey would approve of.

Here was Clark Shacklock groping with her to retrieve the bag from the Cosmati paving ('particularly fine', she had read in advance in her own guidebook). It was herself, however, clawing at Clark as though his solid bulk might save. Under the Pantocrator's eye. Surrounded by the scraggy saints. Words rigid words ascending (... *Tu della luce splendida Creatore mirabile che tra la luce fulgida al mondo desti origine* ...)

'What is it, Ivy? Aren't you well?'

No, she was sick.

'Yes, I'm well,' she snickered. 'It is only – I will tell you – Clark.'

She could have vomited over the brown tripe the two of them were preparing to hang from ancient rust-eaten nails in the glass *duomo*, but instead she was dragging Him (her Lover) into this obscure side chapel, stumbling over the dust-clogged carpet of rucked-up marble.

Clark was panting. 'I'll say you've got an instinct. This may not be in the same class as Caravaggio, but it's not bad for a Reni. Let's give him credit where credit's due.'

In the dark chapel it was almost impossible to see the saint's painted face (her instinctive less than *scarafaggio*) and only from close up the filmic expressions of any human one.

For a reason he too must have begun to understand, they were both filled with a suppressed laughter. She felt his corrugations of fat rub against her pleasingly.

I was never credited with the fat self I have been disguising, Ivy now knew.

Her laughter broke and ricochetted.

One of the emaciated gentlewomen taking part in that other ceremony beneath the high altar pointed her nose in the direction of the irreverent noises she might have heard. Her nostrils scented a blasphemy, the bony structure accused, or as much of it as you could see for lace the colour of incense with which she was coiffed. Till sanctity or partial deafness intervened: the lady was appeased.

Whereas obscene laughter continued to inflate Ivy Simpson. 'Sponge *fingers!*' It burst out of her like ripped rubber.

Clark Shacklock's eyes were glittering between shared hilarity and suppressed horror. Whether he realized or not, the thin and upright worshippers were of a predominating beige powdered with light, the exceptions being the dwarf, whose monstrous head remained a dark world of its own, and of course the blue, larded nuns.

What he could never have understood was that the laughter bouncing her against him was causing her pain, as was memory, dinning into her the words *how a Tyndall ever sired a sponge finger I'm at a loss to know Ivy* after those full lips had rejected the insipid stuff which roused his disgust.

As Clark Shacklock was sucked into the whirlpool of her only half-controlled laughter, he was clutching at Ivy Simpson. Or was it she at him? In the darkened chapel it was hard to tell. Certainly she needed support, however brutally his buttons grazed her.

'We mustn't lose our balance!' she hiccupped.

Several anonymous faces were turned in their direction from the world of light. But faith no doubt protected the worshippers from contagion. Even while the silken ladder spun by the officiating priest was plunging under them, they were in a position to dismiss fantasies. As for the priest himself, his own voice had probably prevented him hearing a word. The voice, becoming increasingly real, hammered on her conscience like fists.

On the other hand her companion, it seemed, had caught her sickness: she could tell from the texture, the fever of his cheek, as they heaved and ducked together amongst the extinguished candles of this infernal grotto. Their surroundings smelt of dead wax. While outside, the glass saints, who should have been recoiling, fluctuating, held their original attitudes of grace.

Wasn't it time, surely, for the faithful to advance and receive their reward?

'When do they communicate?' she asked with fearful hope.

Put that way it would have sounded less reprehensible, more Protestant, if not sociological, to Charles, should he have overheard.

'Never communion at vespers!' Clark Shacklock spoke with authority.

She was convinced he was the RC she had suspected; so she was committing the triple blasphemy: against her honest husband, their enlightenment, and most grievously, their love for each other.

Now only Aubrey Tyndall was laughing: the sensual man who had never recognized her in his lifetime, but whom she had nourished inside her for all of hers.

All that was happening should have been enough, but she visualized the nuns' greed as the pitiful wafer collapsed in their mouths, and regretted her lost opportunity to blaspheme in addition against the Holy Ghost.

Her own hunger, laughter, or whatever, had made her slobber. She could feel it on her chin.

'... Ivy, this is something serious. This is where I fetch the ...'

With bell, book, and candle!

'No, Clark, I am truly – I – you must stay with me and we shall discuss – that is the only way to approach any serious personal matter – can't you see?'

He couldn't, not in the dark.

'But you're not well. You're sick, Ivy!'

At dusk level she could smell his words, those of a frightened man. Like two landed fish, they were lunging together, snout bruising snout, on the rucked-up Cosmati paving. She wrapped herself around him, her slimy thighs, the veils of her fins, as it had been planned, seemingly, from the beginning, while the enormous tear swelled to overflowing in the glass eye focused on them from the golden dome.

So we float conjoined long after the lights are doused at times it is I who sit astride this giant porpoise at others my fragile bones are supporting an intolerable weight strength comes with degradation it appears the lower you sink the easier to survive while actually floating high expelled into an outer darkness which does not obstruct vision since I have become vision itself gaining height through the sooty masses of leaves above the only slightly abrasive towers and dome I can look down always floating I can see inside the box in which He my Dearly Beloved Husband has thrown off the sheet is rising from amongst the limp grey wrinkles on the yellow bed offering Himself afresh for sacrifice under the extinct acryllic object.

She could feel the pattern in the Cosmati paving with the tips of her returning fingers. By now the great edifice would have been in darkness if its glass walls had not given off a perpetual glimmer. That it was not completely deserted she could also tell because somebody was breathing above and around her. She felt what must be a bunch of bananas, or large hand, fumbling with her face, then a cold, heavy – *bracelet*? dangled across one of her cheeks.

'Are you okay, Ivy?' Clark Shacklock was inquiring rather tremulously.

'Where are we?' she asked as it became only too apparent.

'Exactly where we were.'

'But *dark*!'

'Yes. And we've probably been locked in.'

She was so annoyed she almost bit the hand still dabbling in her cheek. 'What? And you didn't stop them?'

'To tell the truth, I was too relieved to find they could overlook us. I lay low.'

She began feeling her way, first past this man's thighs – he was so substantial there was no avoiding Clark Shacklock – then through the faintly luminous darkness.

'What on earth will Charles ...? My husband is expecting his dinner!'

'They'll both be wondering why we're late,' Clark Shacklock chanted back; the walls made plainsong out of it.

Ivy Simpson was charging at chairs: some of them she sent squealing and skittering across the marble on slate-pencil legs; others crashed in blocks, and in some cases, were smashed, it sounded.

The Shacklock voice came bowling after her. 'Put the brakes on, Ivy! If we separate, there's no knowing when we'll find each other.'

She was so desperate she had to blame somebody. 'You could have prevented us getting into a mess like this. So you'll have to get us out. There must be a door, isn't there? for an emergency?' It did not seem in any way peculiar that her voice should be shouting inside the deserted *duomo* at this unreliable, in every way undesirable, stranger.

They continued, separately, assaulting darkness. A metal bird, poised for flight, plunged its beak into Ivy Simpson's shoulder. If she broke a limb it would not be an American but Charles her husband who would care.

'Ivy?'

The noisome *Clark* had found her and was again taking her hand. 'Don't lose your head. We're more likely to find a way out if we stick together.'

Prudence alone persuaded her to accept his advice; after which they blundered as one, though without design. There had never been any, had there? not even by honest daylight – only a hopeful blindness. So they continued stumbling, and stubbing themselves, hand in hand like lovers, the love frightened out of them.

He thought he remembered a minor door, if they could reach it, somewhere near the sanctuary.

'Oh? Well, of course there must be a door – DOORS! What if a priest got locked in?'

When she was almost glad to have him with her, Clark Shacklock said, 'I guess a priest would settle down to a night of prayer.'

She could not bear this man, but had to submit to his sweaty hand.

'Think of waking with the saints,' he encouraged, 'slowly surfacing, like fish in a tank. Then, shaking off the water. And catching fire.'

Oh, she couldn't endure it! At least Charles would know that something unavoidable had detained her. But would he imagine – oh God! as she would in similar circumstances – that she was dead?

She asked as sulkily as she could, because it was this odious American, 'What are you doing?' when it was too evident.

Clark Shacklock had lit his lighter. He was standing holding it below his once rosy jowls, on which fright and sweat must have fertilized the black stubble.

This was the immediate foreground of her vision; beyond it the scraggy legs, the sculptural skirts of the canonized, stood flaming in their glass eternity.

And the little bronze door.

'Oh, Charles – *Clark*,' she whimpered, 'do you think we'll be able to open it?'

If necessary break every nail of her hitherto ineffectual

fingers never expect anything of anyone else least of all this incidental male.

Actually, she only slightly grazed a knuckle, and it was Clark Shacklock who drew the bolts. She needed no further help in escaping from the smell of dark, dormant mould, into the other, stirring and spreading, fungoid darkness.

'Wasn't it too easy in the end?' he shakily asked.

She tried to mump an answer, and finally succeeded, 'I can't think what my husband will be thinking – poor darling – and his tooth – waiting for dinner. He tries to eat, but even *pasta* is painful in the state he's in. You can imagine,' she concluded, out of convention.

Clark Shacklock said, 'Imelda isn't likely to worry. I'm what you'd call erratic in my habits. She's conditioned to it after all this time.'

Mrs Simpson was feeling weaker by now. Well, it wasn't any wonder.

Mr Shacklock remembered while sorting his keys beside the rented car, 'You frightened the shit out of me. But it was fine, baby, wasn't it? San Fabrizio – in any circumstances. The Dionysiac overtones are something Imelda has never learnt to appreciate.'

Above them a dirty, misshapen moon was throbbing back. Mrs Simpson could not see, but knew, that his disgusting teeth must be grinning at her over the moist roof of the car.

'I don't quite get what you mean,' her level voice confessed.

She might not have spoken at all if she had thought he would offer to explain; explanations were for herself and Charles, with whom she had always been in agreement on almost every point.

The lounge had never looked so empty or so impersonal. A night porter (the rude one) had decided to withhold individuality from the two persons who were pushing at the glass doors, coming in from the outer world. Mrs Simpson was grateful for her anonymity. She could not remember that either she or Mr Shacklock had in any way tidied themselves since their escape from the *duomo*, and as one who set store by neatness, she could suddenly imagine the state of her hair, creases in her frock, dust – no, positively rocks, jostling and rumbling as they clung to her frail shoulderblades.

She settled her shoulders. Her companion was fortunately no more than a vague sponginess galumphing behind her.

Almost at once she caught sight of Charles's head, his neck. Seated where he was, he had his back to her. The fact that his swollen cheek was hidden made the situation more normal. She would have pounced on him, and shown her affection and relief by kissing the nape of that neck, only she might have trembled, and the neck itself deterred her with what she recognized as a Byzantine austerity. (Remember to share her insight with Charles; it amused, more, it impressed him whenever she translated perceptions of actuality into terms of art.)

Then, too, Mrs Simpson was restrained by her glimpse of the farthest corner of the lounge, directly opposite the position her husband Charles had taken up. Mrs Shacklock was reading – no, she was studying a book. The smaller volume could have been a dictionary, only a pocket one, however. Mrs Simpson envied the composure, she was impressed by the concentration, in the round, creamy face, while equally, she felt repelled by the full, stockingless calves pressed against the skirt of the chair as the woman continued sitting, sideways and oblivious.

Under the nose of the grumpy porter, and herself aware that her stiff figure always made spontaneity appear somewhat artificial, Mrs Simpson decided to risk the large gesture. 'You poor things, you can only have imagined we had some dreadful accident!' She could almost feel her skirt twirl as she stretched her mouth as wide as it would go.

Just then Mr Shacklock advanced into the spot waiting for him. 'We ran up to San Fabrizio – it seemed a pity to waste the opportunity when Ivy here hadn't seen it.' He too was smiling, but with a physical conviction which came more naturally to him.

If Mrs Shacklock smiled less, it was because she had remained half with the book she was laying down on her lap. 'That's what I expected,' she said, and at the same time raised her face and her lowered eyelids, not so much towards the individual mortals dependent on her grace, as for a more abstract audience

Mrs Simpson decided she had been right in the beginning, and that Mrs Shacklock was congenitally stupid.

The Shacklocks! Her poor Charles was her first and only concern. She turned and he was coming towards her. If she had meant to see whether the swelling in his jaw had to any extent subsided, it was his eyes she looked at: to confirm that their respect for truth had remained undamaged.

Charles said quite simply, 'You've come! But a good thing you went when you had the offer.'

He put out a hand, and she took it, more casually than she might have if the Shacklocks had not been present. She identified the dry grasp and the finger joints (both the Simpsons were dry-handed, and in the early stages of arthritis, so Dr Simpson had diagnosed).

If she decided not to inquire after the toothache, for the moment at least, again it was on account of the Shacklocks.

Instead she said, 'What I'm looking forward to, more than anything, is a bath!' She laughed because the most banal statements frequently embarrassed her. 'How cool you manage to look, Mrs Shacklock!' She laughed some more.

After weighing her reply just perceptibly, Mrs Shacklock must have decided she could lay no claim to virtue. 'I have done nothing all evening to overheat myself,' she declared.

'I've been sitting here improving my Italian – we hope – on a night when the air conditioner works.'

'But you didn't tell us you know Italian!' Surprise and enthusiasm prevented Mrs Simpson from sounding put out.

'Why should I? It's the least of my accomplishments,' Mrs Shacklock answered.

Mrs Simpson, who always restrained her immediate desire to look at the titles of books she caught her friends, and even strangers, holding, in this case couldn't resist asking, 'I do wonder what you are reading.'

'*I Promessi Sposi.*'

'Ah yes, one of the classics.' Gravity had settled on Mrs Simpson. 'But tedious, I've heard. I've been told that Italians themselves are often unable to stay the course.'

'I shall try,' Mrs Shacklock said. 'And am something of a stayer.'

It seemed that each couple had been waiting for the other to take the lift; from the vacuum the lounge provided for them, there could not have been any other way out. Finally it was the Simpsons who pressed the button, fumbling at it simultaneously.

The narrow aluminium booth jostled them worse than ever tonight. The glare made Ivy close her eyes.

While Charles suggested, or the lift jerked it out of him, 'I don't see why we should stay on and let bloody Sicily destroy us. You look a wreck, Ivy.'

This was the point, their being at last alone together, where she should have inquired about the toothache; but she didn't: she was too grateful for his concern.

'Yes, it would be foolish, wouldn't it?' she had to agree.

She would have the rest of life in which to caress a throbbing cheek – mentally, that is; physical demonstrations were not in their line.

'Yes,' she repeated, when her throat had become fully

unstuck, 'I did book – tentatively – seats on the midday flight tomorrow – in case we decided we couldn't endure it any longer.'

She opened her eyes. The narrowness of the lift made it more or less inevitable that Charles should be looking at her. Her tendency to prudence was a quality she knew he had always appreciated.

'But the laundry, Ivy – don't forget the laundry.' He looked quite anxious.

'No. I haven't forgotten the laundry.' She had, in fact, forgotten it completely. 'We'll ask for it early. They'll have to give it to us.'

'They'll have to give it. Though there's nothing like the twenty-four-hour service the brochure promises.'

As they were standing with their backs to the door, they might not have noticed it had opened if the faintest sighing had not invaded their aluminium inferno.

If she had forgotten to inquire about his toothache, it was because she must remember to ask for the laundry in the morning, and because on this, their last night (pray God it was) she must compose the letter to Clark Shacklock. There was no real reason why she should write a letter to a chance acquaintance in a foreign hotel, except that it happened to be the way Mother had brought her up (*to tidy dear as much as to express formal appreciation doesn't cost anything*). Well, nobody could accuse her of untidiness; and as the wife of a professional man, she could not afford to give way to a vulgar impulse of any kind, cultivate forgetfulness, or indulge in the blowsier emotions.

At one point she awoke from her night of exhausting semi-sleep, with such a thump and in such a position, it was not surprising she was left with the lingering impression of a long, slippery fish. She must have made a noise, too. But Charles – *my dearest* – continued to sleep as only men seem able.

Dear Mr Shacklock she would write. Or expand it to include the woman? Of course she might write to Mrs Shacklock, and leave him out altogether; she didn't know why it hadn't occurred to her before: make it a polite but impersonal note. She did not think she would, though. Imelda Shacklock was such an impersonal person. And sitting reading *I Promessi Sposi*, in the original, in public! Who could swallow that?

Dear Clark, then? Oh God, never! She shudderingly only half slept.

And succeeded, after all, in waking early. The slats of light, which later on would solidify into its resinous, daytime consistency, still looked comparatively pale and innocent lying on the dust of the carpet.

Dear Mr Shacklock ... Ivy Simpson began, without altogether knowing how she would continue. That she did, fairly easily, was partly due to her using hotel paper, which made the act seem less private, at least for some of the way, and partly because she must have resolved a few of her difficulties, she realized, in the course of the night.

... this very short note is to let you know that my husband's health is forcing us to leave sooner than we had hoped and planned. We are flying this morning to Rome. You can imagine our disappointment. Indeed, to miss Erice and Piazza Armerina is more than a disappointment – an actual blow!

Thanks to yourself, and Mrs Shacklock, we shall be taking with us more agreeable memories than might have been the case if you had not steered us past some of the more dangerous Sicilian shoals ...

She wasn't happy with that. Was she going too far? Or being too abstract, while venturing as far as she had?

Charles, whose judgment I respect whenever it is asked for – it is almost always identical with my own – might consider some of my Sicilian reactions bizarre. You, with whom I visited San Fabrizio ...

(Oh, she didn't want to admit the Shacklock man into her private world of molten glass.)

... may be better able to appreciate its impact on a nervous system made more sensitive by the strain and repugnance of the last few days.

After that she recoiled and wrote,

Ever sincerely,
IVY SIMPSON

If she had been less sincere she might have enjoyed meandering on, writing a university essay. Instead, she sealed her – you couldn't call it 'shame': nobody, unless a Shacklock, was in a position to accuse her thoughts. She licked the envelope. The gum gave off a perfume of a sort, but tasted bitter.

In spite of Charles, who was against troubling the Americans with the news of their departure (mightn't they turn up at the airport?) she thrust her letter at the *portiere* after they had paid their bill.

'*Per il Signor e la Signora Shacklock,*' she began in her prim-mest Italian, and although the letter concerned only one of them.

The porter replied in English, without referring to his records, 'Mr and Mrs Shacklock have checked out already this morning.'

'Oh? Are you sure?'

'If he says they have, Ivy.'

'Oh, but darling, we all make mistakes, don't we?'

She had thought this day porter sympathetic, when he wasn't at all.

'If, as you say, they've left, they must – surely – have given a forwarding address where their friends can reach them?' The Signora Simpson insisted on insisting.

The *portiere* did consent to flip through his papers.

'No address.' He was sulking now.

The porter's scowling face and rather greasy lips would have remained the last of her vivid impressions of this hateful city if it had not been for the crowds at the airport: the uncles, aunts, and cousins swarming to meet the planes from Pantellaria, Lipari, Lampedusa, Rome.

And San Fabrizio *oh God* still molten in her.

In one corner of the *piazza*, not far from the hotel where they usually put up, sat an ophthalmiac pedlar from whom Charles bought a horrid little comb.

'Tell him, Ivy – in Italian.'

'*Il signor desidera un pettine.*' Charles's request sounded less stern, more an entreaty, when conveyed in her modulated vibrato.

Over the years he had bought many such combs, from beggars, spastics, hucksters, most of them probably frauds. She had come across these combs in the depths of drawers, in the pockets of coats and suitcases, in the glove compartment of the car, even in the tool shed. The combs, she had realized, must have been one of the reasons she had married Charles, long before she knew about them.

'Don't you think, Ivy, we ought to have a look at our church? for old times' sake?' He laughed to apologize for the suggestion.

'Yes,' she said. 'Why not?' For the moment her only desire was to rest her feet in peace and cool.

She was still dazed with winter sunlight when they left the train for darkening streets. He had made her come with him to the mountains. To walk. That part of it she enjoyed. She could ignore the Aubrey monologue, which at times actually lapsed, unable to compete with the silence surrounding them.

So they walked, and between them hung this blessed silence, and a latticework of blue leaves and light.

The flat air of the city and sleazy glimmer of its streets were intolerable on first returning. Accordingly, she began to sulk, and slouch along behind his back. It was a long journey still by ferry, and at the end, the maths she must try to cook up before morning.

When music and singing from a church she had been taught to dismiss inspired him to drop in '... to see what they're getting up to!' instead of immediately catching the tram to the quay.

It would be vespers according to the painted board outside the portico. She barely understood the Church jargon. In fact, she had only ever been inside a church in uniform, as part of a school exercise; the ceremony confused and mystified her. Now she might have felt elated for the novelty of a more personal experience if it hadn't been for Aubrey's presence.

The church was by no means sumptuous: its stark brick box, in spite of an attempt at vestments and a splendour of lit candles, remained downright ugly ('an aesthetic heresy,' Aubrey called it, not even bothering to lower his voice). But in spite of her father's attempts to destroy both the church and her reactions to it, she felt an exaltation creeping over her.

She would not show it, of course. She sat clenching her hot hands, to disguise her emotions, as well as to hide the wart which wouldn't drop off, and which she had inked over in class, in a moment of desperation or boredom.

Aubrey simmered with contempt. 'Observe the poor in spirit, Ivy, and take warning.' He himself, she had to admit, had a certain fleshly magnificence which made him stand out above the congregation; his looks, still only half dissipated, were gilded by the candlelight.

The congregation did indeed look poor: elderly ladies, the humpbacked spinster in a mackintosh, the club-footed man, gaunt, solitary, hollow-eyed boys. She decided not to look at her fellow men, any more than at her father, but let the words lap around her. The incense crept into the folds of her clothes, to mingle with the scent of wood-smoke from the fire she had lit that same day. The words penetrated a latticework of blue leaves and light, into a mountain silence. She was climbing with them.

She would have joined her voice to those of the reedy priests, the humpbacked woman, the club-footed man, if she had known the language. That was her loss, but not an important one, it seemed.

'... while the King sitteth at His table, my spikenard sendeth forth the perfume thereof ...'

Aubrey turned and winked. 'Good stuff, nevertheless!' his face bursting, every pore overflowing.

The priests and servers were processing down the nave in spirals of incense and columns of piety, when the spotty young man swinging the censer dropped it almost at Aubrey's feet. It clanked and rattled, still erupting, before it was retrieved. Aubrey apparently was too startled to comment.

The thread which had been spun between herself and the devotions of those who belonged had not been broken, she thought. Or had it? The spots on the face of the young man who had dropped the censer were feverishly close. She looked down, and there on her thumb was the inky wart which medicine and magic had failed to remove.

She felt numbed by the rapid descent to the side of her inescapable father, whom she saw, at best, as a shabby corsair.

The voices continued picking their way, unconcerned by the presence of the uninitiated; she herself might have prayed for grace if she had been alone, and if she had known how to form the words.

'... his left hand is under my head and his right hand doth embrace me ...' the voices chanted.

Aubrey, she could tell from the fumes of whisky (he had taken with him a little flask 'for the journey'), was bending in the direction of her ear. 'That's the sort of hocus pocus which sells it to the fairies and hysterical women. Come on, let's leave them to it!'

She had been taught to respond with obedience, possibly all she would ever learn to offer. When she got outside, and Aubrey, just ahead, was relieving himself by spitting on the pavement, she glanced back into the church's brick interior (it had much the same ugliness as a factory) where she was leaving behind, she could feel, something of herself which Aubrey – *nobody* could ever touch, but which on the other hand, she might never dare redeem.

It was still a long journey by ferry. Aubrey fortunately fell asleep, though he jogged her shoulder, from time to time, with his shoulder. The wart on her thumb was hurting.

'Yes,' she said. 'Why not?'

They were crossing the *piazza* through dense sunlight. The church they were struggling towards was their favourite. For archaeological, architectural, historical – all the right Australian-rational reasons, they loved Rome. (You can turn your back on the Vatican; and that monster, St Peter's, can be rather fun.) Grateful for shared opinions, their hands brushed as they went inside their church; their fingers tangled together, she would have dared anyone to say 'vulgarly': their age alone precluded that.

The light had so worked on the prospect of diminishing arches that the columns glowed with an opalescence of illuminated alabaster, while windows offered human faces constantly shifting masks in softest purple and crimson velvet.

Ivy Simpson knew she would have looked more haggard if it had not been for these charitable disguises. She was glad to hide behind them, and to feel her feet gliding with recently acquired ease across marble so black, yet clear, they might have been miraculously walking on benign water.

In the cloister, a cat, a young tabby queen, teats showing through her belly fur, lay patting at a spray of jasmine, claws furled inside her pad.

Neighbourhood clocks recording the passage of time finally drew the Simpsons back inside the church, and at the point where they should have branched off to pay respects at the tomb of a great man, Charles made a discovery which almost jerked Ivy's hand off at the wrist.

'D'you know what? We forgot to ask for the laundry!'

'Yes. We forgot.' Her machinery was so run down she had to admit to her own appalling domestic omission. 'I should have remembered.'

'We both should have.'

'I am the one – if anybody.' She didn't insist beyond that, but Charles had accepted it at last; he too must be feeling tired.

When they flopped down on contiguous chairs in one of the side aisles, it was simultaneously and in silence. That it happened to be level with the grisly saint, permanenuy bleeding in her glass case, was not a matter for comment this morning.

It only occurred to Ivy she should have inquired about the toothache. 'Hasn't the swelling gone down, darling? Your jaw looks almost back to normal.' In the circumstances her eyes could not give it attention enough.

'Yes,' he said. 'The pain seems to have gone since we arrived. So much sanctity around!' It was the kind of joke, flat to anybody else, they enjoyed when feeling tired or run-down.

'Do you think Sicily made us imagine things? Of course I don't mean your toothache – that, obviously, was real enough – but there were stages when I was prepared to think I might be developing the ugliest diseases. Or that my vision was distorting what it actually saw into all kinds of perverse forms. Sometimes they were beautiful perversions.' She snorted, and pursed her lips in a way he associated with Ivy. 'Perhaps I shall have my eyes checked – when we get back.'

'If it puts your mind at rest. Your eyes, Ivy, were always the best part of you.' Spoken by anybody else, not necessarily Aubrey Tyndall, but the kindest friend, it might have reminded her how plain she was.

They were silent after that, seated in a continuum, however short or protracted the rest of their life together might be, sorting discoloured snapshots, listening to uneven tape-recordings of each other's voice, briefly touching hands to convey what the average deaf-and-dumb fail to express by other means, occasionally allowing the sheer weight of recollected experience to carry them out of the familiar shallows into the sunless, breathless depths – when they felt brave enough not to resist.

Till Charles Simpson asked, 'Haven't we sat here long enough?' He had been taught to believe that inactivity is immoral.

'Oh, have we? Yes. I suppose we ought to move on.'

They did, and suddenly she thought she could detect a limp.

'Oh, darling, what is it?'

'What? Nothing. My leg's gone to sleep.'

So they plodded on, over the uneven marble. Nobody should accuse her of resorting to prayer; instead, she *wished* for the physical strength to shore him up if ever it became necessary, and more: the power to exorcize the phantasms each might otherwise continue half believing in.

'Oh,' she protested hopelessly.

As they came out on the steps the sunlight was making her stagger, and he put an arm under hers to support her.

The Cockatoos

Dressed casual for Sunday and his mission, Mr Goodenough ran at the path.

As soon as she opened, he started trying to freshen up his patter, which by now was on the stale side, '... the old door-knock for the Heart Foundation. Care to make a contribution?' He touched the heart pinned to his shirt.

Half expecting Jehovah she frowned at first at the paper heart, then smiled, it was almost dreamy, for remembering the smell of raspberry tartlets aligned on greaseproof in one of the safe kitchens of childhood.

'Oh yes,' she said and sighed and went down a passage to fetch her purse.

She was a tall, thin, yellow-skinned woman. Like most people in the neighbourhood, Mrs Davoren and Mr Good-enough had lived there many years without addressing each other more than ritually and in the street; though nobody held anything against anybody else, excepting Figgis, who had been an undertaker, and was still a nark.

'There,' she said, handing the two-dollar bill, which was as much as you had reckoned Mrs Davoren would part with. 'What with the price of things! Never seems to stop, does it?'

If his smile was more like a tightening of the skin, it was because he was writing a receipt on his knee. 'What initial have we?' he asked.

'O', she said. 'Mrs O. Davoren.'

'What about your old man? Think he's good for a coupler bucks?'

'I don't really know. He mightn't be here.'
'Seen 'im come in. Went around the back.'
'Oh, well, he could be here – at the back.'
'Wouldn't like to ask 'im, would you?'

Clyde Goodenough turned on the smile which made ladies overlook his lack of stature and his varicose veins. He liked to play the charmer with strangers; it was all above board, of course.

Something must have worked with Mrs Davoren: if not charm, an autumn sunlight, or the paper heart pinned to his shirt or, most likely, her own munificence.

She suddenly said, and it was the heart she was staring at, 'Mr Davoren and I haven't spoken for six – no, it must be seven years.'

You could have knocked Mr Goodenough over.

'But there must be things you gotter say – on and off – like putting out the garbage or paying the milk.'

'There are things – yes – and then we write them on a pad – which we keep for that purpose.'

In spite of it all, Mr Goodenough turned on the smile again. 'What about pushing the pad at 'im for the Heart Foundation's Door-Knock?'

'Oh, I couldn't!' she said, her feet shifting on the gritty step. 'No, I just couldn't!' Then, although everything seemed to show how she regretted her impulsiveness, Mrs Davoren confided still more rashly; 'It began on account of the boodgie. He didn't bother. When I went down to Kiama for Essie's funeral – he let my boodgie – die.'

Gawd strewth! 'Anyway, you've got a cockie now,' Mr Goodenough consoled, as he handed the receipt and returned the ballpoint to his shirt pocket. 'Looks pretty tame, too.'

'A cockie?' She couldn't have looked more alarmed if he had mentioned a tiger.

'That cockatoo in front – walking around in front of the tree.'

Mrs Davoren's thin legs and long feet carried her by quick steps along the concrete as far as the corner.

'A cocka*too*!' she breathed.

Under a gumtree, a fairly large one for a front yard in those parts, a cockatoo was striding and stamping. He looked angry, Mr Goodenough thought. The sulphur crest flicked open like a many-bladed pocketknife. Then he screeched, and opened his wings, and flew away across the park. It was an ugly, clumsy-looking action.

'Ohhh!' Mrs Davoren was moaning. 'D'you think he'll come back?'

'Must have forgot to latch the cage door, did you?'

'Oh, no! He's wild. I never set eyes on him before. Though he could have belonged to someone, of course. How they'll suffer when they find they've lost their cockatoo!'

Mr Goodenough made his getaway.

'Do you think if I put out seed?' Mrs Davoren was desperately calling for advice. 'I read somewhere that sunflower seed ...'

'P'raps.' Clyde Goodenough had reached the gate; one thing about the Door-Knock, it was giving him plenty to tell the wife.

Mrs Davoren went back along the concrete and was swallowed up inside her house.

Olive Davoren found consolation moving around through her dark house, unless she happened to hear Him moving around at the same time, in a different part; this was liable to give her heartburn. Dadda had left her comfortable: the house in a respectable street, and the interest in Friendly Loans, which Mr Armstrong the partner managed. The house was in liver brick, not so large as to attract thieves, but large enough to impress those who officially weren't. The tuck-pointing was falling out. She must have it fixed. And woodwork painted, inside and out. But not yet. For the trials she would have to bear, at any rate in the interior, and perhaps for having to face Mick at moments when she least wanted to.

Dadda had been right, she wished she had listened. *That man is you can't say no good but a no-hoper you can't blame him you can't blame a man for the Irish in him.* Hard to believe she had been so headstrong as a girl. Whether it was marriage or music, she was the one that knew. And ended up not scarcely daring to hold an opinion. Except on the one subject.

This evening she could hear Him (*your Irishman*) stalking through the rear part of the house. She heard the wire door twang as he stepped out into the back yard. He liked to pick the grubs off the fuchsias growing alongside the palings.

As for music, her violin had lain untouched these many years on the top shelf of her silky-oak-veneer wardrobe. Whenever she remembered she buried it deeper under the overflow of linen from the press.

She was artistic. Mumma took her to the Eisteddfods, fluffed out her skirt, prinked her hair before the performance. When they found it was the violin rather than recitation, Dadda sent her to the Con. Although she knew that she should love Bach, and did, she decided she would play the Bruch at her first concert with orchestra.

(None of it ever meant a thing to Mick, who liked to listen – in the early days – to his own silky Irish tenor, over the sink, or in front of friends.)

But she, she had her vocation, till Professor Mumberson took her through the baize door, not into the office, but outside in the tiled corridor, to tell her confidentially *I have had to fail you Olive in the circumstances ...* What those circumstances were she hadn't asked, because she couldn't believe. It was Dadda who asked and got the answer, but never told, because he was a kind man. If he had a belief in money and what it would buy he didn't succeed in buying Professor Mumberson. Dadda couldn't believe in his own failure, just as she would never (till she married Mick) let herself believe in hers.

She took a few pupils at first, kids from the neighbourhood who acquired an accomplishment of sorts and got it cheap. Most of them hated it: sawing away, all elbows and fingers, in a front room overlooking the park. Her own demonstration of a theme often seemed to sound as deadly thin, its tone as yellow, as the grass around the araucarias.

Not that it mattered: those were war years, and everything could be blamed on the War. (Mrs Dulhunty fell downstairs and broke a hip the night of the Jap sub in the harbour.) It was only when the War was over that you realized the great excuse it had been.

Once while they were still speaking, after they became man and wife, He told her how the War had given him the best years of his life. A sergeant-pilot in the Middle East, he kept his medals in a tin box. He told her he would always hope to take part in another war.

She had just put the food in front of him. 'It doesn't say much for me, does it? I'm to blame, I suppose. Because somebody is always to blame.' She would truly have liked to accept it, not out of spite either, if not from what you would call love; it was as simple as that.

He cocked his head to one side, and laughed at the plateful of overdone steak (it was how he liked it) and she couldn't see his light-coloured eyes for the angle at which he was holding himself. She had wanted to catch sight of the eyes, of a slate blue, or more sort of periwinkle, as she worked out while they were still what people call 'courting', and herself still craving for love or hurt. At that time he was driving the inter-state passenger buses. They met at Mildura, or it could have been Wagga, where he took over. She forgot what she ought to remember.

He was always telling her, still friendly, 'What sort of head have you got? To forget!' She never forgot the chill thrill of the slate – or periwinkle – eyes; she could remember whole sonatas she would never have the ability to play.

Olive Davoren sopped up her nose with a mauve Kleenex she found down her front. On account of the cockie – she remembered that – she tiptoed past the glass doors. Perhaps because of the brown Holland the light the blinds allowed from under them sat on the lino as solid as bars of yellow soap.

She twitched aside the blind from a bow-window, to see whether the cockatoo. There were two of them. Stamping and striding around the tree. Her heart was beating. Sometimes the birds got so angry, she could hear them screeching through the glass. She wouldn't have dared open the window: she might have frightened the cockatoos. Who tore at the lawn with furious beaks, or calming down, composed their crests along their heads, eyes tender with a wisdom which, like most wisdom, threatened to become obscure or irrelevant.

Oh dear, Olive Davoren moaned beneath her breath, *the sunflower seed is what I must remember ...*

And what would He have to say when he found she was coaxing cockatoos? *Mick!* Her scorn rose above her pallid hair; she had rinsed it Thursday, though to what purpose?

She had told him, 'You let it die on purpose. Because I was gone. You knew I loved the bird. You was jealous – that was it!' Her grief made her forget the grammar she had always been respectful of.

'It was sick,' he said. 'Anyone could see. A person only had to look at its toenails.'

'I should have cut his claws,' she admitted. 'But was afraid. He was too frail and small.'

'Sick to anyone else.'

(She had asked to see what they had taken from her – you couldn't have called it a child. She had even touched it. And wouldn't ever let herself remember. He certainly wouldn't be one to remind her of it.)

She must have cried at that point. She had called her boodgie Perk, but the bird hadn't lived up to it. And died.

So they seemed agreed not to speak. At any rate, for the time being, for a few days after the burial. It probably surprised them both that their decision should have hardened into permanence. In her case, there was a wound left over, from which all the blood hadn't flowed; some remained to suppurate. When at the secret burial – she would have died if anyone had seen – she had cried everything out of her, she thought, at the roots of Mrs Herbert Stevens.

It was seven years since Perk died; before that they had it – more or less what people call 'good'. Dadda took *this Irishman* into the business, but he couldn't stick it. Had to lead an outdoor life. He was happiest on the buses, she guessed, meeting people and leaving it at that. Girls offered him lollies, girls he had never set eyes on. They called him 'Mick' soon as ever they found out. He had black hair and a strong neck, yarning into the mike about the historical places they were passing through. Yes, the buses suited Mick.

As soon as they were seated at the café table he complimented her on her hands. Well, she knew her hands were fine from seeing them at the violin, but it hurt rather than flattered hearing it from the Irishman; her throat tightened, and she could not look at him for some time. It didn't seem to worry him: he was telling her about his boyhood at Lucan, how he used to sit, legs dangling, on a stone parapet, watching the water flow beneath the bridge of a Sunday.

'Why?' she asked. 'Was there nothing better to do?'

'That's what you do in Ireland.' She couldn't help noticing his teeth when he laughed. 'Waitin' for somethun to turn up!'

Beyond the window, under the tree, the two cockatoos had raised their crests, not the violent flicking of knives, but gentle almost as ladies' fans. Their currants of eyes looked sweet and moist.

Somebody was coming from around the corner. It was Him, she saw. She made to open the window, by instinct, against her principle, to call out and warn Mick not to frighten the cockies.

But he was walking down the path, not exactly tiptoe, keeling over on the edges of his soles, looking in the opposite direction, as though he hadn't seen, or didn't want to let on that he had.

He passed by, and the cockatoos held their expression of sweet, black-eyed wisdom.

He had reached the gate, his blue suit shiny around the shoulders and the seat, that he must have been wearing for best ever since he left off being the sergeant-pilot. His body was that of a younger man, his hair greyish, such of it as you could see. For he was wearing the hat which made it look as though he was going farther than a few doors along, to Her.

Olive Davoren got so cranky she jerked the Holland blind to shut herself off from her thoughts. She must have frightened the cockatoos. She could no longer see, but heard them as they gathered themselves, wings creaking at first, then beating the air, steadily, till faint.

Probably they would never come back however much sunflower seed she put. She snivelled a bit, before cooking the tea He would not be there to eat.

'Six years – no, seven, she told me. Without exchanging a bloody word! If they have to, they write it on a pad.'

'Waddayerknow!' Gwen Goodenough stirred the pan. 'That's a way, Clyde, it'll never take you an' me.'

The boy had come in with some kind of old bottle he kept on stroking and looking at.

'Who didn't speak for seven years?'

'Somebody,' the father said.

He had unpinned the paper heart. His legs, his varicose veins, ached. He was tired by now, and ready for a beer or two.

'Lots of people don't speak,' said the boy, still stroking what looked like an old medicine bottle.

'I never heard of anybody, Tim. Not when they live to-gether.' The mother was more concerned about the contents of her pan.

'Lots,' said Tim. 'They speak, but don't say.'

'Mr Clever, eh?' Clyde Goodenough had taken offence, though he could hardly have explained why.

'I don't know anything, of course,' the boy answered, too quick for parents.

'Here,' said the mother, 'don't you cheek your dad!'

For the moment Tim hated his dad. An old man in shorts! He hated his father for showing his varicose veins from door to door the day of the Heart Appeal.

After Dad had knocked back his first beer, and Mum only a sip of sherry, and they were all eating the gristly old stew, Tim Goodenough continued fingering the bottle he had stood on the table beside his plate.

'What's this?' the father asked. 'I'm blowed – a dirty old bottle at table!'

'It's an antique liniment bottle. Found it in Figgis's inciner-ator.' He held it to the light. 'Look at the lovely colours in it.'

If you looked hard, you could see a faint tinge of amethyst, even a burnish of incinerated green.

It troubled the father: what if the boy turned out a nut? or worse, a poof – or artist?

'That's not anything to keep,' he advised. 'You oughter throw the filthy thing away. Carrying home useless junk out of Figgis's back yard!'

'I'm going to put it in my museum.'

'Museum?' the mother asked, in a voice which would have sounded severe if she hadn't remembered to make it chummy. 'You never told us you have a museum.'

'I don't tell everything,' said Tim.

The father sucked his teeth; he looked as though he might have been going to throw up, till he got the better of his disgust. 'D'you know what? There's a wild cockatoo in Davorens' garden.'

'Someone must have left the cage open,' Mrs Goodenough said because it was her turn.

'That's what I told 'er. But she said it was wild.'

'How could she possibly know?' Mrs Goodenough wasn't all that interested in cockatoos.

Tim said, 'There's mobs of wild cockatoos in the park.'

This was something the parents couldn't contradict: they couldn't remember when they had last been in the park. Mr Goodenough sighed; he wondered why his charm never worked at home. Mrs Goodenough sighed too: she suspected her monthly was coming on.

When he had finished the IXL peaches, Tim Goodenough got down from the table, taking his antique bottle with him.

'You're in a hurry tonight, my lad.'

'I'm going to Davorens' to see the cockie.' It sounded younger than he was, and sickly, because that way he often pacified them.

Mum said, 'I'm not a naturalist, but know that cockatoos don't take root. It's more than likely flown off.'

It was true, he knew, but also as stupid as truth can often be. The cockatoo's presence in Davorens' garden was only the half of looking for it.

He went out humming, first to the garage, to put his bottle in the museum.

It did exist, in a disused bathroom cupboard, stashed away behind a roll of Feltex and several of wire-netting. In it he kept the skull of a small animal, probably a rat, found in a storm-water drain which emptied itself into the park. He also had – still a matter for surprise – a silver Maria Theresa dollar.

'Vis is from Ethiopia,' said Mr Lipski, the old gentleman from whom he had got it.

'Will you give it to me – please?'

Mr Lipski laughed because caught off his guard. 'Sure,' he said, 'vhy shouldn't you keep it? May be ze start of somsink.'

'Ooh, Tim, d'you think you ought? Something so valuable!' Mum pretended to be shocked, or was; greedy herself, he had noticed she suspected others of greed.

But in this case you couldn't honestly say it was that. He had never owned what he recognized as a talisman – well, there was the rat's skull perhaps. But he badly needed this coin as well.

Now in the dusk of the garage and the stink of damp Feltex, he could only explore the shapes of the silver dollar and the rat's skull by touch. In their mystic company, he left the liniment bottle he had churned up out of Figgis's incinerator.

There were several mobs of kids with mongrel dogs playing in the dusk after tea on the pavement and in the road. A lot of the owners of the houses which made an island between the parks were old and childless, but several large families had migrated to the neighbourhood so that their children could benefit from the parks. Tim Goodenough didn't often play with the mobs of other kids. Being an only child made him superior, or shy. You couldn't say the others disliked, but they didn't like him. Nor did he encourage them to. Not that he despised them for being stupid (several of them never stopped doing well at exams and already thought of becoming doctors and lawyers). It was just that they didn't know what he knew though what he knew he didn't altogether know – but knew.

Sometimes the mongrel dogs belonging to the large, con-solidated families followed him wagging their tails, licking the backs of his hands as they never did to their owners. He liked that.

This evening one of the boys shouted, 'What are you up to, Tim-the-Snoop?'

'I'm sauntering,' he called back.

Because it was unexpected and peculiar, the girls giggled, several of the boys jeered, and somebody threw a seed-pod at his head.

When he reached the Davorens' the house was dark; the brown blinds were down, making it look deserted, though the old girl was probably inside or round at the back. There was no sign of a cockatoo. But he climbed the fence and lay for a while under the spread of a hibiscus bush. Some of the white flowers had grown immense with the gathering dusk; their red pistils glittered with a stickiness which looked like dew. In the west, above the liver-coloured house, the sky still dripped red where it wasn't streaked with green and gold.

Of course any cockatoo would have flown to roost by now, but he didn't need one. He could make the whole mob spread their wings, exposing that faint shadow of yellow, claws clenched tight and black as they veered against the netted sky, then flew screeching past the solid holm-oaks and skeleton-pines, into space.

He lay awhile longer under the hibiscus, gathering one of the white flowers to taste the stickiness on its feathered pistil. It tasted of nothing to explain its attraction for bird and bee, but he felt content.

Miss Le Cornu was leaning on her gate. She was wearing the jeans she always wore, and a pair of sloppy old moccasins. Her shirt white against the dusk. It made Mr Figgis snort: a mature woman dressing like a teenage girl; bursting out of the jeans besides.

Did she know, he asked, that wild cockatoos were around? He had seen two of them under Davorens' big sugar-gum.

Miss Le Cornu didn't know, but now she came to think, she might have heard.

Figgis said, 'If there's anything I hate it's a cockatoo. Dirty, screeching, destructive brutes! I'm prepared to poison any cockatoo and be rid of a public nuisance.'

Miss Le Cornu had never considered whether she was for or against cockatoos. 'Don't you think they might look pretty in a garden? Climbing through that big magnolia, for instance.' She stopped short, and sniggered, because for the moment she was feeling high.

Figgis found himself looking into the gap between Miss Le Cornu's breasts. The breasts themselves, though draped with shirt, looked peculiarly naked in the dusk.

Figgis opened and closed his mouth. Having delivered himself on cockatoos, he would have liked to offer a few remarks on Miss Le Cornu's bursting jeans, but as he couldn't very well, he left her. There was an awful lot he would have wished dead, perhaps because he had spent life as an undertaker.

Dur-dur-dur dur-durr, Miss Le Cornu hummed against her teeth.

She couldn't think why she felt so good, except she had taken a handful – anyway, up to five. And He would probably come; it was his time. More often than not he did, so this was hardly reason for exhilaration. Nothing more than habit. Which was why it had begun, and continued. She had needed a habit.

That first occasion, a sleep-walker, he mightn't have been addressing her, '... told me I'd let 'er bally boodgie die ...'

Miss Le Cornu had never kept a bird, but was moved spontaneously to sympathize. 'Well, it's sad, isn't it? to lose something you're fond of. And getting back from her sister's funeral.' When she realized it wasn't Mrs Davoren at whom she was aiming her sympathy; and a bird is a detached, uncommunicative creature.

He leant on her gate, the hair already grey at the nape of his neck. Although he had glanced at her out of social obligation, it was his own predicament he was looking at.

'Why don't you come inside?' she suggested. 'I've got a nice T-bone steak I'll grill.'

That was seven years ago. She had never thought about a man before, or to be truthful, she had, and most men were distasteful to her. After Mother died, she had invited a girl called Marnie Prosser to share her life; but it hadn't worked: Marnie picked her nose rather too ostentatiously, and smeared honey on things: there was honey on all the door-knobs.

While he sat eating the steak in the sun-room which opened off the kitchen, it occurred to her: this is more than a neighbour's face I've seen a hundred times in the street, it's Mick Davoren, and an Irishman into the bargain. It was too fantastical to contemplate for long.

'Is it good?' she asked in a voice louder than necessary.

He half laughed and some red juice trickled down from a corner of his mouth. 'A bit raw, isn't ut?'

At least she could admire his teeth.

'That's how my father liked it,' she said. 'Very rare. He was most particular – in everything. He was a colonel, you know. Came here on leave from India. And married Mother. And settled. Not that I remember Father at all distinctly. I was too young when he died. They used to have to press his trousers, always before he put them on. He was hot tempered. That was what made his pants wrinkle.' She couldn't think when she had said so much at one go.

After he had wiped his mouth and pushed away the plate with almost the whole of the rare steak – delicately enough, she observed – Mr Davoren asked her, 'Was it your mother had the money then?'

'Yes. She was a Busby.'

It did not occur to her to explain who the Busbys were. Nor

him to ask. He looked gloomier, though. Like when he told her about the boodgie.

'Mother died – August last. You may have heard.'

He had heard something about it, he admitted, but continued sitting, looking, not at her, but inward, above the unfinished steak.

Miss Le Cornu thought she had never heard the house more silent.

That it was *her* house appalled her. First her parents', then her mother's – still a normal situation. But not *hers*! She had never felt the need for possessions. What she needed was a habit. Father died too soon to become one. And Mother, her great, her consuming habit, had left her without warning, over a cup of hot milk, the milk-skin hanging from her lower lip.

She had tried to figure out what consolation she would find in living. Certainly not freedom – if that exists. But was relieved to realize that, if she took care, no one would again address her by her first name. (They had christened her Busby for her mother's family, and she had grown up big and rather furry.)

Now to her own surprise, Busby Le Cornu was asking this Mr Davoren, again in a voice far too loud for the silence of the house, 'What do you like best? If it isn't raw steak!' Anyone else might have giggled, but she was too serious for that.

He too, evidently; although it became obvious he had misunderstood her intention. 'What I liked best – ever – was the days when I did a bit of prospectun on me own. I was hard up, you see, Miss Le Cornu. And I got this idea in me head. To look for gold. But never washed more than a few specks – that I kept in a bloomun bottle. I must have throwed ut away in the end. After I took the job drivun the interstate buses. But the skies, I remember, of a mornun, and the smell of wood-ash, when I was prospectun down south.'

That was where she began to blubber. She was heaving – and glugging, it sounded. He must have got a fright. He stood

up, and put an arm around her, then thought better, and removed it.

'Are you okay?'

'Yes,' she said.

But it increased her sense of loss, and not knowing what to
do next, she took his hand and looked at it. The strangeness of
her own behaviour, in which she could never afterwards believe, turned the hand into a thing lying in hers: an object
rough enough as to palm, but in its veins and structure singul-
arly elegant. She would have liked to put it somewhere and
keep it.

Instead she said in a voice she made as much as possible like
a man's, 'All right, Mr Davoren, we're not going to eat each
other, are we?'

They both laughed then, and she saw that his eyes were of a
light colour.

Busby Le Cornu had only once slept with a man, and that
was equally unexpected: he had come to mend the dishwasher.
It had not given her great pleasure. There had been another
occasion, earlier, but she preferred not to think about, or had
forgotten, it.

Now, out of deference to Mr Davoren as well as herself, she
did not switch lights on, but lay waiting on her mother's bed.
Her body looked long, strong, and white, her breasts spread
white and cushiony in glimmers from the street lighting. The
fuzz of hair between her thighs – her 'bush' the dishwasher
man had called it – looked by this same light fathomlessly
black. She hoped the Irishman would not become unnerved.
As for herself, she was by now nerveless, or indifferent.

Neither of them much enjoyed it, she imagined. He had
taken off his shoes, but not his clothes. His buttons grazed her
only briefly.

But when he was sitting in the dark, getting back into his
shoes, she said out of need rather than politeness, 'Next time

it will be better. I'll frizzle it up. I only did it rare because that
was the way Father liked it.'

That old chair never stopped creaking, which Father brought
from India, which meant that Mother couldn't throw it out,
although she laddered her stockings on it.

Mr Davoren stamped his foot to help with a shoe, and the
chair creaked enough to give up the ghost. 'That time I was
tellun you of – when I was prospectun for gold down along
the Murrumbidgee – things got so bad I had to look for work
at last. I presented meself to the manager of a station down
that way. It was harvest time. They put me an' one or two other
young fellers stookun up the oats behind the harvester. And as
fast as we built the stooks, the cockatoos would pull um down.'
He laughed; the chair had quietened: he must have finished
his shoes. 'Have you ever seen a mob of wild cockatoos? A
bit what you'd call slapdash in flight. But real dazzlers of birds!
I'd say heartless, from the way they slash at one another. Kind
too, when they want to be. They have a kind eye. And still.
You see um settun in a tree, and the tree isn't stiller than the
cockatoos.'

'Oh?' She yawned; she wished he would go; if Figgis
wouldn't have rung the police, she would have liked to play
a record to herself.

'See you later, then,' he said. 'For the frizzled steak!'

See you later was an expression she disliked, because half the
time it didn't mean what it was supposed to.

But He had meant it. He had become her habit. Here she
was leaning on the gate, after so many years, waiting for him
to approach. Neighbours had stopped seeing an 'immoral relationship', even Mr Figgis and Mrs Dulhunty no longer
hinted at it aloud. And anyway, what was there immoral in
cooking tea for a man you didn't love and who didn't love
you? If you had done it together a few times – no more than
three or four, or five, or perhaps six – it was only as if you

were making a bow to convention. Neither of you referred to it. Had he ever enjoyed it, she wondered? She had read that Irishmen, conditioned by the priests, had little taste for sexual indulgence, which made it difficult for the women, and turned many of them into nuns.

If Miss Le Cornu ever felt immoral it was in thinking of that yellow woman down the street, to whom she had never spoken, not even before taking the weight of her husband.

Miss Le Cornu felt less high. If it hadn't been for expecting Him, she would have gone and put on a record. This was the longest established of any of her habits, and might have sustained her, if you didn't also need the touch of skin. She preferred sopranos, or best of all, a velvety mezzo, and through such materializations of her inner self, would pursue the curlicues and almost reach the pinnacle, that golden cupola, or bubble of sound.

If she had never tried out a record on her friend Mick Davoren, who was just now approaching up the street, hat cocked against the dusk, it was because they said his wife had been a music teacher in her youth. Miss Le Cornu sometimes wondered which of all music Mrs Davoren favoured.

'Thought you'd given it away this evening.' Something had roused her anger; she might even have owned to a slight twinge of jealousy.

'It's late,' he admitted from under the hat he wore for propriety's sake, but which made him look less respectable.

He was staring straight at her too, out of his light-coloured eyes, which blended with the bluish dusk to the extent that he was, once again, not looking.

'A button come off,' he said, 'and I had to sew ut on.'

She grunted leading the way along the path, under the magnolia tree which was rooted on Figgis's side of the fence.

'You should have brought it and let me sew it.' She knew she sounded half hearted: sewing and mending, occupations she didn't care for, had not become woven into the habit they had cultivated. 'The food's in the warmer,' she said more kindly, if not kind; whatever was making her angry, unpunctuality couldn't enter into it, not when somebody liked things frizzled up.

While he was eating the spoiled steak, she sat with her back half turned, rocking, in the kitchen where she served the food, never in the sun-room after they became used to each other.

Would it be the rates that had caused her anger? 'I can't remember whether I paid them – the rates,' she explained, and rocked.

He couldn't help her. If they had received their notice, Mrs O. Davoren would have attended to it.

When he had finished his meat, and laid his knife and fork together, unnecessarily precise, it seemed, he cleared his throat, and told, 'This evenun as I was comun out there was two cockatoos strollun around at the foot of the big tree. I didn't see a wild cockatoo in years. The white ones. Yeller topknots.'

She was rocking furiously by now, and laughed too loud. 'So I heard. Figgis is out to poison any pests of cockatoos.'

'He hadn't better!' She was surprised at such vehemence. 'Not mine – he better not.'

'How do you know these tramps of birds would want to belong to anybody?'

'I wouldn't want um to *belong*! Not more than to be fed.'

She stopped rocking. 'What would you feed them on?'

'Sunflower seed. Accordun to packuts I've seen in the shops.'

As though her friend's eye were a mirror to her own mind, she saw a cockatoo groping after, then balancing on, a chimney-pot; she saw a second, circling overhead; a whole strung-out flight was labouring against the wind. But those which clambered through magnolia branches, themselves like big white drunken flowers in motion, were the most desirable of all.

She sighed, and said, rubbing a cheek on its neighbouring

shoulder, 'Yes. It would look lovely. I could use a few of those cockatoos.' When they were accustomed to her, she would try out some music on them: the mezzo voice most likely to have been hers.

He had got up. 'Not any of mine you can't – Busby,' he said.

Then her anger rose again and, cresting over, rocked the chair she was clinging to. 'How did you know to call me by my bloody name? Nobody knows – since Father and Mother.'

'I heard as somebody saw the electoral roll, and well, ut's your name, Busby.' He was Irish enough to sound tender when it served his purpose, not for her, pleading of course for his birds.

'I wouldn't want to coax away anybody's bloody cockatoo,' she shouted.

Soon after, he left. Perhaps he would tell Her – at any rate write it on the pad – let her know he was sold on cockatoos.

Miss Le Cornu had to restore herself. She opened the bottle, and poured several into the palm of her hand. And would not sleep.

In fact, all around her there was this flashing and slashing of wings, white except where yellow-tinged. She could have shrieked.

In the end she took a sedative.

Olive Davoren had continued cooking tea for Him. She kept it in the warmer. When he didn't come, she might eat a little of it herself, but mostly she had no appetite. She shot the rest in with the garbage. She could afford it, couldn't she? Then she would go to bed.

Tonight she waited up longer, thinking about the wild cockatoos. She had gone back once to have a look – in any case she had to lock up – and for a moment imagined she saw something stirring in the white hibiscus. It could not have been a cockatoo; it was too late for any bird.

She went to bed, early though it was, because there seemed nothing left to do, and heard Him, when he came in, bumping around across the passage.

She had forgotten how fine her hands were. Or thin? She thought of the violin lying buried under linen on the upper shelf of her silky-oak-veneer wardrobe.

And slept.

She woke sweating. The big clam-shell continued shining, under the tree on the lawn, as in her dream. Dry, unless for rainwater reduced to a little slime. She must clean out the slime in the morning with her long fine hands. Her birds would need water as well as seed.

Olive Davoren fell asleep, a pillow-end between shoulder and cheek, like a violin.

She had noticed seed at Woolworths and Coles; it was only a matter of choosing.

One of the birds was pecking at her womb. He rejected it as though finding a husk.

Her hollow pillow was reverberating horribly.

She woke, and flew down at such speed, she could have forgotten something. She had. She returned, and put in her teeth, and began again.

The light was growing transparent around her as she filled the watering-can. Then she noticed that someone else had already poured water in the shell. More, they had cleaned it out first. The clam-shell shone like new teeth.

He used to eat the breakfast she cooked and left for him in the warmer, then go out about his Business. That, she had heard, was how he liked to refer to it. One of his mates from the bus days had invented a patent tin-opener. Mick would go from door to door 'marketing the Miracle Opener'. How successfully she had never been told. All this had happened since they introduced the pad, and she could hardly have written, 'How is your Business doing, Mick?'

He seldom held down a job for long: said it was the War had unsettled him. More likely he considered himself exempt from ordinary human activity. Or dedicated to the open air. When Dadda took him into Friendly Loans, he sat at the desk not above a few weeks. He took to gardening, but tired of digging weeds in. Greenkeeping was more in his line: the unobstructed sweep of the links. He kept at that for several years, and became less fidgety, she could hear. 'Deep-breathing is the secret,' she once found written on the pad, but came to the conclusion it was an observation not intended for herself or any second person.

Now here he was, descending the path in his business suit, carrying the case with the samples in it. Breathing deep, she could see from the action of his shoulders. Hatless (he never wore one unless on his way to Her). The nape of his neck might have made you cry if you hadn't remembered the hat he wasn't wearing.

So Mrs Davoren no more than wiped her nose on the Kleenex she kept down her front. And Mr Davoren continued down the path, looking sideways at the base of the tree where cockatoos had landed the evening before. He had stopped breathing. But there weren't any cockatoos this morning. He went on, still what Mrs Dulhunty called 'a fine figure of an Irishman'.

As soon as the gate squealed, Mrs Davoren couldn't smear the powder quick enough, get herself ready for the supermarket. Or was it a Holiday? The possibility made her heart toll cold for several instants. It wasn't a holiday, though. She bought her seed, both plain and mixed, with a pottery dish to put it in and, loaded with her purchases, she made for home.

Where someone else had already put out sunflower seed. In a pottery dish. Olive Davoren could have kicked it. The tears shot out and she didn't bother to wipe them with the Kleenex.

The cockatoos came at evening, the pair, stamping round

the dish at the foot of the tree. Clumsy, beautiful creatures! On seeing them, her mouth fell open: their crests flicked like knives threatening intruders; then when the first seeds were cracked, the feathers so gently laid in a yellow wisp along the head. She loved her birds.

They *were* hers, surely? whoever had put out the seed. They were given to her as compensation.

In her anxiety, Olive Davoren twitched the blind behind which she was hiding in one of the front rooms, and the cockatoos took fright; they flew up into a tree. She was miserable, but could do nothing beyond wait and look.

She was sitting watching the empty garden, when there in the opposite bay of the other room, who was it half hidden behind the opposite brown blind? She had never accepted herself before as a woman of anger.

Pretending not to see her as he watched her birds!

She might not have felt mollified when they resettled on the grass around the gum, if they hadn't become three – no, five cockatoos!

The two watchers were almost for glancing at each other from behind their blinds in opposite bays.

They were saved by the birds starting to menace one another like human beings. Perhaps it was the original pair who couldn't tolerate the newcomers. Crests whipped open in flashes of sulphur; beaks clashed; breast was thrust at ruffled breast, as they stomped and thumped around the dish on callused claws, rolling as though they were riding a swell instead of flat lawn.

She was so entranced she forgot Him.

And soon it was time to cook tea. When it was done, she put it in the warmer. He hadn't gone out; she could hear him moving in remote parts of the darkening house.

After giving adequate thought to a proposition she would like to make, Olive Davoren wrote on the pad, 'Be considerate for once ...' She crossed it out and substituted, 'I hope you will allow me the pleasure of putting out the morning seed.'

In the morning the sheet was gone from the pad, and she found written, 'Don't forget water, v. important.'

So it was arranged, anonymously.

Mornings became hers, when she removed the husks, filled the dish with striped seed, and the clam-shell with water. She shared his sentiments over the water: it *was* important.

In the evenings, which were his, they sat in their opposite bays, watching the cockatoos feed after he had done his duty by them.

For some time she had not caught sight of him strolling down the path, then along the street, hat cocked for Her. Instead she heard him moving through distant rooms, or sitting the other side of a wall, at least thinking, she hoped, but sighing.

Once as he sat looking out through his window at his birds feeding in the gathering dusk, Mick Davoren realized they had multiplied: he could count eleven cockatoos. All docile for the moment, kindness and wisdom in the currant-eyes. Or if the crests rose, it was like ladies delicately opening fans.

While himself no longer sat looking out: he was the boy outside, who stood looking in through this great window to where the company was seated, in knots on gilded chairs, as well as a wider circle round a curved settee, the meeker, sleeker girls all of them in docile white, their harsher elders ablaze with a white fire of diamonds, as they picked at the words they chose to offer in conversation. When a certain elderly lady shrieked, for some secret perhaps, that she was making public. And all the ladies and meek girls were joining in the general screech. Whirling as they changed position. Diamonds bounding. Some disagreement, but with a fine display of polite temper. Then the gentlemen were coming in, laughing too, some of them stumbling, some arguing, others full of ostentatious consideration for their neighbours. While he, the boy standing in the dark the wrong side of this stately window, retreated backwards into the drizzle, all but tumbling over a giant hound that was lying on the lawn pointing her nose at a watery moon.

Mick Davoren hawked the phlegm up out of his throat.

It must have frightened the cockatoos: they rose in a wave, white to greenish by present light, and broke on the shores of holm-oak and araucaria in the park opposite.

He dared glance at the window in the other bay, where Olive, the woman he had married, sat glaring into nothing.

Mrs Dulhunty had read that birds bring lice. Starlings do for a fact: the lice drop off of them down the chimneys.

Cockatoos! Figgis was becoming ropeable.

Most of the kids in the neighbourhood had been and seen the birds, and *oo-arrr*'d, and shouted, and thrown stones, preferably to hit, or if that failed, to frighten the cockies. If Tim Goodenough hadn't yet seen them in the flesh, it was because he got home from school before the cockatoos had landed, and by the time his mum and dad let him up from his blasted tea, the birds had flown. All he found was Mr and Mrs Davoren looking out from opposite windows.

Once in passing her gate, he asked Miss Le Cornu whether she had seen the cockatoos, and she answered, 'Ye-ehss,' about to share a secret with him, it seemed.

But he didn't need it. As though he had stared at them as deeply as he stared at the people in buses, he knew what would be going on behind cockatoo eyes; he knew about the wisps of yellow feather the books showed cockatoos as wearing, as good as if he had touched these tufts, like people he brushed up against, simply to find out about them, and discovered he. already knew.

The cockatoos were coming less often, then only three or four of them. Occasionally none. Or one elderly creature who hobbled, and at times trailed a wing. It was the children who had frightened the birds, and probably stoned the loner. Mrs Davoren almost suggested it to her husband, not in writing, but in spoken words, then was saved by her principles.

She felt sorry for Mick, however, seeing from the corner of an eye that their birds' defection was making him suffer. She heard her husband fart softly in the dark, the other side of the separating wall, and forgave him for it.

She herself was taking the bicarbonate, you couldn't say by handfuls, but always increasing the quantity.

When Mick Davoren put on his hat and went up the street to Miss Le Cornu, it was still broad daylight, or broad enough for neighbours to revive their interpretation of motives. This evening she wasn't leaning on the gate in accordance with custom. A cockatoo was perched on one of her chimneys, a wing outstretched straight and stiff as he picked beneath the coverts. A second bird, feathers ruffled as he sat clutching a terracotta fireman's helmet, screeched at the intruder. Or was it a former love?

Davoren took the brick path which led towards the back, under the Figgis magnolia tree.

'What – who is it?' she called.

Her shirt was open, which she buttoned quickly.

Several cockatoos, heads bobbing, were cracking seed in a circle at her feet.

Davoren roared with a laughter which wasn't.

The cockatoos flew off. That much he had achieved. (He could even imagine telling his wife.)

When Busby Le Cornu started laughing. 'You bugger!' she cried. 'You bloody – *Irish* bugger!'

He was so enraged, he snatched at her shirt, and again it was open on her. He continued roaring, red with pseudo-joviality.

'Coming,' she was now giggling, while stifling it in her nostrils, 'too early,' she shrieked, 'for the frizzling! If I've got any,' she added in the throes of her convulsions.

All this time she was leading him into the house, away from neighbours' ears and the scene of her deception.

Neither of them was any longer much deceived.

'Those are my cockatoos,' he shouted on the stairs.

'They're free to make their choice, aren't they?' As if anybody ever more than imagined they were.

When they reached the room to which they were being conducted, he did not wait for her to take her shirt off, but ripped it away. She seemed to hear the last of her buttons hit the wainscot.

Davoren was caressing her large but flat breasts, as she had never experienced, or if she had, it was so long ago she could barely remember. He was mumbling on them, about the blessed cockatoos. Then, because he had begun pulling off his clothes (it hadn't occurred to him to make such a move on their other occasions), she took her jeans off, and lay waiting for him on the bed.

In the light just before dark, her own body surprised her. Till Davoren was straddling it. She had never allowed herself to look at a man's cock, though she had seen it celebrated on walls, graphically, as well as in writing. Now she looked and the sight was splendid.

'See here, Busby,' he was hectoring from above, knees planted on either side, 'the violation of a confidence is what I'm objectun to. I didn't tell you about me birds to have you seduce um away from me.'

He became so congested he couldn't contain himself. It spurted on her stomach, burning her.

She sighed from within the crook of her arm, 'I don't see why we can't share what doesn't belong to either of us.'

He was already getting back into his clothes. 'The wife would be disappointed,' he said.

For some time after he had gone, she was left without the power to move. The light was failing. She tried to think which solution she should choose: should it be the sedative? or whether to let the fireworks off. In the end she opened neither bottle, but went down as she was, flat-footed, into the garden. There was moss between the bricks in the path, which at least her feet were able to enjoy. She looked down and wiped away a drop from what the dishwasher man had referred to as her 'bush'.

Of course the cockatoos had not returned, except that in the magnolia tree she thought for a moment she could see one of them moving amongst the giant flowers. Or flowers stirring.

Whatever influenced the cockatoos' movements, Olive Davoren was overjoyed whenever they honoured her with their presence. One morning, when He had gone out early, she counted fourteen of them. They would stand still for moments, wondering whether to be afraid, looking like china ornaments. Then, it seemed, they became reassured, and the kindness in their eyes was directed at her as she stood in the window.

It was on this particular morning that she conceived her idea. She in turn wondered whether she ought to feel frightened as she went upstairs and groped around in the wardrobe, under the linen on the upper shelf.

By the time she opened the glass doors within sight and hearing of the cockatoos she was as brittle as the violin she had not touched in years. Which she began to tinker with, and tune. Fearfully. What if some human being caught sight of her from the street? Her skin grew glossy with anxiety.

She was playing, though: what she remembered of what she had found most difficult. It issued thin and angular out of the disused violin. It sounded yellow. But grave and honest. The composer was collaborating with her. And cockatoos. Whatever penetrated the down, their eyes were engaged, as they continued bobbing, cracking seed, hobbling, and occasionally jumping.

If the composer and the cockatoos had joined with her in the Sarabande, she entered on the Chaconne with deeper misgiving, and alone. But drove herself at her arduous climb. One of the birds flew off. He sat looking back at the scene through a window in one of the holm-oaks opposite. The rest of the flock stayed listening to her music. If they accepted her, it must have been from recognizing something of their own awkwardness.

When a string snapped, her breath tore.

Ballooning upward, the birds spread out, and flew clattering across the park, shrieking back at her, it seemed. She wondered whether she had experienced, or only imagined, moments of exaltation in what must otherwise have been a horrible travesty of the Partita.

Across the brown lino she trailed to put away her violin. In future she would have the excuse that a string was broken.

Unlike Busby Le Cornu. Nothing need prevent her playing another record. She would too, if she felt like it. Just as nobody, not even He, could prevent the cockatoos from coming to her garden if they chose to come.

She played them a record for the first time on an afternoon when, unintentionally, she must have taken the sedative instead. She had dragged out the little table on which the player stood, and there where the shadow of the house cut the sunlight, on the edge of the lawn, she was crouching over what might have been her own lament for a real passion she had never quite experienced.

> '*Mi tradì, quell'alma ingrata,*
> *Infelice, o Dio, mi fa ... *'

she all but sang, herself soaring against reason and the tablet she had swallowed.

The cockatoos shot off into the dazzle. She was alone with her alter ego, the voice.

> '*Ma tradita e abbandonata,*
> *Provo ancor per lui pietà ...* '

Cockatoos, two or three of them at least, were rejoining her in vindicating spirals, white-to-sunsplashed.

> '*Quando sento il mio tormento,*
> *Di vendetta il cor favella,*
> *Ma se guardo il suo cimento,*
> *Palpitando il cor mi va ...* '

Wings aswirl in alighting, the birds were soon striding adventurously back towards the dish she had filled to overflowing. When suddenly she switched off the machine. It wasn't that she feared an encounter with the Don; she could not have faced the moonlit statue by daylight: a pity, because the Commendatore might have appealed to cockatoos.

He had drawn one of the veranda chairs out to where the grass began. The air was growing chillier with early winter. Never before had he sat so close to his birds. His wife would probably have disapproved, but if she was watching from inside the house, he wasn't aware of it.

By this sharpened light the garden looked a deeper, lusher green – unnatural. It intensified the purity of white plumage as the cockatoos cracked seed or stalked around. They were restless today, not on account of his presence (in fact they ignored him) but because possessed with the desire to bash somebody up. Their flick-knife crests grew sinister against the walls of brooding green. One bird in particular, old, or disabled (he trailed a wing from time to time), appeared to offend the majority. Although tough and stoical, the outsider was chased away at last. A flight took off after him, undercarts tightly re-tracted, ailerons reflecting yellow, wings sawing as they man-oeuvred into position, and pursued the enemy, or so it seemed, over the park.

Davoren did not see how it ended. His eyes were hurting. (He had his headaches.) Never been the same since that crash-landing. They got him. He had got the other bastard first; when a formation swarmed on him out of the cloud. It became a hide-and-seek through cloud. He threw them off finally, climbed, and dived on their tails. He pressed the tit and let them have it with the brutality and desperation the times demanded.

But failed. He was losing height. Down down o Lord ohhh a leaden feather could not have fluttered so surely. Then he was bumping over the hummocks of salt bush. Rebounded once. Not much more than a numbness, he slithered free before the flames took over. He lay in the wadi, sand hissing around him. He listened to their bullets ricochet off the surrounding rocks. Afterwards, the silence. He was not – dead.

There were still the times when he had to tell himself he was free. Or was he? The familiar chair in which he was sitting threatened to pitch him out. Those brutal birds, while bashing at one another with their beaks only a few yards away, had given off a stench he hadn't been aware of before. He must get away. Perhaps if he sat awhile alone in a darkened room, he would recover his balance. He was glad nobody had seen. Not in years he hadn't experienced such terror.

Olive Davoren watched her husband drag his chair back to the veranda, away from the scattering cockatoos. She would not have known what to do for him, she thought, even if they hadn't renounced speech. She would never have known her own husband.

From under the hibiscus Tim Goodenough had watched and heard the flap. This old man had frightened the birds, but was himself frightened, you could see. Which in itself was fearful: an old, frightened man! When you had as good as made up your mind to spend the night in the park – on your own – to test your courage.

Not long after, the neighbourhood began asking what had become of the cockatoos. For several days, those in whose lives the birds played a part hadn't caught sight of a single one; no longer the dawn screeching, the ribaldry from finial and chimney-pot.

When she could no longer bear it, Miss Le Cornu went down to Mrs Dulhunty, for whom she didn't altogether care, and called up at her window, 'What do you think has happened to them?'

Mrs Dulhunty left off combing her hair to look down from where she lived above the garage. 'He's poisoned 'em. Figgis!' she said in a loud whisper.

'How could he poison a whole mob?'

'Don't ask me,' Mrs Dulhunty replied, dropping a ball of slag-coloured hair into the lane. 'It's what they're sayin'. Figgis has been creatin' because 'is magnolia tree is practically de-*nud*-ed.'

Miss Le Cornu wondered which side Mrs Dulhunty would be on if ever it came to a showdown. 'I'd have said there were leaves enough left on his tree – privacy on either side of the fence,' she answered feebly for her.

Mrs Dulhunty realized; she knew which side she was on – her own; and minded her own business; so she pursed up, and repeated, 'That's what they say.' After which, she retreated slightly to pick between the teeth of her comb with a pin.

Busby Le Cornu could only return up the lane, hoping she wouldn't bump into either Davoren.

More than anybody, Davorens had not been able to accept the disappearance of their cockatoos. They milled around their dark rooms, on the brown lino, and were often almost brought face to face. Olive was noticeably distraught. Her distress was aggravated by the smell of chrysanths which had stood too long in their vases and which ought to be thrown out. Friday she meant to turn out the whole place, if she remembered. She didn't, for coming face to face with Mick in the most awkward, the darkest corner, outside the cupboard where she kept the Hoover and the brooms.

They were properly caught. In spite of the dark she could see the light colour of the eyes she thought she had forgotten. He remembered the twitch in a cheek now that he met it again, and how it was probably what had decided him to take pity. The cheek had appeared sallow, and only later, after they started writing messages on pads, had it turned, if he ever glanced, yellow.

There they were, trapped, outside the broom-cupboard, where for the obvious reason, there always lingered a smell of dust.

It was her who uttered first, and then only '... the cockatoos?'

He advanced perhaps a step. 'Figgis has poisoned um. That's what they say.'

Then they were leading each other through such an unfamiliar labyrinth they were bumping into furniture. (She hated her own bruises: they ended up the colour of hard-boiled eggs.)

'Who else?' he asked.

'I don't know. Some foreigner could. The Yugo-Slavs shoot the ducks and take them home. Haven't you heard them? In the park? At night?'

He had stopped considering. Stretched on the bed they were trying to comfort each other; memory was becoming this spastic sarabande through which they were staggering together and apart. (Had love been strangled – or worse, deformed, in both of them, at birth?)

Her bruises wouldn't have risen yet; not that it mattered: they had their clothes on. He was mumbling something about his mother: it must have been the dark colour of her dress. She was suddenly ashamed of her long hands for having lost the art of touch, just as her music had left her except in the presence of the cockatoos.

'Do you think it could have been the gas men? Who was flushing the pipes all these days. One of them told me we need new burners on the stove. Said he'd come and put them for me.'

'Don't trust um.'

'Why?' she asked.

'Too affectionate.'

They were laughing mouth to mouth. He was soothing the hands she thought had grown, or perhaps always had been, useless.

They must have fallen into a doze, and might have forgotten the cockatoos if the light hadn't reminded them; it was about the time the birds used to come. Davorens sat up on hinges, and without so much as smoothing the creases out of their clothes, rushed down to put out the seed.

And the sky was awash with cockatoos returning, settling on the gumtrees which grew in the garden. If silent, the birds might have merged with the trees, but they sat there ruffling, snapping at twigs, screeching – cajoling, it sounded; one of them almost succeeded in forming a word.

'Where have they been?' Olive Davoren called recklessly to her husband.

The Irishman shrugged. 'Buggered if I know! Woronora – Wyong – Bullabulla – the *Monaro*!' he shouted.

Then when Davorens had turned their backs to drag out their veranda chairs and prepare themselves for the spectacle, their birds descended. Absence had tamed or made them ravenous. Their plumage was smoothed by concentration; the sulphur feathers in their crests were lying together, at peace.

If Davorens did not comment it was because they had dis-

covered in this other silence the art of speech. Once he touched
the back of one of her hands with an index finger, pointing
out nothing they didn't already share. She hardly breathed for
fear her love might make him fearful of being possessed; she
must try to make it look nothing more than gratitude.

It was different fears which began possessing them both,
before any reason showed itself from behind that hibiscus she
had always meant to prune. It was Figgis; more – Figgis with
a shotgun.

'The bloody madman!' From up on the rise, Davoren
started bellowing as soon as he recovered from the shock.
'Only perverts would dream of shootun at cockatoos!'

'A public menace! Picking at the slates – shitting on the
paths – destroying trees – disturbing the ratepayers' sleep!'

After that, Figgis fired. The cockatoos were already rising,
a fountain of white fanning out into separate wavelets; all but
those who had been hit: a couple were tumbling, flopping,
jerking on the grass, as the life inside them broke up.

Tim Goodenough saw, and it was terrible.

He saw Davoren running down the slope, no longer this
elderly man, but like a boy with windmill arms.

'Murderer!'

'I was never one to neglect my duty,' Figgis was muttering.
He took aim again, at distance.

A whole mob of kids had come running up and were hanging
from the park railings to get a better view of what was
happening.

Figgis would have fired again – he was that mad – if Miss
Le Cornu hadn't run along the street. She would have grabbed
him, if Davoren hadn't got there before her. The two men
were whirled round together on their heels, and as part of the
same whirlwind, the shotgun.

Which went off for the second time.

A bunch of women began screaming. Children giggled.

Lying on the pavement, Davoren was looking skywards, his eyes as still as still water. The blood was running.

'You *sod!*' Miss Le Cornu shouted, it wasn't clear for who.

She and Mrs Davoren, already on their knees, tugged at first, each trying to raise, or possess Davoren for herself; then began a regular stroking. They might have been easing the life out of him: you could see it had started to leave. At moments the women unavoidably stroked each other's hands, and threatened to knot. But continued at their work. Their faces were equally pale.

'Speak to me,' Mrs Davoren said. 'My darling? My husband?'

(*My poor habit! You will understand.*)

Tim was glad his father had come, to organize. (Because it was the evening of a week-day Dad wasn't showing his varicose veins.)

Figgis refused to give up his weapon; he would wait for the police. He was sitting on the kerb, clinging to the gun, slightly dribbling.

A little girl was whimpering.

Ladies told each other what a shame.

The police, the ambulance arrived.

'Look!' one of the kids called.

Some way up the street half-a-dozen cockies had returned to settle on top of a pole and along the wires. Feathers ruffled, still shocked, they sat offering their breasts to the wind. They were a nasty grey colour, more like hens which have been fluffing themselves on an ash-heap.

The police collared Figgis and shoved him in the van after taking his gun for an exhibit.

The ambulance carried off what must have been by now Mr Davoren's body.

Ahhh, Mrs Dulhunty moaned; she was done with it all, and would go to Our Lady of the Snows, Ashfield, where a nun of her acquaintance had promised to take care of her.

So it was over.

Only Mrs Davoren and Miss Le Cornu, along with most of the kids present, had not yet found they could believe in death. Then the two women seemed to realize they were empty-handed. They let themselves be led, ramshackle, groping, on their separate ways.

Soon after, Tim Goodenough remembered the dead cockatoos. He would have liked them for their yellow crests. But somebody must have already collected them for burial or snitched them as souvenirs.

Darkness gathering made the grass look poisonous. He might have let out a long howl, like a dog hit by a car, if he hadn't glanced down and seen the pool of somebody else's blood. In the last light it glittered so splendidly it stopped him howling, and he was glad, because Dad was still looking important, ordering people back to their houses.

Time passes: nothing better can be said of it. All was tidied up: manslaughter established, and the cockatoo murders overlooked. Some said Figgis had been taken north to Taree, and handed over to relatives; while others had it on the best authority that he was locked up in a nut-house – and good riddance.

Tim Goodenough thought the nut-house more likely, from hearing Mum and Dad on nuts. (There's a lot more than you'd believe, and it's only luck if you're not found out.)

On the eve of his ninth birthday he decided he was ready to carry out the plan he had been chewing over for the last few months: to test his courage by spending a night alone in the park. Just the other day he had drawn a cross on the inside of his left arm with the smallest, sharpest blade of his penknife, and had not flinched – or not much: he ought to survive night in the park.

He would slip out after they had sent him to bed, after messing up the bedding to make them think he had slept in it.

He would take provisions in case he felt hungry, and his knife for protection.

When it came to the point, he forgot the provisions: he was that anxious to get away without being heard. Dad had drunk his last nightcap of beer, and Mum more than her usual sherry. They were already otherwise occupied when he crept out and slid between the park railings.

He made first for the storm-water drain in which he had found the animal's skull he kept in the medicine cupboard. Down-and-outs slept in the drains in the park, Mrs Dulhunty said; it was a wonder the lot of them weren't flushed out like rats. He lay awhile knocking on the sides of the drain which came out near the Moreton Bay fig. The moon was up, already a bit lopsided; it reminded him of oyster shells.

He continued knocking, listening to the reverberations. There was a man got regularly inside the drain, and lay there knocking, Mrs Dulhunty said; he was no nut: he was in league with the Redfern thieves, telling them in code which of the houses had been vacated by their owners going to the pictures. What if you hit on the crims' code? They could break in while Dad was on top of Mum. Or murder Mrs Dulhunty before she got round to leaving for Our Lady of the Snows.

Soon after that he climbed down from the drain. He left the park. He would keep to the street for a bit, to the blue lighting which the council put because some of the ladies were afraid they might be indecently assaulted, though the last thing they could expect was rape. He picked up a stick for company and ran it along the railings as he marched.

Some of the houses were in darkness (waiting for the crims) but a light was shining in what must be Mrs Davoren's bedroom window. There was a light also in Miss Le Cornu's – Buz. (Wasn't it what everyone called her? since Dad came across it ruling the lines through the names on the electoral roll.)

He walked slower, to prolong the street. There was time enough for the bloody park if he was to spend all night in it.

Mrs Davoren was lying in her bed watching the moon balanced on a black pyramid which by day became a holm-oak. She wasn't frightened living alone in their house. She would never be frightened: there was no reason for it. There was no reason.

She lay and stroked the pillow where his head hadn't lain in years. It had lain on the pavement. She didn't cry: she was as far removed as the Bach partita she had played to the cockatoos before they were frightened by the string snapping.

Miss Le Cornu was the one. Mrs Davoren often wondered how She was coping with her grief.

As Busby Le Cornu lay in her bed watching the moon netted in the araucarias she was not coping: she had taken the lot, the stimulants, the sedatives. But would never – she had to laugh – die.

She wondered about the yellow woman down the street, not interminably, because there were times when they got together, and that removed the necessity.

Mrs Davoren would walk in. 'How are you keeping, dear?' was what she was bound to say.

'Not so bad, thanks. And how's yourself?' Busby Le Cornu did not give the expected answer; because almost nothing is altogether expected.

They are leading each other upstairs. Olive's hand has a rough palm, though the bone structure is fine enough.

Olive says, 'You'll have to fill in with what you remember scribbled on walls.'

'Oh?' Busby does not say.

Ohhh – euhh Olive has begun to whimper.

Knees planted on either side of the skinny body, Busby stoops to lick with strong, regular, vertical strokes, the yellow belly. In particular, the scar in it.

Of course in actual fact they are seated in the garden below, in the shade of Figgis's fully clothed magnolia tree. Busby has dragged out the record player. She is waiting to play it, not so much for Olive as for their historic cockatoos.

Olive gets up and goes in, probably to the loo, from the look on her face when she returns: a pawnbroker's genteel daughter.

'Oh,' she says, picking up the record-sleeve, 'I would have thought so.'

Though it is plain, from the expression on her face, that Olive has always been wondering which music you have in common.

'Such a glorious work!' She sighs with the resignation she has learnt to adopt for any surrender to ecstasy or martyrdom.

Pish!

Busby sets it off – to turn them on.

> '*Mi tradì, quell'alma ingrata,*
> *Infelice, o Dio, mi fa …* '

it has begun to sing, but the voice is a different one today, and there is no descent of cockatoos.

O Dio! Olive is sitting forward in her deck-chair, holding back a grief she may let fall if you are unlucky enough.

> '*Quando sento il mio tormento,*
> *Di vendetta il cor favella,*
> *Ma se guardo il suo cimento,*
> *Palpitando il cor mi va …* '

Busby switches it off: today she could not have borne the Don, and never the Commendatore.

Presently Olive leaves. Which is what Busby has been hoping for.

Mrs Davoren had heard that Miss Le Cornu 'adored' music. Lying alone in her bed, she wondered whether they would dare discuss the subject of their common adoration. For her part, she did not think she would wish to. She had never been what you could call religious, but there are certain things you can't even write on a pad and leave on the kitchen table for somebody else to read.

For a moment she thought she heard Him bumping around in the next room. It must have been her own heart.

At moments his heart beat thunderously, at others it chugged like suffocating felt. None of these people asleep in the houses would rise from their beds to rescue him from the terrors in store. Which by now he couldn't feel he had chosen to face: they were chosen for him. As far as he could see it was like that day or night You couldn't call not even to your mother and father in the next room: they were too busy discussing the price of meat, or whether the rates would go up, or the Gas Company mend the leak, or accusing each other, or fucking together.

He slid, thin and sick, between the railings, back inside the park. (If he had been just that bit fatter, he wouldn't have fitted, and might have cried off.)

He went first in the direction of the lake where the coot were shrieking. At least it was a sign of life. But wasn't it the thought of finding life which was frightening him stiff – the alkies and freaks and pervs and old women with stockings halfdown and scabs on their faces?

The moon was streaming light around him. It should have given him courage. Instead, everything looked less escapable. Trees were brandishing themselves. Along the lake's edge flashed the steely blades of reeds. All had a perverse truth you recognized from thoughts you could scarcely say you thought: it was more as if they were slipped uninvited into your head. Of cruelty. And death.

He wouldn't think. He began humming to himself, but stopped. Somebody 'undesirable' might hear.

The lake he knew by day as a placid, brown, and finally boring stretch of water was tingling with moonlight; it almost looked like frost. He put his hands in his pockets, and was glad to find the knife there. The moon became temporarily wrapped in a shred of cloud, which turned the water leaden. The – body? Yes, a naked one at that, was floating face-down, hidden, though not enough, by a screen of reeds. He whimpered down his nose and revolved twice on the spot where he was standing. Big and bulging, the corpse must be a woman's, which would make it worse.

He had only once seen a woman's body, and then it was Buz Le Cornu walking starkers down the garden path the evening he climbed into Figgis's magnolia watching for cockatoos. Anyone who could walk naked in the garden only a couple of steps from the street might get herself murdered. Or go bonkers enough to do herself in. Busby Le Cornu!

Of course he needn't let on about what he had found. Nobody would know he had seen it. But he ought to have a look at least. He got a stick and prodded at one of the bulges. It felt neither one thing nor another; but dead. As the cloud slipped past the moon, the body looked so green it must have spent some time in the water.

He prodded again and the thing bobbed. It slid out from amongst the reeds: an old li-lo somebody must have had no further use for, or couldn't be bothered to fish out.

He was so relieved he let out a drop or two of piss. He was glad to feel the warmth in his pants.

If he had felt afraid it was because it happened at night when everything looks exaggerated. He hadn't been afraid at the real thing the evening Figgis murdered Davoren and the cockatoos. It was the mystery of it which made him almost let out a howl at the time. For a conjuring trick which was real.

He walked on. There was a man sitting in the shadow of a clump of flax. 'Hi, sonny, what do they call yer?'

'Tom.'

'Come 'ere, Tom,' the man said. 'I got a surprise for yer.'

'What?'

He wasn't going to be surprised; he walked on, and the man cursed for quite a while.

He walked and came to a couple of women who had made themselves comfortable for the night wrapped in sheets of newspaper. Their carrier bags standing around them made fat shadows on the grass.

'Come on over, Dick,' one of the women invited. 'We've got room for a nice little bolster between us. We'll all sleep the cosier for squeezin' up together.'

The second woman laughed. Their faces were so tanned the moonlight made them look black.

'Nah. I got a long way ter go.'

Even at a distance he could smell their smell: of bodies and spirits.

The first woman advised, 'Fuck off then and get fucked.'

He could hear them hitting or resettling their newspapers, and grumbling, after he had left.

He roamed around. For something to do, he started jumping up and down on a rock, and his shadow, like the goat it was, jumped beside him in the moonlit grass.

He felt foolish, then fed up. He might be getting sleepy, without a murder, not even a rape, to keep him awake. He flopped down beside some paperbarks, wondering whether he might catch rheumatic fever, that Uncle Kev nearly died of. At Noraville.

He's real sick they're telling him to lie quiet and let the snow they've plastered on his forehead take effect otherwise he might die *but I won't Sister I can't I'm alive aren't I criminals must* expect the consequences *but I'm not a crim I only tapped out messages without even knowing the code* they got the message all right *but I'm innocent like Mr Davoren who was murdered for being innocent* not even Mr Davoren himself can tell you can ask him if you're foolish enough it's visiting hour and he's come to see what's left of the criminal patient *I'm not Mr Dav am I or am I worse than* Davoren can't speak he is bandaged up he is one big white bandage except for the light-coloured eyes which perhaps can't see you for being unless you also *I can see can't I so I'm not yet* Davoren can only make these creaking noises through his bandages can't pass on the message perhaps he doesn't understand the code he is already leaving the crim's bedside stomping sideways backwards past the beds the lockers to avoid trampling cockatoos there is a grassful.

Sparkling.

There must have been a heavy dew. The morning was rustling with moisture and small birds. Firetails: he recognized them from the book Mum and Dad had given at Christmas. The finches were picking at something invisible on the underneath of the paperbark leaves. They took him for granted until, in spite of stiffness, numbness, he jumped up. The birds were flicked in all directions.

To throw off whatever was still clinging to him from his nightmare, he ran full tilt at light. It was spinning round him. Above him the whirligig of whirligigs. Under his feet the earth thundered, but held firm. He might have thrown his arms around someone if anybody had showed up – even one of those leathery women of last night, or the man who wanted to show his prick. And run away before complications arose. Today he was fast as light. Zingg! He might have sung if he could have thought what.

In the end he only sang out his name, and it was broken up, to add to the shimmer of the morning.

He was nine years old, he remembered just before catching sight of IT, in the ragged grass, in the paperbark scrub, beside the lake. He thudded to a stop.

It was a cockatoo. Which first screeched, then let out a few rusty squawks, from age perhaps, and dragging through wet grass. Had he been abandoned by the mob? Or couldn't the others run the risk of further human treachery by staying to support what must be an old or sick bird? At any rate, the loner had survived a winter after the mob had flown.

Tim Goodenough made the noises his mother produced for age and sickness, for the 'poor old cockie', when suddenly and unexpectedly, desire spurted in him. He jumped high enough to swing on and bring down a small bough. After a bit of a wrestling match, he succeeded in twisting it free.

All the time the cockatoo was eyeing him, beak half open, one wing trailing.

There was no need to pretend: the bird might have been offering himself.

The boy looked round before swiping. The bird squawked once, less in fear or pain, it seemed, than because it was expected of him, and huddled himself against the grass.

Tim hit and hit. It was soon over. The bird's head lolled when he picked it up; the eyes were hidden behind their shutters of grey skin.

The boy looked round again before taking out his knife to scalp the cockatoo in the way he had read Indians do to whites. Very little blood flowed from under the dry skin, before the yellow tuft was lying in the palm of his hand.

He made off, but remembered, and returned, and took the corpse, and pitched it into the waters of the lake, which were beginning to blaze and steam.

He loped. He trotted. He loped. The yellow tuft he was carrying blew around and threatened to escape. He had to close his hand.

He would have liked to throw the thing away, but it sort of stuck to him now that he'd got it. Blowing inside the half-opened cage of his hand, whenever he dared glance, it made his heart beat, his breath whimper.

His talisman!

After running just a little farther, he came out through the park gate. If he hadn't gone in, he might never have discovered what was waiting to burst out of him.

Miss Le Cornu was leaning on her gate. If she had been more like those who lead ordered lives, she supposed she might have fetched a broom and swept the pavement in front of her. But for the moment, leaning in the sun, she was inclined to congratulate herself on being what that kind of person considers unstable. Habits were not in her line; though you do crave for one on and off.

Out of one of Miss Le Cornu's eyes trickled a tear. She rubbed it off, because down the street she could see the Goodenough boy coming from the park, and from the other direction Her approaching.

Since the event in their lives Miss Le Cornu had watched Mrs Davoren, and had sometimes been on the verge of speaking. Then she hadn't, remembering the touch of hands, and the grief they had briefly shared. Besides, Mrs Davoren seemed to be enjoying her widowhood. That winter she had bought herself a mini-car and learnt to drive it. She had bought the sealskin coat. It was much as if Mrs Davoren had inherited money from her late husband, when everyone knew the money had always been hers.

At any rate, here she was, a widow in a sealskin coat, but this morning she had left her mini-car in the garage.

Miss Le Cornu clenched her somewhat grubby hands. She was only too aware that her jeans were split (and at the crutch).

'Lovely day, Mrs Davoren,' Miss Le Cornu said; after all, why not celebrate the fact that you are neighbours?

Mrs Davoren admitted that it was, indeed, a lovely day.

To meet Miss Le Cornu in the flesh as opposed to conversing together in her thoughts was unnerving Mrs Davoren. She had often thought that if she did come face to face with Her she would introduce the subject of music, and now this idea came into her head, but fortunately she saved herself in time.

'It'll warm up later, though.' Mrs Davoren was quite firm about it.

'Won't you find a fur coat a bit too much?' Miss Le Cornu couldn't resist.

Mrs Davoren hadn't expected that. 'Yes,' she gasped, 'but the weight,' and in her confusion the spit flew out, 'the weight is a comfort – even if hot.'

Mrs Davoren was so embarrassed, and Miss Le Cornu grinning her head off. (You had to remember that Busby Le Cornu was mad.)

'Nicely matched skins – altogether beaut,' she complimented her widowed neighbour; only the grace of God prevented Miss Le Cornu adding, 'if it wasn't for the slaughter of the seals.'

But Mrs Davoren might have heard just that, for the pain showed in her sallow face and transferred itself to Miss Le Cornu's throat, which had knotted itself almost as if she had a goitre.

For a mere instant. Then their eyes cleared. The light was beating gloriously around them. The relief was tremendous.

'Well,' Mrs Davoren said, 'I'm off to the city. Thought I'd start early. Walk. Look round the shops while they're still empty.'

She did this at least once a week, picking up things and putting them down again.

'Have a good time,' Miss Le Cornu recommended.

Mrs Davoren left on accepting this advice, and Miss Le Cornu had no opportunity for shouting more, because here was the Goodenough boy.

'Why, Tim,' she blared, 'what have you been up to? Look at your shoes!'

'The grass,' he muttered. 'It's wet.'

Just his luck to run into old Buz Le Cornu.

Miss Le Cornu had left off her moccasins this morning. She liked the feel of moss beneath her bare feet. She would have liked to hang on to the Goodenough boy and show him something; she would have to think what.

But Tim Goodenough barged on. His left shoulder must be looking out of joint because of what he was carrying so carefully in his hand, which no one must guess at, let alone see.

He could still have thrown the thing away, but by now it felt as much a part of him as his guilt.

At Davorens' the blinds were down, which meant nothing; they always were.

On the only occasion he could remember speaking to the dead man, Davoren had just picked up his paper from the path, and was standing reading it at the gate. He said a war had broken out.

'I used to think that if ever another war broke out I would wanter be in ut.' He spoke in the tone of voice he would have used on any passer-by. 'A war brings people closer, you know.'

'Oh?' Yourself left out of the Irishman's thoughts, your voice sounded such a bleat. 'Did you ever kill a man, Mr Davoren – in the war you was in?'

'Eh?' He couldn't very well help looking at you, but only after a fashion. 'Perhaps – yes – a few. "Kill" is what you'd call ut, I reckon.'

Around the two of you the morning was trembling, or so it seemed.

Now on this similar morning of delicate balance, he went straight round to the garage when he got home, climbed behind the Feltex and wire-netting, and opened the door of the wormy old medicine cupboard. He shoved the limp wisp of a crest in amongst the darkness. He did not bother to feel whether his other 'talismans' were there. He slammed the door. Probably wouldn't open it again. It would open, though; it was already opening, of its own accord, in his mind.

A gust of breakfast and other things came at him as soon as he entered the kitchen.

'It's early for you, isn't it? And what's come over you, Tim, to have brushed your hair so nice?'

He had, it was true, wet it a bit, and given it a bash or two with the brush; he could feel the wad of wet hair he had slicked across his forehead.

'It isn't for your birthday, is it?' She, too, was coming at him. 'Nine! Fancy! Who'd believe it!'

She grabbed him to her apron. He hated this sort of thing: his cheek squashed; his shoulder would be looking more than disjointed – deformed. As she held him, practically suffocated, and him not supposed to resist, any vision he may have imagined having, ever, was splodged into one great, white blur, at the centre of it a smear of sulphur.

When she was at last satisfied, she let him go. 'Dad's running late. We'll have the present when he's finished shaving. He went to no end of trouble getting it. You don't realize, Tim, what you mean to your father. He's that proud of you.'

He sat down, and ate his porridge lumps and all this morning before his misery returned. He was hard put to it not to blubber when she stooped and opened the oven door, and let out a blast of half-baked cake. He did, in fact, start to blubber, but managed to turn it into a bubble or two.